ABOUT THE AUTHOR

Tony Richards' supernatural novels have been published by HarperCollins, Schusters, Tor Books and Samhain in the United States and Pan Books, Headline and Endeavour Media in the UK. He has had enough stories published in magazines and anthologies to fill 6 collections – most of them from Dark Regions Press – and he has been a regular contributor to Weird Tales, Cemetery Dance magazine, Alfred Hitchcock's Mystery Magazine and Midnight Street. His novel 'The Harvest Bride' was shortlisted for the HWA Bram Stoker Award and his collection 'Going Back' for the British Fantasy Award. Dark fantasy magazine Black Static has described him as "a master of the art" and the Horror World website calls him "one of today's masters of dark fiction."

You can find out more about his work by visiting his regular blog: SHADOW REALMS: Fiction from Tony Richards.

HIDDEN

TONY RICHARDS

Shadow Realms Press

Hidden is copyright © Tony Richards 2013. This edition is copyright © Tony Richards 2021.

Cover image by Steve Upham. Cover image copyright © Steve Upham 2021.

This edition is by Shadow Realms Press.

This is a work of fiction. Names, characters, places, and incidents are drawn from the author's imagination or are used fictitiously and are not to be construed as real. Any resemblance to actual events, locales, organizations, or persons, living or dead, is entirely coincidental.

All rights reserved. No part of this book may be used or reproduced in any manner whatsoever without written permission, except in the case of brief quotations embodied in critical articles and reviews.

CONTENTS

PART ONE: SEX, DEATH & BELINDA GRADY

Chapter 1 – Marty – 1
Chapter 2 – Lindy – 7
Chapter 3 – Eric – 15
Chapter 4 – The Morning News – 24
Chapter 5 – The Morgue – 29
Chapter 6 – Kevin – 36
<u>Chapter 7</u> – You? – 41
Chapter 8 – The Ax – 48
Chapter 9 – Red – 55
Chapter 10 – Moving – 62
Chapter 11 – The Junkies – 68
Chapter 12 – Oh, Yeah? – 78
Chapter 13 – The Morning News, Part II – 81
Chapter 14 – The Calliers – 86
Chapter 15 – Daddy's Girl – 91
Chapter 16 – Appointment – 95

PART TWO: ROOM 27

Chapter 17 – Actually Maroon – 103
Chapter 18 – I'm on Duty – 107
Chapter 19 – Only a Silhouette – 113
Chapter 20 – Massachusetts – 119
Chapter 21 – George – 126
Chapter 22 – I Want to See You – 136
Chapter 23 – Bound – 141
Chapter 24 – On the Bed – 147
Chapter 25 – The Blonde – 150
Chapter 26 – Shakedown – 155
Chapter 27 – Falling – 161
Chapter 28 – Harem of One – 164
Chapter 29 – Claw Marks – 168

PART THREE: HUNTED

Chapter 30 – Running – 177
Chapter 31 – Don't You Love Me Anymore? – 185
Chapter 32 – Matchi Manitou – 188
Chapter 33 – Maxi and More – 192
Chapter 34 – True Awaking – 197
Chapter 35 – Smoke – 201
Chapter 36 – Nowhere Else to Go – 204
Chapter 37 – Revisitation – 207
Chapter 38 – Fireflies – 213
Chapter 39 – Phone Call – 217
Chapter 40 – Negotiation – 221

PART FOUR: FIGHTING BACK

Chapter 41 – Up – 225
Chapter 42 – Almost Fully Day – 228
Chapter 43 – Epiphany – 234
Chapter 44 – The Church – 240
Chapter 45 – A Handful of Hours – 245
Chapter 46 – Crusade – 249
Chapter 47 – The Park – 253
Chapter 48 – In Darkness – 259
Chapter 49 – In Dreams – 265
Chapter 50 – In Truth – 270
Chapter 51 – And in the End – 275

EPILOGUE: BEYOND THE NIGHT – 279

PART ONE

SEX, DEATH & BELINDA GRADY

1 – Marty

It was only a patch of fog, that was all, some eight feet high by eight feet wide and as gray as a dead dream. But this was on a summer's night, a sauna-hot night in a New York August, when there was no other fog around and no wind either. So what was driving it?

It came skimming in from the high northeast, pushing its way across the fringes of the Bronx and then crossing the Harlem River, traveling down through the various Heights until it reached Harlem itself. It didn't pause there, although it raised a few eyebrows in sidewalk cafes as it passed. It kept on going till it reached the upper edge of Central Park. Went across a couple of the broad traverse roads and the reservoir.

And finally, it began to slow.

***

The voice had been calling to him for quite a while now.

But it was only in his head.

He'd figured that out gradually, but couldn't understand it.

It was a female voice, a very soft and honeyed one, and so he reckoned after a great deal of consideration that maybe it might be his guilty conscience speaking to him.

And he'd *never* felt guilty before.

Marty Callum was now single, but had been married five times. The first time he had done that, he had been twenty-two and it had only lasted four months. Who knew why he'd even bothered with the ceremony at all? Maybe he was trying to find something he didn't really get. Permanence. Perfection. Some might call it truth. The whole idea of being with one woman and no other was so alien to him, so strange and unimaginable, that it had taken on almost a mystic quality to his way of thinking. It had become what he aspired to down in the deepest regions of his soul, although he knew he'd never manage it. It was his Holy Grail though, something that he kept on trying to find despite the fact he knew he never would.

And these days, let's face it, women only went with him because they thought they could get something out of him. They were right about that. If they had the correct mindset and the hunger and ambition, then they could.

Marty was now fat and bald and nearly in his sixties, and the owner of a string of lapdance clubs that stretched from New York through the Carolinas and then down as far as Florida. Additionally, he was the owner of a publishing house that produced such monthly top-shelf magazines as *Wettest Fetish* and *Kluster*. There was a video section to that business, which had expanded itself in recent years to include several frequently hit websites on the Internet. And if you scoured hard enough through the company records, you would find out that he was the proprietor of several escort agencies as well.

To put it plainly, Marty had done pretty well out of women. He'd never stayed with one for more than half a year, but they had made him rich. They were like a seam of gold that never petered out. Everything that he owned, he owed to their bodies.

The hum of the traffic below him on Fifth was getting gentler now. It was almost midnight. He had the doors to his rooftop terrace thrown wide open since, this being Manhattan, it was as humid as it was hot. And sure, this penthouse had an air-conditioner, but if he left that turned on for too long then his sinuses would clog up and the neuralgia would start. It would work down to his canine teeth and then his lower jaw, keeping him up all night. So he preferred to simply leave the windows open.

"Mar-ty?"

There it was again, that voice.

He turned his head, but there was no one even visible.

He was in his living room and standing up, clad only in a thin robe of Egyptian cotton. He was tapping at the new iPad he'd bought, downloading free apps. There was a glass of cognac on the coffee table at the center of the room, a cigar sitting by it in an ashtray, waiting to be lit. And he knew that he ought to be enjoying them and sitting down. But the voice had made him restless. It could only be coming from inside his mind, and why was his mind playing tricks on him this particular evening? It had never fooled with him before. And so he stayed up on his feet, kept pacing and wandering and finding brand-new things to occupy his thoughts with, hoping his mind would calm down.

"*Marty, I'm still waiting for you.*"

Whose voice was that? One of his ex-wives? But no, it wasn't any of those. This was ... a very smooth voice. Very clear. And yet ...

Strangely sweet. Strangely lustrous. Alluring. Enticing. Filled up with the promises of deep, dark pleasures.

Except it was a fantasy. Only in his head. So when it called to him again, he tried to blank it out, ignoring what it said.

"I'm in the park, Marty. All you have to do is cross one street. Why don't you come to me?"

The soles of his feet struck against hard, warm tile. Without his even realizing it, he'd wandered out onto his terrace. Marty started blinking like a man who'd just been woken, and then wandered over to the edge.

You couldn't even see Fifth Avenue unless you leaned across the parapet. When you stared straight ahead, what met your gaze was the broad expanse of the Sheep Meadow, and then the curling foliage of the mass of trees beyond that. The pond with its Rustic Bridge glinted in the left-hand corner of your vision. You could make out the Trump Tower and several other taller buildings in the distance. But it was mostly Central Park that you were looking at.

He could feel that there was something in his right hand now. The iPad? No, it felt smaller than that, less slick. When he looked down, he saw that he had picked up – in its place – the cigar that had been lying in the ashtray. And he didn't remember doing that. What was *wrong* with him this evening?

"Marty? Please don't keep me waiting."

"Shut up," he grumbled back. "You're not even real."

He jammed the cigar into the corner of his mouth, patted at the pockets of his robe, and realized he hadn't brought his lighter with him. So he went back in to fetch it. It was on the coffee table too.

But Marty wandered past the table without even slowing down, and the next thing that he knew was he was outside in the corridor of his apartment block, closing his front door behind him in spite of the fact he didn't have the key. It was only a short corridor, elevator doors at the far end.

And they were already wide open.

Waiting for him like an open mouth.

***

Steve Fullerman had been the night shift doorman at the Sirius Apartments for the past eight years. He never took time off sick. Never missed a shift. And so – since there was little turnover at an overpriced address like this – he knew the residents like they were family. For instance, Mrs. Tudjenski in 26 was a sweet-natured and privately wealthy old lady who owned six lhasa apsos that she'd never housetrained, so the inside of her place smelled like an outhouse and she carried the smell with her when she went out on the street. Mr. Graves in 59 was not only an art expert who made sure that he looked the part – what with his goatee beard and the leather patches on his tweedy elbows – but also an expert at luring girls who were barely of a legal age back to his home. Mr. Chen in 77 was visited by the same middle-aged redheaded hooker every Thursday evening. And Ms. Eckerhart in 82 had a very responsible job at a large international bank, but was often visited by small huddles of women bearing video equipment, so that it was possible she had a taste for making amateur pornography of the girl-girl kind. She was risking her career if she was doing that, but didn't seem to care.

These were secrets Steve would carry with him to the grave. If there was one word that he thought summed up his job, then that word was 'responsible.' He was *responsible* for the folks who had the wealth to live here. He was *responsible* for their safety and security, their comfort and wellbeing. He couldn't help them once they'd gone out past the front door, but when they were inside this building, why, he kept a careful eye on them and took note of their comings and their goings. Signed for deliveries on their behalf. Called cabs for them as were needed, and was always ready to head up and help them out in their apartments if help was required. He almost thought of this place as some kind of nursery. Its inhabitants were the little kids whose care was in his hands, and it was his job to make sure they were happy and untroubled.

When the elevator bell pinged and its doors came sliding open, he half expected to see Mr. Ross. Mr. Ross had serious trouble sleeping in hot weather, and would frequently head outside around midnight for a stroll. He'd usually come back with the foam of a milkshake in his thick moustache, which meant he'd probably wound up at one of the diners down round 57th. Steve's sharp mind recorded things like that.

But no, this was Mr. Callum from the penthouse instead. The titty bar king. Steve neither approved nor disapproved of the man's business; that was not his job. All he really cared about was that the guy was always civil to him. Called him by his name, and left a good tip when required.

But then Mr. Callum stepped unsteadily into the lobby, and Steve could see that there was something wrong. The man was usually casually dressed. But now, he had on nothing but a flimsy cotton robe. So what was up? Was there a fire in the penthouse?

Steve was on his feet immediately, striding out abruptly from behind his desk.

"Mr. Callum? You *okay*, sir?"

The man's eyes were glassy. His face was blank. He barely seemed to hear the question, tipping his face toward the glass front doors instead. Had he been drinking? His robe was so loosely tied at the front that you could practically see the whole butcher's shop.

"Mr. Callum? Should I call you an ambulance?"

Except the man didn't look sick. Simply dazed, as though he had been caught midway between a dream and waking. There was still no real expression on his round face, and his gaze was fixed upon something that simply wasn't there. He took a slow, faltering step in the direction of the street, and then another.

Steve was right up close, now. He could smell no alcohol on the man's breath. And Mr. Callum's pupils looked completely normal, and there were no bruises and no blood, which meant he hadn't banged his head.

Steve had several important rules. And one of those was that he never made physical contact with the tenants unless it was absolutely needed. If one of the more elderly residents needed help crossing the lobby, fine. But situations such as those apart, he never touched anyone.

The problem was that Mr. Callum was still headed for the sidewalk, his step a little firmer now, his gaze fixed straight ahead. And Steve couldn't go letting one of his charges go wandering out into the city night stunned and practically naked. And so he grabbed Mr. Callum firmly by the sleeve.

The man's eyes finally swung round to him.

"Mr. Callum, sir, do you know what you're doing? If you want to go out, then you need to get dressed."

The man seemed to consider that a short while, and then wet his lips.

"There's no time, Steve," he mumbled. "She's waiting for me."

"She? Waiting?"

"Her voice. Surely you can hear it?"

Steve's head bobbed a moment. "Mr. Callum, there's no voice."

"That's just nonsense," the man said.

And then he snatched his arm away and started moving once again.

There was nothing that could stop him this time so that, in the end, they both wound up on the sidewalk, the larger man still trundling toward the park and Steve still trying to reason with him.

He gave up when Mr. Callum stepped off the curb and started crossing Fifth in his bare feet. A Yellow cab swerved to avoid the man, hooting. Mr. Callum didn't even seem to notice that.

Steve pushed back the peak of his uniform cap and rubbed at his brow, wondering what to do. He didn't want the man to get arrested, but the guy was either drugged in some way or he'd had some kind of mental breakdown. There was far worse trouble he could get into, right now, than being brought to the authorities' attention.

So he stared at the retreating figure, called out to him one last time. And then he hurried back inside and grabbed the phone behind his desk.

2 – Lindy

Red lighting and pounding music. The tight press of bodies, the racket of a hundred conversations trying to outdo each other, the air thick with perfume and cologne.

Freddie's Place, just off Madison, was a well-known meat market. Which was why Lindy came here when she was in the mood. She knew the effect she had on men, how easy it was to draw them to her.

See, Daddy, THEY like me!

She drew so many in, in fact, that all she really had to do was pick and choose.

She'd gotten here before eleven o' clock and had managed to secure herself a stool at the bar. She had been perched on it for nearly an hour and a half by now, her shoulders thrown back, her long, tapering legs gently crossed in front of her, her head going from side to side occasionally so that her flame-red hair brushed idly across her shoulders. In that time, maybe more than twenty men had approached her. She'd allowed a couple of them to buy her a vodka and tonic but had finally sent them all away. She was in no rush, and when you could pick and choose the way that she could you were definitely selective.

A thin guy with a pointy nose came up to her a little nervously and tried to make a joke. It was quite a funny joke, but she was careful to keep her face entirely blank, not even laughing with her eyes. He looked sad and wandered off.

Five minutes later, though, this evening's Guy stepped up to her. She hadn't even seen him in the crowd. He simply emerged from it, looking directly at her. And she knew, the moment that she clapped her pale blue eyes on him, that this was this evening's one.

Tall. Broad-shouldered. Firm of jaw. Worked out regularly. Well-dressed, but nothing flashy about it, except possibly his watch. He stepped up to her side as confidently as if he owned her.

"Buy you a drink?"

"Why? To loosen me up?"

"Only being friendly."

"There's no such thing as 'only' in this place."

He grinned. "Right."

"Let's go," she said.

And if he'd jolted with shock when she said that, then she'd have changed her mind. But he didn't do that thing. He just went very still, his eyes widening slightly.

"Your place?" he asked.

"So you can leave afterward? No, we'll go to your place, and then *I* can leave afterward."

It was a condo on the Upper West Side, very tasteful. In the cab, he told her what he did. It didn't register. He told her his name, but that didn't stick either. He was just this evening's Guy.

As soon as they were in the door he started kissing her, but far too gently. She squirmed away from him, her face becoming angry.

"Oh Jeez, don't be such a pussy."

"What?"

"Slam me up against the wall. Pull my hair, grab my wrists. That's what you really want to do, ain't it?"

For the first time since they'd met, he looked uncertain.

"You don't want me to hit you, do you?"

When she grinned at him, it was the grin of a tigress. "Only if you want me to hit you back. And I hit hard"

Afterwards, her clothes lying all over the floor, she asked him, "Got any blow?"

And he said, "Sure."

And so they did a couple of lines and then wound up in his bed, where it lasted a whole lot longer. She got him to bind her wrists with one of her own holdups. It was fine. And she was just thinking of showering, after he'd undone the knots, when the pager in her purse began to beep. She leapt off the mattress, pulled the pager out and studied it. Then she started hurrying around the apartment, retrieving her clothing.

"What's up?" he asked her, getting out of bed himself.

"Gotta go to work."

"But … it's gone two in the morning. What kind of work, exactly?"

Lindy re-opened her purse and showed him her detective's badge.

He was still gawping at her when she let herself out.

***

A full moon was up beyond the tall skyscrapers.

There was a black-and-white with its beacon pulsing stopped on Fifth when she got there. She identified herself to the two uniformed guys beside it as Detective Sergeant Belinda Grady, Homicide, and they pointed across the park in the general direction of West 72nd. She'd forgotten about the Guy altogether by this stage. She had gone into work mode, where nothing as messy as sex intruded. She went out across the darkened stretch of grass until she found the others.

Detectives Renzo and Hayes were already in place. Peter Renzo was a small, dark Italian-American in his mid-thirties, with a permanent shadow of stubble on his jaw. He always wore a suit, and never smiled or attempted to make light chitchat, but he was a good cop and utterly reliable.

Personality wise, he was chalk to Hayes' cheese. Maxwell – 'Maxi' – Hayes' parents were Jamaican, and he'd lived there in his early teenage years, and it had stuck. He was tall and narrow, dressed mostly in denim, wore his hair in short cornrows, and beamed whenever he saw her. He was doing that thing now.

He also generally talked the Rasta talk, despite the fact that he'd been living in Manhattan for the past eleven years. That shouldn't make you think he wasn't a good cop as well. Far from it. He'd worked several years deep cover with Organized Crime before tiring of that kind of life and transferring to Homicide.

"Lindy gal, what took ya so long?"

"I was otherwise engaged."

"At this time of da night? Wi' what?"

She tried to walk past him, but he grabbed her wrist gently. He was always doing stuff like that. Maxi seemed to have a very slim concept of rank, of chain of command, superiority and appropriate behavior. If she hadn't liked him so much, she'd have bawled him out.

But he was staring at her with genuine concern. Maybe that was why they felt so close … he was like the brother that she'd never had. Maxi lowered his face till it was level with hers, studying her eyes. And when he spoke again, it was in a soft, conspiratorial whisper.

"You bin riding the toot train again? Lindy gal, you're gonna get yourself in serious trouble one a' these fine days."

"I can take care of myself," she came back at him. "Don't need you mothering me."

He could see that she wanted to change the subject, and he let go of her, shrugging as he did so. He really cared about her, that was all. And it was nice that *someone* did that, even though she didn't understand entirely why, but she desperately wanted to put considerations like that far behind her so she could immerse herself in this new case.

She walked over to the body, taking in its nudity with a mild sense of surprise. You saw it all when you were on the force, but dead *and* bareass in the park? You got the occasional drunk or nut or exhibitionist running round here in the nude, for sure. But they generally didn't wind up *sans* pulse. The naked guy was face down, with a fellow from the M.E.'s office – Florette, she thought his name was – poring over him.

"His robe's over here," Renzo told her in that quiet, slow voice of his.

The little Italian had a wife and three small children somewhere off in Queens, she knew. He never stepped up close to her or met her gaze directly. She was his sarge and he respected that. But it was like he sensed that she was trouble, and preferred to keep his distance. He needn't have bothered. He was not her type.

He was pointing at a bundle of cloth that, when she looked closer, turned out to have sleeves and a belt.

"He was still wearing it when he crossed Fifth, apparently," Renzo told her.

"Very considerate of him. And he is?"

"Martin Callum, fifty-nine and single. Owner of a string of strip joints, among other enterprises."

"Rich?"

"Yuh-huh."

"You'd think he could afford some clothes, then."

Renzo just ignored that, turning his face to the east. "He lived over there, the Sirius Apartments. Penthouse suite."

Lindy gazed back at the body.

"And you identified him and learned so much about him how exactly?"

"Doorman," Maxi chipped in. "Over there. Were him put in the call."

Further off, toward a group of boulders, a man in dark livery was standing between another pair of uniformed cops. He wasn't talking to them, which meant he'd already told them all he knew. He was staring over at the dead body, his head tilted anxiously, his fingers wrapped around each other. And the guy looked practically like he was going to start crying.

She'd get to him later.

Lindy stepped right up so that she was standing over the cadaver. Full moonlight was shining down, and it made the dead man's pale, excessive flesh look stark, like a photographic negative. She could make out every fold and blemish. Jeez, but this guy was a blimp. Why did people let themselves go this way? Fifty-nine wasn't so old. She felt her top lip curling with disgust. She could practically smell him from up here, the odor of his blubber, the stink of the dried sweat trapped between his bulges.

Florette pulled out a thermometer from the guy's liver and then started trying to turn him over.

"Need some help?"

Without waiting for a reply, Lindy crouched down and took a firm hold of the corpse's wrist. It was very hairy. The whole arm was hairy. That reminded her of ...

She closed her eyes a second, but then returned her concentration to her job.

When the front of Mr. Callum appeared, her eyes immediately scoured his face and chest. There were no injuries that she could see. No cuts, no bruising, nothing. The face was entirely slack – corpses *have* no expressions, they can't. The eyes were wide open. They were pretty damp, as though the guy was quite upset about his own demise. The upper lip had skinned back from the teeth, giving Martin Callum something of a slight Bugs Bunny look.

Florette was inspecting the front of the corpse too, but a lot more slowly than she had done.

"Opinion?" she asked.

"At a guess, a coronary."

"Not a homicide, then?"

"No. No signs of that."

"Well, I'm not a detective in the Coronary Division, so what the hell am I doing here?"

"It's unusual, is all."

She took that in and nodded.

"Yeah. It's that."

And she was *here*, wasn't she? She was on a callout, wasn't she? So she might as well be thorough about it.

She went across and talked with the doorman, Steven Fullerman. Got him to repeat his entire story, listening carefully as he described the whole encounter in the lobby with the now-deceased, the struggle and the words that had been spoken. How it had wound up.

"And that was all he said?"

"Yeah. He was yapping on about this voice."

"Except there was no voice?"

"No."

"And you gave up when he wandered over Fifth. What happened then?"

"I went back inside to phone you guys. And then I headed here to try and find him, see if he was still all right."

"And ?"

"I only saw him from a distance. I was way back there." He pointed. "Mr. Callum, he'd taken his robe the whole way off. So I was shocked and I stopped running."

"He was moving around?"

"No. Completely still. Facing to that treeline there and standing very straight, which was unusual. Mr. Callum usually slouched."

"And then?"

"This broad – sorry – this woman steps out from the trees. And frig me if she ain't naked too."

This was a new one. Nobody had mentioned any woman until now.

"Do you think she was … a friend of Mr. Callum's?"

"Could be."

"Playing some kind of kinky game?"

"I don't read minds, miss."

"Right. Can you describe her?"

"It was at a distance, like I said. But tall. Yeah. Slim. Nice figure, I'd say. Dark hair. Skin even paler than his. Other than that …"

He shrugged.

"And she …?"

"Walked up to him and seemed to put a hand against his chest, and then he fell."

"She just touched him? Didn't hit him?"

"Didn't seem to. It was a gentle kind of motion."

"Was she holding any kind of weapon? A taser, perhaps?"

"I don't think so."

"And then …?"

"Soon as I saw him going down, I started running again. Reached him, felt for his pulse. Nothing. I've CPR training, so I did that. Still nothing."

His fingers kept on twisting round each other, and a bead of damp was running down from one of his eyes. He was in shock, Lindy figured. She'd make sure the uniforms got him medical attention before she left. But she had one more question.

"What happened to the woman?"

Fullerman jolted, his eyes going wider but his mouth tightening up.

"I don't know. I was panicked, running flat out. All I was thinking about was getting to Mr. Callum."

"So you didn't see her leaving? Which direction?"

He gave a stiff shake of his head. His face was looking very bloodless now, and rather numb. Lindy took one of the uniforms aside and explained to him that the fellow needed treatment.

"Already figured that one out," he assured her.

"Okay, then. So snap to it."

Then she headed back in the direction of Florette.

"Any sign of a taser being used?"

"I'd have spotted that in half a second."

"Still sticking with heart attack?"

"Do you know anything I don't?"

"I'm not sure. I guess we're gonna have to wait for the autopsy." She chewed her lower lip a moment, thinking about how Callum had been acting just before he'd wandered off. "You're gonna need to throw in a full and extensive tox screen."

"I can do that."

"Do it soon."

And that was it, for the moment. There was nothing she could really do until the cause of death was established. This was probably a total waste of time.

She stood there for a moment in the dimness of the park, her head going around, her gaze scanning the distance for any pale, thin outline that might be a naked woman. *And what was that about?* And then she told the others she was leaving. She could trust them to tie up the loose ends. Personally, she was beat.

She persuaded the guys in the first squad car to drop her off back home. It was an easy cruise down Lexington at this hour of the night. The edge of Chinatown was very quiet when she arrived, a lone bum going through trashcans, that was all. She climbed the wooden stairs to the tiny, mostly bare apartment she'd rented for years.

Kicked off her shoes. Threw herself out fully-clothed on her narrow bed. She never brought men back here.

Felt sleep closing over her almost straight away, her head swirling as her eyelids dropped.

Just before she fled the conscious world, she heard as though from a far distance – the same voice she almost always heard before oblivion claimed her.

"No daughter of mine is gonna be a cop!"

A hand was swinging down toward her – she could see it in her mind's eye. It was a big hard hand with reddened knuckles.

But she fell fast asleep a bare instant before it landed, managing to evade it for perhaps the millionth time.

3 – Eric

Almost dawn. The sky to the east was taking on a slight platinum sheen, and the temperature was already on the rise. The air was very still, as though the whole of Manhattan were holding its breath. And you could even feel it through the fine pores in your skin … it was going to be another killingly hot day.

Eric Rochester made his tired, ambling way down Central Park West. He was a slim young man with narrow shoulders and thick, tousled hair. His head was tucked down so that locks of the latter spilled across his wide, pale brow like stuffing hanging from a rip in an old, damaged couch.

You could tell by the unsteadiness of his gait that he'd been drinking. He'd been all night at a party thrown by one of his oldest friends, Cooper Weiss, whose father was a music magnate and whose townhouse was on 66th. Eric's folks' apartment was on 61st, tucked in between Fordham and Time Warner. He was back from his first batch of semesters at Harvard for the summer and – in some respects at least – it was good to be home.

Like, Boston was okay. It certainly had its charms. But it was *small*, so small in fact that to a native-born New Yorker's eyes it barely even counted as a city. It was satisfying to be back in a metropolis that was expansive, towered above you, stretched off in every which direction, offering you limitless possibilities. You could get anything here you wanted.

Except … could you really? Eric had always imagined it was so, but now he wasn't quite so sure. His head remained tucked down, and he was walking slowly because he was feeling like a total failure.

He'd left it until eleven thirty before showing up at Coop's. Fashionably late, you know. The party was already in full swing – you could hear the music and the voices from the street. His pulse had quickened simply approaching the door. And when it had swung open and he'd started pushing his way through the crowds beyond it …

After high school, Cooper hadn't followed him to college. Eric had always imagined that they'd both go off in that direction, but it turned out that that wasn't going to happen.

"*Why even bother?*" Coop had shrugged. "*One word from my Dad, and I'm in on the top rung of the music biz. How's three wasted years and a piece of paper saying you're a Bachelor of Whatnot going to improve on that?*"

So while Eric had gone off to study, Cooper had remained right here and started doing business with the talented and famous. He had his own apartment down in the West Village these days. And was only using the townhouse because it was the larger venue. His folks were away at the Hamptons at the moment.

The press of bodies was incredible. It stretched right down through the house's extensive lobby and then pushed unbrokenly up the stairs to higher levels. Everyone was talking at once, a sound like a waterfall of words. Everybody had a glass in hand. Some were dressed in very modern styles, while others looked like well-heeled hippies.

Eric kept on inching his way through. He knew there was a kitchen on this level of the house, guessed the booze would be in there, and knew from old experience that that would be the best place to get talking with a bunch of people that he didn't even know.

Or was that even genuinely the case? Wasn't that George Eller from the Neon Volumes he was looking at? The guy had a tall blonde with a silver headband standing close behind him, and was talking very seriously with a pair of guys in business suits.

George Eller? *Wow!*

He saw a few more faces that he recognized before much longer. Soozie Spark from Dreamboat. She was far smaller than he had imagined. Michael Ferman of the acoustic duo Ferman & Cole. There were people well-known from the TV here as well, pundits and presenters.

A big grin started spreading out across his face – a rather sappy one, he was aware of that. But this was *unbelievable*! He'd stepped right out of college life into a very different and more glamorous world. This was promising to be one hell of an evening.

When he finally made it to the kitchen at the back, he saw that he'd been right. The booze was in here, piled up like big pebbles on a beach. Bottles of tequila, Scotch, and Pims. Stacks of very good imported beers. There was plenty of champagne too, and dammit if it wasn't Cristal. Coop had to be doing really well for himself, didn't he? But then Eric realized he was being naïve – this all had to be on the company's expenses.

He'd only tried Cristal once before, but had enjoyed the experience and wanted to repeat it. Only problem was, somewhere around forty people were jammed in between himself and those particular bottles. Every single one of them was deep in conversation, and they didn't look like they were going anywhere real fast.

He tried murmuring 'scuse me' and then 'coming through' a few times, except that no one even seemed to hear him.

But then – almost miraculously – a woman with waist-length platinum blonde hair saw what he was trying to do. She turned her face to him and fixed him with a dazzling white smile. And that was when it struck him he had never looked into a more beautiful face before. Her eyes were a perfectly translucent blue. Her nose and ears were very small, her cheekbones high. The lips that framed that blinding smile were the same pale pink as rose petals.

"Tryin' to get to the champagne?" she asked him in a lilting Southern accent. "Here, let me help you."

When she turned away from him, he could see how smoothly tanned her shoulders were, how long her legs were underneath the scarlet minidress that she had on. He was still gawping at those when she turned back to him, handing him a foaming glass.

"There you are. So, how do you know Coop?"

His gaze snapped back to her face. He explained how, then asked her the same question.

"Shampoo."

Eric blinked. "Er ... you're his hairdresser?"

She looked amazed a moment, and then burst out laughing. "No! I do shampoo *commercials*, silly!"

And – obviously dismissing him as some kind of young idiot – she returned to the conversation that she'd previously been having.

Feeling awkward and a little disappointed, Eric wandered off. It hadn't felt good being mocked like that by a desirable woman. But the encounter – at least – had raised the blinkers from his eyes. So far, he'd only been looking out for famous faces in the crowd.

Now he began to notice it was laced throughout with dozens of absolutely gorgeous women. They were slim and beautiful and briefly dressed. And most of them had to be models.

"Eric goddamned *Rochester*!" growled a familiar voice from directly behind him.

He pivoted around and found himself staring directly into Cooper's smiling features. And an instant later, he was hugging the big guy.

"Hey, you're slopping Cristal on me, buddy," Coop mumbled.

But he didn't sound as though he minded, not even a little bit.

"How's life in the lofty halls of academia?" he asked when they broke apart.

"Some sex. Lotta work." Eric waved an arm around at the enormous press of bodies. "This is quite some shindig."

"Biggest industry party in New York this year," Coop nodded proudly, "and the whole thing organized by yours truly."

"You sound like a man who's enjoying his work."

"What's not to enjoy?"

"Lot of pretty famous people here," Eric pointed out.

"Lot of stunning ones too. Where music people congregate, there you will find hotties by the truckload."

Eric nodded. "Dated any?"

"Dating's such a long-term word."

But someone else had come up to one side of Cooper and was tapping at his shoulder quite insistently, demanding his attention. He was a short guy with a thin moustache, his long hair in a ponytail, and Eric did a double-take and recognized him as Andy Barrington, who'd had a seriously big hit with 'Wind Song' earlier this year.

He was saying, "Coop, I need to have a word with you about the publicity for the new single," and he didn't even seem to *care* that Cooper had been talking to someone else.

Except that Coop seemed wholly used to this kind of behavior. He shrugged, threw an arm round Andy Barrington's shoulders, used his free hand to pat Eric on the elbow and said, "No rest for the wicked, right? Duty calls. I'll catch you later."

He and Barrington went wandering off, presumably in search of some quiet corner.

Which, once again, left Eric surrounded by strangers. Only it didn't have to be that way for too much longer, did it? He was young, he was smart, he was reasonably good-looking and was single. And here he was surrounded by a wide selection of the most attractive women in the world.

So he managed to get one of them talking to him, a brunette with hazel eyes set in a round, almost babyish face. He started telling her about his time at Harvard.

But after a bare minute of that, she started looking bored and wandered off.

***

He'd stuck it out to the bitter end, desperately hoping for a lucky break. And almost thought he'd got it.

A lot of the guests had filtered away, the kitchen was much emptier than it had been before, and he found himself talking with a *very* tall brunette with a strong accent. It turned out that her name was Anya, she was from Croatia. She'd been on the cover of Vogue two months ago, but was interested in furthering her education.

So that when he started telling her about Harvard, she listened with real interest and then asked him a few intelligent questions. And the heaviness was lifting from his heart, a smile was breaking out inside him. At last he was getting somewhere. This was great!

Except another brunette sidled up to Anya, casually linked arms with her and then glanced at her silver wristwatch. Anya leant across and pecked her on the cheek before looking back apologetically at Eric.

"Sorry, but I have to go. Most interesting talking to you. Good luck with your studies."

When he wandered through the stragglers and the debris of the party, every last model had gone. He looked around for Coop but couldn't find him. So he strolled across to an older man and asked him, "Know where Cooper Weiss is?"

The man grinned a dirty little grin and tilted his eyeballs toward the ceiling. "Last time I saw, he was headed upstairs with a pair of twins. So I don't imagine that he wants to be disturbed."

And now here Eric was, alone on the street with dawn rising around him. He couldn't quite believe it. An empty cab slowed down as it passed him and then sped on by. There was the rattle of glass bottles being delivered somewhere in the distance. He was crossing 62nd now, and almost home.

Only he suddenly became very much aware of his own bladder. It began to ache badly, and felt like it was going to burst. He'd been drinking all evening, but he hadn't made it to the bathroom once. And now he needed to pee, so very urgently he knew he wasn't going to make it the last few hundred yards to the apartment.

So he changed direction, swerving across the bare pavement of Park West and then off into the park itself. There was a small cluster of trees he could secrete himself between. No one was around, and he would not be noticed.

Once inside their shadows, he tugged at his fly. A stream of urine came arcing out as soon as he'd freed himself up. All that he could do right now was wait for it to stop.

But a minute seemed to pass by, and the flow was still going strong. The ground ahead of him was dry and hard, and so a huge puddle began to form. He had to keep on edging backward just to stop it rushing over the tips of his shoes. Cool way to finish up a glamorous evening, huh?

But finally, the stream died down. He waited till it had completely stopped, and was shaking out the last drops …when he became aware of movement in the trees ahead, a shadow moving and a rustling sound.

His head came snapping up. He found himself staring into a woman's eyes. She was only about ten feet away from him, and peering intently at his face. He registered her presence with a jolt of shock. And only after *that* did it occur to him that he still had his dick in his hands.

He tucked himself away as quickly as he could, almost catching himself on his zipper in the process. Ducked his head, mumbled something along the lines of "Sorry about that," and started walking away quickly, feeling his cheeks flush. It was just one of those unfortunate things. There was no real need for anyone to feel embarrassed. Both of them were adults, weren't they?

"Eric?"

When her soft, sweet voice came floating to him from the trees, his immediate thought was, *Oh God, do I know her?*

And he slowed down again, stopping, turning.

She was still in the same place where he'd first seen her. The shadows from the trees enfolded her figure, so he could only make out her face. And it was not one that he recognized. It was a very lovely face indeed, though wholly different from the models.

Theirs had been like the faces of perfectly wrought mannequins, unreal in their symmetry. Whereas hers was ... 'lived in' was not exactly the right term. There were no lines or blemishes he could make out. But a heat radiated from her features, there was passion and emotion there. The models had been gorgeous in a static, passive way, whereas this woman's beauty went a good deal deeper and was all about embracing life.

He couldn't tell what color her eyes were precisely. But they were dark and warm and liquid, and were fixed on him intently.

"Er – do I know you?"

She stepped out from between the trees and walked slowly across the grass toward him. He thought at first her hair was black, but when a streetlight caught it he could see that it was auburn. She was fully as tall as Anya had been. And she was wearing some unusual looking kind of cloak. It reached right down to the ground, so that he couldn't even see her feet ... that made her look like she was floating. And it had some kind of weird pattern and texture to it, overlapping little sections, all dark green and slightly glossy.

They looked like ... hundreds of leaves, all sewn together. Which could not possibly be.

She smiled gently and then shook her head, and those two things combined seemed to entrance him. The world around him seemed to fade away, so that she was the only thing that he was properly aware of.

"No," she told him as she moved in closer. "You don't know me at all, but I know you. I know your every want and your every desire, Eric. The things you need, but never seem to get."

What was she talking about? Was she insane? How could she know anything about him if they'd never even met?

It started to occur to him how full of crazy people New York City was. And what more likely place to come across one than the park at night? Might she have some kind of weapon on her? He looked down, but couldn't see her hands. That peculiar cloak was covering them up.

"Like this evening, for instance," she was going on.

He ought to back away from her. He ought to turn and run. But when he attempted it, he couldn't move a muscle. And why was that?

"You tried and tried for hours, Eric. You made every effort that you could to get those women interested in you. Because you wanted a relationship with one of them? No. What you really wanted was this."

And suddenly, a hand came snaking out from underneath that cloak. Its fingernails were very long, he couldn't help but notice. The hand went to some kind of small clasp at her throat.

And she didn't stop walking. She kept on moving to him at the same unbroken pace. But her cloak fell away to the ground behind her. She was wearing nothing underneath it.

He could feel his eyes go very wide, his pulse starting to beat up against the front of his throat. She was *nuts*, she *had* to be. Although …

The beauty of her figure seemed to scorch his retinas. He couldn't look away from her. The height and fullness of her breasts. The swaying of her hips. There was a large black triangle between her legs, and you never saw that these days except in Seventies movies. So perhaps some kind of crazy hippy chick, practicing free love and all that?

He wasn't thinking straight, he realized. In fact, he was struggling to think at all. Her naked figure had filled up his vision, and provoked the kinds of reactions that you would expect. His skin felt hot. His breathing had gone ragged. And there was plenty going on between his own legs.

She finally stopped in front of him. Her smile transformed itself into a tiny but delighted laugh, like a bubble bursting from her lips. He could finally see the color of her eyes, the sky above them lightening very slightly. They were a clear and perfect green, brighter than he'd ever seen that color.

They were sparkling with amusement.

"Touch my heart, Eric," she said.

Do *what?*

"Touch my heart. Don't be afraid. You need to do it, and I want you to."

He thought 'no,' but his hand was already moving. It was almost like one of those dreams in which you had no control over

22

your own motions. His palm drifted up across the woman's left breast, stopping at the engorged nipple.

"Yes, that's right."

He applied his thumb and forefinger. She was no longer smiling gently but was grinning, her white teeth bared almost savagely.

"And now," she said, "you've partly gotten what you need. And now, I'm going to touch *your* heart."

The same hand that had unfastened her cloak came out toward him. He was so transfixed by her he barely noticed it. He felt it press against his shirt. But after that, there was a truly odd sensation, quite like nothing he had ever felt before.

Eric snapped partway out of the trance that he was in and peered down quickly. Couldn't understand what he was looking at, at first. Her hand had gone in *past* his shirt and seemed to have buried itself, right up to the wrist, *inside* his chest.

There was no pain. There wasn't even any blood. His fuddled mind tried to take in what was happening, and he finally guessed it had to be a matter of perspective – he was looking downward from an awkward angle and the fabric of his shirt must have obscured her hand.

And he was still trying to tell himself that was the case, when he felt – with perfect clarity – those long fingernails of hers start digging fiercely right into his heart.

His chest exploded with excruciating pain which quickly filled up his whole body.

Then it went away completely.

He was dropping to the grass.

And by the time his head was bouncing on it, his life was already over.

***

A touch of gold had added itself to the platinum in the sky a moment later. The woman stared down satisfiedly at Eric's corpse, then backtracked and retrieved her cloak. She wandered back into the trees, disappearing among them, the shadows swallowing her up so totally that she could not be seen at all.

Just before the sun finally rose, two more large patches of fog came sailing in across the Harlem River till they reached the park as well. They wandered in between the copse of trees where she had disappeared, and then dispersed.

4 – The Morning News

There was a timer mechanism on the small portable TV in her bedroom, and at just after seven it turned itself on, the volume pitched blaringly high, which was what was required to wake her.

The morning news was on. The first thing that Lindy was aware of was the authoritative voice of anchorman Matt Hamer filling up the air around her bed.

"Imagine you are walking home at night down a familiar street, sleepy houses all around you, when you are suddenly attacked …"

Huh? What kind of news item was this? Lindy sat bolt upright, trying to open her eyes properly, except they were gummy and the lids were stuck together.

"Well, that's what happened to a promising young freshman just last night."

Had something else been going on while she'd been sleeping? She pawed at her eyelids with her knuckles and finally got them to unstick. The TV came into focus. On the wall behind Matt Hamer was the caption *Terror in the Dark*. But the accompanying photo wasn't of New York – it looked like somewhere way out west.

"Eighteen year old Robert Plummer of Hastings, Nebraska enrolled at Arizona State last fall. He immediately became popular with his fellow students and a favorite with his teachers. A young man with a bright future stretching out ahead of him, in other words. But last night, walking home to his lodgings in Tempe after a party in neighboring Chandler, he was set upon and savagely mauled by a pack of coyotes, right out on the street of a well-populated city. We're going to our southwestern correspondent, Karen Todd."

The photograph behind him gave way to live feed. A woman in her thirties, clutching at a microphone, was stood in front of a large glass and concrete building. A sign beside the entrance read *UA Department of Emergency Medicine.*

"Good morning, Karen."

"Very early morning here, Matt."

"Do we have any idea of Bob's condition yet?"

Karen gave a sad shake of her head. "His condition is still being officially described as 'critical.' He has already had to lose one leg, and might well lose the other, but the real concern here is to whether he'll pull through at all."

"A difficult time for his family, then."

"Oh, sure. His parents and his brother and two sisters arrived in Phoenix just an hour ago. They were immediately ferried here, and are with him now. Naturally, they haven't made any statement yet, and aren't expected to for quite a while."

Matt nodded empathically. And then he settled back a little in his leather chair, his expression becoming thoughtful. "Does anybody have any idea how a pack of wild coyotes wandered in from the surrounding desert quite so far into a busy city?"

Karen's chin came up. "That's not thought to be the case, Matt. This is believed to be the work of a pack of 'urbanized' coyotes. That is, wild creatures who have moved into an urban environment for good. It's an increasing problem right across the States, with raccoons and foxes encroaching into the suburbs of almost all our cities. But here in the southwest, I'm afraid it's coyotes. This boy's not the first person down here to be attacked that way, and almost certainly won't be the last."

Jesus Christ, of all the awful ...!

Lindy dragged herself out of her bed and switched the TV off. There were so many bad things waiting for you out there in the darkness of a night-time city, and she knew that. But being actually ripped apart ... the very idea gave her the shudders.

She was still fully clothed. Her top was sticking to her, and her skirt kept getting caught between her legs. So she pulled down her blind and stripped off, went into her bathroom and switched on the shower.

When the warm water hit her skin, she remembered the Guy from last night. She couldn't even conjure up his face any longer, but recalled the firmness of his touch.

But when she was toweling herself down afterwards, when she was rubbing at her hair, she found herself holding both arms at a certain angle.

Which made her remember something else.

***

"Pick up the bat, Lindy."

"But Daddy, it's too heavy!"

"Pick up the bat!"

He was drunk again. Sometimes, when he got so drunk, he forgot that she was not a son and started showing a real interest in her, trying to teach her stuff. Except that wasn't necessarily a good thing.

It was mid-October, gray overhead and blowy. The promise of rain was on the air, but it hadn't arrived yet. They were out on the weed-strewn plot of dirt behind their apartment block in Brooklyn. He had a softball in one massive fist.

She strained and heaved and finally beat gravity, getting the bat up off the dirt. It wasn't any kid's bat he had given her. It was a genuine Louisville Slugger, almost as big as she was, and the weight of it made her wrists ache, but she held on tight.

'See,' she thought, 'I've done what you asked! Aren't you pleased with me?'

"You're not holding it right. Up across your shoulder, at a slope."

He grabbed hold of her wrists and forced the bat into the right position, the same way you saw on the professional games on the TV — he watched a lot of those. But then he let go. And gravity kicked in again, very fiercely, so her arms and shoulders flared with pain. Tears were pricking in her eyes. But she set her jaw and tried to hold to the position he had put her in. It didn't matter that he was being unreasonable ... she'd do anything to please him.

"It's wobbling!"

"I'm trying, Daddy!"

"What the hell is wrong with you? You're useless!"

And he had suddenly struck her out of nowhere, slamming her so hard across the ear that she went down.

When she finally managed to lift her head and look around, he'd gone stumbling away. She was alone out here.

***

She was still damp, but the hell with it. The apartment was plenty warm enough. She pulled on a robe and then padded back into her bedroom, opening the top drawer of her little nightstand. At the back was a small twist of paper. She opened it carefully and dipped her pinkie into it in such a way that her fingernail came back lined with powder, which she snorted. Just a little of it. Just to get her day off to a start and drive the old demons away. Her most recent drugs test had been a couple of weeks back, so she was safe for a good while.

And she was very good at getting around tests. She'd had three mandatory psych evaluations in the course of her career, and had passed each one with flying colors. When you grew up the way she had, then you very quickly learned to modulate your voice and control your expression, never seeming guilty or evasive, looking people calmly in the face and telling them what they wanted to hear.

Lindy went into her kitchenette and started coffee brewing. There was a window here that looked directly down onto the edge of Chinatown. Some of the food stores and restaurants were taking deliveries, and a few people were sitting at the sun-washed tables.

Personally, she didn't bother with breakfast these days. There was just the coffee and the coke.

She could hear some of her neighbors moving in the apartments round her. Lindy didn't know them, didn't even speak to them when they met on the stairs. She had no real friends. No one seemed to like her except Maxi, and God only knew why that was. Outside work she lived alone, except for nights like last one, and there'd been plenty of those.

She poured her coffee, staring out again. At a round chrome table, a young man was chugging at a paper cup of soda. As Lindy watched, a woman in a red beret came hurrying across to him. He stood up quickly and they kissed. He put his arms around her and she did the same. They were both beaming, lit up by each others' presence.

What was that like? Lindy pulled a face and turned away.

There were just a larger TV and old two-seater couch and a small coffee table in her living room. The walls were the same color they'd been when she'd first moved into this place. The only picture on them was a photo of her graduating the Academy. There was a small row of books on a shelf in one corner, almost all of them by Georges Simenon. She didn't like most authors, but she liked his stuff. He really understood people, how petty, how ridiculous they were, the nasty, selfish impulses that drove them to do hurtful things.

Then her thoughts turned to her work.

Work was her salvation. It was the only place she could put everything behind her, forget the way she lived, forget her past, and involve herself in something that was rational and almost pure. One case came hard on the heels of another, and you either solved them or you didn't, but you followed the same route with each, looking at forensic evidence, interviewing witnesses, toying with the separate pieces of the jigsaw you had been presented with until you finally built it up into a complete picture. It consumed her.

She was trying to bring some order and some sense into the world. It was the only decent thing that she had in her life these days.

And if she hung around in this apartment long enough, then the old memories would start hitting her, hard.

So she had better get to work.

5 – The Morgue

It was already getting pretty hot by the time that she arrived at the morgue. The street was sharply divided between brightness and shadow, and the windowpanes on the sunshine side were all like burning mirrors.

Doc Morris was standing outside on the sidewalk, leaning against a wall, smoking a cigarette and chatting casually with Maxi. He was a jowly older man with very fine gray hair that flopped down occasionally across his eyes. When he noticed her approaching, his pale brown gaze pinned on her face and stayed there. There was something rather insolent about the way he looked at people, like he didn't really trust them and he wanted them to know it.

Maxi was his usual self, standing very casually, his whole frame relaxed, although his eyes were gleaming with a razor sharpness that was almost always there, taking in everything around him. He noticed her as well and turned and grinned, but she ignored him, concentrating on the coroner instead.

"Am I seriously to believe you haven't started work on Martin Callum yet?"

Doc Morris shrugged, unconcerned, turned his head and blew out a stream of smoke.

"I thought you'd want to see it for yourself." He dug into the pocket of his stained white coat and came out with a sheet of paper. "Here's your tox report."

She snatched it from him, scanned it quickly. Apart from nicotine and a minimal amount of alcohol, there was nothing. Damn.

"Can we get *on* with this?"

The doc threw down his cigarette and ground it with his heel. "Your every wish is my command, my queen," he said with open sarcasm.

Except that when they went in, there were *two* corpses waiting to be examined. One was Mr. Callum from last night. But the other was a whole lot younger, a tousle-haired and slightly girlish fellow of about eighteen.

"What's this?"

"They brought him in around an hour ago," Doc Morris grunted.

Lindy finally turned to her colleague, looking to him for an explanation. And to her surprise, Maxi had become uneasy almost to the point of nervousness. What the hell was going on here?

"I dunno how to tell you this," he mumbled, "but he were found in the park too, a few hours later on th'other side, up near the start a' the West Sixties."

Seriously? Two corpses in Central Park in the course of a few hours?

So far as she knew, such an occurrence hadn't even been that likely back in the bad old days before the city had been cleaned up. Her gaze was already moving steadily across the young man's corpse, looking for some sign of injury and finding nothing.

"Was he naked too?"

"Nar. He only got that way when he were brought in here. He got found fully-clothed."

"What killed him?"

"Florette reckons it another heart attack."

"At his age?"

But she understood it happened. Twice in a few hours in the same general location, though? She swiveled back to Doc Morris and indicated he should start.

His assistants shifted Callum onto the slab first. Doc Morris yanked on a surgical cap and gloves, turned on his recording equipment, then picked up a scalpel and dug deep, cutting a big Y in Callum's chest. The separators came next, the corpse's ribcage being pushed back with a sickening cracking sound. Nothing else quite makes that noise.

The smell of the man's insides began to fill the room. Maxi coughed gently, but held his ground. Lindy didn't even react. She was staring fixedly at Callum's interior. Spread open the way he was, she was put in mind of some enormous, dark red flower. Only there seemed to be more congealed blood in there than there ought to have been. Like he'd bled out internally. Which was very odd.

She stared at the heart, leaning in slightly to do so. It looked ... *flatter* than it should have done. Could coronaries cause that?

"What the hell is *this*?" Doc Morris was grumbling.

His set down his instruments and placed his latex-covered fingers gently round the heart. And then he lifted it slightly.

"What the *fuck*?"

His thumb went to a left-hand valve and pushed a flap of muscle back. Lindy could see a straight edge, and she knew that wasn't right, since there are no straight lines inside a human chest.

Morris was still swearing like a drunken trooper, fumbling roughly with the heart right now, his eyelids widening with disbelief.

"What is it, doc?" Lindy broke across him.

She had never seen him act this way, and it made her feel genuinely anxious.

When Morris's face snapped toward her, the look in his brown eyes was shocking. There was genuine panic in them. There was something close to fear. And perhaps the suspicion he was going crazy.

"This organ has been incised, and several times," he snapped. "That's the reason that there's all this blood."

Lindy felt herself take a step back. The next time that her eyelashes batted, they sounded very loud. All that she could manage was a rather throaty, "Say again?"

"This man's heart has been repeatedly cut with something very sharp."

"And how's that possible?"

"It's *not*! There are no slightest lacerations on the outside of his body. No indication that his chest's been opened up, and even if it had ..."

The doc's voice petered off. He was shaking his head with absolute dumbfoundment.

The only thing to do, in the end, was get Eric Rochester up on the table. Lindy was holding her breath while the doc worked and, although she didn't look around at him, she knew that Maxi had to be the same.

Eric's ribs came slowly open like the jaws of one of those peculiar Venus Fly Traps, until there was enough light getting past them to take a look inside.

"Fuck me with a rusty shovel," Doc Morris blurted, for the benefit of the recording equipment.

***

There was a diner nearby that they often visited when they came here. She and Maxi usually sat beside the plate-glass window, but the sunlight was pushing through it so fiercely today they opted for a table near the back. A friendly waitress came across.

"I'll have a glass of water," Lindy told her.

She was often like that when she was on the job – in the mood for things that were unsullied.

"Still or sparkling?"

"Tap will do."

"I'll take a double latte," Maxi added.

Lindy waited till the waitress had gone before smirking at him and remarking, "Double latte? Wuss!"

All he did was smirk back at her. It was hard to believe that he had once worked undercover, hanging out with Yardies and the like ... he was always such a pussycat around her. Except she knew from past experience he was no pushover, and damned good when the need arose to throw your weight around. And *everyone* had different aspects to their character. Lord, didn't she know *that* for a fact?

But then their smiles faded, the mood of before returning. And they eyed each other carefully, wondering who was going to speak out first.

"So then," asked Maxi, "where d' we go from here?"

"How d'you mean?" Lindy came back at him. "We see if CSU's come up with anything. We talk to anyone who might have seen anything or been involved. We do our job, the same way that we always do."

Maxi shook his head.

"No, you don't seem to unnerstan'. Did you not hear what Morris said? The way those two guys died ... it be impossible."

"Well, now it's possible, because it's happened."

Maxi blinked, not understanding. "Uh?"

"Uh what? Do I look like a scientist to you? Some kind of explanation has to turn up, surely? Some medical condition so obscure that Morris hasn't heard of it. Or some kind of poison that attacks the heart."

"Can you even hear what you're sayin', gal? Something *that* unusual, twice in a few hours in th' same location?"

"Well, yeah, it's a pretty huge coincidence, for sure. But it has to be something along those lines, because there's nothing else it possibly *could* be."

"You certain a' that?"

She felt her brow furrowing.

"What are you saying exactly?"

Then she watched while Maxi struggled to find the right words.

"When I were growin' up in Jamaica, when I were a teenaged boy ... I remember some of the stories used to be told at night, when the moon were up an' the air were very still and quiet."

And she couldn't quite believe this. Had never once had any indication he was capable of this kind of thought. He was single, just like her. Rented a small downtown apartment the same way that she did – it was somewhere near East 14th, she believed. And – his little quirks and mannerisms aside, which were mostly cultural – he behaved like any other hard-working detective. He lived a wholly modern life, in other words. Who would have guessed he carried older stuff around inside him?

She practically smirked again. "Stories huh?"

"The kind that used to be told in hushed tones, by me grandma and me aunties."

And Lindy was so amazed she pulled a clown's face, straightening her lips and raising her thin red eyebrows up as high as they could go.

"Voodoo and zombies?"

"That be Haiti."

"That be bullflop and you know it, Maxi. Stories are made-up stuff. And people love that, but it's not our job. Our job is to get to the truth." She stopped a moment, eyeing him warily. "You haven't lost sight of that, have you?"

Maxi hitched his shoulders up. "Ain't quite sure." He decided to avoid her gaze, staring down at the tabletop, and Lindy could almost hear the cogs in his mind working. "You ever *been* to Jamaica, Lindy?"

"No, never."

She'd only ever known New York.

"When I were there, I lived out at the far edge of Montego Bay. Look out from my porch, and it were only hills and trees. Jamaica has ... bad history, ya know? A lot a' pain and sufferin'. A lot a' blood spilled in the ground. And some nights, standin' on my porch and starin' out across that landscape, I could sense it, feel it. That the blood had fed and watered something, makin' it put roots down. That the pain and sufferin' had caused something to grow. I could almost *hear* it sometimes, Lindy. Somethin' lurking out there."

"Sure there was. There was the imagination of a teenaged boy lurking out there. Maybe a few robbers too. There's only human evil, Maxi, nothing else. Tell me you know that?"

He shrugged again, more tiredly this time, but he didn't look convinced. In fact, a faint annoyance creased his brow. A slight pale glassiness dulled those sharp eyes of his. He'd been trying to communicate something to her. Not an everyday thing, no, but something that he genuinely believed in, deep down at the hard core of his being. That there was more to this world than could go into a case report. Only trouble was, she didn't want to hear it.

They were quiet for a while, sipping at their drinks. But finally, Maxi began staring at her in a slightly awkward, slantwise fashion she found puzzling.

And he said, "Arl we ever talk about is work these days."

And here it was again, another one of his intrusions. They were supposed to be colleagues. In point of fact, she was *supposed* to be his boss. Her back began stiffening, but she tried to act casual.

"Okay. What do you want to talk about?"

"You okay? On a personal level?"

"Why shouldn't I be?"

"Which be neither a yes or a no. You were spun when you showed up last night. Hardly the first time that has happened."

"Am I going to get a lecture here?"

But he started getting rather agitated.

"It not the *only* thing I've noticed, Lindy. Ya never mention any guy. Ya never mention friends at any time. Seen a movie, lately? Been out for a meal with a big bunch a' people?"

"What's your point?"

"That what everybody else does. But I've known ya years – ya never seem to do it."

"So?"

"So what *do* you do?"

He was really pushing right over the line this morning, wasn't he? She fought to hold down her annoyance, with just partial success.

"What do you *imagine* that I do?"

And she asked that aggressively enough that it ought to have made him stop. But it didn't – he simply got more het up.

"Ya turn up some mornings lookin' like you gone several rounds wit' a Mexican wrestler. Bruises on ya wrists, even bruises on ya ankles sometimes – think I don't notice? A few weeks back, you were in the office the entire morning and you didn't sit down once. So what was that about?"

That was when he realized he'd gone too far, and stopped, looking embarrassed. But she could see the other questions floating there, behind the gloss of his dark irises. *What did you let some guy do to you, Lindy? Did you let him spank you? Did you let him sodomize you?*

Frankly, she didn't remember. It could have been either, or it could have been both. On evenings when she found the Guy, she made a gift of her body to him, goading him to use her in whatever way he wanted. And the type of men she usually chose … they didn't need a great deal of persuading.

She was very, very practiced at controlling her expression, even the expression in her gaze. And so she kept it blank and stared back at him, daring him to voice those kinds of questions.

Which, of course, he never would. In the end he turned his head away, let out a rattly sigh and mumbled, "I think ya ought to have a boyfriend at your age, is all."

A boyfriend?

She'd only ever had one of those, and only for a sparse few days. And that had been an awfully long time back. In spite of which, it was still vivid in her mind.

6 – Kevin

Fourteen and awkward. What could be worse? Her bright red hair had always made her a target for teasing at school. But as she entered puberty, two other things started happening that made her stand out. She started getting taller, fast. That earned her the nickname 'beanpole' among others. And her breasts sprouted and kept on swelling until, by the age of fourteen, she had the figure of a full-grown woman.

That made a lot of the girls jealous of her. But it was the boys' reactions that were truly weird. Some of them would gaze down at her stupidly for a whole age, not looking at her face at all. Others would make dumb jokes regarding jugs and melons. And once in the playground, Danny Pearson had come up behind her, reached around, grabbed her right breast and twisted it so hard that it pained her the rest of the afternoon. He ran away immediately he did it. But why had he even behaved like that?

Except that then Kevin Mitchell had turned up at her school. His folks had moved up here from Charleston. He was two grades her senior but they were roughly the same height, and when they looked at each other that first day that he arrived she felt something click between them.

It was another couple of days before he came across and spoke to her.

Kevin was handsome – she was already aware of that, but up close it was even more pronounced. He had sandy hair and light hazel eyes and very even features, a dimple in his chin. He was muscular, but not in any heavyweight way, more like he swam a lot. And it turned out he was smart too, and polite, and softly-spoken.

They found themselves wandering away from the other kids, off to the far edge of the school yard. And they did the same the next couple of days, talking for ages about almost any subject. He asked her what her father did. She said he was a cop, but added nothing more. And Kevin seemed to accept that.

He smiled a lot, but it was only ever gently. Kevin was gentle the whole way through, and she felt very safe around him. So that when, on the fourth day, he reached out and took her hand, it was like some large butterfly had alighted on her fingers and she didn't pull away. She could feel a strange new kind of warmth flowing along her skin.

On the fifth day he was waiting for her by the gate when class broke up.

"I thought I'd walk you home."

Her instantaneous first thought was, 'My Dad'll see,' and her face went stiff and her heart started pounding. But then she remembered he'd be out on patrol. He never got back until after six. So she calmed down and smiled and nodded.

Hand in hand, she took him a route to her home she rarely used, through a labyrinth of intertwining alleys. She wasn't quite sure why she'd chosen this way. Except ... there was no one here, they were completely alone and were not overlooked. She was interested to see what he might do. Might he suddenly push her up against a wall and kiss her, like she'd seen in the movies? That looked so exciting. Might he even lay his palms against her breasts?

All he did was keep holding her hand and keep on talking to her, listening to her. So he was a gentleman, and that was pleasant too.

They finally wound up on the weed-strewn lot behind her block.

"Well, here we are."

"Fine. See you tomorrow," he smiled.

And her heart dropped at that remark. Was he simply going to turn around and walk away from her, without doing anything?

But the next moment, he'd leaned in toward her. Leaned in with his face, and pecked her gently on the lips. A butterfly alighting once again, but on her mouth this time. Her first kiss. She could feel her heart trying to leap out from her chest. It was a perfect moment ...

Broken by an enraged roar behind her.

Oh my God, she'd completely forgotten! He'd been transferred to the night shift just yesterday evening!

Dad came bursting out of the rear exit of the building and then surged across the empty lot, coming at them like a locomotive. She was so shocked that she was frozen to the spot. She couldn't look away from him, not even to check how Kevin was reacting.

Dad had on his uniform pants and boots, but was in his undershirt. His broad, hairy shoulders were lifted high, and the mass of muscle in his heavy arms was clenched. As he got closer, she could see his lips were skinned back from his teeth, and he was making snorting noises.

She cowered when he reached them, covering her head. But what her father did next startled even her.

He went straight past her. Grabbed Kevin by the front of his denim jacket.

And landed the hardest punch he could, square in the boy's face.

Kevin flew back and sprawled out on the dirt, blood pouring from his nose and mouth. Lindy shrieked and tried to protest. But Dad just grabbed her by the hair and started hauling her inside.

Once back inside their apartment, he proceeded to beat the living daylights out of her.

***

Half an hour later she was lying face down on her bed, still crying her eyes out, when the front bell rang. She got up, wiped the strands of mucus from her nose, then leaned out of her window. The agitated man down there on the porch was apparently Mr. Mitchell, Kevin's father.

Dad flat refused to let him up, going down and confronting him instead. He was still in his undershirt, had his hands on his hips. She couldn't see his face, only the top of his bald head, but could imagine his expression from his voice.

"Do you know what that son of yours was trying to do to my girl?" he was yelling, loud enough for the whole street to hear. "He was trying to do her! I'm not even gonna dignify that with the term 'statutory.' I'm gonna call it what it is, attempted rape!"

Mr. Mitchell opened his mouth to protest, but her father was having none of it.

"If I ever see that lousy kid of yours anywhere near my daughter again, I'm not only gonna see to it that he winds up in juvie, I'm gonna make sure it's the worst one in the goddamn state! Ever heard the term 'gladiator academy'? How long do you think your pervert son would last in one of those?"

And that had been it. When she'd next seen Kevin – with his heavily bruised face and bandaged nose – he'd turned and walked silently away from her. And after word had gotten round, the other boys started avoiding her as well. It was like people had learned she was the carrier of some awful plague. Her life was something no one wanted to become involved with.

And hers being the kind of neighborhood it was, that word kept spreading out beyond her school's front gates.

She was turning gradually into a full-grown woman, but no one would come near her.

Except that – before she'd even reached the age of twenty – she'd discovered there was one type of place where they would.

Away from Brooklyn, right across the river, in those establishments where no one had a family or history.

In crowded singles bars.

***

"Are we going to get to work or what?" she asked.

Maxi looked relieved that she'd suggested it. "Yar, let's do that."

They split the check between them, throwing down some extra change, then headed for the door. Just as they were about to step out onto the sun-blasted sidewalk, though, Lindy caught a glimpse of a reflection in the plate-glass window. Some guy – sitting at a table on his own – seemed to be staring at her retreating back.

Or perhaps her retreating ass? Part of her hoped so. This guy was the total business. Tall – she could tell that even though he was sitting down. Broad-shouldered, in a tailored suit. Dark thick hair, cut in a way that looked a little wild and spiky. A face that was mostly square. Black, dense eyebrows and a neatly shaped beard of designer stubble.

If this had been *Freddie's*, she'd have turned around and walked over to him instead of waiting for him to approach, and she almost never did that. But this wasn't *Freddie's* and she was on duty. Damn!

She glanced back all the same, hoping to catch his eye and even get a smile from him.

Except the table she'd been looking at in the reflection … it was empty.

Lindy blinked surprisedly.

Was she starting to imagine the Guy in her waking dreams now? It was a slightly troubling development.

And the best thing to do with *those things*, she knew, was to get on with her job and push them to the far back of her mind, where they wouldn't even bother her.

7 – You?

A call on her cell confirmed that forensics had come up with nothing. And not a single witness had stepped forward yet in either case.

Which left them with interviewing the people who'd been nearest to the two potential victims just before they'd died. Which in turn meant that she and Maxi were forced to split up. He took the East Side, Callum's direct neighbors. She took the West, the party Eric Rochester had attended last night. Someone at her office had already cobbled up a partial list of people who had been there, and it took some reading.

The phrase she kept on using on them most was, "Look, I'm not going for a drugs bust here. I couldn't give a damn about that aspect."

But she wanted to find out which drugs had been consumed. Poppers? Amyl nitrate could damage the heart, although she was pretty sure it couldn't shred it.

The interviewee who irritated her the worst was the party's host, Cooper Weiss. He was sad and solemn at first, obviously shocked by Eric's sudden death. But once he'd gotten past that, he started noticing the way she looked. He kept on glancing at her figure when he thought she wasn't looking. He grinned insipidly while they were talking, throwing in a couple of stupid little double entendres, as though at any moment she might jump into the sack with him. As if. In the first place, she was working now. And in the second, he was way too young, and rather doughy-faced.

The weird thing was – leaving his house – she thought she saw the guy that she'd imagined in the diner once again. Or rather, she saw his reflection. She was stepping out onto the sidewalk, sighing with relief that she had gotten away, when she caught a glimpse of the very handsome dark-haired guy standing directly behind her … his reflection was right there, in the window of a Lexus that was parked against the curb.

So she pivoted on her heel. But there was no one there. Apart from her, the street was empty.

Lindy shook her head and carried on.

She broke for lunch at just gone one. Bought herself a cheeseburger and Coke and went into the park and ate them on a bench. But she kept on staring round the whole time she was eating. People in sunhats were strolling. Dogs and kids were being walked. A group of Latino teenagers was playing a languid game of softball. What had genuinely happened here last night? The two realities weren't matching up.

She peered tiredly at the list that she'd been given. By this time, there were dozens more names at the bottom of it in her own handwriting, the residual result of the enquiries she'd made. *Hundreds* of people had been packed into that party. There was no way she could talk to all of them in just a single day.

But she knew she had to interview as many of them as she could. Police work wasn't about inspiration, the way it was portrayed in books and movies. Police work was largely legwork and digging. You kept on moving around, prodding at a seemingly impenetrable surface until a crack appeared and something gave.

She was in the shade of a small tree, where she was sitting. Out beyond its shadow, the park seemed to be almost melting in the heat. Each individual blade of grass was reflecting the sunlight. The air shimmered, and the huge grey boulders that protruded from the turf looked to her like big slumbering beasts.

How could anything that awful happen here, in this day and age? Was she simply chasing ghosts?

The burger was finished and the Coke was done. She balled the greasy paper up, stuffed it in the cup, stood up and tossed them in a nearby bin. Her heels clacked on the pathway as she walked out of the park.

As she reached the street, a bus went by. Its windows were gleaming, and she could see her own reflection in it.

The very handsome dark-haired guy was right behind her once again. Except that – when she turned around – he wasn't.

Was she going nuts? If she didn't know herself so well, she'd say she wasn't getting laid enough.

By the time that evening fell, she'd had enough. She'd run down slightly more than a dozen other people, and all she'd really gotten was a lecture on vegetarianism from Soozie Spark, who'd smelled the burger on her breath.

She was still uptown, a long way from home. The heat of the day had drained her, her clothes were sticking to her, and the straight fringe of her red hair was plastered to her brow. She needed to shower, but was too tired to care. And so she wandered down through the Upper West Side until she came to Broadway.

Twilight had transformed the city round her to a phantom of its former self. There were just as many cars and just as many people, but they were far less substantial now, appearing out of the surrounding grayness and then vanishing back into it. Only the moving lights around her had any real presence, the headlamps and taillights of the passing taxicabs, the flashing neon signs above the eateries and stores.

It wasn't too much longer before she knew that she needed to eat again. The burger at lunchtime had done little but give her appetite a boost. That was the way it was with the essentials of life – get a little taste of them, you needed more.

She chose some kind of Middle Eastern takeout place with a couple of ratty little tables tucked away into one corner. Studied the menu board above the counter, and then asked the kid behind it for a shawarma with salad in pitta bread. He could only have been seventeen, curly-haired and long-faced, his cheeks pockmarked, his teeth uneven. But he kept on glancing at her as he worked, his eyes sparkling.

"Like chili peppers?" he asked her, his accent so thick that the words were difficult to make out.

"Love 'em."

He shoveled two scoops of the little green torpedoes into the bread envelope, then beamed at her, handing it over.

"Extra chili peppers for the pretty lady."

And she almost threw back a retort at him, but stopped herself. He was from a different culture and was only trying to be kind.

There was no one else in here. She sat down on a wobbly chair and began to eat. Out on the street a truck went by, so large and heavy that it made her table shake. She really ought to have ordered a soda with this meal. Her mouth was burning.

She paused with the sandwich halfway to her lips.

The world around her went away, and her old life came back.

***

This was the day when everything was going to change. She'd finally worked out what he wanted from her. She had just completed high school and was home on break. And he was home too, since he was back on night shift once again.

He was sprawled out on the couch in his underwear and socks, watching a rerun of a Mets game, a beer in his fist and several empty bottles on the floor. When she edged herself into the room, he glanced across at her boredly a moment, then ignored her.

"Daddy, can I speak with you?"

He didn't even look at her again. Simply jerked his shoulders, tipping his forehead at the screen as if to tell her 'can't you see I'm busy?'

"Daddy, it's important."

He let out an angry sigh. Thumbed the remote and the TV went silent. Finally, he turned his face toward her.

"What is it?"

"I've decided what I want to be. I want to be a cop, like you."

When he responded with a "What?" it was a startlingly loud bark, and made her jerk back. He began standing up. It was like watching a tower raise itself up straight. She couldn't understand why, but something was going very badly wrong.

Her birth had been a terribly difficult one. She wasn't certain of the details, but at some stage surgical procedures had been involved. And when she was merely a few days old, the doctors had sat her parents down and explained to them that Momma would never be able to have another child.

And Daddy had wanted a son more than *anything*. A boy to carry his name forward and achieve the things he'd never done. It was one of the main reasons his life disappointed him, frustrated him so much.

How differently would this conversation have gone if she'd been a son?

"No daughter of mine is gonna be a cop!" he yelled.

There was a strange look in his eyes she'd never seen before. She couldn't figure it at all.

"But Dad, I want to do what you do. Help people. Protect them."

He advanced on her, his arms long and heavy by his sides and his palms open.

"You don't know the half of what I do! It's no work for a woman!"

Except he worked with women all the time. He'd taken her down to the station house one time, when she'd been almost ten, and she had seen it. Full-grown women in their dark blue uniforms and shiny boots, with guns strapped to their sides. They'd cooed over her for a few minutes, but had then gone back to being brisk and solid and efficient. And she'd admired them so much.

So she tried to tell her Dad a lot of that. But he simply wasn't listening. That peculiar look was growing stronger in his eyes, as though it were blinding him.

"You're gonna do a proper woman's job!" he yelled. "You're gonna be a secretary or a clerk! If you think for an instant I'm gonna let you wander round on these damned streets –"

"But I want to make a difference!" she cut across him.

He gawked at her.

"You?"

"I want to be *someone! I know I can!"*

An astonished, warmthless smile spread out across his lips. And then the top one twitched back, and he said slowly, "You'll never be anyone, Lindy. Don't you know that?"

Anger flared in her.

"You're wrong!"

And he hit her so hard that she went straight over. Then he squatted over her and pounded at her belly with his fists. However brutal he had been with her before, he'd only ever used his open palms, since he reserved his fists for Momma.

Momma was a very devout Catholic. She believed in 'till death do us part,' with no exceptions. No leaving and no divorce. And what kind of religion was that, where you thought God wanted you to get used as a punch-bag on an almost monthly basis? Lindy had stopped believing in Him years before, although she'd kept that to herself.

And maybe it was that – the fact he'd used his balled-up fists on her, and doubtless would again – that finally drove her out. She'd left. Spent the first week living rough, sleeping on a park bench, till a hostel took her in. Then she got herself a couple of evening jobs and she enrolled at the Academy.

When she graduated, she was top of her class. Once the ceremony was done, a tall guy with thick salt-and-pepper hair wandered over to her, smiling paternally, clutching her gently by the shoulder. His badge identified him as a captain of detectives. He said quietly, "Quite a few of us are going to be keeping a close eye on you. I can see a bright future ahead."

And then he tried to make a pass at her. She brushed him off as gently and as diplomatically as she was able, pointing out he still had on his wedding ring. She was already visiting the singles bars on a regular basis, but had never fucked a cop and never would. She needed to keep those two halves of her life entirely separate.

A couple of days later, in full uniform, she'd headed back to Brooklyn. She'd already figured out a while back why her father had reacted that way when she'd told him her ambitions. What the strange look in his eyes had been about.

It had been pure and simple fear that drove him. He had never been promoted. He was terrified that if she joined the force, she'd quickly overtake him. Become his superior, this stupid girl he'd never even wanted.

Only she was going to give him little choice but to accept it now. She'd defied him and had gotten what she wanted. So now, he was going to have to look at her and see that she had won. Recognize that she was someone after all.

And perhaps – once that had sunken in – his frame would slacken and his big shoulders would drop. And he'd look ashamed of himself, casting his gaze to the ground. Then finally look up at her with tears prickling in his eyes and murmur, "I was wrong."

She stopped outside the old apartment block, staring at her bedroom window. Reached into her pocket. She still had her keys.

She let herself in, and the familiar smells of stale, cheap cooking hit her. Not a thing had changed here. Time was still.

She went up the stairs carefully, her service revolver bumping on her hip. The building was silent round her. All she could hear was the soft clump of her own boots and the occasional creak from the risers under her.

And then she heard his voice. Only faintly, but he was yelling again.

It was far louder by the time she'd reached the apartment door. She was finding it hard to breathe. There was the crash of wooden furniture being overturned, and then a smashing noise that sounded like glass breaking.

Lindy somehow fumbled the other key into the lock, and she went in ...

8 – The Ax

The meat and bread were heavy in her stomach by the time she'd finished off her meal. She was feeling bloated and she hated that, so she decided that she'd walk it off.

She went back out onto Broadway and started heading south again. The air around her was as warm as a bath, and night had fallen fully now. The indistinct blurriness of twilight had given way to hard, dark edges all around her, shadows that had proper form, the rectangles of lit-up windows only making the darkness look more solid. People hurried past her on their way to theatres. Couples were sitting in restaurant windows, on display like they were part of the décor. There were bars too, the customers going in and out. And she knew of *one* bar, less than a block from here, where …

But no. She stopped herself. Last night had been sufficient for a while, and she genuinely was exhausted. She was happy to simply amble along, her step gentle and her head tucked down, anonymous, no expectations being made of her.

Someone laughed loudly, and she looked around in that direction. There was no one there, but she caught sight of her own reflection in the window of a little store.

The dark-haired guy was standing directly behind her once again.

She spun around and, again, found herself alone. Jesus, what was *this* about? She'd never had such strange, vivid imaginings before. Maybe it was down to tiredness. Or maybe she ought lay off the cocaine for a few days. It couldn't cause hallucinations, but could make you paranoid.

Lindy was down into the mid-Fifties by now, and Broadway was getting crowded around her. She tried to tell herself that she was practically invisible, that no one who was pushing past was even noticing her. But that turned out to be not entirely true. Some men's faces jerked toward her momentarily as they went by, their eyelids widening, their jaws becoming slightly slack. They weren't seeing a detective sergeant who investigated homicides. All that they could see was a tall, slim redhead with big boobs. Who knew what fantasies went through their heads in the couple of seconds that it took them to walk past her?

Who cared? Fantasies were like cheap tissues that you blew a tiny part of your thoughts into and then threw away. If only one of these men who were grasping at her with their eyes would have the nerve to go beyond that, summon up the courage to stop in front of her, making her stop walking too, and then say, "I want to get to know you better."

But they never had. They never would. She had to sit on a barstool and offer her body as a gift to get them interested.

A sudden instinct took her head round to the left. Why it had occurred to her to look in that direction, she wasn't quite sure. All there was across the street was another mob of people like the one that she was passing through, a thousand strangers packed in intimately closely, weaving round each other on the sidewalk. Nobody was doing anything unusual. No one in particular stood out.

But then ...she *saw* him again. The guy who she'd been spotting intermittently for the best part of this long, hot day. The guy she'd seen reflected in the glass.

Except he wasn't a reflection this time.

She stopped dead and her lips dropped apart. And for the first few seconds, she tried to tell herself that it was simply a trick of her sight. But no ... he was right there, right in front of her – she was *certain* of it.

He was striding down the opposite sidewalk in the same direction she was going.

That dark, slightly spiky hair. That same beard of stubble. Broad-shouldered and in a beautifully tailored suit. He had to be easily six foot six, and was standing out clearly in the crowd that he was walking through.

And what was going on here? How could a man who she had simply been imagining suddenly turn real? He just kept marching down his side of Broadway with his face fixed straight ahead, like he had very important business somewhere.

She kept on trying to tell herself that there were plenty of good-looking, urgent natured men in New York City. He was moving away from her now, the jam-packed sidewalk beginning to swallow him up like a river.

Except she had to know. She didn't understand this, and she needed to.

There were no stoplights anywhere near her. So the next second, she found herself stepping out onto the pavement. The asphalt had gone slightly tacky, sticking to her heels a little. Then a bus came rushing up at her, its horn blasting, and she was forced to jerk back violently and almost lost a shoe.

But on her next attempt she made it over as far as the central line. And then another dash and she was on the opposite sidewalk.

She looked south. A darkened, slightly spiky head bobbed for a few seconds and then vanished.

She was going through the press of bodies after him, not quite running but going fast. And more people were glancing at her now, men and women both, with curious expressions. What exactly was her rush? She went past them as quickly as she could, because she had to know the truth.

He was closer than he'd been. All that she could make out was the rear-side of his silhouetted head. But if she made him turn, looked at his face …

How could it *possibly* turn out to be the same one she'd been seeing? Something about this was very wrong.

He was coming up on the intersection at 52nd, where a crowd was waiting for the lights to turn. And she thought at first that he was going to join them, so she'd easily catch up. Only he didn't.

He swung abruptly to the left, almost like he was aware that he was being followed. And then disappeared around the corner.

Lindy sped her pace up even more, a sudden tightness in her throat. Went around the corner herself. Came to another dead halt.

There were a few people abroad on 52nd, but none of them were in a suit. None of them were broad-shouldered and six foot six.

The man was gone.

***

She was still trying to figure out which doorway he might have disappeared into when a black-and-white went past her back, its siren blaring. Followed by a second one, and then a third. Something else was going on. And she came out of her daze and jolted back into reality.

The squad cars were screeching to a halt barely a block and a half away. More sirens – a lot of them – were howling toward that same spot from other places in the city. And the weariness had left her several minutes back. She felt sharp and alert now. So she slung her badge around her neck and then started running, shouting, "Police! Coming through!"

She reached the edge of a broad circle of onlookers. It was moving backward slowly, some patrolmen yelling stuff along the lines of, "Clear the area and let us do our work!"

When she shouldered through she could see that – at the center of the circle – was a man waving an ax. He was short and stocky, rather dark-skinned, clad in a checkered shirt and baggy shorts. His round, flat face was screwed up with an insane kind of fury.

There was blood on his shirt, but it didn't seem to be his own. There was blood on the sidewalk in front of him too.

Everything went into slow motion for Lindy.

She looked around at what the uniforms were doing. About eight of them had surrounded the guy with their revolvers drawn. They were stopping him from going anywhere, but they were also giving him a good wide berth, yelling, "Put it down! Put that thing down! We don't want to hurt you!"

Glancing off to the side, she could see that more patrolmen were huddled around the open trunk of a black-and-white. They were pulling on protective vests and readying tasers. But why were they taking so long about it?

She knew the core truth about axes. They had an unstoppable momentum which even worked against the people who were wielding them. Once that sharpened iron head had started swinging, then it kept on going in a huge wide arc. And so there was an easy way to overcome a guy like this. She started walking forward.

One of the armed cops appeared to recognize her, shouted, "Sarge, get back!"

She paid him no attention, since it was already too late. The axman had noticed her by this time and was staring at her fiercely.

His eyes ... were the weirdest green. She'd never seen such a bright, distinctive version of that color. It was like being stared at by a pair of rounded emeralds, and it froze her for a moment.

What unfroze her was the ax head coming past in a swift downward stroke. She could feel the gust of air as it went by her face, and realized she'd stepped back before she'd even known it.

The edge of the blade clanked against the sidewalk – there was that momentum for you. And she tried to push herself forward and get a foot down on it, but the maniac was already lifting it again.

She was watching the guy like a hawk. There was drool spilling from his lips. His face was creased up like a twisted ball of card. There were so many lines around his eyes they looked like a kid's drawing of stars. But the greenness at their center seemed to burn and sparkle.

He bared his teeth. Murmured something that she couldn't hear properly and then stepped in again, swinging the ax at her from the side this time.

Which was what she wanted. *Attaboy.* She jumped back and it passed her and continued on, that unstoppable momentum taking it away from her. There was no way that he could bring it swinging immediately back.

And so she simply stepped right in, grabbing hold with both hands on the wooden shaft. In the same instant, she brought her left elbow slamming up under the man's chin. That made him loosen his grip a little.

And a little was enough. She shoved the handle upward, and it slipped through his grasp and hit him on the chin as well. Those very bright green eyes rolled backward, and his knees were buckling, and she was yanking the ax away from him, and the uniforms were rushing in ...

***

As soon as Lindy stepped away, cold sweat started running down her body. Her skin was shaking. She was trying to gulp in breaths of air, but they weren't going the whole way down.

What had come over her? Why'd she even *done* that? This evening was panning out like some kind of weird dream.

She stared at the sidewalk beneath her feet, and for a few seconds she felt that she was standing alone in the darkness, confused as to where she was, or why. But then she looked back up, all the lights of Broadway rushing into view. And could hear a new sound that she'd certainly not been expecting. It was applause, from the watching crowd.

A hand came clapping down on her left shoulder. She glanced around, and found herself staring into the aging face of the patrolman who had recognized her. His name was McGurk, and he was staring at her with open wonder.

"Damn good work, Sarge," he was saying. "Wouldn't go that route myself, but damned good work."

And he nodded and moved away from her.

Well, this kind of praise was another first, like nothing in the least that she was used to. She felt her cheeks flush and ducked her head again.

But – face it – this was why she had become a cop in the first place, wasn't it?

Was it?

Face it, mostly no.

***

She wanted to get away from here as quickly as she could, but simply walking off would look odd, so she hung around a little while. The uniformed guys had the axman cuffed and had dragged him to his feet and propped him up against the side of one of their patrol cars. He had his face tucked down, his shoulders heaving. God, he looked like he was crying. He was repeatedly shaking his head, denying something or protesting something.

His checkered shirt had a front pocket, and one of the patrolmen reached into it and pulled out a slim little rectangle that looked like a passport. Stupid place to put it. Another cop was talking to a storekeeper in a blue apron up at the front of the onlooking crowd. Ambulance sirens were wailing now. She hadn't even seen the people who this guy had hurt.

McGurk came ambling back to her, his mouth tight and his bushy eyebrows drawn together.

"His name's João Martinez. A tourist from Brazil. Claims he don't remember a thing about what happened."

"So where did he get the ax?"

McGurk jerked his thumb. "Hardware store just round the corner. Mr. Martinez here asked to see it, and then ran out onto the street with it."

"Just like that?"

"That's how all the worst things happen – just like that."

Martinez was protesting even more strenuously by this stage. She could hear his voice, and he sounded quite convinced what he was saying was the truth. That made her mildly curious, and she wandered across.

As soon as she was standing close enough, he seemed to sense her presence. He stopped shouting and his face came up. He stared at her mournfully.

With a pair of very watery *brown* eyes.

Which made her draw up rigidly, her face freezing with violent shock.

McGurk, who had been following her along, asked, "What's up, Sarge?"

She gave her head a baffled shake.

"His eyes. When I first looked into them, I thought that they were green."

"When he was still holding the ax, you mean?"

Lindy nodded.

"Heat of the moment," McGurk told her. "Everything looks different in the heat of the moment."

9 – Red

She finally broke away and got out through the ring of onlookers. Except that while she was doing that, several people tried to shake her hand. Hell, were any of them going to try and follow her as well? But they didn't, thank God. She was aware of a few cameras flashing, but that was all that really happened.

She walked briskly another block, then found a cab and directed it to the edge of Chinatown. She'd only been in it for a few minutes, though, when she saw that there was very little point in going home right now. There was no way that she was going to be able to rest or relax. Her heart was still pounding, pumping adrenalin through her veins. She was shaking, vibrating, completely wired. And she needed to let out all that energy somehow.

So Lindy banged the heel of her palm against the Perspex separator.

"Stop here, okay? Let me out."

A squeal of tires. The city drew her back onto its lamplit streets as though she were a mote of dust, sucked into the maw of a heavily breathing giant.

She was somewhere in the low Twenties. Damn, she should have let the cab carry her down into Chelsea at the very least. There were none of the right bars she knew of around here. The only one that she could see – half a block down and across the street – was full of youngish office workers.

But opposite it was a nightclub's entrance. And that made her mind up.

She went into the office worker bar, pushing her way through toward the washroom at the back, staring straight ahead and trying to ignore everyone around her. But not all of them ignored her. She had to make her way past a large gaggle of guys in their mid-twenties, rather drunk, their ties pulled loose. And just as she had gotten by them, one of them called out after her.

"Hey, beautiful, come here! I've got a knee that you can sit on!"

She shot "Go fuck yourself," across her shoulder.

Which got a loud "*Whoo!*" and then a peal of laughter from the entire group, like they were a bunch of schoolboys.

Which they still pretty well were. Early on in her life, she'd made the mistake of going home with a couple of guys like this. They didn't know how to take charge, and when she goaded them to treat her rougher they got all stuttery and limp-dicked. She'd slice her own wrists before she went that route again.

She finally got to the washroom, which was very clean and bright, and she was grateful for that. She went into a cubicle and peed, then went to a basin, rinsed her hands and examined herself in the mirror. She'd been walking around in the heat all day, and it showed. She unstuck her clothes from her body, shaking them gently till they lost most of their adhesion. Then she ran the cold tap again, cupped some in her hands and sluiced her mouth out as well as she could, trying to get rid of the smell of grilled meat.

She washed her face, unsticking the fringe of hair on her forehead. Then she went across to the hot-air blower, upped its angle and used it to dry herself off.

She went back to the mirror, rearranged her hair and then applied some makeup.

She still looked a good deal less than perfect, but she'd have to do.

Heading for the street, she had to pass through that same group of guys again. And as she went in between them, one of them muttered, "Bitch."

She didn't even bother coming back this time. None of them were worth her words.

She began crossing the pavement to the nightclub. There was a queue waiting outside it, but the doorman took one look at her and waved her through.

***

Once you got in past the doors, you had to go down several steps. This wasn't a big club. More like an intimate place, booths around the walls, soft shadows everywhere. The bar was over at the far side, lit subduedly like some antique jewel.

The music wasn't really that, more like just a pounding noise, like a heartbeat. She looked round slowly. The place wasn't particularly full and two thirds of the people in here were women. The men all seemed to be accompanied by someone.

She felt her high start to deflate a little, her adrenalin level starting to drop. But ... this wasn't the first time she'd been disappointed by the nightlife scene. At least she ought to get a vodka and tonic out of it. And so she wandered over to the bar, but found that she was having to wait behind a cluster of three couples who were all ordering elaborate cocktails.

And she was starting to think of leaving, when a deep voice with a Southern accent said, "Thank the Lord you finally showed up."

Her brow creased and she turned around.

And didn't recognize this feller. This was no one that she knew.

But she realized in the next instant she'd *like* to know him. He was really tall, and had what she'd always characterized as 'Texan good looks.' Hair cut short. A big square jaw with a dimple at the center of it. A wide mouth that was crooked into a smirk. Gunmetal blue eyes that had genuine laughter in them. He was a little jowlier and thicker round the waist than she was used to. But what the hell, she was adaptable.

He was wearing an expensive suit, and had a watch on his wrist that made Rolexes look cheap. Some high-flyer in oil or finance, maybe?

Only he'd just talked to her as if he knew her. Why'd he talked to her like that? She asked him.

"I've been waiting for a genuinely attractive woman the entire past hour, bored out of my tiny gourd. I was about to give it up and leave, but then *you* walked in through the door."

She let her gaze wander out past him. It flickered around the club briefly and then went back to his face.

"There are plenty of attractive women here."

"Sure there are. But only on the outside. None of them are fun like you."

Who the hell *was* this guy? She smiled at him a little tautly.

"Why'd you think I'm fun?" she asked.

"I recognize my own kind when I see it."

And the next moment, he'd clasped one of his massive hands gently around her wrist and was towing her across the dance floor in the direction of an empty booth. And she was a little startled at first, but finally recognized this was some kind of game that he was playing. He was eager to show her something.

He set her down on one of the benches with a comically courtly flourish and then sat across the narrow table from her. The benches here were deeply padded leather, and the smell of it filled up her nostrils.

At the center of the table was a small white dish with dried patchouli or some such in it. He emptied it onto the floor between his feet, then set it back down where it had been. Then reached into the inside pocket of his jacket and produced a little silver box. Two tiny pills clinked down into the dish.

Drugs?

"Designer," he said. "Brand-new, so they're not even illegal yet. And only mild, rather like drinking a little too much champagne."

Lindy raised her eyebrows at him. "Mild?"

"The drug's not the pleasure, sweetheart. Just the overture to that thing."

And that was a sentiment she thoroughly agreed with.

He picked up one of the pills between his thumb and forefinger. Said, "To fun," and waited for her.

She picked up the other one. "To fun."

But she watched him carefully until he'd swallowed his one before she knocked down her own. It seemed okay.

So far, he'd been making all the running. So she decided to see if she could actually wrong foot him.

"Want to know the truth about me?" she asked slowly. "I'm a cop."

He burst out into laughter, so much that his face turned red. "No, darlin', I don't think so."

"No. The truth is, I'm a hooker."

His head shook vigorously. "You're not one of them gals either."

"And how do you know?"

"I spend a great deal of my time in top hotels, and not even the most expensive escort girl looks halfway as alive as you."

Which clinched it.

***

Back out on the street, she followed him across the asphalt, back past the bar where the grown-up schoolboys were still yammering among themselves, then further up along the sidewalk.

But then suddenly, he stopped.

She looked around again.

"Where are we going?"

"We're here."

They were standing at the opening to a narrow alley. Lindy raised a single eyebrow this time.

"What? You can't afford a hotel room?"

"I can afford a whole hotel. That's not the point." And when he saw that she was still uncertain, he asked, "Ain't you as much fun as I thought you were, Red?"

She'd been called that before and liked it, and she smiled at him again. She'd already had sex in public places several times. And on one level that was crazy. Because if a uniformed cop happened by and caught her, then the consequences would be too dreadful to contemplate. But it was that, the risk, the danger, that made her pulse quicken and her entire body seem to salivate.

It was a narrow alley, largely empty, with just a very small light on at the end above a metal door. If any passer-by *did* happen to glance in, all that he would make out was a pair of moving shadows. And the thought of being reduced to an erotic silhouette excited her. So that, when he stepped in, she went with.

They stopped three quarters of the way down, turned to face each other. He reached into his pocket. *More pills?* She didn't need more. He'd been right about the first one, it was coursing through her blood like good champagne, extremely nice.

He produced a length of cord.

And her excitement faltered.

"What's that for?"

"Hell, I didn't think you'd need to ask."

She felt her face go slack.

"You're kidding." And she tried to study him again, but it was difficult in this level of darkness. "Doing it in an alley isn't good enough for you? You want to restrain me as well?"

But he said, "If you're diving into a pool, why not do it from the highest board?"

Which got her pulse driving again.

She let out a breath and then pivoted away from him and crossed her wrists behind her back.

And this was *totally* insane. She knew it. Working homicide, she came across women who had died taking one twentieth of the risk that she was. But the danger was the drug now, far more powerful than the pill she'd dropped. Her knees had started trembling. She waited.

His weight pushed up behind her, bumping her against the wall so that the rough brick grazed her cheek.

At times like these, the barrier between the two halves of her mind broke down, and she could hear what her subconscious mind was thinking. It was whispering:

Hold me. Want me. Need me.

It was whispering:

I make a gift of my body to you.

And then the cord started curling around her wrists, and her conscious mind thought *gift-wrapping,* and she almost laughed.

Didn't, because he was tying her way too tight, the cord digging savagely into her skin. He had already fastened the final knot and was turning her around again, and she opened up her mouth to protest. "*Hey!*"

And that was when he stuffed a linen handkerchief into it.

She couldn't see his face anymore, just the dark shape of his head. It moved closer to her ear, and he said to her, in a tone entirely different to the one he'd used before, "I knew you were a stupid slut from the first moment I laid eyes on you."

And this was no longer fun. This wasn't a game. His hands started moving very roughly down her body, tracing her waist, squeezing her breasts, but there was little sexual about it. And she went completely numb for a second, trying to pretend that she was somewhere else. But then the truth hit her. She had finally gone and done it, hadn't she? After all these years of picking men in bars, she'd gone and chosen someone she thought was the Guy, but who was actually a predator and just wanted to hurt her.

His palms settled themselves around the hem of her skirt and then began pushing it aggressively up. Which was when the shock gave way to panic and sheer terror, because she understood the mindset of this kind of guy. As soon as he figured out she had no underwear on, it would confirm his first impression of her and he'd spiral upward into overdrive and really do a number on her.

Every time she blinked now, she could see her pale, bruised body lying naked on Doc Morris' slab. And she'd better start doing something about that, before it was too late. So she brought her knee up very sharply, aiming for his crotch.

She could hear him grunt with pain, but not enough. She'd missed the target.

He hissed out the words "What did you do that for, you fucking bitch?" And then his hands were round her throat. His thumbs were compressing her larynx. She tried using her knee again, but he had stepped back out of reach, his arms held straight.

And this was it. She could feel how very wide her eyes were. And she was staring around at the alley she was going to die in. How'd she gotten this so wrong? She could feel tears running down her face. The pain in her throat was awful, and her lungs were burning. Her mouth couldn't scream, and so her mind did it for her.

A kind of fog seemed to fill the alley. It wasn't really that, she realized. She was blacking out. A one way trip into the final darkness. Oh my God.

But then the light above the metal doorway abruptly went out.

And she could hear a new voice, directly behind the man who had hold of her.

She couldn't make out what it was saying. But the very next moment, the grip on her windpipe slackened. She heard a wild, high yell, and it was coming from the guy who had been strangling her.

The moment after that, he went away.

He didn't *step* away. He wasn't *forced* away. He just ... suddenly went shooting back, his feet leaving the ground and his entire body hurtling off toward the far end of the alley, disappearing into deeper blackness.

Where'd he gone? *How'd* he gone?

There were no further sounds coming from the direction he'd vanished, only Lindy wasn't bothered about that right now. She was trying desperately to suck some air in through her nose, trying not to choke because her head was filled with mucus. Her knees were crumpling. Her hair was flopping down across her dampened face. Her back was sliding down against the wall.

Still alive.

Somehow saved, but not undamaged.

10 – Moving

She wound up sitting down, sort of. Her back still pressed against the wall, one leg buckled underneath her and the other sticking out across the ground. Managed to spit out the wad of cloth and gasped, then began coughing.

Who had rescued her? She couldn't see far into the alley and her eyes were wet, her vision blurred. But so far as she could tell she was alone in here. That made no sense.

Some footsteps went by, out on the sidewalk, and she could hear people chattering and laughing. And at first, she thought of shouting out for help. But if they called 911 and a squad car arrived, how was she going to explain how she had gotten trussed up in an alleyway? It didn't work. She'd have to help herself.

It took her nearly ten minutes to get loose of the cord, the knots had been tied so brutally tightly. How could she have been so idiotic, so wildly and absurdly reckless in the first place? She usually had a damned good inner radar when it came to this kind of stuff.

Did I get born *this dumb? Goddamn!*

A loop slipped free, and she was tugging at it urgently, moaning with relief as the bonds began to come undone. And then she was staggering to her feet, wobbly, her legs numb underneath her. She seemed to be making a great deal of noise now, her hard heels clattering against the alley's surfaced and her breath ratcheting in her throat. Her face was soaked with sweat. And her neck hurt as though she'd been suspended from a hangman's noose, which was actually pretty close to what had happened.

But the question that kept on coming to her was, *Why am I even still alive at all?*

She had managed to steady herself by this time and quiet herself down. She was no longer being deafened by her own breathing. And so she went as still as possible, listening, her eyelids wide. She could hear the faint murmur of distant traffic, but nothing on this street. And there was absolutely no one in this alley, not so far as she could tell. She needed a few minutes wholly to herself, to try and figure out what had truly happened. Why that murderous assault had come to a halt so abruptly.

She took both her handgun and her cell out of her purse. Gripped the latter in her left hand, turned on its flashlight function and – by its faint, pale beam – began to work her way toward the far end of the alley, her gaze switching from side to side, watchful for any sign of movement. There was none. The light over the metal door was still out – it looked as though the bulb had been smashed, although the glass dome covering it was still intact. That was just a small thing, but made no sense either.

She'd almost reached the dead end with its blank brick wall when she noticed something she had not before. The square, deeper black shadow down at this end, which she'd thought was just a product of the high surrounding buildings, was actually a Dumpster. It was pressed against the brickwork with its lid propped open. Lindy checked the open spaces either side of it first, the muzzle of her gun traveling where her gaze went. There were no crouching men or dead or injured bodies.

And then – as if caught up in a scary dream – she stepped up closer to the Dumpster's gaping maw.

She took a breath and peered inside, half expecting her original attacker to come rearing out and seize her round the throat again. But all that she could make out were a few crushed cans and candy wrappers, nothing else.

She could scarcely believe it. She played her light round every corner of the bin. There was barely any trash in it at all, and certainly no human being.

And she was just relaxing when a terrified instinct took hold of her. Because if there was nobody *in there* then there had to be someone outside, maybe coming up behind her. And she whipped round, almost yelling out, both hands shaking furiously, the light shaking, so that the alley looked as though it had some kind of strobe lamp in it.

But there was still no one there. She was completely on her own. And how could that be?

Then she reminded herself how long it had taken to free herself up. And how long after that had she simply sat there, stunned and breathless? Plenty of time for her attacker to flee and her rescuer to leave the scene. She was getting all riled up over nothing.

Her arms dropped to her sides, her finger slipping from the handgun's trigger. Felt her shoulders slump. Let her head drop, so that her red hair flopped into her eyes again. She felt such an utter dope. How'd she gotten into any of this? A fourteen year-old would know a whole lot better.

As a final act before she moved away, she reached out with her left hand, which was still holding the cell phone light. And hooked her index finger round the Dumpster's lid, giving it a light tug so that it dropped shut.

It did so with a heavy bang. The sound reverberated round the alley like a gunshot. Lindy raised her cell phone to switch the light off. And then paused, gawping at the section of the wall that had been covered by the Dumpster's lid.

There was more than simply brickwork there, a patch of something darker on it. As she watched, the bottom edge appeared to move a little

And her pulse was suddenly racing anew, her breath was rasping in her injured throat.

The dark patch was some four feet wide, unevenly shaped and apparently red.

It was blood.

***

What the *hell*? What *was* this? She found herself turning in circles several times, shoving the light every which direction that she could. But she could still find nothing. Aside from her, this alleyway was utterly deserted.

But no! If there was *that* much fresh blood, then there had to be a corpse. Except there was no sign of anything like that. Lindy played the light across the ground, going forward several yards at a time and then backtracking. There was no blood here, no trail across the concrete. Where had her attacker gone?

As for the back wall, it was a good fifteen feet high. No way to climb it. Certainly no way to drag a body out of sight behind it.

The metal door! That *had* to be the answer! Except she found there was no knob or handle, only a brass keyhole. And when she gripped an edge and tugged, it didn't budge a fraction, firmly locked.

The light from her cell was beginning to fade. Lindy thumbed it off, then stood there numbly in the darkness, trying to pull her muddled thoughts together. Maybe the drug that she'd taken was considerably stronger than she'd thought. How much of this had even been genuine? There was no proper way of knowing.

The pain in her throat was real enough. But after that?

She stared back at the patch of blood. It was glossy in the dimness. But that much of the stuff ... no one walked away from losing that much, or at least not very far.

And she was stupidly considering calling this in, her cop's instincts taking over, when the reality of what she had to do leapt up and hit her.

Oh Jesus Christ, I've got to get OUT of here!

She had a badly bruised neck. She had deep ligature marks on both her wrists, and any cops called in would notice. She had heaven only knew what kind of narcotic in her bloodstream, and no slightest idea how it would make her act or talk. Bring any of her colleagues into this and she would find herself in trouble deeper than the damned La Brea tarpits.

She had to distance herself from this. She had to go away and not look back. She returned to the spot where the attack had taken place and used the last of her cell's light to find the cord she had been bound with. Stuffed it in her purse – she didn't want to do this but she had no choice. Brushed her clothing down and got herself as calm looking as she could manage, and then went out of the alley.

Several of the grown-up schoolboys were staggering out of the bar she'd been in, yucking and guffawing to each other, so she turned smartly the other way. Her first thought was to find a cab. But once again, she saw that that was a really bad choice. If a body *was* eventually found and her office started canvassing the local cabbies, one of them would certainly remember a tall, shapely redhead who'd been acting oddly and looked shaken up.

When she reached the next intersection, a crosstown bus was sitting against the curb a few yards further down. So she ran for it and managed to jump up before the doors hissed shut, dropping her face low as she went in so the security camera didn't catch it.

There was no one else on board, thank Christ. One small mercy at least. Lindy staggered almost to the rear as the bus moved away along its route. She finally dumped herself into a seat and sat there at a huddled crouch.

There ... finally away. Finally able to stop, be very still a while, and try to figure out what had gone down. She sifted the events through her thoughts, trying to keep them in perfect order, the same way she did when she was at work.

For a start, her attacker *couldn't* have gone flying backward. That simply didn't happen. He had been yanked off her, by somebody far stronger than he was. As for the light above the doorway going out like that – it was merely a coincidence, the bulb had burst.

By the time the bus was nearing First, she thought that she had a far clearer picture mapped out in her head.

A passer-by had glanced into the alley and seen her plight. He'd come up behind her attacker, pulled him off, and they had fought. At some point, her rescuer had either broken the guy's nose or split open his scalp, either of which injury would let flow a good-sized quantity of blood.

Her attacker had been driven off – he'd fled the scene. And as for the guy who'd saved her ...

He'd simply walked away and left her there, still tied up and struggling for air? That made no sense, any way she turned it over.

Unless she wanted to wind up by the river, she had better get off this damned bus. She disembarked at the next stop, and as it rolled away she stared downtown in the direction of her home. It was at least twenty blocks away. But it would be perfectly okay to take a cab from this point. Only thing was, she couldn't see one.

Wearily, her throat still throbbing and her whole body starting to ache, Lindy began making her way through the Lower East Side. The streets were largely quiet, and as she walked she kept on surmising.

There was one other thing that she was missing. Just before her rescuer had made his move, just before he'd pulled the strangler off, he'd murmured something. And she struggled to remember what it was.

Something about 'head'? *What's going through your head?*
Something about 'dead'? *Keep that up and you're dead?*
And then it came to her, between one footfall and the next.
She was convinced that he'd said, "No, she's mine instead."
But she discarded that with a brisk shake of her head. Why on earth would someone who was helping her say anything like that?

You're being absurd. You were dying, being choked, losing consciousness, your pulse like cannon-fire in your ears. How could you remember any *words, let alone words that were spoken softly?*

No cab had appeared as yet, and this far downtown at this time of night it probably wasn't going to. All she wanted was to get back home and close her door behind her, and she wasn't even going to be able to do *that* for a considerable while. Her stride was very heavy now. She was mentally as well as physically exhausted.

Great going, she told herself as she pushed out across the next deserted intersection. *But where would you be now, if sheer chance hadn't brought that other guy along?*

Any way you looked at it, it was a very curious kind of luck.

11 – The Junkies

For the past three days, Neil Waller and Milo Boyles had had a roof over their heads. That is, they had managed to break into a basement storage locker at the rear of a tall building on the edge of the Garment District and proceeded to use it as a home.

Nobody had come down here and bothered them so far. The little room was lined with metal shelves, each of them with massive rolls of fabric on it. So, for want of anything better to sleep on, Neil and Milo had unraveled a couple of those and piled the cloth at the center of the room before sprawling out on it. It resembled a nest built by intruding rats, which was appropriate, although they weren't even aware of that.

They had managed to trade in enough stolen goods by midnight yesterday to buy themselves a quantity of low-grade scag, which they had injected between their toes. And they were still sleeping it off.

They started to come to around six in the evening, grunting and mumbling and wondering for the first few minutes where they were. Neither of the men had reached their thirties yet, but they behaved like they were pushing sixty half the time. They yawned copiously, sat up painfully, tried to stretch but then gave up on that. Milo started fumbling around for his socks and boots. He tried putting on Neil's instead before realizing his mistake and throwing them away into a corner.

"Hey, watcha do *that* for?" Neil complained.

But he didn't go after them. He sat there staring at his bare feet for a while.

Neither of them was in any particular hurry. Midtown Manhattan, the way it was these days, was not a particularly welcoming place for people such as they were. Once, it had been different, and they knew that and resented it. But these days, what with the city being cleaned up and all these extra cops, it was better that they started moving only when the shadows fell, when twilight blurred their features and hid what they were genuinely about. So they took their sweet time getting ready. It was practically an hour before Neil cracked the basement door and poked his face out.

"Jesus fuck!"

He pulled his head back in again, squinting, his eyes watering. There was still enough sunlight outside that its intensity had struck him like a blow across the nose. And the heat out there was so fierce that his throat felt like it might close up for an uncomfortable few seconds. He doubled over, hawked and spat.

Mumbled, "Let's leave it a while, okay?"

But Milo was complaining now. "I need to use the can, man."

And if there was one rule that they had, it was that they literally didn't shit in their own nest.

Out on the street, they walked about five yards apart, the way they usually did to minimize attention, their heads tucked down and their backs bent, their hands shoved deep into the pockets of their old frayed jeans. A cop car went by at one intersection, but it was already heading somewhere and did not slow down for them. And so they made it to the MacDonald's they normally frequented without being bothered. The place was packed, big queues at the tills, and so they went into the washroom without even being noticed.

While Milo was still locked up in a cubicle, Neil went over to a basin, ran the cold tap hard, rubbed some of it into his face and – finally waking up most of the way – stared at his own reflection.

He didn't recognize the face that was peering back at him. It was ridiculously thin, the bones practically showing through, the nose longer and more hooked than he remembered, blotchy at the end. His hair was wild and unkempt and his jaw was thick with stubble. Had he always looked like this? He couldn't quite recall.

Man, these were uncomfortable thoughts that he was having. Shit, he needed to get high again.

He made a deep cup of his hands, filled them with the water, slurped it, swirled it round his mouth, then spat it out again. Milo had still not come out of his cubicle.

"What, you fallen in?" Neil shouted. "An alligator climb up out of there and bite your ass?"

But Milo was constipated. They both were, always. It went with the territory.

Breakfast, when they finally got it, was a single small fries shared between them. That didn't bother them too much, since they rarely had anything that could be described as an appetite, not for food at least.

But by the time they reemerged onto the street, evening was starting to bleed the color from their surroundings. They walked a little closer now. It was time to start getting busy. So they headed over to the Port Authority, to find out if there was any luggage they could snatch.

Problem was, the way they looked made people immediately wary of them. Heads started twitching round, gazes hovering on them. And then – as though by some horrible dark magic – a uniformed cop appeared, stared at them aggressively, then began talking on his radio. So they forgot about the luggage bit, heading up along Eighth instead.

A year or so back, they'd have bee-lined the big department stores and tried their luck there. But that had been when they had still been able to afford a room in some cheap hotel and keep themselves a little cleaner and a little neater. These days, they didn't have a snowflake's chance – store security began to follow them the second they walked in and usually asked them to leave before they'd even wandered a few yards. And so they wandered up to 57th instead. Plenty of smaller stores, far less security.

Except ... what the hell was there to steal here? Neil could have reached in easily, grabbed a handful of clothing off a rack and run away with it, but what would that get him? Anything of any real value was tightly buttoned down, and where there were laptops or cameras there were people watching and alarms.

Night was falling now. They went on up into the Upper West Side, and they finally got lucky near the Y.

Here was a quiet, leafy side street, empty save for one fat guy who *had* to be a tourist, because he was wearing a goddamn Stetson on his big round head. In this fucking city? What a blast! They'd show this idiot who the *real* cowboys were.

He had one of those big, professional-looking digital cameras slung around his neck, and Neil understood that they were priced from several hundred dollars upward.

Not a word passed between he and Milo. They both knew the drill. Milo peeled off to the opposite sidewalk and began circling around the tourist so that he could come back from the other side. Neil simply waited until Milo was in place. The guy in the big hat wasn't even moving. He was staring at the skyline beyond Central Park, off in the direction of the Sherry-Netherland, as though he'd never seen anything like it in his entire life.

Milo started moving in. Neil did the same, and he was actually grinning now, enjoying this. He was thin and scrawny and homeless and broke, and he was going to make some well-heeled fucker pay for all of that in one fell swoop.

The tourist didn't even notice them until it was too late. And when he did, his flabby body went as rigid as it could. His eyebrows rose up on his big round face, and he tried to mumble something about, "Only minding my own business, guys."

The knife came out of Neil's back pocket. He believed that it was called a Harpy, and he'd had it for a while. It only had a short blade, but one with a nasty curve, like some raptor's beak. And it looked as sharp as a straight razor that had just been stropped. The kind of knife that would open up a wound if it so much as breezed against your skin. The kind of knife you didn't argue with. The tourist's eyes went very wide.

"Guys, I've just got credit cards. I've barely any cash."

"But you got that." And Neil jerked his forehead at the camera.

"Yeah, sure. Okay. You're welcome to it."

And the dumbass started trying to slip it from his neck. Except that he'd forgotten to take his hat off. Neil lashed out with his free hand, knocking the Stetson off the tourist's bald and shiny head. The guy twitched like a frightened child when he did that.

And the camera was in Neil's hand in another second.

But the truly hilarious thing was – as he and Milo were beating their retreat – he distinctly heard the tourist mutter underneath his breath, "I thought this place had been cleaned up?"

Neil had real trouble not bursting into laughter.

That's only statistics, man. Don't let bull stuff like statistics fool you.

***

Gerard, of course, tried to stiff them. He sat torpidly behind the thick wire cage at the counter of his pawnshop, turned the camera over in his fingers as though inspecting an entirely unremarkable chunk of rock, and said, "Thirty."

"What are you *talking* about, man? That's a professional fucking camera!"

"Don't shout." Gerard peered at him, his face a big dull blank, and then his head shook, his ponytail quivering. "This *looks* like a professional camera. But seriously, it's not. It's got a good zoom lens, I'll give you that. But the other features you'd expect – they're just not here. All that this is is a fancier-looking version of those small, pocket-sized digitals that you see everywhere. Whoever bought it is a schmuck."

"You're trying to gyp me!"

"Okay, take it back."

"No, hold it. No. You said it had a good zoom lens, right? That has to be worth something."

They wound up with thirty eight.

"What the hell are we going to do with that?" Milo was grumbling as they made their way over to the corner where Frankie dealt.

Neil shrugged philosophically. "We'll figure something out."

What they finally settled on was a reasonably sized lump of 'brown' – black tar heroin, nice and strong, but cheaper than the powdered stuff. Frankie even threw in a square of tinfoil and a half-filled plastic lighter. Neil and Milo headed back toward the park, going deep inside it this time. They found a clump of bushes they could hide behind, and chased the dragon till three quarters of the brown was used up. Then they fell asleep behind the shrubs.

What time it was when they reawakened they had no idea, since neither of them had worn watches for a good long while. But it was *deep* into the night by now, the moonlight shining down.

Somebody was moving out there nonetheless. A lone figure.

A slim blonde woman.

***

They sat up as quietly as they could, rubbing at their eyes until most of the residual blurriness was gone. Who the hell was *this*?

When they finally took a good look around they could see that, apart from the woman, there was no one else at all in this broad section of the park. Barely any traffic noise was coming from the streets beyond, so the hour had to be extremely late. The air had cooled down a reasonable amount, and Neil started feeling more alert than he usually did. Both of them levered themselves up onto their knees, so they could take a better look at the approaching woman without revealing themselves.

She appeared to be following a footpath. She went under one of the globe-shaped lights, and abruptly they could see her very clearly. She was fairly short, but slender and young, no more than twenty. And she had very straight gold-blonde hair that reached almost the whole way to her waist. Her skin was very white. Her legs were bare, and so were her feet. She was ambling along in an extremely casual fashion, her gaze fixed on some imagined distance.

Her face was heart-shaped and lovely, her lips full and pink. In fact, she looked like she'd just stepped out of a photo shoot. What was she doing here?

The next moment, she wandered off the path onto the grass. She changed direction, and Neil was concerned at first that they'd been spotted. But she hadn't sped up, didn't look alarmed. She was wandering along at the exact same pace.

She got close to another light. And Neil finally took in what she was wearing.

What the ...?

All she had on was some kind of very thin green smock. It went right up to the bottom of her throat, but left her shoulders and her arms entirely bare. And as she passed this second light, Neil took in the fact that it was practically translucent. He could see the high tilt of her breasts.

He hadn't thought of sex in quite a long while – junkies rarely did. But now he felt a hardness growing in him.

And Milo was obviously having the same type of idea, because he reached across and rapped Neil on the elbow with his knuckles.

"Thinking what I'm thinking?" he hissed.

"I'm not a mind reader, man."

"Aw, c'mon. Seriously? We could jump 'er."

They had gone that route one time before, with a student chick they'd happened across – drunk out of her gourd – stumbling late at night down the Cathedral Parkway. They had guided her confused ass into this same park and ...

Neil grinned hungrily, remembering that. I mean, shit, it wasn't like they got too many dates. She had been out of it the whole way through, and so it wasn't like they had been hurting her or nothing.

"I mean, look at her," Milo was pointing out. "Wandering round the park in her nightie at God knows what small hour? She's either nuts or drummed out of her skull. Either way, she won't even remember by the morning."

Their heads went around again, a final check. Any slightest sign of any problem and they would be gone like ghosts. But there was still nobody here except for them and the cute blonde. She was ambling around in broad circles now, like she was waiting patiently for something. Maybe this was what she really wanted – a couple of strange guys, down on the grass under the clear night sky. Some chicks liked that – Neil felt fairly sure of it.

They did the same as with the tourist, splitting up and circling around from opposite directions. Only they were going to have to play this thing a little different from a mugging. What Blondie here needed was being distracted until Milo had grabbed hold of her.

So Neil went through the bushes till he was in front of her, and then stepped out. She stopped dead. Didn't look scared, though. Didn't flinch back. Her face was a perfectly pale blank in the moonlight. Milo had been right. She was either very dumb or flying high on something.

Neil raised one hand in a placating gesture.

"Sorry. Didn't mean to startle you there. I was just out – you know – jogging, while the park is nice and quiet. Wasn't expecting anyone else to be here."

Smiling, he began to step a little closer, very smooth and gently. Milo had emerged from cover and was coming up behind her at a crouch.

"I've not seen you here before," Neil remarked casually, being careful to keep his gaze firmly on her face. "I'm sure I'd have remembered."

She was still not moving, not a muscle, and was peering at him calmly. Now that he was closer, he could see what color her eyes were. And he felt a faint amazement. They were the most piercing green he'd ever seen. Looked more like a cat's eyes than a person's. Maybe they were contacts and she *was* a model from a photo shoot, because it was a pretty damned unnatural hue.

But the next instant, every thought like that went straight out of Neil's head. Because Milo had gotten right up behind her and was preparing himself.

He lunged suddenly. He could move fast when he needed to, and was stronger than Neil. One arm went round both of hers, pinning her elbows to her body. And his free hand clamped itself across her mouth, pulling her head back onto his shoulder.

Trapped in that position, Neil could see her breasts perfectly clearly through the filmy garment she was wearing. Hunger flooded through him, and he started moving in himself.

That was till he realized something.

She wasn't struggling in the least little bit. She wasn't even trying to shout out against Milo's greasy palm. And when he looked into her eyes again ...

There was laughter in them.

The shock of it struck at him like a thunderclap. God, she really *did* want this. It took him a few seconds to absorb that, then he exhaled gently, hardly daring to believe his luck.

Started reaching for the high neck of her nightie. He was going to rip the thing in half. And then, he was going to split *her* in half, since that was what she was expecting. This was all panning out like some wet dream.

Till Milo started howling.

Neil jolted back. Was she biting his hand? *For chrissake, just pull it away, you dope! No one's going to hear her scream out here!*

And if she was going to start fighting after all ... his right hand tightened to a gnarled up fist. One punch to her belly ought to do it.

Except that Milo was now yelling like he'd caught on fire. How hard was she *biting* him, for chrissake? Neil was already drawing his fist back when he noticed a dark fluid splashing down onto the grass between them.

Milo's hand was pouring blood. He was trying to yank it back from the girl's mouth, but couldn't seem to do that. His whole body was shuddering as though convulsed by an electric shock. His eyes were as full of white as a scared horse's. And his shrieks kept on resounding out across the grass.

Abruptly, the blonde woman gave her head a shake, and Milo's hand was free. Except it came loose in a massive spray of blood, and two fingers were hanging oddly, partway severed.

Neil went stumbling backward, stunned.

The woman had turned Milo round, grabbed hold of him by the front of his T-shirt, and was dragging him toward her. Her right hand came up. Paused by her shoulder, like a hawk about to swoop. Then …

Plunged the whole way into Milo's chest. Whose screams abruptly stopped.

Neil went rigid with dismay. This couldn't be *happening*! How'd she *done* that?

The blonde woman let Milo drop, then turned her face to him. Her green eyes were glowing, lambent now. Her pale chin wore a beard of blood. Her mouth came open a short distance, and the canines at the top were long and curved, like daggers. Fangs.

Neil went flailing back still further, trying to put some space between this thing his eyes were seeing but his mind could not absorb. He was yelling something, only he was not sure what. Every muscle in his scrawny frame had turned to Jell-O.

But then instinct took over, and he turned and ran.

He couldn't even tell in which direction he was going. He couldn't even see straight, goddamit. Trees and rocks and stretches of open turf went past him in a darkened blur.

All that he could hear was his own ragged breathing. Vaguely, through his muddled panic, he could make out clustered lights ahead, and so he made for those. It seemed like he'd already been running for miles, as though the park would never end.

Finally, his strength gave out entirely. His lungs were burning so bad that they felt like they were going to explode. He came stumbling to a halt, doubling over, setting his hands on his knees and wheezing furiously. He *had* to have run far enough by this time, didn't he? Enough to put that crazy bitch a good long way behind him?

Sweat was dripping off his nose. He waited till his breath began to slow.

Sounds came drifting back to his ears. When he managed to lift his head a little, he finally saw where he had stopped. He'd wound up on the Rustic Bridge. A few dozen more steps and he'd be back into a city, like a sailor returning to dry land. He could do that and then think about what had happened later.

Neil glanced back across his shoulder, checking he was in the clear.

Unruffled, as calm and casual looking as before, the blonde woman was standing directly behind him.

12 – Oh, Yeah?

She'd finally gotten back to her apartment, crawled into her bed and fallen fast asleep. And in Lindy's dream, her past history was unspooling again in all its awful glory.

Once more, it was two days after she'd graduated. She'd returned to Brooklyn, to the scene of her torments, to show him what she'd gone and done. To finally prove her point. She'd let herself into the building, climbed the stairs. Stopped outside the apartment's front door, and heard the all-too-familiar sounds of domestic violence, him bellowing, stuff being overturned and smashed ...

Lindy swum back into semi-consciousness a moment and thought, "Maybe he started taking it out on her worse once I'd left?"

It was a thought that had occurred to her before, and it frightened and sickened her, leaving her confused and guilty. Then she sank back down into the murky memory-dream again.

She still had her key. Opened the door. Went through in the direction of the kitchen.

Stopped in the open doorway.

And here it was again, the never-ending nightmare.

Momma was halfway down on the linoleum floor. She was only half on the floor because he had her by the neck of her blouse and was yanking her face up to him, where his fists could reach it. Her eye was bruised, and there were thin trails of blood coming from her nose and mouth. The truly insane thing was that he seemed to believe that he had won some kind of bar fight, that he was standing straddling a male opponent who he'd gotten the better of and was now teaching a lesson. Except that wasn't the case. What in all hell did he think that he was doing?

Her training took over, and she was vaguely aware she'd popped the clip at the top of her holster. She hadn't meant to do that thing – her fingers had done it all by themselves.

But then she moved her hand away from the gun and shouted, "Stop it!"

And to her amazement, he actually did. He stopped dead still, freezing like a statue, not even so much as turning his face to her.

"*Let her go!*"

He did that too, Momma dropping to the floor.

Her father remained in the exact same position, except that a small grim smile had lit up his face now, a strange and oddly knowing smile, like he'd foreseen that this was going to happen.

And he confirmed that by muttering, "Always thought that you'd be back some day."

"*I'm not here for you! I'm here for me!* Look *at me!*"

He didn't do that straight away. Took his own sweet time. He pursed his lips and furrowed his brow and hitched his shoulders slightly up. But finally, his big bald head came swinging round. He took in how tall she was standing, and the cap on her head with its shiny new peak, and her boots and her belt and her crisp fresh dark blue uniform and the silver badge gleaming proudly on her chest.

And he said ...

And Daddy said ...

And her own goddamn father said ...

"*Oh, yeah?" He thrust out his lower lip, his eyes glittering in a peculiar way. "And who'd you have to open up your legs for to get to wear that thing?*"

It was worse than any physical blow that he had ever landed on her. And her gun was out in both her hands next instant, hot tears streaming down her face ...

Lindy woke up sharply. She was in her bed, but lying in an odd position, her elbows almost pressed against her knees. She couldn't see the room around her. She was wrapped up in her quilt, she realized. And there really were teardrops running down her face.

The memories kept on spilling through her mind, not as a dream this time.

He'd not been afraid of her gun. In fact, he'd moved toward it, spreading his arms out widely to his sides, a huge and ridiculous smirk on his face.

"*Go on! Do it! Show me how tough you've become! Shoot your old man! Shoot your daddy!*"

"*Shut up!*"

But he hadn't stopped. He'd begun capering from side to side like some absurd jester, dancing, prancing, his chest wide open to her bullet.

"Go on, go on, do it!"

He was a monster. No, he was insane. The whole while she had been a little child, he'd called her ugly. What kind of father was that? And once she'd hit puberty, he'd simply looked disgusted and ignored her as much as he could. He was out of his mind. He was deranged!

"Shoot the guy who brought you into this world!"

"God, I wish you never had!"

Which was when it occurred to her that ... maybe he really wanted her to do it. Maybe he wanted her to really shoot him. Maybe a part of him was looking down at himself from a higher angle, could see what he was, and hated himself far more than he hated her.

So finally, she'd holstered the gun. And turned. And walked away, refusing to give him what he needed, since it would destroy her too.

And she'd never, ever once gone back. How could you deal with that kind of madness?

She was getting blurry again, sleep sucking her back into its careless depths. She rubbed her cheeks against the inside of the quilt, trying to dry them.

Just before she tumbled back into unconsciousness, she heard his voice again.

"Who'd you have to open up your legs for –?"

And the answer sprang up full-blown in her head.

"Everyone. I open up my legs for everyone, you bastard, and I do it mostly just to flip the bird at you."

It was a rare moment of insight, and it left her feeling bad.

But it was the last thought that she had before unconsciousness reclaimed her, and she let it go like some unwanted scrap of paper, secure in the knowledge she'd forget it by the morning.

13 – The Morning News, Part II

"... two degrees hotter than yesterday," anchorman Matt Hamer was saying.

The timer on her portable TV had switched on the news, as usual.

"Now let's take a look at some of this morning's headlines. The *Times* has ..."

Lindy struggled into wakefulness, her dreams forgotten. The quilt was still wrapped tightly round her. She'd been sleeping curled up in a ball, but not on her side, on her elbows and knees, her head tucked down between her arms. Which meant that, when she tried to move, her lower back ached terribly and cramp flared through her thighs. And she was still fully clothed. *My God!* The only times she'd ever woken up like this was when she got extremely drunk the night before, and last night hadn't been like that.

What kind of morning was she waking to? Did she still have her job? She pushed her face out tentatively from beneath the covers and the sunlight hit it and she groaned.

"Whereas the *Post* is running," Matt Hamer was saying, "with HERO COP FLOORS AXMAN."

Lindy sat up dead straight, her eyes going wide as they took in what the TV screen was showing. That was her own photo, right there on the cover of the *New York Post*.

So much had happened yesterday evening. The headline might as well have read NYMPHO COP IN ALLEYWAY SCANDAL. Or maybe BAD COP COVERS UP POSSIBLE MURDER. But instead, it didn't say any of that. In the eyes of the world, she was officially a hero.

This was happening too fast. And so she shut her eyes, clasped both her hands across her face and breathed in and out slowly. It was only the heat of the sunlight on her bed that finally made her move.

She stumbled through into her little bathroom. And there it was, starkly in the mirror. The middle section of her throat was a mass of dark purple and yellow bruises. She could swallow fairly normally by now, but the evidence of last night's brush with death would not go away anything like so easily.

There was nothing she could do about it except cover it up, she saw. The last thing that she needed was for her colleagues to know.

Lindy began stripping off, throwing her clothes out carelessly onto the bedroom floor. She ran the shower just as hot as she could take it and then clambered in, keeping her head under for the first full minute before pulling her face clear and soaping down her body. And she went at that for a good long while. Every time she blinked, she could see the silhouette of her attacker still in front of her. But even that was fading by the time that she climbed out and started toweling herself down. She'd been a cop more than a decade, and this wasn't the first time somebody had tried to kill her. So she'd recover far quicker than a civilian ... she was sure of that.

You were wrong about me, Daddy. I am special. I am strong.

She stopped toweling her hair and inspected her wrists. There were only the thinnest of pink lines around them from the cord. No one would notice, save for Maxi perhaps.

By the time she'd gotten a robe on, by the time she'd tooted a little more coke than was usual, by the time she'd phoned in to say that she was coming in a little late this morning and then fixed herself a second cup of coffee, she'd gotten it all figured out. Living the lifestyle that she did, she'd always known – deep down – that something like last night might come along. And now it had, except she'd gotten through it safely to the other side. The storm had passed. She was home free. She'd lay off the bars and clubs for maybe a week or so, and she wouldn't let any man tie her up for a good long period. But she was safe now. Somehow.

Lindy felt the bridge of her nose crease, thinking again – momentarily – about the stranger who had saved her. Maybe he had been a criminal himself, and hadn't wanted to get caught. But the query only lasted for a second in her mind before something else replaced it.

The TV was still yapping fairly loudly in her bedroom.

"In further breaking news, the body of socialite Kendra Callier was discovered in front of her parents' home on Fifth Avenue in the early hours of this morning."

The park again? Lindy stuck her head through.

"Kendra came to public notoriety two years back when a video of her with several young men was released onto the Internet. She went on to become the 'ultimate wild child,' with stories of her ceaseless partying the constant talk of tabloids right across the world. Several spells in rehab …"

Kendra had been the only daughter of Orson Callier, the property magnate, Lindy knew. She was – Lindy struggled to remember – just twenty years old. So why was she dead?

"… from a high balcony of her parents' home. According to police reports, no one else's involvement is suspected."

She'd been the heiress to a fortune topping several billion dollars. She could go anywhere and do anything and be anyone she wanted. And she'd gone and killed herself instead? How nuts was that?

Apparently, not everyone had been so lucky last night.

***

When she finally walked into the office, all her colleagues who were at their desks stood up and started applauding. Her second round of applause in twenty four hours. Her first two ever. Lindy did her best to duck her head and look modest. She was in one of her lightweight suits with a thin cotton top on underneath it but had added, this particular morning, a brightly colored neckscarf – canary yellow, with red and blue spots – that covered two thirds of her throat. She also had on a pair of pale green shades, so that Maxi couldn't look into her eyes and see she had been using.

Except Maxi wasn't here. And neither was Renzo.

"Banhoff wants to see you in his office, right away," Bob Collins told her.

Captain Ronald Banhoff – crouched behind his desk over some papers – was a short, rather squat man in his early fifties. He had a full head of wavy hair so black that everyone could see he dyed it. Reddened cheeks and a slight strawberry nose. He had a penchant for colorfully embroidered waistcoats, which he doubtless thought made him look interesting. He was wrong.

But there was a copy of the *Post* lying at one side of his desk, the front page on view. And when she tapped on his door and he looked up, his face broke out into a wide, delighted, toothy grin.

He pushed himself up, hurried over to her, shaking her hand vigorously.

"Here's the hero, home from the wars!" he crowed.

Lindy had never liked him much, but it was hard not to respond to this kind of praise. She felt a childish smile break out inside of her. But then she began looking for the faults in what she'd done.

"I wasn't following proper procedure," she pointed out, knowing how keen Banhoff was on that kind of stuff.

But he didn't even seem to care this particular morning. He simply slapped his palm down on the copy of the *Post* and announced, "This makes us look good! This makes the whole department look good! You can't even *buy* publicity like this!"

He circled back around and took his chair, then invited her to sit down opposite. Lindy slipped her shades off. A windowless office, it was dim in here, and Banhoff wasn't observant enough to notice the way her pupils were.

He tented his knuckles underneath his chin, still beaming.

"There's a commendation in this, obviously. Probably a medal too."

"That's great."

"And I must say, you're very nicely turned out this morning. I wish more of my people …"

Then he faltered to a nervous halt.

She could almost hear the small wheels turning in his mind. He was wondering if what he'd said could be construed in any way as inappropriate. Banhoff was actually a hapless dope. Word was, they had bumped him up to captain just to get him sat down in a nice quiet office, off the streets and out of the hair of the taxpaying public.

He finally decided he was fairly safe, looked newly serious and cleared his throat.

"Anyway, to business. This whole Kendra Callier brouhaha."

"I thought that it was suicide?"

"So did we. But we'd originally believed that she was alone in the house, and it now turns out there was someone with her. Hayes'll fill you in on all the details. He's waiting for you downstairs."

Lindy felt her brow go wrinkly.

"I'm already working on another case."

"Do you know how much pull Orson Callier has?" Banhoff came back at her sharply. "Jesus, he and Mrs. Callier had to come back from the Hamptons at five o' clock this frigging morning. And so naturally, they want our very finest on the case. You're our hero cop. The papers say so. So you're it. *Capice?*"

Who even said that anymore? He sounded like an old movie, and Lindy could feel her irritation growing.

"So there was someone with her? What does that prove? I'm dealing with a double murder here."

"Quadruple, as of a few hours back."

Which jolted her.

"Two more stiffs have been found in the park," Banhoff continued. "Both with the same cause of death."

"But then I –"

"Pair of junkie scumbags, both with sheets like Marge Simpson's 'to do' list. City's better off without 'em. Renzo's on it."

"But I –"

Occasionally, Banhoff got a hard and nasty gleam in his small eyes, and today was one of those occasions.

"As of this morning, sergeant, you represent the very best that the NYPD has to offer. That being the case, you'd better act like it and do exactly as you're told."

14 – The Calliers

Maxi was waiting for her in a mud-brown Buick in the basement garage. She put her shades back on as she approached the car, which earned her a curious squint.

"You okay there, Lindy gal?"

"Any reason why I shouldn't be?"

She got in. Maxi kept on looking at her sideways without turning his head fully, his hands set firmly on the steering wheel.

"Saw the headline. I believe congratulations am in order."

"Thanks."

"Why the shades, then? Celebratin' last night?"

"Right."

"'bout a headline that you wouldn't ha' seen until this morning?" he asked dryly.

Damn, why did he always do this to her? Why was he always studying her so very closely? He glanced briefly at her wrists, a little longer at her gaily-colored neckscarf, and then rolled his eyes and keyed the engine and they trundled out into the New York sunlight.

"How come we now think Kendra wasn't alone?" she asked.

"Her bed, freshly made at three o'clock th' previous afternoon, were all mussed up."

"And?"

"CSU found a hair in it. Short, dark, curly one."

And Kendra Callier was a natural blonde.

"Cleanly lasered too, an' so it definitely weren't hers."

At last, here was her chance to get back at him a little. Lindy smirked and lifted an eyebrow.

"So you've watched that famous video, huh?"

"You not?"

Before much longer, the high towers of midtown were giving way to the lower structures of the Upper East Side. There weren't too many pedestrians about, but there were a load of doormen hanging round the entrances to the grand apartment blocks. The Callier residence wasn't exactly hard to find, but they had to circle for five minutes before Maxi found a parking spot. Which was why Lindy generally preferred to go on foot or else use public transportation. Owning a car in Manhattan was like trying to keep a horse in your back yard – considerably more trouble than the thing was worth.

'We're sorry for your loss,' was the mantra that kept repeating through her head as a flunky let them in and showed them up a flight of marble stairs. The Calliers were waiting in a grandly-decorated reception room on a huge Regency sofa all done out in pink damask.

Orson Callier got slowly to his feet, his wife following suit and clutching at his forearm. Maxi hung back while Lindy stepped forward, stretching out her hand. There was an unspoken formality to meetings such as these.

"I am truly, genuinely sorry for your loss."

Callier was a big man, in his mid-sixties but still very fit and deeply tanned. Twenty years younger, ten even, and she'd immediately have seen him as the Guy. As for Mrs. Callier, she was his third wife and had once been Miss Wisconsin. She was half his age and normally looked fabulous, but grief had aged her now.

They were both dressed in expensive sweats. They'd obviously dragged on what was quickest before getting down here. Callier's face crumpled up into a lined, weary expression that was neither a smile nor a frown, and then he shook her hand and murmured, "Kind of you, detective."

Both the couple's eyes were red-rimmed. They looked utterly exhausted. They had the flunky pull a couple of smaller chairs across before he left, and then they sat back down on the big couch. It was like they were waiting for something else to happen. Except they were not sure what.

Lindy settled back in her chair. But Maxi perched uncomfortably on the edge of his, already aware that he was not going to be too much of a part of this discussion.

Lindy turned her gaze to Mrs. Callier.

"Alexandra, is it?"

"That's right. Allie."

"You weren't Kendra's natural mother?"

"Obviously not. There was barely more than a decade between us. We were more like sisters. She was a sweet kid."

Lindy immediately switched her focus to Orson Callier, who had raised his chin and taken on a slightly defiant look.

"All most people knew of my daughter, detective, was her reputation. But there was a damned sight more to her than that. She was bright, and she was very kind. And she could be pretty amazing sometimes, seizing every opportunity to get the best out of her life."

"She lived here?"

"No. She had her own place in the Village. She preferred to hang around with ... less conventional types than you tend to find in this neck of the woods."

"Paid for by herself, or you?"

Orson set his teeth for a few seconds.

"She paid. Her doting grandpa left her a big trust fund, see, that kicked in as soon as she hit eighteen years of age. Not a single thing that I could do about it, and – believe me – I tried."

"What was she doing up here, then?"

Callier's defiance evaporated and his chin went down.

"Her lifestyle ..." he started, then gave up.

Mrs. Callier took over.

"Her lifestyle could be very wearing. Kendra would sometimes find herself on the verge of burning out. Any time that happened, we made it perfectly clear that there was always a sanctuary for her here. She could come here and remain here any time she wanted."

"Which was what she was about last night?"

"Yes," Orson growled.

"There were no other people that you know of in the house? Some servants?"

"The only one who lives in is Armando, our cook. And he was visiting his mother last night, in Jersey City."

Orson Callier went on to explain that, though it might not look it, this house had a security system that was pure state-of-the-art. The whole place was alarmed, naturally. But beyond that, every time a door or window opened it was recorded on computer, both the time and the duration of that point of egress staying open. And there were hidden cameras all over the lower levels of the house, on the porch, around the front door, in the lobby and up the first flight of steps.

"But none in the higher rooms?"

"Of course not. Privacy becomes an issue."

Lindy turned to Maxi. "Have we seen the footage yet?"

"We've looked at it several times," Maxi told her with a weary nod. "It shows no one except Kendra comin' in."

His expression told her that this entire business made no sense to him. Nor her either. *Someone* must have gotten in, since they already had the evidence to prove that.

Then Maxi's cell phone started humming in his pocket. He excused himself and walked out of the room before he answered it.

Lindy returned her attention to Callier. "Did Kendra seem depressed?"

And he began looking a little angry. "She was *never* that thing. She was tired. Flaked out. She'd been burning the candle at both ends as usual, and …"

A tear suddenly went rolling down his cheek and he sucked in a wheezy breath.

"People always used to act like it was my fault. Like I ought to have controlled her better, put my foot down, made her stop. But they didn't know her. You could no more control my daughter than you could grab hold of a bolt of lightning. And once I'd accepted that, I came to see the only thing that I could do for her was be there when she needed me, help her when she asked for help, and simply …"

Then he really started crying.

"Lindy?" Maxi called from the partly open doorway, before remembering himself. "Er … ma'am?"

It occurred to Lindy to apologize, except that Orson Callier no longer seemed aware that she was even in the room. And his wife was huddled over him, trying to comfort him but descending into tearfulness herself. They made an awful sight. And in a way, an enviable one. Who'd cry for her?

So she got up quietly and went over to the door, which Maxi motioned her through, out onto the landing.

"The preliminary DNA be back," he told her. "And the short and curly? It be female."

"No shit?"

Lindy glanced back into the room. What a picture. One of the richest and most powerful men in the United States, doubled over, his huge body racked with sobs, mucus dripping from his nose, his trophy wife reduced to an old woman by the agony of this.

Maxi looked where she was looking, then said quietly, "I t'ink they just found out that money doesn't stop ya bein' mortal."

"They've had more than enough," Lindy nodded. "They don't need this as well. We need to speak to those who knew her other life a whole lot better."

Back in the open air, the sunlight burned at them so hard that it was like a swarm of flies attacking them. Maxi's cell phone hummed again while they were returning to the car.

"Doc Morris' report has come back too," he told her.

"Wow, he moved fast for a change."

"Found absolutely no indication a' Kendra being forced off of that balcony."

"Okay. Tox?"

"Practically clean."

"She wasn't pushed. She wasn't drunk or drugged up. Still an apparent suicide, except that where was our mystery lady when it happened?"

They reached the Buick and climbed inside, but it was even hotter in the car than out of it. And so they left the doors wide open.

"What we need is a list of Kendra's friends and close acquaintances."

"Already got a partial one," Maxi told her, reaching for an envelope on the back seat.

He handed it to her. It was page upon A4 page of single-spaced typing.

"You kidding me! We might as well start working through the phonebook!"

"How da we approach this, then?" Maxi asked.

"How do you eat an elephant?"

"What?"

"One bite at a time."

He grinned. Lindy scanned through the addresses.

"You got another copy of this?"

"Yar."

"You take uptown, then. I'll take downtown."

15 – Daddy's Girl

Since he had the Upper West Side to work on as well as the East, Maxi drove her through the park and dropped her off at Columbus Circle, where she could catch a bus into the Village. Once on one, there were no seats you could sit on where the hot sunlight could be escaped. Out through the windows, the city was so bright it looked almost like a photographic negative of itself, bleached and rather unreal.

The narrower streets of Greenwich Village were a little cooler, and they smelled of summer leaves.

This was a Saturday, and most of the people on her list were at home and available. She found herself among the realms of the young, well-heeled and amazingly pretty, whether male or female. They'd all heard what had happened. Kendra Callier finishing her life was news on the scale of the Titanic being sunk by a burning, falling Hindenberg. Everyone in New York knew about the suicide, and it was barely noon.

Some of her friends were genuinely upset. Others were numb, the truth of it not sinking in yet. And a couple were philosophical and somewhat unsurprised. But when the question came up of a possible female partner, their answers were all pretty much the same.

"She *did* kiss girls when she was round fourteen, but that was just for show. She was boy crazy."

"Kendra? She'd try anything, I guess. But *I* wasn't aware of it."

"She'd strike poses with girls. For fun, you know. But she never kept any secrets from me, and she never mentioned that."

"You could never tell what Kendra would do next. But whatever it was, she always made sure everybody knew about it. And so ... no."

The only thing that Lindy found out in the end was that, if you really wanted to know about a lesbian relationship, the best person to ask by a long chalk was a lesbian.

Dee Dee Tanner was a young African-American with huge Seventies-style Afro hair to prove it. She was clad in a pale green tank top and a pair of tight gray running shorts, the better to show off her gym-honed limbs. Her studio on Houston was filled with her sculptures, all in a version of the style of Southern Africa, groups of vague-shaped women wrapped around each other.

They sat opposite each other on a pair of beanbags. Dee Dee was obviously deeply into retro.

"Kendra?" Her hazel eyes were burning angrily at the cruelty of what had happened to her friend. "Knew her six years. Absolutely loved her. Never made a pass at her. Never even thought about trying except – you know – in daydreams. She was straight as the rain falling down from the heavens. Daddy's girl, in her own style."

Lindy shifted uncomfortably at those words, but tried to hide it.

"Pretty wild, though?"

"*Very* wild, when her blood was up."

"And so ... not exactly adverse to experimentation?"

"But girl on girl just wasn't her. And besides, she had her career to think of."

This was something she'd not been expecting, and Lindy took a brief moment absorbing it.

"Career?"

Dee Dee's wide, flat brow creased up. "You have to know how infamous she was. And these days, infamy can be the biggest kind of fame. She had TV offers coming in, even movie offers. She was about to launch herself on a career that would've made Paris Hilton look like Daisy Duck. Everyone's seen that video. Every guy in America, straight or gay, was fascinated with her. Women too. And girl-girl is acceptable in some circles, but not in *all* of them by any stretch of the imagination. Kendra wanted to be bigger than Paris, not some runner-up to Lindsay fucking Lohan."

"But I'm talking just one night here. And I'm talking just in private."

At which, Dee Dee curled her lip up.

"Girlfriend, are you kidding me? People photographed her everywhere she went, and not just paparazzi. We're living in the age of the video cell phone, right? So how'd she even pick a woman up without everybody knowing?"

She lowered her head and rubbed tiredly at the corners of her eyes.

"Besides, you know how many people spent a night with Kendra and then went running to the gossip papers the next morning? She had no such *thing* as private."

All of which might be the case, Lindy reflected as she finished up and headed out. But maybe Kendra Caller had been like her. Maybe it was taking chances, putting herself at risk, that genuinely turned her on.

A soft hand closed around her shoulder. Dee Dee had followed her onto the landing. And her face was gentler than it had been before.

"You look tired. Tense. And I'm the same. So maybe it would be better for both of us if you stayed here a while."

Lindy smiled back at her weakly. This was an avenue she'd explored a couple of times, but not today. She was on duty and had too much work to do. And besides, there was still the matter of the bruises underneath her neckscarf.

By this time, it was midway through the afternoon. When she walked out onto the wide, flattened expanse of Houston, the hot air hit her like a bowl of soup. The sunlit windows opposite her were so dazzling you couldn't look at them directly. A truck went roaring by, its muffler cracked so that it left a stinking plume of blue exhaust behind. There was no breeze, and so the stench-cloud didn't move.

Walking back in the direction of Bleecker, she came across an Internet café. And Dee Dee had been right – she felt exhausted. Last night's sleep had hardly been a restful one. She needed a break badly, so she went inside, got an iced tea and a muffin from the counter and then sat herself behind a computer that was tucked away in a far corner.

She'd heard enough about Kendra by this time that she wanted to see the video for herself. Googled it, and found it pretty well instantly. It was right up there at the top of the list. She made sure nobody was looking in her direction, and then clicked it on.

It wasn't what she'd been expecting. No close-ups ... no camera movement at all. Somebody had simply propped a digital device on a nearby dresser and then left it running, so that the people in the video kept moving in and out of shot and having one half of their head cut off.

A bare mattress. Four people moving on it. Kendra Callier was at the center, pretty and flawless, her blonde hair reaching down to the small of her back. Impossibly lithe, not an ounce of spare fat on her except for her smallish, conical breasts. The three guys with her were all of her own age and were attractive too, tanned smooth bodies, chests and armpits cleanly shaven.

They weren't being rough with her, but they weren't exactly holding back either. One of them took her from either end. The other guy massaged her titties. There were no speakers on this computer, but when Kendra's mouth finally came free it immediately started moving, and the guys changed positions straight away.

Someone else might think that she was ordering them around. But Lindy recognized, almost immediately, the gentle way her lips were moving and the taut, haunted expression on her face. She was pushing them to greater heights, goading them to keep on doing more and more to her.

Kendra had only been eighteen when she'd made this.

I make a gift of my body to you.

Lindy switched the movie off, then put a call in to the office. Moxi hadn't come up with anything yet either, so far as anybody knew. Nobody had come up with a scientific explanation for the punctured hearts out in the park. No one had come up with nuttin'.

Back on the parched street, she went through half a dozen more of the friends and close acquaintances on Kendra's list and then gave up. She was getting nowhere. No one was. What was it with this case that made it so impenetrable? It occurred to her for a brief moment that the four other deaths and Kendra's suicide might somehow be linked. But that was absurd, wasn't it? God, her brain was fried.

By now it was gone five, the shadows of the curbside trees beginning to stretch out. She could take the subway home from here. So she found the nearest station, started going down the steps, feeling annoyed and frustrated by her utter lack of progress.

But her cell phone started ringing in her purse. She took it out.

16 – Appointment

It was Bob Collins from the office.

"Do you know any guy called John Hunter?"

Lindy took a short while spooling back through the Rolodex of her memory, trying to recall that name. Somebody shoved past her coming up the subway steps, despite the fact that he had plenty of room. She scowled.

"I don't think so."

"Well he says he has some information on the Martin Callum case, and he's insisting that he only speaks to you."

"Weird. How do I get in touch with him?"

"I've got him on hold right now."

"Then – *duh* – put him on."

There was a click, a dead pause on the line.

And then: "Detective Grady?"

"Mr. Hunter?"

"You can call me John."

After the couple of days that she'd had on these cases, she was in no slightest mood for pleasantries.

"I understand you have some information?"

"Regarding the death of … Mr. Callum, is it? Yes."

This was a very masculine voice, deep and vibrant, strong. She was weary and frazzled and halfway down a flight of rather dingy concrete steps, but in spite of all that she felt a sudden tightness in her chest.

"Go on."

"It would be better if I spoke to you in person."

"Why?"

"I'd just prefer that."

She almost came back with a sharp retort, but kept a lid on it, trying to understand where he was coming from.

"Okay then, we can meet up somewhere, if you like. Where do you live?"

"Not in New York, certainly. I'm simply here on business for a few days."

"Your hotel?"

"Are you familiar with the McKinnon on Madison?"

Only from the outside. It was a ritzy-looking little boutique hotel just up from the Sherry-Netherland. Not too far from the Sirius Apartments, where Martin Callum had resided. She glanced at her wristwatch.

"I can be there in half an hour."

"But I'm not there at the moment, sergeant. I'm taking a break from an important meeting, and after that I have a function to attend."

"Mr. Hunter, need I remind you that this is potentially a murder case?"

And why'd he taken so long to call her, for that matter? But his deep, rich voice took on a sympathetic tone.

"You sound tired. Sounds to me like you could use a break."

And yes, she could. But how'd he known that?

"Get yourself rested and freshened up. I'll meet with you at my hotel at … let's say ten thirty? It's room 27."

What – his hotel didn't have a lobby? But he seemed to sense that question too.

"I'd rather that we kept this thing entirely private."

"Ten thirty, then," she agreed.

***

The subway train, when it came along, was packed with shoppers and tourists, and stifling too. It was only a few stops, but her feet were aching. So she managed to wedge herself into the only remaining seat, between a fat Germanic-looking guy and a woman who had half a dozen bags from the cheap clothing stores on lower Broadway piled up on her lap.

A guy across the aisle – sharp-chinned and unattractive – kept on glancing at her. But she ducked her head and just ignored him.

The events of last night had dissolved from her mind like some heavy pall of black smoke that had looked like it might hang around a while, but which a gentle wind had blown away. She was past that now, busy with her work, getting on with her life. And the plain truth was, John Hunter's smooth, chocolate-dark tones had stirred her slightly. When was she ever quite that accommodating to the wishes of a witness? Combined with which, the film she'd watched had left her feeling slightly aroused.

There were maybe five, six waking daydreams that she carried around inside her head, fantasies she could repeat over and over whenever she liked in the same way as playing singles on a jukebox. She'd been having this particular one since she'd been seventeen.

I am in a large, tastefully furnished room, standing at the very center of it. There is a cocktail party going on around me, except that all the other guests are men. They're older than me, but not too old, not a thinning hairline or a wrinkled brow in sight, no flabby guts. And they are all very successful older men, all wearing formal dinner suits. Businessmen, congressmen, doctors, lawyers, judges. They are confident and powerful – you can tell that by the way they're talking and the way that their hands move.

Since I'm wearing bright red five-inch heels, my head is above theirs. I am in a backless dress of the same color, slashed to the hipbone, and with my red hair I am like a beacon, only nobody is talking to me.

The conversation rolls around me like an ocean. They are talking about politics and law and world affairs, and none of them is even looking at me.

Finally, I get frustrated. I walk across to a laughing, joking guy who people keep on calling 'senator,' tap him on the shoulder to get his attention and he looks at me with sparkling eyes. His tuxedo is ivory white

"Excuse me," I ask, "but I don't understand why I am here?"

He immediately forgets the people he's been talking to and, without a word, takes hold of my wrist and makes me follow him across the room toward a door.

There's a bedroom inside, the bed very large, the room very small, so that there's barely a foot of carpet space around it. He shuts the door behind him and then takes off his tuxedo and drops it on the floor.

I'm about to ask him why he's done that, when he puts his hand lightly to my neck and undoes the clasp of my red silk dress. Gravity takes hold of it, and I'm nude between one second and the next.

He takes a step toward me. Instinctively, I move away. The backs of my knees hit the top edge of the mattress, and gravity grabs me as well. I bounce down on my naked back, try to push myself up on my elbows, but he's already pulled off his bow tie, torn away the buttons of his shirt and –

The carriage shuddered to a halt. The doors hissed open. This was her stop.

The first thing that she did when she got home was go into her little bathroom, untie her neckscarf and inspect her throat.

And she thought at first her eyes were playing tricks on her. But she rubbed at them, then looked again.

The bruising, which had been very bad this morning, looked to be more than halfway gone. It was about a third of its original size and had barely any purple left in it, only faded yellow. And how could *that* possibly be? Unless it hadn't really been as bad as she'd first thought.

Last night? When she tried to conjure up the exact details of it, Lindy found she couldn't. There were only splintered fragments left, that came to her in no particular order. Maybe she was in denial, blanking that part of her past right out. And if so, then perhaps it was a blessing. There were few things worse than being haunted by the bad parts of your life.

She started the shower running and stripped off, then soaped herself for practically a quarter of an hour.

Once dry, she went through into her bedroom, setting her TV alarm for 21:30. She lay down naked on her narrow bed, put her fingers between her legs, and finished off the fantasy that she'd been having.

The confident way that the senator made love to her. And, when he was almost done, she glanced across at the bedroom door and saw, to her shock, that it was now wide open. Every man who had been talking in that other room was pressed up against the doorway, staring in at her, and not a single word was passing between them.

They had been rendered mute, their wisdom and their erudition turned to dust by the sight of her body.

Lindy came. She fell asleep.

For now, those two things were enough.

***

"Authorities are still scratching their heads over a vicious fight that broke out in a swanky midtown restaurant a few hours back.

Customers were ordering their *hors d'oeuvres* in *Belatinni's* on Fifth ..."

Her eyes snapped open. Hell, she knew the place. It was four blocks above the Rock.

"... when several of them simply turned round and attacked the rest with – wait for it – dinner knives. At least half a dozen people have been hospitalized, and the police are reported to have made several arrests. The attackers allegedly include the editor of a well-known fashion magazine, the co-director of a charitable foundation, and ..."

Lindy rolled across and slapped the TV off. More craziness. What the hell was happening to this city?

She sat up straight, dropping her legs off the mattress. Took in the fact she felt remarkably refreshed after a couple of hours sleep. The tired graininess of earlier had vanished.

She went back into the bathroom and stared at her throat again. There were only some very tiny yellow marks left by this time, barely visible unless you knew where to look.

Too strange. But not a bad thing.

It was now nine thirty five. She washed her face, brushed her teeth, put a little make-up on.

She chose another of her lightweight suits, pale beige this time, with a very thin pale yellow cotton top on underneath it.

Checked herself in the mirror, took a breath. Then went out onto the darkened, balmy street to keep her appointment with John Hunter.

PART TWO

ROOM 27

17 – Actually Maroon

The double front doors of the McKinnon were dark, polished wood, with very ornate, shiny brass handles and rows of little squares of glass above those, so you only got fractured glimpses of the interior as you approached.

Lindy went inside.

It was the smallest, narrowest hotel lobby that she'd ever seen. The paintwork on the walls was that kind of beige that keeps on trying to phase through to pink, a light terracotta. The features were art deco and might well be original. To her right-hand side were a few low chairs grouped around a glass-topped table that had some kind of bluish-green Lalique bowl on it. To her left was a long, shiny mahogany reception counter.

A girl in uniform was standing behind it. She couldn't have been older than nineteen. Very thin, with smooth black hair that was cut extremely straight. She was busy with some paperwork. Glanced up at Lindy quickly, favored her with a brief smile, but then her head went down again.

A discreet place, in other words. People could come and go here as they pleased. Lindy checked the higher corners, but could see no cameras.

The elevator cage was at the far end of the lobby and was quite literally that, a cage. One of those old-fashioned jobs you rarely saw these days, made up of intricate twistings of metal, with a cantilevered front gate that you had to pull open manually.

She went across to it, her heels clicking on the pale cream tiles. Room 27 had to be on the second floor didn't it?

But not in a hotel of this size. There was a guide etched into a brass plate beside the elevator door. 27 was on the fourth story.

The machinery creaked as it bore her up. The metalwork around her shuddered faintly. As she rose …

A most curious sensation started coming over her.

It wasn't tiredness exactly. No, the weariness of before had not returned. There was no blurring of her vision, and her shoulders remained high, her back straight, nothing in her slumped. But …

Back when she had been nineteen, she'd dropped a couple of ludes, given to her by a kind-looking middle-aged man who'd started talking to her on a bench in Bryant Park. And this was rather the way that had been, a feeling of floating and detachment, like she'd fallen into a gentle doze while still apparently awake.

She moved her head from side to side, trying to shake it off, but couldn't. What was causing this?

The elevator cage stopped with a heavy jolt. She grasped the handle of the gate and yanked it open – it was rather stiff. And then she was out onto the fourth floor landing.

The paintwork up here was a much darker terracotta. The lighting was dim. She stared around, and there were only four doors that she could make out.

The one marked 27 was hanging very slightly open.

***

She approached it carefully. The gap between door's edge and the surrounding woodwork was only whisper thin, and she could see no illumination beyond it.

She stopped in front of it, then rapped with her knuckles. The door swung back another half an inch, and now she could make out there was a small light on behind it.

But otherwise, there was no answer.

"Mr. Hunter?"

Back in the far distance she could hear water running, a faucet. So perhaps he couldn't hear her.

Lindy set her hand against the door and gently eased it open.

***

Red. Most of the room was red, or actually maroon. There was only one small lamp on, at the nightstand by the bed. The wallpaper was of an abstract design in which brushstrokes of differing shades bisected each other. That was hard on her eyes at first, making her squint, until it softened out and turned into a slightly lustrous fog.

The carpet was evenly toned and thick. The bedspread, which had been folded most of the way back, was the same color. Out of this whole room, only the sheets and pillowcases were a brilliant white and stood out starkly in the dimness.

The headboard of the double bed was softly gleaming brass, upright rods of it, so that it resembled a gate before a railway crossing. And there was a shorter version at the other end.

There was a closet, and a dresser with a chair in front of it. No other places you could sit. No obvious signs of luggage or of habitation, which was odd. Her experience was that, when people got inside a hotel room, the first thing that they did was spread their stuff around.

A full-length mirror was screwed into one wall, and when she glanced at it she could see the bed reflected. Which went a good way to explaining the extremely discreet welcome in the lobby. The McKinnon seemed to be the kind of place where well-off people came for assignations. Why'd a visiting businessman choose this kind of hotel?

The faucet was still running. The bathroom door was a few inches open too, the light in there a harsh fluorescent white. There was another mirror just beyond the gap, and in it she could see the reflection of a tall man's back.

His hair was dark, a little shaggily cut. He seemed to be wearing … a formal dinner suit, an ivory white tuxedo. Which was exactly like the daydream that she'd had.

She brought herself up short. She was here on business, here to do her job.

The water stopped.

"Mr. Hunter?" she tried again.

"Would that be Sergeant Grady?" he asked her in that deep, smooth voice. "Excuse me. I was using a pen earlier, and I seem to have gotten some ink on my hands."

She watched his back as he reached out for a plain white towel and dried his palms and fingers. Then, when he turned, he vanished from the bathroom mirror altogether.

He was silhouetted in the doorway the next second. Around six foot six tall. Broad-shouldered.

But she couldn't see the details of his face until he took another step toward her.

A face that was mostly square. Small ears, but a nose that was slightly longer than it should have been, a Roman nose. Black, dense eyebrows, and a neatly shaped beard of designer stubble.

He had on gold-rimmed reading glasses, and the lenses were reflective, so she couldn't see the color of his eyes.

But this was the *same guy* she'd been imagining seeing most of yesterday.

The same guy she actually *had* seen on Broadway, and had gone running after.

She'd not managed to catch up with him.

So ... had he caught up with *her* instead?

18 – I'm on Duty

Her mind had gone blanker than she'd ever known it.

She couldn't have managed a straightforward thought if her life had depended on it.

She felt *more* than dazed. As though she had stepped outside the boundaries of reality, like stepping off a moving train while it was crossing a high viaduct and suddenly finding yourself with only empty air around you.

This couldn't possibly *be*. Was she remembering things right?

"Sergeant Grady?" he was asking her, looking rather puzzled.

He took his glasses off, setting them down on the nearest flat surface. It was hard to be certain in this weak light, but his eyes appeared to be the sharpest shade of green that she had ever seen on a human being. And that stirred something in her mind, trying to warn her of something, though she couldn't recall what.

"Are you all right, sergeant?"

His deep tone was concerned. Lindy blinked hard, several times. If she could only get rid of this drugged, drowsy sensation. But it wouldn't lift from her. She tried to turn her mind to what she ought to do. Except … there was no way that this made any sense. Which meant that she had gotten something badly mixed up somewhere down the line – there was no other explanation.

"Sergeant?"

He used the word loudly this time, and it snapped her back into some kind of focus. She was acting like a moron. She was here representing the NYPD. Officially, as of this morning, New York's very finest. Any confusion was her business and hers alone. And she would have to sit down quietly later, try to work out what had really happened. Because this man and the guy she'd been imagining could not *possibly* be the same person.

But the next question he asked her was, "Do we know each other from somewhere? Because you're staring at me like you recognize me."

Which gave her the opportunity to clear this matter up. And so she took it, cocking her head to one side.

"I thought I saw you last night, on the street."

"You noticed me among the vast and thronging crowds of Manhattan? Well, how very flattering."

"Around nine pm, on Broadway. Were you there last night, near 52nd?"

He thought about that, then shook his head gently. "I was at a business dinner in Tribeca – not a particularly good one, I'm afraid."

And so that cleared it up. She *was* mistaken. She had only noticed somebody who *looked* quite similar to Mr. Hunter.

At which point, she lightened up enough to ask, "You seem to do a lot of business dinners?"

One thick eyebrow rose.

"The tux," she pointed out.

He looked down at it as if noticing it for the first time, then smiled.

"Yes, the formal engagement that I talked about. Much better food."

"It must have wound up early?"

"No. I left early to meet with you."

Which was when something else occurred to her.

"Why did you insist you had to talk with me? There are other detectives working this case."

"I saw you on the morning news. And when I found out that you were in charge? You'll have to forgive me, but I was ... intrigued."

He'd wanted to meet her because she was briefly famous? What was he looking for here, an autograph? She couldn't help but smirk ironically, but she felt slightly flattered too. Her gaze met his, then moved away with a soft jerk.

"Okay. To business, then."

He pulled out the chair beside the dresser for her, and then sat down on the corner of his bed.

Lindy took a notepad from her purse, and was about to ask him her first question when the soft click of a latch off to her right caught her attention.

The door to Room 27 had slipped the whole way closed.

***

She put it hurriedly out of her mind.

"Okay then, you're ...?"

"John Egon Hunter."

"Egon is unusual."

"It doesn't get used much, fortunately."

"You're from …?"

"Let's just say New England. A little place you've never heard of."

"And you're here in New York City for ….?"

"As long as it takes."

He was pulling off his white tuxedo as he talked, folding it neatly and draping it over the end rails of the bed. His head turned as he did that to show her his profile. He was actually amazingly handsome. Lindy felt her inner thighs tighten a touch, but kept her mind on her job.

"So, we're talking about two nights ago, right?"

"That would be correct."

He'd taken off his bow tie and was unfastening the top buttons of his shirt. Men looked massively relieved when they did that, like the clothing that tradition obliged them to wear kept quietly strangling them for hours. She couldn't even imagine what *that* was like. How did they stand it?

"Why'd you take so long getting in touch with us?"

"I wasn't quite sure what I saw."

Which made him an honest, open witness, and that made a change.

"Go on."

"It was around midnight. I wasn't quite ready to sleep yet, so I took a walk along the edge of Central Park. I was heading up toward the Zoo. I could hear one of the animals calling – I remember that quite clearly."

Her pen stopped.

"I suddenly noticed that a man was walking out across the grass. He was quite a distance off, but I could see that he was older than me, quite bulky, and oddly dressed. He looked like he was in a robe, in fact. And then he took it off. I assumed that this was some kind of aberrant behavior."

"New York being famous for that."

Hunter smiled again and nodded. "Yes, exactly. And I was about to look away, it being none of my concern, when a woman appeared from the trees. Tall. Slim. Dark-haired. She was naked too."

So far, she'd heard nothing that she hadn't already been told by Martin Callum's doorman, but she waited.

"I supposed it was some manner of bizarre *triste*. And I didn't stop to watch it, since I've never been a voyeur. But – when I turned my gaze away from them – I noticed a second woman standing further back."

Lindy's heart started bumping over lightly and she began to scribble.

"Are you absolutely sure of that?"

"Quite certain."

"Can you describe her?"

"She was at a greater distance than either of the other two. But ... shorter than the dark-haired woman. And I'd say a few years younger. Very long blonde hair."

"Dressed?"

John Hunter shook his head, another gentle smirk alighting on his lips. And was he kidding her?

"Are you trying to tell me there was some kind of orgy going on?"

"I can't be sure. I didn't stick around. I turned around and headed back to this hotel."

"So ... you didn't see either of the women approach Mr. Callum?"

"No, I'm afraid not."

"You didn't notice any kind of weapon?"

He looked puzzled, his dark eyebrows drawing together. "No. But ..."

Once again, she waited.

"Just before I moved away, I got the definite impression that there was a man back there as well."

God, they had a whole perverts' convention going on here, didn't they?

"You're *sure* of that?"

"I could only make out a vague shape. But it wasn't female."

She wrote down KINK? CHECK WEBSITES! She wrote down CULT? The moon had been full that night, after all.

"No description of him?"

"He was a *very* long way off, and heavily in shadow. But ... possibly tall. Maybe even round my size."

"Clothed?"

"I couldn't tell you."

"And you didn't stick around? You didn't take a second look, with all that going on?"

"They were all fully-grown adults, and their business was their own. Like I said, watching's not my thing. Not at all."

Except that he was watching *her* now. She had crossed her knees and propped her notepad on them, and he was pretending to be interested in what she was writing. But he wasn't really doing that, no. He was looking at her legs.

She felt her thighs tighten a little more.

But *no, no, no!* She was on duty, and she didn't mix things up that way. She was uncomfortably self-conscious though, and drew in a long breath.

"Is there anything else that you can add?"

Hunter turned that over very carefully, his eyelids squinching and his bright green irises becoming distant.

"I'm afraid not. I really wish that I could be more use."

"No, you've been ... I've learned more about this case in the past few minutes than the last two days. This has been invaluable, Mr. Hunter."

He smiled warmly, staring only at her face.

"I'm glad that I could be of help."

What a smile. One of the best-looking guys she'd ever seen. But a witness, maybe central to this case. She had to bear that in mind and get out of here.

She fished a card from her purse, stood up, handing it to him.

"If you think of anything more, my number's on the back."

"Of course."

"You're gonna be in New York for a few more days?"

"At least."

"Okay. Then maybe we'll talk again."

She offered him her hand. When he took it, his touch was firm but gentle. Very, very warm.

"Why go rushing off?" he asked her out of nowhere. "Can't I offer you a drink?"

Before she'd even *started* to think how to reply, he'd stepped over to the closet doors and opened one of them. There was a cabinet inside, a bottle of red wine and two elegant glasses propped up on it.

"Mr. Hunter, I'm on duty."

He glanced at his big platinum wristwatch.

"It's getting on for eleven in the evening. And our interview's complete. Sounds to me as though your working day is done, Belinda. May I call you that?"

19 – Only a Silhouette

A moment of complete disorientation.

She was not really sure – at *all* sure – where her mind was going.

She knew perfectly well that last night's encounter with that big Tex-looking guy ought to have been weighing down on her heavily. Controlling her thoughts and limiting her actions. But that drowsy, drugged sensation she'd first started feeling in the elevator grew a little stronger, blurring her mind and driving away her recent memories. Not her old ones, though.

That kind-looking, middle-aged guy who'd persuaded her to follow him home from Bryant Park. They'd both dropped the ludes which he'd produced.

"*How Seventies!*"

"*I'm Seventies!*" *he'd laughed.*

Once the drug had kicked in, they had done it on the bright yellow cushions of the sun-bed on his balcony. Afterwards, he'd produced a camera and taken photographs of her in various poses, her pale body with its rose-pink nipples and its flame-red hair against the fire-yellow of the cloth. It had been a very long while since anyone had made her feel that gorgeous.

She pulled away from the image. Stared at John Hunter again, and got the distinct feeling he might be the man to do it.

And heard herself saying, "Lindy. I prefer that."

A small crease appeared at the bridge of his nose.

"Not Bella? That means beautiful."

Her shoulders drew back a little. "I *know* what it means."

The blurring hadn't rendered her completely stupid. And she'd been around for long enough to watch him carefully while he opened the bottle. It was a metal screw-top cap, and gave a satisfying crack when he twisted it, which meant it had not previously been opened. When he offered her a glass, she took the one in his other hand nonetheless, and waited till he'd swallowed some before she did the same herself.

The crease on the bridge of his nose was still here.

"Lindy Grady? It sounds like someone from a nursery rhyme."

"But I like it. Perhaps because of that."
"How so?"
"I prefer to keep things straightforward and simple."
"Well then … in that case, I like it too."

She took another gulp of wine. Her drowsiness took on a softer, warmer texture.

***

"Can I point something out?" he asked her.

Oh Lord, what was coming now? More and more these days, she liked to keep the talking to a minimum.

"I used the word 'beautiful' a little while back. And you didn't react well."

He had noticed that?

"Women are rarely comfortable with that word, applied to themselves. They look in a mirror and all they see are the imagined flaws, the things they'd like to change. Whereas the truth is very different."

He set down his glass and turned to face the full-length mirror.

"Come over here a moment, will you?"

They'd only known each other a very short while, and he was already trying to boss her round a little. Or perhaps this was some kind of game? She liked games, the way that you could lose yourself in them and forget who you really were. And so she thought 'okay' and set her own glass down and went to stand beside him.

"No, in front of me."

She did that slightly warily, wondering where this was leading.

Once that she was in position, she could see barely anything of him but his hair and brow and eyes above her own. The dimness of the room was such that it intensified his green irises and the whites surrounding them. She tried to relax, but couldn't quite manage that, tensing up a little. His gaze smiled when he saw that, crinkling at the edges. His palms brushed against her elbows, cupping them a moment.

"This is beauty, right here."

One of his hands went up to her hair and raked it very delicately. But she only went a little stiffer.

"This is beauty." It moved down to trace her neck. "Like a swan."

But he was losing her. This was turning out like something from a lousy European movie.

"That's the best you can do?" she asked. "Compare me to waterfowl?"

The drowsiness was lifting. And Lindy was starting to wonder what the hell she was still doing here.

But she'd practically snapped at him and he hadn't even flinched. That held her in place for a few seconds longer.

"You can be hard on people, can't you?" he asked quietly.

"Right."

"Life has made you that way. Tough."

"Yeah. Right again"

One of his arms encircled her waist and pulled her to him.

"You get what you want from people, then you leave."

"From men? Right a third time."

His lips suddenly pressed against her neck, firmly and with no slightest hesitation.

And *this* was far more like it. She didn't want anyone eulogizing on her looks. She wanted to be flesh and heat, immediacy, the moment, her job forgotten, her childhood gone, everything but this direct time and place swept away on a cresting, foaming, brilliant wave of sheer carnality.

She'd wanted him from the first moment.

He was still kissing her neck, had pushed her jacket to one side and was moving his lips to her shoulder, sending sparks of heat down through her body. And when the arm around her waist tightened she pushed herself against him.

And after that – thank heavens – there were no more words.

***

After the second time, she pointed to her purse – which was tipped over on its side in front of the mirror – and said, "Look inside."

John padded across to it and crouched, then glanced up at her with his heavy eyebrows scrunched together. "A phone? A badge? A gun?"

"Look underneath."

He came back with a pair of handcuffs looped around his index finger. And his eyebrows were raised by now.

"But Lindy, I don't like being cuffed."

"Tonight's your lucky night, then."

***

It had to be two in the morning, by this stage. She had showered and re-dressed herself. John was in a thick navy blue robe with the McKinnon's logo on it. His spiky hair was all mussed up, and she felt pleased about that.

He stopped her at the door, grabbing her gently by both wrists and kissing her again.

"Come back tomorrow night?" he asked.

She gawped at him. What was he *talking* about?

"I'm in town a while," he told her, "but have no more business dinners planned. I'm busy in the day, but I have absolutely nothing to do with myself in the evening."

"I can think of one thing you can do with yourself."

Again, he didn't flinch. "You're being mean again," he smiled.

"So what am I supposed to be, an unpaid escort?"

"You could arrive a little earlier next time," he said, ignoring that.

And she hadn't been expecting anything like this. But she'd been telling herself, just this morning, that she ought to stay away from the singles bars a while. Which, since she had no friends outside of Mari, meant condemning herself to an entire week at least of being at home alone each night.

Wasn't this a better option? Two strangers meeting in a room and having sex each night, like something out of *Last Tango in Paris*?

She found herself grinning gently.

"I'll consider it," she told him.

Then she turned away. Didn't even bother waiting for the elevator – headed down the stairs instead.

Out on the street the air was still hot, but not as oppressive as it had been. She took several deep breaths and then headed south, looking for a cab.

She could smell the park from here, the odor of the grass and leaves. The sky above was very clear, although the light from the city meant that you could see few stars. She loved nights like this, and was not in the least bit tired. The drowsiness had gone, her pulse was humming nicely, and she decided she'd walk a while.

She was just approaching the intersection with 61st when someone came around the corner. Lindy frowned gently, wondering who it was.

Only a silhouette at first, tall but with long hair, so probably a woman. But her shape was difficult to make out. Was that some kind of long coat or even *cloak* that she was wearing, in this weather?

Lindy's step faltered slightly, her heels clicking unevenly on the flat paving stones. She was a cop, was armed, and had nothing to be afraid of. But – for some reason that she could not define – she suddenly felt a little unnerved.

As the two of them drew closer, she began to see that her instincts had been wrong and there was nothing to concern her. The streetlights started to reveal a proud and lovely face framed by long, slightly twisty auburn hair. The woman was *indeed* wearing some kind of cloak – it was green, and looked extremely lightweight. She was not even bothering to look back at Lindy, staring straight ahead instead and walking very smoothly. Her nose was slightly too long, and there was a faint patina to her features that made Lindy think she might be Latin.

The hem of her long cloak was almost brushing on the sidewalk. It was only when they were right up close that one of her feet flashed into view. And Lindy felt surprised, because it looked completely bare.

Passing each other, they finally both glanced across and their eyes met. And Lindy got another small surprise. This woman's eyes were an intense, bright green, not dissimilar to John's. She'd never seen that hue of iris in her life before, and now she'd seen it twice.

The woman's lips – which were unpainted but very full – pursed into the briefest smile. Then she looked away again, and was disappearing into the background.

Lindy kept on walking. But at the corner of 61st, she glanced back.

The woman had receded to a silhouette once more, and was making her way in through the entrance of the McKinnon.

So ... a relative of John's, perhaps?

Visiting him ... at *this* hour?

Maybe she would ask tomorrow. That is, if there was even going to *be* a tomorrow.

Lindy stayed in place a while, then finally moved on.

20 – Massachusetts

Banhoff phoned her the next morning. By the sounds of it, he was calling from the office, despite the fact this was a Sunday. But that was no great big surprise with so much going on.

"I've been talking to an opposite number in the MSP."

The Massachusetts State Police? Lindy's brow creased curiously.

"They've had another death like your four, just a couple of weeks back," the captain explained. "Same thing with the heart."

"Okay."

"A backpacker this time, name of William Derham. Twenty-five, single. His body was found in the middle of plain nowhere, deep woodlands some twelve miles outside a little town called Alberly."

"All news to me."

"MSP is waiting for you now. Get over there and check it out."

"I ... drive to Massachusetts? Are you kidding me?"

"I don't see what the problem is."

"I thought Kendra Callier was the huge frigging priority?"

He made a rumbling noise to remind her how she ought to talk to a superior. Lindy chewed her lip uncomfortably.

"It's starting to look like Kendra was a genuine suicide, isn't it?" the man was saying. "Her parents are beginning to accept that, so the pressure on the department's off."

"Thank God."

"And are you getting anywhere with those four other cases?" Banhoff asked her. "No, I thought not. So you might as well try checking it out from a completely different angle. Ask around, see if anyone was with Derham or approached him. Trying to find stuff in the middle of plain nowhere might turn out to be a whole lot easier than trying to find it in New York."

"By the way," he stopped her with, just before he hung up, "ever come up with any theory as to why Kendra Callier would kill herself? She had so much to live for. Why would she do that?"

"Why does anyone do anything?" she answered quietly.

She dressed and snorted a little more coke before heading out. She knew someone in Medical who tried to warn her when a drugs test was coming. The one time she had ever been caught out, she'd been working a case involving nightclub owners, and had been able to claim she'd taken the stuff to fit right into that environment and get people to trust her.

Down in the station house's garage, she chose a dark-blue Pontiac from the pool. The sergeant in charge found a satnav for her, and she punched in 'Alberly, Mass.' The sunlight almost blinded her when she drove out, so that she put on her green shades again. She headed for First, winding her window down.

All she got for that was hot air rushing past her face and the stink of exhaust fumes. Thinking about it, it would be nice to get out of the city on a day like this. She would have almost felt grateful of Banhoff if he wasn't such an idiot.

Before she knew it she was sailing across the Triborough Bridge, the river below her like a sheet of mirrored glass. Reaching the Bronx shore, she started heading quickly up the Bruckner Expressway, but that didn't last for very long. There were red brake lights ahead, hundreds of them. She slowed to a halt. An ambulance went pushing past, so there'd been an accident somewhere further on.

Lindy only traveled a few dozen yards over the next five minutes. But she finally reached an off ramp, doing that. She didn't know this neighborhood, but there was still a good long drive ahead of her and she felt no desire to stay here any longer. So she took it.

Low white wooden houses started going past her. They were nondescript, no real indication if this district was a poor one or not. She kept her eyes fixed on the road, turning left at the next intersection.

She was riding parallel to Bruckner now. This street was good and straight, and if she kept on going then she ought to skim right past the pile-up, rejoin the expressway and be heading out into the greenness of Connecticut before a whole lot longer. There were no signs of human life around her. But there *was* something moving up ahead, she noticed, something reddish brown. It ambled along a little while, then seemed to sit down directly at the center of her lane.

A dog? She began slowing down again.

Jesus, no! It was a goddamned fox, a big one. It was sitting perfectly still and upright in the middle of the pavement, watching her as she approached. There was no other traffic, and she could have simply steered around the thing, but she was so astonished that she stopped.

It still didn't budge. A big mothering Pontiac had been bearing down on it and it wasn't even fazed. As though it felt some strong entitlement to be here.

It lifted its head a couple of inches, studying her with hungry yellow eyes. Its mouth came open the same distance – she could see its whitely pointed teeth, the deep red of its maw.

It seemed to think it owned this place. What was it even *doing* here?

Lindy recalled that news broadcast she'd listened to a while back. That unlucky kid who had been mauled by urban coyotes down in Arizona. And wasn't this a version of the self-same thing? Thank God she lived on an island. She was unused to wild animals, perhaps a little nervous of them.

What the hell d'you think you're up to? she thought at the fox. *Why don't you go back into the wilds where you belong?*

Obviously, it didn't respond, and so she jammed her hand down on the car's horn, thinking that would make it bolt. Except it didn't. It just got up rather languidly, shook itself at leisure, and then wandered off with the same kind of attitude as a large, disdainful cat. Vanished underneath a fence. Did people even know that it was living near their homes?

But she forgot about it and got moving again. And it turned out she was right. When she rejoined the expressway she had left the traffic jam behind, and before much longer she was heading up across the state line, keeping her speed at an even sixty-five.

The sunlight was still powerful, but the air was noticeably cooler, so she wound her window down again and left it there. She fiddled with the radio for a couple of minutes, not finding anything she liked. Took a peek in the glove compartment – someone had left a pack of L&Ms in there with three smokes in it and a half-filled plastic lighter. This was something that she hadn't tried in ages. Lindy lit one of the cigarettes, but it was stale. She tossed it and the remainder of the pack out through the window.

Sighed.

There were signs to little towns going past her. It sure was pretty as all hell out here, but there was absolutely nothing going on. And in circumstances such as these, she'd usually descend into one of her familiar daydreams. Except, when she tried ...

Something about a room, a cocktail party? Something about a red dress? She wasn't certain. Every time she tried to call the fantasy up it kept dissolving in her mind, the elements of the dream refusing to come together.

It was the same thing when she tried to recall that middle-aged man from Bryant Park. She couldn't remember what he looked like. And as to what they'd actually done ...?

A flash of bright yellow exploded behind her eyelids and then just as quickly vanished.

This was so strange. What was wrong with her? Only it didn't feel like it was anything that she'd done. More like something had intruded deeply into her most private thoughts, leaving them in disarray so that she could find nothing.

And *that* made no sense at all, now did it.

There was little other traffic on the road by now. This was mid-morning on a Sunday, after all. Lindy took a casual glance up at her rearview mirror.

And thought she saw a pair of bright green eyes – John Hunter's square face framed around them – staring at her from the back seat of the car.

She yelped. The Pontiac wobbled badly, crossing into the next lane. She got a grip on herself and hauled over to the ditch and stopped.

Her heart was banging wildly and her breath was seething in her lungs. She dragged her palm across her upper lip, which was beaded with sweat, then looked into the mirror again.

There was no one there. Of *course* there wasn't, but she turned her head, confirming that.

Wow, John had really had some kind of powerful effect on her. Only she couldn't think about him now. She couldn't dwell on the approaching evening. She still had a case to solve.

***

The odd thing was, by the time that she arrived near noon, her surroundings were darker than they'd been before. That had nothing to do with the weather or clouds. There were none. The sky was still a clear, harsh blue.

But she'd gone so deeply into the New England woodlands that it might as well have been approaching evening. Ranks of massive trees around the road were baffling the sunlight.

Up ahead of her, a gas station signpost drifted into view. She already knew that it was just outside of Alberly, and it was where the MSP were going to be waiting for her.

Lindy pulled onto the lot. An SUV was sitting there, two-toned, pale and darker blue, with a big badge painted on its door. She killed the Pontiac's engine and got out.

The driver's door of the SUV clicked open and a woman emerged from it who was even taller than she was, narrow as a stick and with a slightly elongated, horsey face. She was in full uniform, a Smokey Bear hat and light blue shirt and dark blue pants. Her pale hair was braided back behind her cap. When she smiled, her teeth were very white but a bit too large. She walked across to Lindy eagerly.

"I'm Trooper First Class Ellen Hamp," she beamed. "You must be Sergeant Grady. I have to say, I was expecting a man. What a nice surprise."

She kept on looking Lindy up and down.

"A real live Manhattan detective. Wow! Never met one of *those* before. Did you find your way here okay?"

Lindy pointed to the satnav on her dashboard.

"Fascinating little gadgets, ain't they?" Ellen chirped.

Oh boy, but this girl was chipper. Lindy simply hated chipper.

"I've wanted one of those ever since I saw 'em," Ellen Hamp was going on. "Only problem is that I know every street round here for sixty miles, and I never go anywhere else."

She stopped and reflected on that, then added, "All the way from the Big Apple, huh? But *wow*!"

And Lindy was about to ask the woman her first question, when there was an abrupt rattling sound from the rear of the lot. She glanced across.

Up against the paybooth's wall there was a large gray Dumpster, and the sliding lid was tipped partially open. As she watched, a furry face with black around its eyes came poking out, something wedged into its mouth.

Ellen looked where she was looking, stiffened up annoyedly and muttered, "*That* shouldn't be open."

Then she advanced on the surprised raccoon, clapping her hands and shouting, "Scat!"

It scurried off into the undergrowth. Ellen got the Dumpster shut and then came back, looking apologetic.

"Hell, we get that all the time."

"We even get it in New York these days."

Then they discussed the case a little while, and agreed between them they should go and take a look at the location William Derham's body had been found.

"You can even have a word with the guy who found him," Ellen told her, except Lindy wasn't quite sure what she meant by that.

"Okay."

"It's better if we take the SUV. You can leave your car right there – don't even need to lock it."

They both climbed in and headed off, driving back some quarter of a mile the same way Lindy had come before turning off onto a track. Low branches scraped the windows of the SUV. It was almost cold this far into the woods. The forest up ahead of them looked even denser than the forest that they'd left behind. It was a totally alien landscape to Lindy, like they'd plunged beneath the surface of the sea or something.

But Ellen definitely knew her way around, steering with confident precision. Which gave Lindy time to think about the raccoon that she'd seen, and then the fox back in the Bronx.

"Why now?" she asked.

Ellen glanced across at her. "Why now what?"

"These wild animals coming into cities? I mean, cities have been here a while. And the animals have been out there … forever, I guess. So why'd they wait so long before deciding to come take a look?"

"It's the smell," Ellen explained to her.

And when Lindy responded with a puzzled squint, she pushed the idea further.

"For a good long while, the strangeness of the cities kept them off. The unnatural surroundings. The weird odors and the constant noise. But in the end, they couldn't resist the *other* smell that's coming out, and they steeled themselves and moved in closer."

"Other smell?"

"Easy pickings, see? The trash in cans. The garbage in the dumps. The stuff thrown out from diners and the stuff that people simply drop. Animals can't fight it. Nothing is more tempting to them than the promise of some easy pickings."

So it was down to hunger finally. And didn't a load of things in life break down to that, when you got to the nub of it?

"I'd hold on, if I were you," Ellen told her.

And the next second they were crashing over exposed roots, then heading down an even narrower track, the SUV barely slowing down at all.

Leaves were rattling against the windows. Undergrowth was murmuring and scraping down the vehicle's flanks. There was barely any light at all, where they were going. Lindy felt her chest contract.

"How'd anyone even *find* a body this deep in?" she asked.

All Ellen did was grin. "You'll be understanding soon enough."

She switched on her headlamps, then abruptly slowed.

"Well, there he is. He must have heard us coming."

Standing in the yellow beams was a squat figure in silhouette, its long hair forming a pale, glowing halo round its head.

21 – George

The figure squinted as the lights hit it, its flat brow creasing up. But then the man stepped sideways out of the beams. Only Lindy got a good, clear look at him before he did that. A small guy, maybe only five foot three, rather dumpy, gray of hair, his face so lined that it resembled an aged baseball mitt.

He was dressed in a plaid shirt topped off by a dark green jacket. Faded blue jeans and a pair of heavy boots. He waited patiently while Ellen killed the engine and switched off the lights, his dark gaze studying them impassively.

Lindy found her own eyesight adjusting as soon as she was out. It wasn't quite so dark as she had thought inside the SUV – the leaves overhead were dappled with light like they were a membrane, sealing her off from view of the world but not excluding it completely.

"This is him," Ellen told her, walking over to the waiting man. "Sergeant Grady, I'd like to introduce you to George Greentree, a First American of the Nipmuc Nation."

"Personally," George corrected her, turning his attention fully to Lindy, "I prefer the term 'redskin.' It makes me sound more colorful."

His voice was very harsh and croaky, but his eyes – which were practically jet-black – had started dancing with an impish light. His withered lips broke into a broad smile. Lindy immediately – for some reason, she was not sure why – took a liking to him.

"And ... you live out here?" she asked him.

"In a shack a little further back," Ellen answered for the man before he could respond. "George likes to keep to the old ways and stay close to nature, don't you, George?"

"Yeah, right." George hawked on the undergrowth between his boots. "Offer me a Lexus and a house on Beacon Hill and I'd jump on 'em with both feet. I live this way because I'm poor."

Ellen let out an impatient sigh and then began walking away from them. George and Lindy followed.

"George grumbles a lot," the trooper was explaining, "but he does okay. In season, he's a hunting and a fishing guide."

She was talking about the man as though he wasn't even there, the way you'd talk around a child. Lindy stared across at George. There was a look of weary resignation on his face, so he was used to this.

"I think we're getting to the spot right now," Ellen announced.

"You're almost standing on it," George informed her.

All three of them stopped.

It was merely another section of forest, like the rest that they had walked or driven through. High tree trunks surrounded them on all four sides, with moss lining the bark. Under their feet was mostly ferns, a few pale heads of fungi pushing up between them. It was no lighter or darker here than anywhere else they'd been. You'd never know a man had died.

But then – when crime scenes were cleaned up – you never did. They looked entirely normal. There was so much in this big world that just managed to get hidden.

"You've processed this place?" Lindy asked.

"With a toothcomb. We may not be Manhattan, but we're well-trained and we're thorough."

"And you found …?"

"Precisely zip."

Lindy stared at the ground in front of her, trying to imagine a fresh corpse lying there.

"He was a backpacker … I've got that right? That means he had to have equipment."

"Sure."

"And he set up camp here? Except that I can't see any peg holes or abrasions in the dirt."

It hadn't rained in weeks – she knew that. And the forest cancelled out the possibility of wind erosion. And there was nothing else out here that could have covered any telltale signs up.

"When we found his camping gear, it was still all packaged up. So our guess is that he was just about to strike camp when the killer got to him. George found him at break of dawn next morning, and saw no one around here when he passed through the previous afternoon. So our presumption is that William Derham got here around twilight, then was killed while night was falling."

"By cover of darkness," George muttered, nodding.

Lindy wasn't sure what he was talking about and stared at the man curiously. The humor had entirely vanished from his mouth and eyes.

"Something like *this* would never happen in the daylight," he explained. "Only at night."

Which left her no slightest bit the wiser. Had her first impression of this guy missed out the fact that he might be a little touched? She looked across to Ellen Hamp for guidance. And to her surprise, the trooper was now smirking.

"You're going to have to excuse George. He thinks William Derham was murdered by an evil spirit."

"A wendigo," George grunted. His dark gaze took in their surroundings slowly. "Not uncommon for a couple of them to come wandering through this section of the woods."

Lindy could feel her eyebrows pushing up, and looked again to her colleague for an explanation.

"Old native mythology," the woman shrugged. "Flesh-eating monsters."

"That's a misconception," George said. "Wendigos sometimes eat flesh, but –"

"That's quite enough now, George. The nice detective didn't come the whole way out here from New York just to hear your stories."

And the trooper pursed her lips.

"George gets lonely out here sometimes, don't you, George?" she murmured. "Starts imagining stuff."

George stared at the ground between his feet.

"How does your science explain his shredded heart?" he asked.

"We'll figure it out," Ellen came back at him rather brusquely.

All George did was shake his head.

***

"Anyone see Mr. Derham the day he died?" Lindy asked.

"Yup. He went into a store and tried to buy himself some coffee."

Tried?

"You mean in Alberly?"

"No. About a mile over there." Ellen jerked her thumb in an easterly direction. "Tiny little place called Rowan's Nook. No more than a hamlet. We've already spoken to the storekeeper."

"I'd like to have a word with him as well."

"If you want to waste your time, you're welcome. Coming, George?"

They walked back to the SUV and George and Lindy both got in the back.

"What do you mean, *tried* to buy some coffee?" Lindy asked Ellen as the trooper turned the vehicle around and headed off.

"There's only one store in Rowan's Nook, and it don't sell coffee, alcohol, smokes, or any other kind of stimulant. Not even Coca Cola."

"What, they're Amish or something?"

"Not exactly, no."

"They're afraid, and always have been," George murmured quietly.

They followed a new track until it intersected with a broader one, then turned eastward, the forest still surrounding them like prison bars. Except that this new route was particularly bumpy, which meant Ellen had to concentrate and leave them to their own devices.

"The real food of wendigos," George continued in a barely audible whisper, "is human souls."

Lindy turned her full attention to him, studying his face up close. She could scarcely believe that she was hearing this, but his features were grave, his eyes were clear and earnest. He appeared to be entirely serious.

"The one who killed the backpacker was probably a young un," he was saying, "only two or three hundred years old. Those kind are impatient and they kill real fast. Rip the heart up. Grab the soul and eat it while it's still emerging from the victim's mouth."

Lindy recalled she had read somewhere that that was how Native Americans thought the spirit left the body.

"But an *old* wendigo, one who's been around for say a thousand years or more? That's a different matter. No impatience. No concept of time at all. He enjoys what he's doing, the hurt that he's causing, and he takes it carefully and slowly."

George blinked a couple of times, peering deep into her eyes. He could see that she did not believe this stuff. Only her disbelief was not enough to shut him up.

"Wendigos like that know people all too well. Their weaknesses, their flaws, the things they want and cannot have, and they exploit that. An old one, he will choose a victim and then toy with that person like a kitten with a ball of string, just batting it about a while. He won't *snatch* a soul the way the young ones do. He'll maul it slowly, one shred at a time. And by the time the victim figures out what's going on, it's far too late to stop it."

How could anyone give credence to this stuff? The only kind of evil was the human kind – she knew that all too well. But she'd left the normal world behind her, now. She'd set foot into his world, and did not want to offend him.

"You keep saying he?" she asked him carefully. "Are these guys always male?"

"They're genuinely neither. They don't even count as animals really. No, they're something different, from the dark side of the veil. But they can look like humans if it suits them. Can appear like anything they want. An old wendigo is a master of deceit. You won't even know he wants to hurt you till it's happened."

"Fearsome creatures indeed," Ellen Hamp broke in with a slight laugh in her voice. So she'd been listening the entire while. "And yet they wander through those woods a lot, and you're still safely here, George, aren't you?"

He could hear the cynicism in her tone. His threadbare gray eyebrows bunched together.

"I've protection," he replied.

And he reached under his plaid shirt, pulling into view a leather thong.

His eyes were back on Lindy's face – in fact, they'd scarcely left it since they'd met. And was he trying to convey something to her?

At the end of the thong was a flattened piece of iron, crudely worked into the shape of a proud native face, surrounded by a feathered headdress.

"My gramps gave it to me," George told her. "It's Matchi Manitou."

Which conveyed precisely nothing.

"The Great God," Ellen explained from the front. "Actually, some people just say 'God,' like – you know – our one."

"And that keeps them away?"

"For sure," George nodded, smiling gently.

"So you wear it all the time?"

"Of course."

"And they can't trick you into taking it off?"

"They visit sometimes and they try, but when you have the Great God on your side then you can see right through them."

"That's *enough* now, George," snapped Ellen.

When the trees finally opened up, they still cast their long shadows across the scene that was revealed, so that the whole place looked like it was caught up in the grip of dusk.

There was nothing here except a double row of wood-built houses, the track passing down between them. And there was actually a wooden sidewalk either side of the uneven dirt. Lindy had only ever seen that thing in movies.

Ellen had to swerve going in, because a huge wooden cross, some twenty feet high, had been planted directly at the entrance to the place. There was no indication what this small village was called, no 'welcome to' or 'population' signs.

Another large cross reared against the wooded backdrop at the far end of the hamlet, from the steeple of a church this time. It was by far the largest building in sight.

Ellen parked. All three of them got out, and Lindy stared around. This was barely like leaving the forest at all – every building round them was the same brown color as the tree trunks. There was nothing around except a big crow perching on an eave. The houses all had small, square windows. They were glossily reflective, so she could not see the rooms beyond, only the drapes tucked in neatly by the edges, which were uniformly beige and plain.

Who in God's name chose to live in a place such as this?

The crow peered down at them, then took off, flapping away until the treetops swallowed it completely up. There'd been more sound out in the woods than could be heard in Rowan's Nook.

Except a door came open to her left, and her head jerked in that direction. A woman was peering out from it, directly at her. She had mousy hair that was tied up in a tight bun. Her face was blanched as though sunlight had never touched it. Her thin lips were tightly clamped together, their corners downturned. And she had on some manner of shapeless black dress, with long sleeves and a skirt that almost brushed against the floor.

Lindy studied her carefully, taking in the fact uncomfortably she couldn't tell what age this woman was. Early thirties, or late forties? It was near impossible to tell.

The woman yanked her head back in her home and slammed the door.

"Quite some welcoming committee."

"They're not exactly the friendliest folk you're ever going to meet," Ellen admitted.

Then she jerked her chin toward a sign that just read GENERAL STORE.

There was wooden shelving inside with a meager range of produce. There was also a large metal crucifix – bronze this time – on the wall behind the counter, and two smaller ones on the opposing walls. No pictures. No decoration of any kind.

A thin man of medium height stepped out behind the counter from a small door at the back. His crown was bald, but he had reddish hair and a neatly trimmed beard of the same color. Like the woman that she'd just seen, he looked very pale and glum. And he had on black clothing too, a waistcoat and pants, with a plain white shirt buttoned the whole way up.

The moment he laid eyes on her, his head went down. He stared fixedly at the top of his counter, and did not look up when she approached.

"Mr. Foreman?" Ellen asked him, from behind her. "You remember me?"

"Yuh-huh."

But his face still did not rise, not a fraction of an inch.

"This here's Detective Sergeant Grady from New York. They've had a couple of incidents like the one out in the woods. She'd like to speak with you."

"Don't know why. Only saw that feller for a minute. I've already told you everything I know."

"Mr. Foreman?" Lindy tried. "The deceased went by the name of William Derham – did you know that?"

"So I'm told."

"Did he say anything unusual to you that you recall?"

"Asked for coffee. Told 'im that we had none."

"Anything else?"

"He was surprised we didn't have none. Then he left."

"And there was nothing more?"

The man's head shook, his face remaining down. And ... what on earth did he think he was doing? He was openly refusing to meet her gaze, but God knew why.

And she was starting to get rather peeved about it. Lindy was used – when interviewing someone – to looking out for body language and facial expressions. Whereas none of that was possible with this strange guy. Even his voice was a flat monotone, cadenceless, remote, impossible to read. Her skin crawled with annoyance

"Sir?" she tried asking, in a sharper, more authoritative tone. "Would you mind looking at me while we speak?"

His jaw twitched, but that was all the movement she got out of him. Ellen laid a soft hand on her shoulder.

"Nice try," she whispered, "but it probably won't work. He won't so much as look at *me*, and I'm not half the peach that you are."

What *was* this? All that Lindy could do was press on.

"Did anybody else come in here after Mr. Derham left?"

"Not for a couple of hours, as I recall. And then it was a local."

"Did he speak to anybody else in town?"

"You'd have to ask them that thing, because I don't know."

Lindy glanced enquiringly at Ellen again, and the trooper shook her head. MSP had obviously already canvassed this whole hamlet and come up with nothing.

She could think of no more questions to ask.

"Okay, then. Thank you so much for your invaluable help, sir," she told Foreman, not even trying to hide the sarcasm in her tone.

They headed back to George, who was standing by the doorway. He grinned at Lindy in an odd, slightly triumphant fashion.

"He won't look at you because you pose temptation," he told her as soon as they were back outside. "The people in this place, they keep their lives holy and pure. Allow no weaknesses or hidden flaws ... nothing that the wendigos could use against them."

Lindy tried to smile and failed.

"George, I like you. Honestly I do. But if you keep on talking that way then I'm going to lose my patience. There are really no such things – you have to know that, don't you?"

He didn't look the least put out, but merely thoughtful.

"I know what I know."

Her eyes rolled in her head and she let out a groan.

Driving back the way they'd come, the forest appeared even darker still. It was now gone two in the afternoon, the sun changing angle and the shadows growing denser.

"Let me out here," George said when they reached the smaller track.

"You'll walk from here?"

"George likes to walk," said Ellen.

Lindy turned round in her seat. George was smiling warmly at her, his leathery face all crinkled up. She reached across to shake his hand, and the man cupped her smaller one in both of his.

"Pleasure to meet you, George."

"More than that on my part, sergeant."

George pulled out the thong again, lifting it from off his neck. And placed the small amulet in her palm. She blinked at him, astonished.

"What?"

"If those things have arrived in Manhattan, then you might find yourself needing this."

She almost laughed, but stopped herself.

"Well, what's gonna protect *you*, George?"

"You think I live out here and I've got just the one? I've scads of stuff to ward off evil creatures."

He gently forced her hand shut. And his gaze when it bored into hers was deadly serious again.

"I get it that you don't believe a thing I said. So let's just call this a souvenir from your trip into the woods. Okay?"

She turned that over.

"Okay, sure."

His grip tightened noticeably.

"Keep hold of it. Promise me?"

"I will," she nodded.

"Then take care of yourself, sergeant," he said, letting her go and opening the door. "I'd wish you luck, except I hope that you don't need it."

He climbed out. And a second later he was gone, the undergrowth not even moving in his wake. Lindy's head swiveled around.

"How'd he do that?"

"That's First Americans for you," Ellen shrugged, putting the SUV into drive again. "No making any sense of them."

Lindy slipped the amulet into her jacket pocket. And both women went silent until they'd rejoined the blacktopped road.

***

"Like to see the corpse? They want to look at it in Boston, so we've still got it on ice."

"Nah," Lindy frowned. "I'm not a scientist – I wouldn't know what to do with it."

She felt relieved to be out of the woods, like a heavy weight had been lifted from her. Or a wide gauze bandage had been removed from her eyes and she was able to see properly again.

"Your guys in New York come up with any explanation for the condition of the heart yet?"

"Nope."

"Everybody's flummoxed, then."

"That's the word."

"So it's what? Back to Manhattan for you?"

Yup, another three hour drive. This was so goddamned frustrating, hauling all the way out here, staggering round the forest like fucking Gretel in search of Hansel, and *still* coming up absolutely empty. Not a single aspect of this case was getting any clearer. It was like trying to find a small thread of pale gray cotton in a heavy fog.

"Sure," she muttered tightly, "back to the Big Apple."

She immediately thought of John.

22 – I Want to See You

She was starving, and stopped in at a roadside diner halfway through the journey back for a late lunch – chargrilled chicken, a side salad, and a calorie-free Seven-Up. Most of the guys in here were truckers, burly guys with baseball caps and – in some cases – thick mustaches. And they kept on glancing at her, taking in her looks and figure. But she simply acted like they weren't even there.

The waitress who bought her her plate was pushing her sixties, walked with a slight limp, and didn't even manage a smile when she mumbled, "Enjoy your meal."

A lot of people's lives didn't exactly wind up happily … Lord, wasn't that the truth?

The skyline of Manhattan began coming in sight sometime after six in the evening. The inward lanes were busy, faster cars continually slamming by her. It was still fully day, except the sunlight had taken on a slightly amber hue, the shadows stretching like they belonged to a different, darkly-reflected world, the air as dense and full of energy as ozone. Lindy was looking at nothing in particular, simply keeping her eye on the road ahead, when her gaze lifted a little and she noticed something that oughtn't be there.

There was a large and curling pall of smoke hanging like a blackened query mark over midtown Manhattan. And what in Christ had happened now? She abruptly remembered where she'd been on 9/11. Came back to full alertness in an instant, switched on the Pontiac's radio again and fiddled with the dial until she found a news station.

"… had to be evacuated when one of the guests managed to set fire to himself in his own room."

A hotel? She got the sudden, awful feeling that it might be the McKinnon.

"Fire alarms and sprinkler equipment somehow failed to work, and estimates put the number now hospitalized at between twenty and thirty, many of them foreign tourists. A spokesman for the Colari chain …"

Lindy turned that over in her mind and then let out a long, slow breath. The McKinnon was not part of that group. But the Colari International was also near the park.

By the time that she was back on the Triborough Bridge, the pall of smoke had thinned and flattened out. It didn't look so much like a punctuation mark by this time as a bruise, as though some giant had jammed his fist against the sky.

She got back to the garage, checked the car back in, then went up to her office to see if anything new had transpired regarding any of the cases she was working – nothing had. So she went out onto the hot street and found herself a cab.

By the time she'd gotten home and showered and dried her hair, the light at her windows was beginning to fade a touch.

She went to the cabinet where she kept her laptop, pulled it out and got onto the Internet. It was something that she didn't do an awful lot. She *certainly* never used this thing for meeting men. You could find yourself having a conversation with some four hundred pound shut-in who was passing himself off as the next Robert Pattinson ... why did people fail to understand that?

She looked up 'wendigo.' Got the spelling wrong at first, but the machine corrected her. She wasn't even sure why she was bothering with this, but the intensity of George's belief had left her slightly intrigued.

They were listed here as flesh-eaters, not soul-eaters, so perhaps George knew something that the general public didn't. They had all the qualities that he'd described – shape-shifting, the ability to take on a human appearance, and a penchant for deceit. But there was more.

According to one site, they could possess a human being, taking over that person's mind and controlling his actions, often in a violent manner. She remembered that Brazilian tourist up on Broadway who'd gone crazy with an ax, but afterwards could not remember why.

Then she thought, *Nah, people go nuts the entire time*, and snapped the laptop shut.

Her shoulders were aching. She hated driving, always had. The long road out to Massachusetts was imprinted on her memory. She saw it every time she blinked. And normally, when she was feeling like this, she'd have gotten dressed up and applied a little perfume and a touch of make-up and gone heading out to one of her regular bars, so she could put all this behind her and forget it.

But the plain fact was that she was just too damned exhausted.

Except her mind turned back in the direction of John Hunter.

If he was true to his word, then he'd be waiting for her in that hotel room. Maybe he was sitting on his bed right now and staring at the door. He'd been terrific, strong and assured and expert, guiding her taut body up from one height to another. She'd certainly have gone back under any other circumstance. But if she failed to show, would he believe that she'd declined his offer? That wasn't the case.

She had to let him know that. So she got directory to put her though to his hotel.

"The McKinnon. How may I assist you?" came a pleasingly gentle female voice at the far end.

"You've a guest in Room 27, a Mr. –"

But John's deep, smooth tones suddenly broke across that.

"Why, if it isn't Lindy Grady from the nursery rhyme."

"I … John? I was speaking to reception."

"And they passed you up to me immediately. They're very good like that."

Which *sort* of explained it, but seemed a touch unusual.

"They didn't even ask me who I was," she pointed out.

There was a brief silence, and then, "I was expecting you in person, not a phone call, Lindy."

Which left her feeling awkward.

"See now, that's the thing."

"Oh dear. Work is getting in the way of fun?"

"Sort of. I had to drive the whole way out into New England today."

"How charming. My own stamping ground."

"And – honestly, John – I'd *love* to see you, but I'm way too tired."

"You wouldn't have to do much. I'd do all the physical exertion."

And she grinned tightly at that.

"I appreciate the offer. But seriously, it's gonna have to be another night."

"Too fucked for fucking, huh?"

"Yup."

"I don't believe that."

Oh, come on now!

He said, "I want to see you *so* very badly, Lindy. I'm not sure that I can wait another night."

"You're a grown-up boy. I'm sure you'll manage. Your hotel has movies, don't it?"

"I don't want a movie. I want you."

Ah hell! She felt faintly irritated with him, for sure, but the weariness was lifting from her, a tingling sensation beginning to run around her body, like a mild electricity or a dash of Tabasco added to her blood. She felt more energized than she had been, but tried to fight against it.

"I'm sitting here in my bathrobe, John."

"A very pleasant sight, I'm sure."

"I'd have to get made-up and dressed and find another cab."

"You don't need make-up, and I'll send a car."

And was he kidding?

"What are your address and number?" he was asking her.

She gave them.

"A driver will be there in half an hour."

She heard herself saying 'okay' as though from some enormous distance. And then he hung up.

Why had she agreed to this? She had been comfortably resigned to a quiet evening a few minutes back. But urgency had filled her now. She went back into the bathroom and dried herself off fully. Then she opened up her closet, to select something to wear. Another suit? But no, she had a few dresses, and one of them was a bright red one. Just like in that fantasy she couldn't properly remember.

No need for make-up? Hell, a touch of mascara and a little liner couldn't hurt. And she was poised in front of her bathroom mirror, ready to apply them, when she stopped herself.

Let's see if I can take him at his word?

Precisely half an hour after John had rung off, her phone chimed again. And when she answered, there was a driver at the other end, telling her he was downstairs.

Lindy crossed to her living room window and stared at the street below. A stretched black limousine was parked against the curb.

And by this time, the sky was fully dark. She locked her front door and then hurried down.

23 – Bound

"You didn't put on make-up after all."

His knuckles brushed very softly against her cheekbone, his thumb tracing the eyebrow above it, and he smiled.

"I'm pleased."

He was already in the dark blue robe he'd had on last time, his bare feet showing. She moved in to kiss him. But she caught sight of what was on the bed out of the corner of her eye, and that stopped her dead.

Like last night, the covers were peeled back, the stark whiteness of the sheets displayed. Only there were narrow bands of dark across the white. She felt the corners of her eyelids crinkle, took a moment to identify what she was looking at.

These were leather cords, four of them. Each had been knotted to one of the brass railings top and bottom of the bed, and they were the same length and spaced very exactly.

Her heart seemed to knock up against her ribs and stay there. She wasn't looking at John Hunter anymore, but was still aware of his presence. He had moved around behind her and had placed a hand on either of her shoulders. Once again, Room 27's door had clicked shut of its own volition.

Lindy fought to keep her voice from rising when she asked, "What's this?"

"After last night, I assumed ..."

"Making a big load of assumptions, aren't you?"

"You liked being handcuffed."

Her chin tipped down. Her mouth came open silently.

Then: "Handcuffs are a game. This is something ..." And she hunted for the right words. "Different. Bigger."

"Are you telling me you don't like different? Are you telling me you don't like big?"

Once again – exactly like before – the drowsiness came over her. It wasn't tiredness, wasn't a resurgence of the sheer exhaustion she'd been feeling about an hour back. It was more like being drugged again. A feeling of detachment. The outside world seemed very far away. Within these red walls was another world entirely, she and John the only people in it. And she genuinely found herself warming to the idea of that.

Her gaze went to the nightstand. There was something white and narrow on it, which she imagined was a face towel or a handkerchief. Except it wasn't either of those things, simply a long strip of white cloth with a tight knot at its center.

There was a damned good reason why she oughtn't be considering this. A part of her brain kept on trying to tell her that. Something that had taken place – not last night – but the night before. It seemed important, and it kept on pushing at the outer edges of her consciousness. But she only got vague images. A struggling sensation and a silhouette in front of her. Except ... she couldn't quite remember what had happened.

"*Big* load of assumptions," she could hear herself saying. "Do you always act like this?"

"Only with a woman who can handle it."

"And you think that's me? How do you know?

"I knew it from the first moment I saw you, Lindy."

"And you think that this is what I want? Kink?"

"No, that's not what this is really all about."

"What then?"

"I want to see the truth of you. I want to see the *real* you, Lindy."

She took another deep breath, then yanked a strap of her bright red dress off of one taut shoulder.

"No, please," he chided her. "Please, do it slowly."

***

"Have you ever considered," he asked her quietly as he tied the knots, "the similarities between this and your own profession. People do wrong, you hunt them down to punish them. And you do that by restricting their freedom, putting them in cages, putting them in chains."

"Yeah. I'm just a sadist, I guess."

She grinned a little boredly. Her wrists were tied, but not her legs yet. Why was he taking so long about this?

"There's a very strong parallel –" he started saying.

"Please, please, please, *shut up!*"

To her relief he did that thing, and moved down to the foot of the bed, finishing up the job he'd started.

She looked down along her body. He had bound it up so it was perfectly displayed, her long, tapering legs pulled out to their full limit, her waist tautened so that her belly was completely flat, her breasts pulled up high by the tension in her shoulders. It was very rare for her to look at herself and think herself gorgeous, but this was one of those occasions.

Someone else had made her feel this way a good long while ago. Something about a park, a yellow bed. But her mind couldn't get a proper hold on that particular memory either.

Except it struck her. With her legs out straight, her knees couldn't bend. And if that was the case, how were they going to …?

She looked past her feet. John had taken off his robe and was coming up along the bed toward her like a jungle cat, an impression that those bright green eyes of his only served to reinforce.

He made his way halfway along her. Then his head disappeared between her legs, and their tiny world contracted to a microscopic dot.

***

It had to be almost half an hour before he got up. She was shuddering and bathed with sweat. John climbed up her carefully and set one knee down either side of her shoulders, then reached down and lifted her head off the pillow.

Quid pro quo. Okay, then. She'd never had the slightest problem with this.

As she worked, she watched his face. His eyelids were closed, the lashes fluttering, and his expression was very distant, far away, like he'd gone to some different place altogether, except he'd absentmindedly left a part of his body behind in her mouth.

That thought made her want to laugh, which was – under the circumstances – difficult. But he must have felt the tightening of her jaw, the fluttering of her tongue.

He yelled out like he was in pain. His features crumpled as though he was going to cry. She was watching his face very intently now, amazed at the power she could exert on him even while she was tied up.

He rolled off her and disappeared into the bathroom. She swallowed, and the saltiness burned at her throat. She needed to get up from here so she could drink some water.

The shower started running, and her head came jolting up.

"John?"

She could hear him climbing into it, the pitch of the spray changing. Lindy craned her neck around as far as she was able.

"Er ... John? Haven't you forgotten something?"

But maybe he couldn't hear her. Which was his own fault. She lay back again, trying to relax, but could feel her cheeks flushing. Of all the dumbass things to do. What was he *playing* at?

She was starting to feel slightly cold. That was only psychological, she knew – this room was a perfectly warm one. Except that, trapped like this, she felt exposed. Her nipples had gone as hard as pebbles. But she had no choice except to wait until the shower stopped. That took about five minutes.

"*John!*"

He was toweling himself down and she could hear that clearly. So why couldn't he hear her?

"Hey! Remember me? I'm still where you left me, *obviously*!"

To her utter amazement, he suddenly began talking, only not to her. It took a few seconds for her startled, fuddled mind to take in what was going on. John was talking on his cell. He had to have had it in the pocket of his robe. Lindy stiffened up with fright initially, yanking at her bonds. Who exactly was he speaking to, and what precisely was he telling them? But that fear evaporated quickly, since it merely sounded like a business conversation.

"What d'you think you're *doing*?" she moaned.

His head came poking out the bathroom door, and he now had his robe back on. He peered at her, his expression admonishing. And he had one hand flat across the mouthpiece of his cell phone.

"This is a very important call," he told her in a lowered tone. "Please do not embarrass me by shouting out behind it."

And he said that thing as though it were the most reasonable request in the entire world. Was he *nuts*? Did he think she was a piece of *furniture*, for God's sake? But it was better to get this over with, let him finish up and then untie her, then get out of here.

So she went completely slack again and peered up at the ceiling.

John's business conversation just went on and on.

By the time that he had finally wound it up, she was genuinely fuming. Her head snapped up again. And she was filling her mouth with invective to spit out at him, when he moved in on her very quickly, snatching the strip of white cloth from beside the bed and gagging her with it.

The anger in her started melting and reforming into something else. John began again, like he had done the first time.

***

This *was* his idea of game playing! *Goddamn!*

The second time they finished up, he produced a laptop from his closet and sat down at the dresser with his back to her, tapping idly at the keyboard, bringing up charts onto the screen. The gag was gone, since he'd required her to use her mouth a second time.

"John?"

His head shook and he raised one hand and wagged the fingers gently without looking round at her.

"John, I need some water."

He got up smoothly, went into the bathroom. She could hear the faucet running and he returned with a half-filled glass. He lifted her head carefully and let her sip. And then he reapplied the gag.

Was this a power trip, him telling her that she was only really there for sex? She tugged against the bonds at her wrists – the knots hadn't loosened in the slightest and the cords would only stretch a little way. But he noticed the way her body tightened, and was on her with his mouth a third time.

Afterwards, he actually switched on the TV in the middle of a Mets game. *For fuck's sake!*

"This is *crazy*, John."

That only got her gagged again.

He seemed to be watching the baseball quite intently, but she figured out that was an act when – bottom of the ninth – he suddenly clicked the set off and returned to her.

She'd almost bitten through the gag by the time he had finished. And he finally removed it, but he didn't require her to use her mouth this time.

"We done?" she asked breathlessly, as he clambered off the bed.

He went back into the bathroom. She could hear the water in the basin running once again. When he stepped back into the main room, he crossed over to the dresser. Opened a drawer, selected a pair of boxers, pulled them on.

"Hello?"

He was getting dressed. What was he up to now? She squirmed against the leather cords, peering at him anxiously.

He had on a pair of jeans, a pair of sneakers, and a white muslin shirt within another minute. He came over to the nightstand, not even glancing at her. Took his room key from it.

"*John?*"

He turned his back on her. Crossed over to the door.

Opened it, flicking off the light as he did so.

"*No!*"

But he went out, slamming it behind him.

24 – On the Bed

What the ...?

How long was he planning to keep her here like this? When, if ever, was he coming back? That last thought scared her, and she struggled furiously against the cords. But all she succeeded in doing was tightening the grip of leather round her wrists and ankles. So there was no getting out of here without somebody's help.

Lindy let her head drop back. John had switched the bathroom light off as well before he'd left, but the room was not entirely dark. The drapes were open some eight inches, light from the street spilling in and illuminating a wall and the dresser, but only in monochrome, so that she felt like she was trapped in some black-and-white movie. When she stared at the world beyond the window, none of the opposite ones were lit. Nobody could see her. There was nothing moving out there, not on this high level.

She squeezed her eyelids shut, infuriated. And when she opened them again ...

She jolted with shock and started to let out a yell before calming back down and going slack. It had only been her eyesight playing tricks on her, but for the briefest moment she'd believed she'd seen ...

A pair of faces. Women's faces, staring in at her from past the drapes. One of them had seemed to be the same woman she'd walked by in the street last night. The other's features had been unfamiliar, younger, more petite, and blonde.

Except that this room was at the *front* of the hotel. There were no fire escapes out there, no balconies, no way of getting up. So no one could be standing out there unless they were floating – not exactly likely. And both faces had vanished between one second and the next. It was only her imagination, which was – understandably – becoming pretty fevered, her mind rushing every which direction since her body couldn't. She wriggled her back against the mattress. What in God's name was she going to do?

Sometime later – she could not be sure how long – she heard a group of people climbing up the hotel stairs. It sounded like four of them, and they were chattering, laughing, obviously coming to the end of a nice evening. People lived in their own little bubbles, unaware what someone else's evening might be like.

They started passing by her door. She thought of calling out for help. Then she considered what that would result in. A spare key clicking in the lock, worked by a member of the McKinnon's staff. Then the door coming open on her bound, spread-eagled nudity. And she didn't want that.

She ground her head against the pillow and gritted her teeth. *Oh fuck you, John! You've really got this figured out!*

She was a police officer, for chrissake! She had a life, a dozen other things to do! She wasn't only here for his amusement and his pleasure!

Then why, a voice seemed to ask her very quietly, from somewhere deep inside her head, *did you put yourself in this position in the first place?*

The passers-by were gone. She could hear them saying goodnights to each other on the floor above and then their doors opening and closing. Lindy felt like screaming out an oath, but was afraid that that would also bring someone uninvited here. And so she screamed it in her head instead.

There was a small electric clock there on the nightstand, bright green numerals flashing on it. She hadn't even noticed it until this stage. But when she first looked at it, it was half after one. When she looked at it again, only a minute had passed. This whole thing was driving her insane. What was John even *doing*? How long would he *be*?

The numerals on the clock filled up her vision, flashing rhythmically, the final digit only changing very slowly. She was still staring at them when she drifted into sleep.

***

She was awoken by the room's door banging shut. John was standing by it, but he hadn't switched on any lights. She felt blurry and disoriented, and had trouble taking in the fact that he was kicking off his shoes, then pulling his shirt off along his muscled arms.

The clock said 3:25. He'd been away for hours, but she was still too dulled with sleep for emotions like annoyance.

"Where were you?" she mumbled.

But he didn't even bother to reply. His pants and shorts came off, his body pale in the glow from the window. And his eyes, catching the intruding light, appeared to sparkle luminously for just a second.

And then he turned into a silhouette, advancing on the bed. He was ready to go again, and not just with his mouth this time.

"For God's *sake*, I've got work in a few hours," she tried to complain.

But his hands were already running over her thighs, down across the backs of her knees and smoothly down her calves, and he was untying her ankles.

25 – The Blonde

By the time she finally got out of the McKinnon, night was beginning to lift from the city like a black glass bowl being eased away, light filtering in around the lower edges so the buildings round her were silhouetted and two-dimensional looking. She was utterly exhausted. Felt simultaneously satisfied and somehow hollowed out. John hadn't played his stop-start games for a single other moment once that he'd come back. He had attended to her constantly, parting her legs firmly, pressing their bodies so closely together that toward the end it felt as though their flesh might meld.

A silver ray of sunlight shot up from the east, making Lindy squint. And so she turned away from it, and found herself wandering in the direction of the park.

She took her shoes back off. The grass felt springy underneath her feet. In one direction was the Rustic Bridge. In the other was the Sheep Meadow and then the trees and tall buildings beyond that. She was basically pretty well dead center of a good number of possible crime scenes, but that didn't impinge too much on her consciousness. All that she was genuinely aware of was the fact that she was very tired and aching. And she wished she'd not quit smoking since – right now – she could seriously use a smoke.

What *was* it with that guy? He seemed to enjoy playing with her in the same manner as – what was the term George Greentree had used? – as a kitten with a ball of string. It was infuriating in some ways, but on a deeper level she quite liked it. It made her feel like she was really being noticed. How long had it been since anyone had bothered with her outside of taking her back to his place and fucking her and then forgetting her? John noticed her an awful lot, even when he was pretending to ignore her.

On the other hand, she'd barely gotten any sleep. She was now becoming starving hungry – hadn't eaten once since yesterday mid-afternoon. She had to start work again in a bare few hours, and she scarcely even had the time to get back home.

Once again, the question reared itself inside her head. *Why'd you put yourself in this position in the first place?*

She reached one of the park's broad boulders, sat down on its edge and tried to work her head around that thought. *Because I have to? Need to? Trying to find something that I've never known?*

Her mind recoiled immediately, like a snake drawing back from a flame. There were many things that she indulged in, but self-analysis was rarely one of them. What was the point of thinking about what you did when you were going to do it anyway?

Her skull felt so heavy, she let it drop down practically the whole way to her knees. Out of nowhere, she felt terribly alone.

But then she realized that was not the case. Out of the corner of her eye, she caught a glimpse of movement, turned her face toward it.

It was hard to be certain in this poor light but ... a pale and vaguely human shape was advancing in her direction. Just a pallid strip against the park's dimness, at first. But then it began to take on substance.

She made out the top and bottom first. Bare white legs and straight blonde hair. And then the rest came slowly into focus. It was a young woman she was looking at. A rather rounded face, although she couldn't make out the small details. Bare arms hanging slackly by her sides. And she was wearing ... what was that, some kind of shift? It was very short, looked extremely filmy, and left Lindy with the impression that this might be some kind of retro Flower Child.

Whoever she was, she was moving inward at a swift and steady pace. Her pale legs scissored underneath the shift. Her feet were bare, so far as Lindy could make out. Her face turned neither left nor right, but remained fixed ahead.

She could definitely see that someone was in front of her. And yet she didn't slow. Her stride didn't falter. She was homing in on Lindy like some guided missile.

Abruptly, all the tiredness went away. Lindy stood up, but *still* the woman kept on coming. And when she'd first spoken to John about the Callum case, hadn't he mentioned a second woman, young and fair-haired just like this? Blondie here had an entire goddamned park to walk through, so why was she heading fixedly to this particular spot?

Lindy took a couple of steps forward. But *that* didn't stop the woman either. Didn't even make her stall. Adrenalin had started pumping by this stage. Lindy stared down at the woman's hands and couldn't see a weapon. But she started opening her purse and reaching for her gun.

Wasn't this ... now that it was closer ... wasn't *this* the blonde face she'd imagined briefly, staring in at her between the half-drawn drapes of Room 27? Lindy gave her brow a shake. That simply wasn't possible. She closed her fist around her sidearm, but she didn't take it out.

The blonde woman had to see she was being reacted to. Except she took no slightest notice of it. If anything, her tread became a little faster. She was moving in on Lindy in a perfectly straight line. The word here seemed to be 'relentless.'

Four people had died in this park in the past few days. Five, if you counted Kendra Callier out at the edge. And here was someone who'd been noticed at one of the scenes. Lindy pulled her gun out, aimed it.

Still the woman didn't slow. She was close enough now that the details of her face could be made out. A blandly pretty one, with small and even features. The kind of features that might peer out at you from the glossy cover of a magazine. There was no expression to it Lindy could discern. No spite or anger or determination nothing. And no apprehension either, so she wasn't frightened of the gun.

What did this young idiot think that she was doing? It was so hard to grasp that Lindy almost felt the marrow loosen in her bones. But then she got a grip on herself. She was more than capable of self-protection.

She was sucking in a breath, preparing to shout out a warning when ... the blonde woman drew to a halt.

Except it didn't seem to be on account of anything in front of her. The gun, the person holding it – she seemed unfazed by those. But she abruptly held herself extremely straight and her head lifted on its thin white neck, her face tilting around to the left. She was staring at where Lindy had just come from. In fact, she was gazing at the block where the McKinnon stood. A line appeared on her smooth brow. Her head tipped slightly to one side. It was as though she were listening to something.

And then she suddenly smiled, a noticeably hungry grin. After which she turned around and headed back the other way. And had disappeared entirely into the folding shadows in a bare few seconds, which couldn't be right.

Lindy blinked, trying to make her out again, but couldn't. The shock had frozen her by this stage, and she had to fight to break away from that. She scrabbled for her cell phone, her breath hissing fast.

"This is Sergeant Belinda Grady, Homicide." She gave her badge number. "I need to close the park down. Send me every cruiser that you can. Murder suspect. Blonde Caucasian female in her early to mid-twenties."

Sirens were closing in around her several minutes later. And she thought of setting off into the shadows, trying to find Blondie once again. But in this kind of dimness, she might even get mistaken for the person she was after by the other cops. And so she sat down on the boulder once again, but quite unsteadily.

**

Closing down a place as big as Central Park was one hell of a tall order. Practically impossible, in truth. The sun started to rise, casting her shadow on the rock below her. She was checking in every few minutes on her cell, only to be told that there were no reports of anyone as yet.

Some half an hour later, a small group of uniformed officers began strolling toward her across the sward. The air was already getting pretty hot. The windows in the higher towers round her shone like they were trying to melt.

The cop leading the way was another one she recognized, an overweight and thick-lipped individual called Robson. He always had a smug look and an attitude to women. And he came swaggering across to her like she was insignificant, some kind of joke.

"Got anything?" she snapped at him, not even bothering to stand up.

"Got zip. Not even a stray dog." His upper lip curled back a little. "You sure that you saw this blonde dame?"

"Of *course* I'm sure."

"You live downtown, don't ya? What were you even doing this far up at this time of the morning?"

That was none of his damned business. But his gaze had already gone to the clothes she was wearing, and she remembered that she still had on the bright red dress.

"Visiting your poor sick grandma, huh, Little Red Riding Hood?"

She almost sprang up to her feet, but realized how much satisfaction that would give him. So she fixed him with her gaze and said, "That's 'sergeant.' Don't forget it."

"Sure."

And he went wandering back to join the rest and started up a conversation with them. Only, what it was about was something she could only guess. Several of them kept on glancing over at her with tight little smirks, like they thought that it was funny that she had some kind of private life. And she'd always been careful to avoid encounters like this. Her work colleagues had never even *seen* her in a dress.

But that was when she finally remembered. She had a court appearance this morning. Some gangsta she'd put away four years ago was appealing his conviction. And she couldn't stand up in a witness box looking this way, could she?

She made her excuses, backtracked hurriedly to Lexington and took the IRT back home. Didn't even bother showering. Simply pulled the red dress off and dumped it on the floor, hauling on one of her plainer suits instead. Applied small touches of make-up.

Went back out into the heat and found a cab to take her to Tribeca.

She had half fallen asleep by the time they that they were pulling up outside of 346 Broadway. The cabbie had to tell her they were there.

Which was not a great start. This was turning out to be one hell of a day.

26 – Shakedown

"What the *fuck* were you doing in there, Lindy?" New York County ADA Stuart Bellman asked her furiously, as soon as they were back outside the courtroom.

Her eyelids were crinkled like well-used tinfoil, and she knew it. She had stuttered and stumbled in the witness box. She'd forgotten certain pertinent facts, and since she had neglected to bring her notes along she'd had to stand there trying to dredge them from her memory with the whole court watching her. It hadn't been her finest moment.

Stuart looked as if he wanted to hit her, and he'd never looked like that before. He was a hard-working and handsome young attorney with a promising career ahead of him. They'd always gotten along fine. In fact, he'd asked her out one time – she'd naturally declined.

But now, his eyes were blazing and his smooth features were all screwed up.

"What were you *thinking* of?" he hissed. "Not this case, for sure. Not keeping Duwayne Davidson where he belongs. He almost *walked*!"

And then he looked down and his eyebrows knitted together.

"What the …?"

He grabbed hold of one of Lindy's wrists and yanked it up. She yelled 'hey,' but that didn't stop him.

There was a red ring on her skin where the leather cord had bitten into it last night. Stuart peered back up at her, his whole expression going numb and slack. She pulled her hand away, then shifted with embarrassment. There was a certain dullness to the lawyer's gaze now that had never been there before.

"Look, I don't know what you've been getting into," he told her, considerably more quietly than before. "And it's none of my business, sure. But if it's starting to affect your work, you're going to have to choose. I always thought you were a good cop, Lindy. Don't go spoiling that."

Then he turned on his heel and marched briskly away from her, shaking his head as he went. Lindy watched him rather sadly and then re-inspected her wrist.

John had really left his mark on her. And in more ways than one. What she'd done last night was starting to impinge on what happened the day following that. And she wasn't warming to that notion so much as a tiny bit. She started to think seriously of not ever returning to that room in the McKinnon. Except the thought of more abstinence pained her.

She went back out into the searing sunlight, heading north. Before much longer, she was on one of the busier parts of lower Broadway. There were stalls at the intersection with Canal, cut-price clothing stores past those, and the area was full of shoppers. In the dazzling yellow light, they kept on going by her like a swarm of ghosts. Their faces were largely blank. Their eyes went past her without even registering she was there. She felt as though the blinding brightness had reduced her to a pale negative of her former self. Exhaustion was closing over her again, the heat making it worse so that she felt light-headed.

If Stuart had noticed the state of her wrists, then other folks would do the same. She needed to fix that before she got back to the station house. She fiddled with her watchstrap till it covered up the mark on her left wrist almost completely. Then she went into one of the discount stores, selected a wide, cheap bracelet, put it on her right. There was nothing she could do about her ankles but, hey, this wasn't the Nineteen Hundreds. People didn't pay them much attention these days.

The weariness was something else, not so easily hidden. But she kept on moving up till she was through SoHo and past the Village, heading into Chelsea.

There was a strip club that she knew of that was open day and night. She didn't even bother with the front door, simply went round to the back exit and stepped into the shadows. Waited there until a tall, young black woman came hurrying up the concrete steps. Her head was down – she didn't even notice anyone was there till Lindy grabbed her by the elbow.

"Hey, keep your damned hands to yourself!"

Lindy showed the girl her badge.

"What? I ain't done nothin'!"

"No? Well, I'm willing to bet you've got a little cocaine in that purse of yours."

Lindy reached into her own, produced a few tens and fanned them out.

"We got a deal?"

It took a short while to convince the stripper that this wasn't an entrapment. But she finally produced a small vial of the stuff.

***

By the time she'd arrived at the office – clear-headed and wide awake – she had her shades back on. Face it, she was always hiding *something* these days.

Bob Collins stood up from his desk and told her, "Looking good, as always."

Lindy ignored that.

"Anything else come up? Any more mayhem?"

He squinted thoughtfully. "Like the axman, you mean?"

"Like the axman. Like the hotel guest setting fire to himself. Like the people going crazy in that restaurant."

"It *has* been pretty weird the past few days. But here's the even weirder thing – it only ever happens close to evening, when the light is starting to fade. How'd you figure that?"

And then Bob glanced across at a small, portable television that was playing silently in the far corner of the office. The news was on, a different channel to the one she watched. A brunette anchorwoman's lips were moving. A huge photo of Kendra Callier was being displayed behind her, and Bob Collins smirked.

"She was butt naked when she hit the sidewalk. Did you know that?"

"Yeah, I knew."

Lindy turned away, feeling briefly depressed. Even in death, people were obsessing about Kendra Callier's state of undress.

But the feeling didn't last for long. The coke was still singing through her system. She moved toward her cluttered desktop. And had almost reached it … when some instinct made her glance off to the right, in the direction of the glass pane in the captain's office door.

And she thought she saw John Hunter's face reflected in it for a second, his bright green eyes staring at her carefully.

She spun around, but there was no one there.

Except that when she blinked, those same green orbs were looming in the darkness right behind her eyelids. He seemed to be right there inside her head, and she could almost hear his voice.

"Can't you do something to liven this place up a little?"

What? She was imagining this, had to be. There was no other explanation. But the impulse suddenly came over her to do exactly what the voice had said. Yeah, stir things up a little. Her gaze swept across the office, and she saw the perfect target.

There was a small bare room adjacent to this one that had a drinks vending machine, another one for snacks, a couple of plastic chairs and a low coffee table. And the only person sitting in there right now was Peter Renzo, besuited as usual, stubbly as usual, with a sandwich in one hand and a paper cup clasped in the other.

Little Peter Renzo, who never even allowed himself to get too close to her. By-the-book, goody two-shoes Peter Renzo, a staunch Catholic with a wife and family in Queens. What, was he convinced that he might catch something if he allowed her to touch him? This was something that had gone on too long. And it needed redressing, didn't it?

She hitched up the waistband of her skirt, adjusted her top so there was cleavage showing and then sauntered through into the little room.

"*Peter!* Haven't seen much of you the past couple of days. How's it going with those two stiffs in the park?"

She set her palms down on the back of the chair across from him and leaned over to give him a good view. His gaze came up, then darted quickly off, and his throat jerked as he swallowed.

"Scumbags, the pair of 'em. Not too much to go on as to how they died."

"Peter, why're you talking to the floor? I'm over here."

His brow furrowed. She had never spoken to him like this before. But his head came slowly round – he stared directly at her face, venturing no lower.

Was his marriage so fragile he was afraid of what might happen if he looked too long at an attractive woman? Lindy lifted her right foot and set it on the chair, so that her skirt slid halfway down along her thigh.

His cheeks colored when she did that. She beamed.

"We don't know each other particularly well," she said,, "even though we work together. That's a pity, isn't it? Don't you think we ought to be a little closer?"

And he cleared his throat.

"I'm ... not really sure how that would help anything."

"Ah, you men. So impersonal. Why does everything have to be about the job? We're not machines, we're people."

Lindy brought her foot back down, wandered slowly over to him, put one hand on the back of his chair and leaned forward again.

"Do I look like a machine to you, Peter?" she murmured up close to his ear.

He dropped his sandwich and was up on his feet in another second. Turned and started making for the door. And at first, she thought that he was simply going to storm out through it like some startled kid. But no. He pushed it shut, being careful not to slam it so his colleagues outside would notice. He came back toward her, anger darkening his face, and halted just out of her reach.

"What's going on, Lindy?" he snapped. "I mean, you're spun again – I can tell that by your voice. But I've never seen you act this way toward another cop."

Her grin became a saccharine one. "You're not just any other cop, Peter."

His head shook fiercely.

"You're completely losing it, can't you see that? I mean, what you do in your off-hours, that's your concern, none of my damned beeswax. But when you start bringing that stuff in here, when you start letting it affect your relationship with those you work with –"

"We have a relationship, Peter?" she smirked. "I only wish. Don't you get bored with your little wife in Queens sometimes?"

And that really blew it. He went stiff as a mannequin, his features taut.

"I'm bored with nothin' except you right now. I have a *great* wife and three terrific kids. And yeah, we go to church each Sunday and we try to live clean and decent, like the Bible tells us. And you might think that's a little old-fashioned. You might think that's dull and even laughable, but it suits us fine. It suits *me* fine. I don't understand what you're doing with your life, and I don't want any slightest thing you're offering, not ever. Get it?"

Which was when he registered how loud his voice had lifted. Which was when they both looked through the window to the rows of desks beyond. Several of their colleagues had stopped working and were peering round. Bob Collins was staring at her with an open expression of shock.

Oh God.

Oh my God!

It hit her like a bucketful of freezing water. What in holy hell had she been thinking of? It was like someone else had gotten inside her head, making her behave in the exact same way that she had always been so scrupulously careful to avoid.

Peter seemed to sense the change in her, like he was watching someone who had woken from a trance. His eyes narrowed, his features crumpling up, and he took a backward step.

He muttered, "What?"

And she tried to think of something credible to say to him. Some kind of explanation for what she'd just done. But she was so confused, so horribly embarrassed, that her mind wouldn't work straight. Her head went down. Her cheeks were burning. Christ, she needed to get out of here before anything else went wrong.

She was past him and out of the room in the next instant, weaving in between the desks and heading for the front door. Collins called her name out, but she didn't stop.

And she was halfway down the stairs when Maxi appeared, heading up the other way, taking the climb at a loose-limbed stride, two steps at a time. He looked up, noticed her and grinned. But then he saw her face and his expression changed. His eyes started gleaming with concern. He tried to grab her wrist again, but she snatched it away.

"What's up, gal?"

"I'm not well, Maxi. I have to go home."

"What be wrong wit' you?"

"I'm not sure. Don't know. I ..."

And then she was hurrying past him, the only person she was close to in this entire world. Out beyond this building was a city of some nineteen million people. But when she stepped into the open air again, she was alone.

27 – Falling

Chinatown was beginning to smell. The heat had been pounding down for so long, so persistently, that the odors and aromas of that part of Manhattan had begun filtering out into the surrounding streets. So that, as soon as you were halfway close to it, you began catching scents on the air around you, of ginger, five-spice, fish oil and soy sauce and squid. Chicken fried with garlic. Lemon grass, and something indefinable and quite unpleasant just behind that.

On her way back from the subway station, Lindy stopped at a convenience store and asked the turbaned man behind the counter to hand her the largest bottle of vodka on display. This was no cocaine moment.

What in *God's* name had made her act like that, with *Peter Renzo* of all people? She'd lost count of the number of times colleagues had come on to her. But she'd always brushed them off, and she had never, *ever*, acted the same way.

Her tiny apartment – when she finally reached it – was like a furnace, the sunlight coming in through the windows at such an angle that the entire place was yellowed like a piece of very aged parchment. She had nothing even vaguely resembling air-con, and so all that she could do was haul the windows open as wide as they'd go, then yank the drapes shut. That gave her place a curiously shadowed look, like it was caught between two worlds. Lindy stripped down to her underwear, then took that off as well and pulled on a long white shirt that she'd acquired a while ago, not even bothering to button it up.

She sat down on her bedroom floor, her back pressed against the base end of her bed, and took her first swig of the vodka, not even bothering to use a glass. Her life was starting to unravel – she could already feel it. The two separate existences she had created for herself and so assiduously kept apart were clashing with each other and coming to pieces like two big tidal waves suddenly crossing paths. And she wasn't sure what she could do to stop it.

Stop it?

How'd it even started? She tried to think back.

Two nights ago. It had begun when she'd first stepped into Room 27 and met with John Hunter.

Except that had to be a coincidence, surely. A mere trick of timing. She'd never met a man who could move her the way John did. Never met a man who knew exactly how to rock her boat. The way he'd treated her last night – it had been callous and impersonal on one level, but it had only been a game that he'd been playing with her. Once he'd returned, once he'd untied her ankles and then climbed on top of her – she'd never known such passion. Or longevity, for that matter.

She smirked at the memory of it and took another swig.

Might this be what the beginnings of love were? She had no idea. She'd never felt that particular thing, and wasn't even sure she could. But this was pretty damned close, she was certain of it.

What, she asked herself, lifting the bottle to her lips a third time, *you're going to get drunk* now, *on top of every other stupid thing you've done?*

And so she screwed the cap back on, set the bottle by the wall and then clambered into bed. She'd feel more sensible and more alert if she could only get a few hours' sleep. Couldn't remember the last time she'd slept in the middle of the afternoon, but she was plain exhausted and she sank into a slumber very easily.

Dreams immediately started rushing at her, most of them created by her miserable past. Dad roamed through the hallways of them, his shoulders bunched, his bald head gleaming, his voice stentorian as a bull's roar. His fists clenched.

But there were others too.

The first time Momma had ever taken her to church. She had been only five, her tiny hand clasped tightly in Momma's grip so that her whole right arm was stretched, her shoulder aching from the strain of it. She tried to complain, but Momma wouldn't listen.

Maybe years of Daddy's version of affection had left her numb – or even cruel – herself.

They'd walked up the front steps side by side and stepped into the echoing gloom. The first thing that had struck her was the smell of it, an ancientness that went beyond the true age of the building. The second thing ... it was the way the lighted candles looked so very bright inside this dimness, like yellow stars so large that you could even see them in the twilight.

Then her gaze alighted on a painting of a pretty woman.
"Who's that lady, Momma?"
"That's the Blessed Virgin."
They'd been the first to arrive, but other people were now filtering in behind them.
"What's a virgin, Momma?"
"Keep your voice down, girl!"
"Is it a bad thing?" she whispered respectfully.
"No, Belinda. It's a very good thing. It means 'untouched by men.'"
Untouched? She'd pondered on that for a while. Did 'touched' mean hit, the way that Daddy touched?
But when she asked that, Momma cuffed her round the ear.

The scene faded away to black. The blackness filled her head so utterly and so completely that it baffled her, began to frighten her. She could feel herself shifting around on the bed, her forearms pressing against the mattress, almost physically trying to lift her out of sleep. Except it didn't work.

The darkness in her skull was like a huge well she was falling down. She tried to grab the sides, but they were out of reach. Panic filled her, because she'd realized she had only two choices left. She could either keep on dropping endlessly, the idea of which terrified her. Or ... the only way that she could stop was by hitting the bottom, which would kill her.

Her mouth was open. She was trying to scream.

When suddenly, two points of light appeared in a far distance and then moved in her direction, smoothly, swiftly. And as they got closer, she could see they were bright green.

They were John's eyes, and became so massive they were looming over her within a few more seconds.

They blinked.

She woke, sitting up sharply on her narrow bed.

It was already night. She could scarcely believe it. God Almighty, for how many hours had she been asleep?

Her phone was ringing.

"Ms. Grady?" an unfamiliar voice asked when she picked it up.

28 – Harem of One

"Uh?"

Her mouth tasted awful. She couldn't get her eyes open properly and her skin was bathed with sweat. She tried to listen carefully to the voice coming from the receiver, but it sounded like it was a continent away and barely comprehensible.

"I'm parked downstairs. Mr. Hunter sent me for you, same as last night."

Lindy tried to understand what she was being told. Was this the driver of the limousine again?

The yellow of the sunlight at her windows had been replaced by the streetlamps' ochre glow. And a warm, slow breeze had sprung up so her drapes were fluttering gently, sending faint ripples of artificial light dancing through her room. When she tried to move, her joints ached at first. But she forced herself to get up and hobbled across to look down at the street. Her shirt was open at the front, and so she held it shut with one hand before leaning out.

The black stretched limo was up against her curb again, its lights off. She struggled to collect her thoughts.

"I was asleep. I'm not sure –"

"Mr. Hunter asked me to wait for you, as long as it takes."

"That might be an hour. Maybe even more."

"Which is what 'as long as it takes' means, Ms. Grady. Take three hours, if you want. I'll still be here."

He wasn't even kidding.

***

John was in the same navy blue robe again when she stepped into Room 27. He smiled at her, but then his bright green eyes went puzzled. In the first place – in *this* weather – she had on a light fawn raincoat. In the second, she was carrying in her left hand a large paper-and-string shopping bag from one of the better stores. His gaze fixed on it.

"Dare I ask what's in it?" he enquired.

"A gift. For you."

"A gift? That's nice."

But his expression was still quizzical.

That partly changed when she took it out. Her police cap with its polished glossy peak. Lindy set it atop her head at a jaunty angle.

"*Very* nice," he said, although he still looked slightly puzzled. "But I thought you were a plainclothes cop?"

"We still have a uniform, for ceremonies and stuff. I've had this since I graduated the academy."

And when he said nothing in response, she added, "Want to see my other gift?"

She undid the cloth belt on her raincoat and shrugged so that the garment tumbled off her shoulders. She was wearing nothing underneath.

***

He'd already gagged her, and was binding her again. He'd produced the leather cords from a drawer of his nightstand – only two of them this time – and was tying her wrists firmly to the brass rails on his bed. Every time their grip got tighter, she drew in a stifled breath.

But something was discomfiting her in the background. What was she even *doing*, using a part of her uniform like this? She'd been so damned proud of it when she had graduated, so damned pleased with this cap with its stiff and shiny peak. What it represented. What it stood for. What it made her. Now, she was reducing it to this?

But then she thought, *To hell with it. There aren't two Lindy Gradys any longer, there's just this.*

John had grabbed hold of her ankles and was lifting them. And at first, she thought that he was going to dive down with his face again. But he was raising them too far, pushing her legs up over her body so that, finally, her knees were squashed against her breasts, she was uncomfortable and struggling to breathe properly. What precisely was he doing?

Next moment, her eyes went wide. He was already pushing into her, but not in the same place that he had pushed last night.

She yelled against the gag, first in protest, then with pain.

Then all that vanished in a white light as the first orgasm took her.

***

"You shouldn't have done that."

She was angry with him, so much so that she could feel the heated redness on her cheekbones. So why – now that he'd untied her – was she lying with her head across his chest? It made no sense.

She watched him grin in a self-satisfied manner.

"You've never done *that* before?"

"Not in that position. And never without being asked."

"Would you even be here if I was the kind of man who felt the need to ask permission?"

She went silent after that.

***

He was tying her again. Four cords this time. Face down on the mattress.

"Jesus, John, not again. I'm sore."

"There are a whole load of different ways to be sore."

What did *that* mean?

Once he'd secured her, he stood up and went over to the closet. Selected a suit, taking it out on its hanger, draping the hook over the top edge of the closet door. Christ, was he planning to walk out on her again?

But all that he was doing was pulling off the black belt that was hanging from the pants waist. He returned to her with the buckle wrapped around his fist and the length of leather dangling.

She wanted to yell out, *"No!"* She'd never done anything like *this*, or even wanted to.

But that strange, drowsy, detached feeling came over her again, so that she simply buried her face in the pillow.

***

While he was unfastening her knots a second time, Lindy tried to figure this out. Or rather, she *struggled* to think this through. She had never come during anal before, not even when she'd enjoyed it. And she'd *certainly* never come from pain, her body jerking as the belt struck it, tears streaming down her face. Her chin was still damp, and the pillow beneath her was soaked through. What did this mean? What was this effect that John was having on her?

The last cord slipped away. She tried to move, but her back was still killing her. Lindy sucked in air between her clenched teeth.

And John appeared to notice that. He leant across and ran one of his big palms very slowly, very gently, down across her spine.

The pain faded away and was gone in a few more seconds.
What the ...?

Except the drugged, detached feeling closed over her more strongly than it ever had before, swallowing her the way the black well in her dreams had done and driving away any questions. She felt so light-headed she was almost floating. Nothing mattered anymore. There was barely even any need to think what she was doing.

She spent what felt like the next couple of hours wandering between the bed and the room's full length mirror, where she'd examine the narrow wale marks on her back with open fascination. It was almost as though John had changed her physically.

He was sitting naked on the chair by the dresser, and every so often he'd call her across to fellate him. Her knees turned red from being on the carpet and her throat stung with salt, but she didn't care. She felt like a slave in a harem.

The walls would shudder gently once in a while as a truck went by, and that was an intrusion she resented just a little. So far as she was now concerned, there was no other world beyond this place.

There was only Room 27.

She kept on believing that right up to the point when John asked her to leave.

***

"I need to sleep now, Lindy."

"We can *both* sleep."

"I can't. Not with you around."

"But ..."

His fingertips caressed her chin and jawbone. "I'll see you tomorrow evening."

"I ..."

"The limo's waiting."

She was practically in tears on the ride home. And it was only when she was opening her apartment door – struggling with the key – that she remembered she'd left her police cap behind. *Goddamn it!*

Sitting on her narrow bed, she hit the vodka bottle hard, downing it nearly to the halfway mark. By the time she had passed out, it was two thirty in the morning.

29 – Claw Marks

I HAVE TO STOP THIS!
The thought was so violently loud, her own voice screaming in the confines of her skull, that it woke her up with an abrupt start. Her whole body spasmed. Her eyelids snapped open very wide and stayed there. She was staring at her bedroom window. There was still darkness and amber streetlight out beyond the drapes, but a mild platinum glow was suffusing its edges.

When her gaze slid across to the numerals on her TV, it was not long after four o' clock.

Lindy tried to move. Pain tore through her, ripping her apart as though she were a scrap of muslin cloth. The tortured skin of her back had tightened up while she'd been sleeping so there was no slightest play in it at all. It felt as though her shoulder-blades had fused together, and her spine had arced like a bow and was refusing to relax. Every time she tried to even shift her weight, it killed her.

What in God's name was I thinking of? I have to stop this!

She could now see very clearly there was only one word that described what was happening between she and John. They'd gone – in a bare couple of days – from passionate, reasonably straightforward sex to forcible sodomy and serious pain. She took in the fact numbly that it wasn't merely her back that was hurting. Even her throat felt swollen and sore where he'd repeatedly probed it.

The single word that described this? *Escalation.* It was as though she'd climbed aboard a runaway train that had no brakes and was accelerating furiously. If he'd done this to her tonight, where would they arrive at next on his itinerary? Why'd she even let him go this far?

Gotta stop.

Slowly, very carefully, she managed to ease herself into a half-seated position. The vodka was still flowing through her system, but the skin on her back felt like it was going to split nonetheless, the whole while she was doing that. Tears sprang up in her eyes again, mingling with the perspiration that was running down her cheeks. But she gritted her teeth and straightened herself up.

As soon as she had done that, the amount of booze she'd downed kicked fully in. Her head swam. Nausea swept over her.

Somehow, she got up to her feet. Somehow, she made it to the bathroom and hawked in the basin.

Looked in the mirror, when her head lifted back up. Her red hair was a tangled, plastered mess. Her shoulders were bent forward like a woman several times her age. And as for her face, it was so creased she didn't even recognize it.

Her skin went abruptly hot and she began to shiver.

You are ill.

She staggered back and fell down on her mattress. Dragged the duvet halfway over her, and then lost consciousness again.

***

Vaguely, she remembered waking up again sometime around mid-morning – heat and sunlight streaming in – and managing to scrabble around blindly till she found her purse beside her bed and fumbled her cell phone out of it. Called the office, mumbling something about being sick. She thought that it was Peter Renzo she was speaking to, and thought he sounded more concerned than usual, but she was hung-over as well by this stage and she wasn't sure of anything.

Her back was burning hot now, and the fever stemming from it swept right through her body. She fell back asleep, but was aware that she was thrashing around, in the grip of some kind of delirium.

Her dreams overlapped each other, wild and dark and full of soundless screams. Silhouetted figures stalked across dim, shadow-filtered landscapes. Wild animals sprang from cover, baring their ferocious teeth. There were a whole coyote pack somewhere in there, and it was hunting her. Urban coyotes.

But there were other things as well. Green eyes. They came rushing at her continuously.

And then, out of nowhere, she could hear George Greentree's voice.

She couldn't see the man, but he was saying: *"They know people all too well. Their weaknesses, their flaws, the things they want and cannot have, and they exploit that. An old one, he will choose a victim and then toy with her like a kitten with a ball of string, just batting her about a while. He won't snatch her soul the way the young ones do. He'll maul it slowly, one shred at a time. And by the time she figures out what's going on, it's far too late to stop it."*

She felt herself roll over and then set her teeth with inner pain. Was that a wendigo that George had been describing, or John Hunter?

She needed to puke again. She stumbled up, but didn't even make it to the bathroom.

***

The next time that her eyes slid open, it happened gently, no suddenness to it. She drew in a long, deep breath. She was still aching, but the fever appeared to have passed. And when she checked the time again, she saw that she had slept till gone five in the evening.

Her bedroom was baking hot and smelled of vomit. But there was nothing she could do about either of those things right now. Lindy eased herself to her feet and hobbled through until she was facing the bathroom mirror.

Her hair was plastered flat against her scalp, and her skin was so slick that it looked as though it had been varnished. When she turned her back to the silvered glass and craned across her shoulder, she could see that the narrow marks on it had turned to ugly, livid bruises, crisscrossing each other. Was she insane? Why'd she allowed this?

She realized that she couldn't take a shower in this state – the pain would probably be blinding. But she got her head under the spray and managed to wash her hair – that woke her up a way – then wet a towel and carefully cleaned herself with it.

Every movement sent a fresh stab through her. Even breathing hurt. But she was starting to get angry with herself by this stage. After the childhood she'd endured, why would she consider anything like *this*?

Or perhaps it was because of that, some deep-down craving that she'd never understood.

It occurred to her John Hunter knew that. But she saw that thought for what it was – completely crazy – and dismissed it, since there was no way that he could know about her past.

By the time she'd cleaned the bedroom floor and got some clothes on, dusk was closing in over the city. Moving around carefully had eased the tightness in her skin. She was far from in good shape, still sore and fragile, but she wasn't immobile or helpless any longer. She took a couple of aspirins and watched the light beyond her drapes gradually fade, then pulled them open.

True nightfall remained a couple of hours off. In the meanwhile, Manhattan was becoming like a hollowed-out shadow of its daytime self, the traffic noises slightly louder than they'd been before, the electric lighting going flat and dull, the distinction between sky and city skyline blurring, the alleyways and other narrow places sinking down into a deeper gloom like darkness had already fallen. Twilight was neither one thing nor the other, was a no-man's land where few people belonged.

Except she felt she *did* belong there now. She was trapped between her two lives, caught immobile in the middle, and that had to stop.

She would talk to John and call this off. Except she wasn't going to be a wuss about it and just use the phone. She'd do it in person.

***

The same skinny, pretty teenager with her straight fringe of black hair was back behind the counter when Lindy walked stiffly into the lobby of the McKinnon. She was speaking on a phone herself. She glanced across, smiled briefly and discreetly and then went back to her conversation.

Lindy rode the creaking elevator up. No drowsiness closed over her this time. Her back had hurt her a great deal on the way here, but that had only cleared her head, making her more focused, more determined. This was going to come to an end, right here and now.

She glanced at her watch. Lindy knew that John had business to attend to in the day – he'd told her so that first evening they'd met – but he ought to have returned by now. Reaching the fourth floor, she yanked the metal grid open, then made her way to the door marked 27.

Put one hand either side of it, dizziness suddenly taking her. She'd begun shivering again, and moisture had started dripping from her upper lip. And she instantly recognized symptoms like these. You got such physical reactions from a hardened addict.

If John were to open this door in his robe ... if he were to smile at her, his green gaze piercing hers ... smile and then invite her in ... to the bed again, the leather cords again ...

She squeezed her eyelids shut and shook her head, banishing those images. If it had been pain last night then what was next? The runaway train was still accelerating, and she had no choice but to jump right off it.

She steeled herself and held her body ramrod straight. There was no bell push to the room, so she rapped on the woodwork with her knuckles.

Waited. Tried again.

Lowering her head, she could see no light coming from beneath the door. Had she come all this way for nothing? It occurred to her to wait here for a while, except that that would make her passive again, awaiting John's presence.

She could at least leave a message. And at the same time find out if he'd left her uniform cap at the desk. She went back down. The pretty thin girl was no longer on the phone and smiled at her mildly as she approached.

"Good evening. Can I help you?"

"You have a guest here, a Mr. Jonathan Hunter?"

A line appeared on the girl's brow. She didn't seem to recognize the name.

"In Room 27? He's been here the past few nights."

Which only made the girl's confusion grow.

"I don't believe that room's been occupied all week. Are you sure we're talking about 27?"

Lindy grimaced. What was she dealing with here, some utter idiot?

"I've been up there myself. I *know* which room it is. If you could ..."

But the girl had reached for her computer keyboard, and her head was shaking.

"No, I'm very sorry, but that room is vacant. And there's no John Hunter staying with us. Is it possible you've got the wrong hotel?"

This was insane. What kind of trick was being played on her this time? Her heart had started banging up against her ribs again.

But Lindy produced her badge, demanding to take a look inside herself.

The girl accompanied her up, opening the door with a spare key. Lindy reached in, flicking on the light. The bed was made, the red bedspread pulled up across it. There was not the slightest sign that anyone had been here.

She marched over to the closet doors and yanked them open. There were only bare hangers dangling from a rail.

Had John fled? This was completely nuts. Or else – it started to occur to her – she'd been the victim of some kind of con man.

Her heart was beating double-time now, and her breath had hardened in her throat. As a last desperate measure, Lindy went into the bathroom.

Saw it in the mirror before she even looked at it directly. A large disc of navy blue, suspended high against the white woodwork in there.

Her uniform cap was hanging from the bathroom door. She went to snatch at it, then stopped as the shock hit her.

It had been mangled, the peak busted up in several places and the headband ripped and twisted.

And in the fabric at the top, there were several long straight parallel cuts.

They looked like claw marks.

PART THREE

HUNTED

30 – Running

By the time that she emerged back onto Madison – shaken, drained of heat and blood, and fighting hard to hold her panic down – the city was in that stage of half-light, neither evening nor proper night, where nothing seems quite real. As though a massive fire were burning somewhere in the unseen distance and its detritus, its smoke and ashes and its blackened smuts, were all descending on the city and obscuring it. The taillights of cabs and cars were humming past like reddened fireflies. The long apartment blocks that lined this district reared up all around her, blocking every other thing from sight.

Lindy wobbled as she hit the sidewalk. She blinked several times, trying to remember where the nearest subway station was. Then she turned in its direction and hurried toward it, her mind working furiously.

What exactly might be going on? Who precisely had she been to bed with several times? She'd left her cap behind, since it was no use to her now. But claw marks? That couldn't be right.

It had to have been done with a knife. But to what end? What had she gotten herself involved in?

As to how John had gotten in Room 27 without so much as registering at the desk … that had been done before, and she knew it. Certain types of con artists could insinuate themselves into an unoccupied room, stealing keys or picking locks, then treat the place as though it was their own.

But to what *end*, on this occasion? She had no money he could part her from to speak of. There was the sex of course, but someone with John Hunter's looks and assured presence would never go short of that. Which left …?

She'd never experienced anything quite like this. *She* went after perpetrators, not the other way around. And she kept on thinking furiously what she ought to do about it.

Report it, was her first thought. But then she took that idea further down the line, and started to imagine what it would entail. Some other detective gawping at her while she told her story. His gaze turning lustrous as he read between the lines and saw that there was sex involved. Then word drifting around the station house – "Lindy's been humping a perp." She would be done. She would be finished.

Except that she still couldn't figure out what John Hunter's motive might be – if that was even his real name – for treating her this way. Had he filmed her, or recorded her in some way? Why?

If she could understand the reasoning, she might feel slightly better … but she *couldn't*. All she drew, when she tried to make some sense of what was going on, was a total blank.

She was almost at the subway now, the maw of the steps leading down into the earth. And relief was beginning to take partial hold of her. When footsteps started coming up behind her, fast.

It was a man's stride, long and heavy. Someone closing in on her with the focused swiftness of a predator. She got the idea in her head immediately that it was John. Her hand went to the weight of her gun inside her purse, and then she turned.

There was no one there. She looked quickly around, but she was alone on the sidewalk. Nobody was near her. No one was emerging from the subway station either.

But she could still hear footsteps. She was *sure* of that.

They moved right up to her, so that she practically flinched back.

And then …

They seemed to pass right *through* her. She could feel their vibration on the paving stones beneath her feet. She was *certain* of that, and her entire body quivered. Then they passed behind her and had faded and were gone. She gasped for breath, doubling slightly over.

You're imagining this, she tried to tell herself. *You're all riled up, your mind's gone hyper, you are hearing things and feeling things that are not there.*

She knew she needed to calm down, except that knowing and being able are two different things. Her heart was banging like a drum now and she could no longer think straight.

The lights had changed on Madison. A fresh slew of traffic was rushing past. The yellow-white of headlamps and the different colors of the cars filled up her vision for a few seconds. But then she thought that she saw something on the opposite sidewalk.

Women, two of them, staring across at her. One dark and tall. One shorter, blonde.

A city bus went past, blocking them from view. And by the time her line of sight had cleared, the two women were gone.

***

The worst thing was, she wasn't even sure if they had really been there. She'd encountered them both before of course, one passing her on Madison, the other in the park. But had she really seen them this time, or was it her imagination spiraling out of control completely? That was the real problem when your mind began screwing up on you – how precisely could you tell?

There was no one else around at all, if you discounted the vehicles. Nobody abroad on foot in this whole part of the Upper East Side. It was different where she lived, but this far up much fewer people walked. She felt like she was standing in some built-up, urban desert.

The subway entrance still awaited her. She turned around, took a couple of steps forward and then stared into its depths. No one down there either, not that she could see. Just a few posters, a faint gleam from the metal turnstiles. The platform was more than likely empty too.

And she had never been afraid to ride the subway in her life, any time of day or night. It had never bothered her an instant. Yet going down into that hollow dimness now …

She wanted to be home. Wanted to be behind a locked door in her own small place. Except that home was half an island off. She had to get there somehow. How?

A cab approached her and she hailed it.

***

Passing through midtown now. Merging with the heavier traffic, and the sidewalks filling up. The cab kept catching reds and stopping, so that she ached with frustration. The lights on the avenues didn't *work* this way. They usually let you go at least a dozen blocks. So this oughtn't be happening either.

Every time the cab slowed down, Lindy peered out at the people on the street. Some of them looked downtrodden and tired, others alert and happy. Couples of various ages went by, a few of them hand in hand. A young woman with yellow hair was pushing a stroller.

She caught the briefest flash of bright green in among a cluster of young men all in their mid-twenties. Just the tiniest flash of green, but it immediately captured her attention, her gaze swinging toward it.

John Hunter's face and his bright green eyes suddenly became apparent in the crowd. He was looking straight at her and smiling gently.

She didn't know how he had found her, but her body went rigid, her spine snapping up. She started shaking. Lindy managed to edge her gaze in the direction of the stoplights, and they were still red, the traffic around her immobile.

When she looked back, the group of young men had moved further along. She could no longer make out John among them ... couldn't see him any way her frightened, jerky stare went. But that didn't mean that he was gone. He might be circling around behind her.

The lights turned to amber.

"Move!" she shouted at the driver.

"Huh?"

"I'm a cop, on duty! So get going!"

And he did as he was told.

Lindy turned around in her seat and peered back through the cab's rear window at the block that they had left behind, just in time to see a tall dark silhouette step off the curb and stare in her direction.

They traveled six more blocks before the lights brought them to a halt again. This was a less populated area, the sidewalks almost empty and the frontages of the surrounding buildings dark. Her pulse was still thumping and her breathing felt constricted like the muscles round her lungs had tightened up. And she was still fighting to understand what had happened. It couldn't be a coincidence, surely, that she'd run back into John that way?

These lights stayed red for half an age, crosstown traffic slipping by in front of her. This was a part of town she barely even knew, unwelcoming-looking, shadowy and only thinly populated. A few lights shone in small windows, but no one moved behind them. A streetlamp was out, and there was trash in the gutters.

Home. She wanted to be *home*. She needed the escape of sleep, so she could put all this behind her. If there were consequences, then she'd face them in the morning. But this was not the time for anything like that. Her mind was trying to shut this whole thing out.

"What is it with these lights?" she blurted.

All the driver did was shrug. But then they switched to amber.

Just as the cab started rolling forward again, Lindy thought she caught a movement in the corner of her eye, and her head swung around. There was a large and darkened doorway off in that direction, blackness gathered in it.

John Hunter stepped out from it at the same moment that the cab moved off, still staring at her face, still smiling.

***

He was left behind a moment later. All she caught was a flash of his expression, then the night reduced him to a featureless outline again, dwindling in the back distance. But she saw him step up to the curb. She was sure his face was turned her way.

And her entire body cringed involuntarily. Her brain felt like it was banging around loose inside her skull. Felt bruised.

Her mind had to be playing tricks on her, her imagination running wild. There was no possible way a man could be at one intersection six blocks up, then at another one a minute later. Not even if he'd hailed a cab himself. Not even if he had some form of transport and was tailing her.

Lindy grappled for some rational explanation.

Pull yourself together!

She almost screamed it at herself.

Calm down and straighten up! Get some sense into that head of yours! This isn't happening because it cannot be!

Another yellow cab pulled out in front of them at the next intersection, making her own driver honk and swerve. As they went around it, Lindy glanced at the intruding vehicle's back seat.

And when she did that, John Hunter stared back at her.

His taxi turned away at the next block, and he was gone into the night again. But for how long?

***

By the time they'd reached the edge of Chinatown, she was doubled over, both hands clasped across the back of her head, not wanting to look out through the windows anymore. And her mind was coming to a terrifying realization. The booze, the drugs, the wild nighttime forays – they had all backed up on her, and she was actually going crazy.

She could feel a whimper pushing its way up her throat, but wasn't sure if she'd released it or not until the driver jerked round in his seat and asked her, "You okay?"

Her face was damp again, and she wasn't sure if it was sweat or tears. Her hands and forearms were vibrating. *Please don't let me lose my mind!* Except who was she talking to when she begged for things like that? She was a rationalist, an atheist. She could remember discussing such things with Maxi just a couple of days back.

So she forced herself to uncurl. Wiped her face dry with her sleeves and straightened up. She looked around slowly. And there was no one staring in at her.

"You sick?" the driver asked her.

She could feel how bloodless her face was, but forced a crooked smile.

"No. I'm okay."

She yanked a twenty from her purse and was about to ask for change, when a thought struck her. She said, "Keep it."

"Thanks!"

"But can you watch me till I'm inside my front door?"

There was a small gaggle of tourists off toward the Chinese lights, but no one else apparent. And the driver looked puzzled, but he shrugged.

"Yeah, sure. Whatever."

Her legs were shaky as she clambered out onto the sidewalk. She was painfully aware of her heels tapping on the slabs, loud as gunshots in the night. The air around her still had to be warm, but she couldn't feel it anymore. Her skin felt chilled. Her fingertips were numb. When she reached her door and tried to find her keys, she fumbled, dropped them.

Just as she was bending down, the cab moved off.

Hey ... dammit!

Her fingers scrabbled against the rough sidewalk, trying to retrieve her keys. She finally got them back in her palm, stood up and pressed one in the lock.

For some reason, it jammed halfway. She jiggled with it angrily.

The noise of a sanitation truck drifted to her, working the blocks further downtown, the thrum of its motor and the whirring, scraping racket of its loaders. It was a familiar enough sound, but – in the state that she was in – her face went angling off in that direction.

The tourists by the Chinese lights were gone. But slightly beyond where they'd been, on the opposite corner, two figures were standing. Quite immobile. Gazing at her openly.

It was the tall, dark woman and the blonde-haired girl again.

Lindy shoved at the key and it slid fully in. She was in through the door and slamming it behind her in another instant. She seemed to have lost the ability to breathe.

Call for help, for backup, was the first thought that occurred to her.

And have to explain all of this? Get yourself revealed as being insane?

Her hand was in her purse again and closed around her gun. She banged a light switch with her free palm before heading quickly up.

And she was two-thirds of the way to her apartment door, when the hall lights suddenly went out.

They were on a two-minute timer, and had been so ever since she'd moved into this place. But pitch darkness engulfed her and she stopped, her head swimming as she lost her sense of balance.

She had to get inside her place. She gripped the stair rail, felt out with her right foot until she found the next riser up. And kept on that way, as rapidly as she could, until she reached the landing just below her own.

Heavy footsteps started coming up behind her, though she hadn't heard the door to the street open up or close again. Her heart slammed hard inside her chest. Lindy reached along the wall for where she knew there was another light switch.

Felt the touch of plastic. Jabbed at it frantically.

The bulb above her only lit up for a second before going out again.

But that second was long enough to see John Hunter climbing up toward her.

And – even when the blackness returned – Lindy could still see his bright green eyes.

She could make those out clearly, since they were glowing like a pair of tiny colored lamps.

31 – Don't You Love Me Anymore?

And after that, her mind was registering nothing, shocked into blank muteness by the sight advancing on her. She could no more form a cogent thought than she could spread her arms and fly.

It was all reaction now, her instincts taking over where her conscious mind could not. She was turning away and stumbling up, tripping and half-falling but not stopping, keeping going.

Instinct slammed her up against her own front door. Pressed her palm against it till she found the lock. She couldn't even make out which key was the right one, but her grasp fumbled across the bunch until it found a familiar shape. Then she was in, and slamming that door behind her too.

The last thing that she saw was John's illuminated gaze reaching her landing, so his eyes were almost level with hers. And she only saw it for a split second, but it chilled her to the core.

It was shadowy in her apartment too, but some streetlight was filtering in through her living room window. She grappled with the security chain and got it fixed in place, and then backed off.

The door shuddered as something hit it from the outside. She had dropped her purse on the floor by her feet and had her pistol in a double-grasp by this time.

"Lindy?" John's voice drifted to her, soft and coaxing. She could almost hear him smile.

Her gun came snapping up straight-armed. Her hands were shaking so hard that she almost fired unintentionally.

"Lindy, don't you love me anymore?"

She never had. She'd been obsessed with him. Beguiled by him ... he'd tricked her into that.

She grit her teeth.

"I've got a gun!"

"Of *course* you have."

"It's pointing right at you!"

"And what good do you think that'll do you?"

The woodwork of her door shuddered again, and she let loose a shot. Smoke swirled around her and she saw a hole appear. John's only reaction was to laugh.

Conscious thought started returning. It began vaguely occurring to her ... where were her neighbors? There were people living above and below her, and they couldn't all be out. They ought to have been shouting at the very least, once they had heard a shot inside their building.

But she listened hard and was rewarded with utter silence. There was nothing going on out there. No tiniest response. And she got the strangest notion. This was like being back inside that goddamned hotel room. She was alone with John again – the outside world had faded back, and was not part of their world.

Call for backup! her mind was screaming at her. *Doesn't matter if you lose your job, or even get turned to the city's biggest laughing stock! This is your* life *at stake right now!*

Keeping her gaze pinned hard on the door, she bent from her knees and retrieved her phone.

Thumbed the 9 of 911. John had gone entirely quiet out there, and that scared her as badly as anything had done so far.

She was moving her thumb across the keypad when she yelled out and jerked back upright. The cell phone skittered from her grasp, went clattering away across the floor.

She'd gone numb again, her mind not moving. Because both of John's hands had suddenly appeared.

They'd passed right through the door.

***

She didn't believe in stuff like this. But she had seen it – she was *looking* at it, wasn't she? Reality was coming apart like a length of soggy tissue paper, everything she thought was true being ripped up into little shreds. And there was nothing she could do about it. The sheer awfulness refused to stop. For a moment, it occurred to her to simply give up, throw the towel in. Sit down on the floor and close her eyes and let whatever was going to happen to her simply happen.

It would be an end, at least. All this would be over.

But then old George's words started returning to her. Something in her bellowed, *"No!"* Something in her hardened up. She would not fold that easily. She'd not be treated as a toy.

She was digging deep by this time, trying to draw on every strength she'd ever acquired or learned.

Find some other soul to shred! Mine's no longer available!

Both John's forearms had come through the wood by this stage. And his palms were spread. He kept on coming very slowly, taunting her with his approach. She aimed directly between his hands and let fly three more close-grouped shots.

His arms didn't drop away. His hands did not so much as twitch. Despair took hold of her. Either this was a dream, or her life was nearly over.

His shoulders were appearing now, the front of his body, his tuxedo-clad chest. All that she could do was back away, still wondering why no one was reacting to her shots.

His face appeared, and she sucked in a painful breath.

But then he stopped.

32 – Matchi Manitou

His smiling expression transformed in an instant, becoming a puzzled blank at first, then changing to a worried frown. It was as though he had seen something in the room that bothered him. Only … if four bullets hadn't given him a moment's pause, what could possibly be stopping him right now?

When she pointed her gun directly at his brow, it was because she couldn't think of any other way to act. She stood her ground for the same reason.

"Come on, fucker," she heard herself growling. "What exactly are you waiting for?"

His eyes flickered away from her in the direction of the bedroom, paused there a moment, then came slowly back. But otherwise he did not move.

Was he going to stand there all night? The mere idea ground at her. But her mind had readjusted itself by this stage and was moving along brand-new channels, wondering why he'd glanced toward her bedroom.

Think.

It was very difficult, because she'd never guessed at anything like this before.

Why there? Think!

There was nothing in there that could stop a creature like this, surely? Only her bed, her clothes, her portable TV, some make-up and …

Her clothes! When she'd driven into Massachusetts, she'd been wearing one of her lightweight suits, the pale green one if she remembered straight. And – since she'd not been subjected to Manhattan's heatwave that particular day – she had simply hung it back in her small closet when she'd gotten home.

George's voice came drifting to her inner ear again.

"If those things have arrived in Manhattan, then you might find yourself needing this."

And he'd handed her a piece of shaped iron on a leather thong, describing it as a protective amulet. She'd forgotten all about it, but it was still in her jacket pocket.

John seemed to hear that thought – perhaps he could. His green gaze went toward her bedroom door again, then returned to her angrily. His face creased up with frustration. He made a strong, visible effort to get the rest of the way into the room. And for a second, she felt certain it was going to work ... more of his tall body shifted forward into view.

But it was as though he was being stopped by an invisible wall now. He got a couple of inches further in, but then was forced back, his whole frame subsiding. And he wound up trapped in that position, only halfway through the door.

Lindy snapped into a sudden, taut alertness, her muscles tensing. The next moment, she was bolting for the closet in her bedroom, snatching her green jacket out and fumbling through its pockets, nearly ripping them she was so insanely urgent.

Her hands were trembling once again, since she was coming up with nothing. Maybe in this half-light she had gotten the wrong coat. But then her fingers closed around cool metal.

She pulled the amulet out. The proud face of the Matchi Manitou stared back at her. And hadn't that state trooper told her this was one aspect of God?

She'd never believed in *any* of this stuff. Which proved that there genuinely were no atheists in foxholes.

Holding the thing in front of her, she returned to the living room.

John's face hardened, but his glowing eyes went duller. He appeared to take a lengthy backward step and slid away from view, the solid woodwork of the door returning.

Lindy doubled over, gasping with relief. She squatted down on her haunches, both hands pressing the cool amulet against her throat.

And stayed down there for an unmeasurable while. The night was not yet over.

***

She'd driven him away, but couldn't even *start* to think what she ought to do next. Her mind racked at the problem but came up with no solutions. John was almost certainly still out there – she could almost sense his presence. But he wasn't human. He was some kind of wild, supernatural force. He and his two female chums were almost certainly responsible for the deaths in the park.

And that meant they could shred a living heart. So if she called for backup now …

She pulled herself around enough to stare down at her watch. It was only coming up to midnight, hours of darkness left to go. The shadows seemed to fold around her, trying to absorb her. And she thought it best to let them do that and refused to move.

Except her calves began to flare with pain. She took that for as long as she was able, but finally stood up.

Paused a moment, and then slipped the leather thong around her neck, the metal cold against her breastbone. Very cautiously, she edged toward her window.

The world beyond it was an odd mixture of gray and amber, the streetlights warring with the night. Everything looked strange out past the glass, robbed of proper color, of genuine substance, merely a faded ghostlike image of the daylit world.

The Chinese eatery across the way was closed. Its round chrome tables had been taken in. But standing where they had once stood were the two women. They were staring up at her. Their gazes shifted slightly when her face appeared. But otherwise, they did not move.

Lindy fought against the urge to flinch back, then studied them carefully. These things weren't even vaguely human. Neither was John Hunter. And she felt waves of revulsion running through her when she thought about the stuff she'd done with him. But she killed those kinds of emotions dead in their tracks.

The women didn't make the tiniest move toward her, and she guessed she had the amulet to thank for that. But their eyes remained pinned on her hard, not even blinking. The intense brilliance of their irises seemed to leap out at her through the gloom.

Her head shook involuntarily and she finally backed away until they'd disappeared from view.

In her door, above the bullet holes, there was a spy-hole. One of those little rounded lenses that gave you a view of whoever was standing out past your threshold, brass gleaming around its outer edges. She could see the light was still off on her landing – there was no glow coming in under the woodwork. But it was so breathlessly quiet out there that perhaps John Hunter had gone away. She had to risk a look.

Her heartbeat started throbbing as she got closer. She kept on remembering the way he'd appeared through this very door. And she was terrified that, if she got too close, he might suddenly snatch in at her through the woodwork. Shred her heart before she'd even realized what was happening. The amulet ought to prevent that, but she was not entirely certain.

When she tilted her head toward the lens, she felt her body arcing back. Like she was being pulled in two directions at the self-same time. It was awkward, almost painful, but she kept on going.

Her eye was to the glass. Shortly afterwards, her neck jerked back and her whole body followed suit. Because she'd seen nothing in the darkness of the hallway save a pair of bright green discs, as brilliant as stars. And they were completely motionless. Not a tremor from them. Not so much as the merest twitch.

George Greentree's words came back to her again.

"But an old wendigo, one who's been around for say a thousand years or more? No impatience. No concept of time at all. He enjoys what he's doing, and he takes it carefully and slowly."

Which meant that John Hunter would stand there for as long as this was going to take.

But then it struck her. He might have no concept of time, but that didn't stop time flowing. The world still circled round the sun, and there was no way he could stop that.

You can stand there for as long as you like. For the rest of the night, if need be. But all nights end. The sun'll rise. And what'll you do then, you creep?

She risked putting her face to the lens again, just in time to see him blink. And then his green eyes vanished.

So perhaps he'd heard what had been going on inside her head, and left.

Or maybe he had simply closed his eyelids.

33 – Maxi and More

She was back on the floor in the middle of her tiny living room again, since there was nowhere else to go. Not squatting this time – that was too uncomfortable. Her knees were pulled up to her chest, both arms wrapped around them. Her back was starting to ache gently, the wales on it starting to smart again, but she could endure that.

It had never struck her before quite how claustrophobic her apartment was. But then, she'd lived most of her life outside of it, only ever using it as a retreat. She'd never been trapped in here before. The walls seemed to press in on her, and the ceiling looked slightly lower every time she stared at it.

And her triumphal thoughts of earlier had practically evaporated by this stage. Because – of course – this night had to end. But it was going that way at an extremely painful crawl. Time was passing like a thick wad of molasses. In counterpoint to which, her mind kept churning furiously.

It was still trying to deny that this was really happening. There had to be some other explanation. And it scrabbled around angrily for what that thing might be, but it found absolutely nothing.

She was wide awake. She wasn't drugged. She hadn't really gone insane so far as she could tell. She was in the middle of downtown Manhattan in the modern day, and there were unearthly beings parked outside her front door and her window. *This could not be.* Only it was and she had little choice … she needed to accept it fully.

If only she'd listened properly to George. He'd said that he'd encountered them on a regular basis, hadn't he? And he had the vital knowledge to keep them at bay. She needed to head back into the Massachusetts woodlands and seek his advice. But not until the sun had risen, and that still seemed a whole eternity away.

A sudden loud bang on the door halted her mind in its downward spiral. She twitched and practically cried out, terrified that John was getting past the amulet somehow.

But then a familiar voice came skirling at her through the woodwork.

"Lindy, gal? You okay?"

Her body tautened and her head came up. And at the same moment, the light came on out on the landing.

At first, she was getting to her feet, taking the first proper breath in what seemed forever, her head whirling with the intoxication of it. Then she stopped herself, the becalmed feeling and uncertainty returning.

"Maxi, is that really you?"

"Who else would it be?"

Which was followed by another hard thump on the wooden frame.

He'd never even visited her place before. Lindy forced herself to look down at her watch and saw that it was only a few minutes after two in the morning. And what was he doing here at this kind of hour?

"How'd you get past the front door?"

"One a' ya neighbors buzzed me up."

And she wanted so very badly to be wrong. Was in such desperate need of saving. But ...

"But they can look like humans if it suits them. Can appear like anything they want. An old wendigo is a master of deceit. You won't even know he wants to hurt you till it's happened."

She couldn't take a chance on this. She had to go at it extremely cautiously.

She got slowly, carefully, the rest of the way to her feet. A floorboard creaked under her. She wondered if whoever was outside had heard that.

"Why won't ya open up this door, Lindy? What be wrong?"

"What brings you here?"

"I were concerned you was still sick."

"At this time in the morning?"

"Couldn't sleep. You don' *sound* sick. So what be goin' on?"

"Something's after me."

"Don't ya mean someone?"

"I meant what I said. The only thing that's keeping it off is this amulet that I got hold of."

A pause. And then a laugh.

"This supposed to be some kinda joke?"

"No."

"You musta been dreaming, gal." Maxi's tone was amused at first, but then concern started to fill it. "Or else you be delirious, sick in the head. Open up this door, Lindy, 'cause you need help."

"And what form will that take? Persuading me that I've got everything wrong? Convincing me that I don't need this amulet?"

The man outside went awfully quiet.

Lindy made her way over to the spy-hole in the door again. The lens revealed Maxi's short cornrows and denim clothing, but his head was bowed so that his face was hidden.

She called out his name, suddenly and loudly. And his head came jerking up, revealing his familiar features.

Only thing was, his irises were now bright green.

She recoiled, just as the light on the landing stuttered out again. Lindy teetered away, practically falling, her legs nerveless.

Finally – for want of any other place to go – she resumed her position in the middle of the floor. And a waiting age turned into a whole waiting forever.

***

Was there a little touch of light at the edges of the skyline now, that softest hint of iridescent gray that heralds the approach of dawn?

Lindy wasn't even sure. Every time she looked out through her front window, she thought that she could see it for a moment, but it faded off to black again. Perhaps it was only the streetlights causing that effect. Or more likely, it was wishful thinking. She checked the time again, and only half an hour had passed since 'Maxi' had shown up. So she was *still* nowhere near morning.

There'd been absolutely no sound from beyond her door this entire while. So when she heard another thump, she jolted.

It was footsteps coming up the stairs, and for a panicked moment she thought it might be one of her neighbors, walking blindly into John's sharp claws. Except the lights were still switched off out there. In spite of which, the footfalls were coming up smoothly and confidently toward her level.

She took in how heavily the stairs were being pounded. These sounded like boots.

A brutal suspicion sunk its talons into her next second, making Lindy shiver. The pace of this ascent. The measuredness of it. This was a familiar sound from way back in her past. Back from the days in the Brooklyn apartment.

The boots reached her landing and halted outside her door. The woodwork creaked, like someone had set both his hands against the frame, leaning his full weight against it.

Her eyes had gone extremely wide and sweat was pouring down her neck, staining the shirt that she was wearing. She could already imagine *him* standing out there, his thick, muscled arms and hairy shoulders.

But that couldn't *be*. The violent bastard was *dead*. Both her folks had passed on *years* ago, both from cancer, merely seven months apart, as though they'd been somehow bound together by a seal made out of anger and spilled blood.

The heel of a big hand – at least, it sounded like that – slammed up hard against the wood.

"*Lindy?*" bellowed a familiar voice. "You let me *in!*"

She was being deceived again – she knew that. But the sound of that enraged bull's roar sent tremors running through her. She was suddenly a little girl again, tears pricking her eyes because she knew that, whatever she did, she'd never please him. Life had disappointed him, and he blamed that on her.

Was it her fault? She went rigid. *Might* his life have been a whole lot better if she'd never come along?

She fought against that notion, like she'd done a thousand times before. He was a coward and a bully and a worthless s.o.b.. But he wouldn't go away. Would not let her alone, and never had.

The woodwork shuddered to another thump.

"Do as I *tell* you! Do it *now!*"

And what she felt like doing was to scream out a response. Except that that would be submitting to this whole illusion, wouldn't it? Treating it like it was real? Her father wasn't on that landing, he was in the ground in Brooklyn. This was just a new deception, yes, a crude attempt to throw her off her balance.

What alarmed her worst was how well it was beginning to work. And she couldn't see how that was possible. She knew *precisely* what this was. But it still sent her memories rushing back, the gulf between the past and present being bridged, so that part of her was nothing like a full-grown woman any longer. She felt herself begin to shrink. She felt her whole body tremble, and she ducked her head. Tears dripped off her nose when she did that.

The third blow against the door was the hardest yet.

"Why aren't you even *answering* me? You *stupid* or somethin'?"

She set her jaw and clenched her teeth, terrified that if she answered, the illusion would turn somehow real.

"You're *useless*!" the voice outside roared. "*Ugly, weak, and pointless!*"

And this was all too much to take. Lindy got up from her tight, huddled position, easing herself to her hands and knees, and scrabbled through the dimness till she found the vodka bottle that she'd purchased.

And then, she began to drink.

34 – True Awaking

Daylight only pushed in very gradually at first, slivers of yellow so sharp at their edges that they hurt her brain and she retreated from them, plunging dizzily back into the depths of her intoxicated sleep again. Dreams came rushing up at her when she did that, and they hurt her too, in different ways. She was aware of several things about her body as she slept. She was lying on a hardened surface – one whole side of her body ached, but when she tried to roll over she couldn't. That was mostly because she was hunched up in a fetal position, but she couldn't seem to change that either. And her back was smarting once again.

None of that bothered her half as much as the words reverberating over and over through her head. And they weren't in her own voice. They were in John's. He'd spoken to her through her door, just before the dawn had risen.

"Ah, well done. I didn't think you'd make it quite this far."

He paused to chuckle softly.

"So you've reached the sanctuary of daylight, yes. And are protected by the sunrise now. In doing so, you've bought yourself a brief handful of hours. But think, Lindy. What is it that always follows daylight, as inevitably as the dawn? Can you prevent the sun from setting again, any more than I can stop it rising?"

And the next moment, he'd faded and was gone.

***

She woke.

After what seemed like hours of struggling to prevent that happening, her eyelids abruptly snapped wide open and the world came slamming back at her. And not merely the sight of it either – the sounds and smells, the heat. It was like an oven inside her apartment, so she'd slept a good long way past dawn. Her clothes were plastered to her body. She could hear the traffic beyond her window, the cars going by on her street and the more generalized murmur further off, an ambulance going past in the distance. The queasy stench of alcohol filled her nostrils, but it wasn't coming from the bottle that was lying on her floor – that was empty. No, the smell was coming from inside of her.

She blinked several times, then tried to move her head. And that was when the pain struck at her. Her brain felt like one massive bruise.

Except she had to get up. Had to move.

Had to do something.

What?

That was a question for later. Getting to her feet came first. She took it an inch at a time, her whole perspective rocking like a ship caught in a violent storm.

Made it to the bathroom. Turned the shower jets on at full blast and freezing cold. She didn't even bother to undress, just sat down in the bottom of the little tub until her mind began to clear, and that took some fifteen minutes.

Had she gotten dead drunk and imagined the whole incident?

Hung-over, in the light of day, that seemed entirely credible. Her thoughts kept trying to cling to that idea. Nothing else could be possible, could it?

She let her head drop, and when she did that something bumped against her sodden cleavage. So she stared down through the moisture in her eyelashes to see that she was still wearing the amulet George Greentree had given her. She put her fingers to it and turned it around, so that the crudely shaped face of the Matchi Manitou was staring up at her.

And she suddenly realized the truth.

She didn't even know how much time she had left before twilight started thickening again. And so she hauled herself to her feet and went stumbling through into the bedroom.

It was already gone noon. She had been unconscious for hours.

She had barely half a day to do the things she needed. So she'd best get on the move.

***

Just before the hire car was delivered, her phone started ringing, but she let her machine take it.

"Lindy, gal?" came Maxi's voice. "You there?"

Was it really him? But this was daytime, so it ought to be. She waited.

"I'm worried about ya. What be wrong with ya, exactly? Please pick up."

She stared at the phone blankly, thinking, *Leave it, Maxi. Please don't get involved in this.*

But to her plain exasperation, the next thing that came out of his mouth was, "Something be wrong. Can feel it. So I'm comin' over."

There was a toot from downstairs, just as he hung up. The hire car had arrived, a little Nissan. She let out her first huff of relief in ages.

The Bruckner Expressway was fairly clear this afternoon. She headed down it quickly and went back into Connecticut. Everything was green around her. Everything looked clean and bright, and that made the horrors of last night seem far more like a dream. She had to hang on to the knowledge it had not been that. It was incredible, the way her mind was trying to repair itself, the sunshine acting like a salve and trying to drive the lurking shadows from her brain. Shape-shifting monsters with glowing eyes … they didn't seem the least bit real in this kind of setting. But if she let herself believe that, then she wouldn't live past nightfall.

Her cell phone started ringing. It was Maxi once again and so she switched the damned thing off.

She kept on going. And would have made it into central Massachusetts in a flat three hours, except a roadwork crew had set up pylons and stop signs on the route approaching Hartford, and that delayed her considerably. It was well past four in the afternoon by the time she was approaching Alberly.

That familiar gas station sign came back in sight, and she understood she'd driven too far. The road was empty and so she performed a hurried U-turn.

As before, it was far dimmer in these woods than anywhere else that she had passed through. As though the whole landscape around her was immersed in twilight. Lindy struggled to remember how far Ellen Hamp had taken them before they'd left the blacktop. She kept looking out for a dirt track off on her left-hand side but – as it turned out – there were plenty of them. They all looked similar as well. Some of them were bare of any marks, but others had tire treads on them. Most of those impressions looked like SUVs. She had no slightest idea which to choose.

So finally, she took a guess. The Nissan started jiggling furiously as soon as it had left the road. The undergrowth scraped against the car's paintwork. And tree trunks went by so closely she was worried that she'd hit them. But she kept on going into the prevailing gloom.

And finally reached a dead end, the pathway simply petering out. She had to reverse for several dozen yards before she could even turn.

Her second try got her the same result, except she came back to the blacktop with a dented fender this time. Lindy stared bewilderedly around and then got out.

There was a solid wall of trees to either side of her. The higher ones were so tall she could only make out a thin strip of the sky above. George was somewhere off to her left – that was the only thing that she was certain of. But she walked across the pavement, moving as far to her right as she could manage. That got her a better look up at the sky, in the correct direction.

Either it was her imagination playing up again, or it had already turned a deeper shade of blue. Only a few hours of daylight were remaining, and her pulse began to thump. If those creatures caught her out here, and at night …

She moved up to a tree that had a low, reachable branch and climbed that. From her new perspective, something she'd not seen before came into view.

And as soon as she had fixed the location in her mind, she jumped down, ran across to her hire car, then drove off toward it.

35 – Smoke

A faint breeze was blowing from that direction, and George could hear the car approach. It didn't sound big and heavy like the vehicles you usually got around these parts. In fact, it was struggling with the terrain and crashing around wildly on its chassis. But it finally reached the same spot where Ellen Hamp had parked a couple of days back and then the engine stalled.

He could hear the clack of a door coming open, and then a single set of footsteps began moving in toward him. What puzzled him was, they weren't moving confidently at all. They were stumbling, occasionally veering off the wrong way before coming back. And the kind of footwear sounded wrong for these woods.

A city dweller.

Then he realized who it had to be and frowned concernedly. He'd had the feeling when they had last parted that she might return.

He found himself wondering how she'd even managed to locate him. But after a few moments' thought, his gaze turned to the tidy little fire burning on the ground in front of him. His withered lips formed a soft smile. Clever girl. She had been following the smoke.

He was sitting cross-legged on a patch of dry grass, and waited patiently, listening to her gradual approach. It would have been much easier for her if he had shouted out, but he was sure this Lindy was a smart one, so he let her find him on her own.

Finally, some bushes rattled and then parted. Lindy's face burst into view. Only that George could see at his first glance that there was something very different about it – it had changed since they'd last met. There was a hard, cold pallor to the skin, a dull sheen that had not been there before. The woman's jaw was firmly set, her mouth a flat, unsmiling line. Her nostrils were slightly flared, and in her pale blue eyes …

They were glazed with real hurt, and an awful kind of fear was burning like a flame beyond that.

Staring at her, the realization sprang up fully blown inside his head.

A wendigo's been fucking with her – perhaps literally.

George didn't say it, though. He just shot her a gentle smile instead.

***

She was sitting down across from him before much longer. Didn't even seem to care that she was seated on a patch of dirt and messing her clothes up. But she refused to look him in the eye. Her head was bowed, her red hair flopping down. Oh, some creature had really done a number on her, hadn't it? He could feel the fear, confusion and disgust rising off her like the heat off a radiator in cold weather.

"Why a fire in August?" he could hear her mumble.

George shrugged. "I don't know. I like to sit and stare into the flames. I have visions sometimes. Better than TV."

"I would never have found you without it."

"There's your answer, then," he grinned. "Matchi Manitou must have made me light it."

And then he reached under his shirt and pulled out a larger version of the amulet he'd given her. Three white feathers were depending from the base this time.

"Still got yours?"

She hooked out the leather cord from around her neck so that he could see it. And George nodded quietly. That at least was good.

The shadows were a little longer, now. The air had the smell and feel to it of a day that was beginning to expire. Dusk came earlier in these woods than in the outside world. George tilted his head back to look at a small fragment of sky, then returned his attention to the huddled woman.

Waited for her to speak again, and waited a long while.

But finally, she stirred and said, "I practically laughed at you, the last time that we met."

George nodded again, unjudgmental.

"I couldn't believe … had no way of knowing …"

A shudder ran through her, from her shoulders to her toes.

"One of them looked like a handsome man. I was … I did …"

And the words failed her altogether and her head went further down.

"You most likely got a very ancient one," George told her softly. "The young ones only care about killing. But those who are far older learn about elaborate pleasures down the way. Like you said, you had no way of knowing anything. It's not your fault. So let it go."

"I can't."

He'd been expecting her to say that, and he waited once again.

"These amulets … they keep those creatures off. But that is all they do, right?"

"Isn't that enough?" he asked.

And then he listened as the woman described how she'd been taunted all last night, and how this 'John Hunter' had promised to come back.

"I need to kill him. How?"

And George had never once even considered that. It was not part of his culture, had never been mentioned in any of the stories he'd been told. Beings such as these were part of nature, like the wind and rain. And you couldn't kill the wind or rain, only protect yourself against them. That was what he'd always understood.

Except the woman's face had finally lifted, her gaze fixed upon his own. Her cheeks were as bloodless as chalk, her eyelids puffy and red-rimmed. She was caught between exhaustion and insanity, and absolutely desperate. So he turned it over.

Finally, he came to a conclusion. Fingered the larger amulet again, holding it up.

"The iron that made this and the one you're wearing? It comes from a mine on sacred ground. I guess that if a wendigo were ever to feel its touch …"

And then he let the sentence die.

"It might destroy them?" Lindy asked.

"It might."

But then he went on to explain how doing that thing was pretty damned unlikely. And it took him quite a while.

36 – Nowhere Else to Go

Gradually, as the gloom deepened, Lindy began to take in her surroundings. She'd been so immersed in misery and fear that she had barely even noticed them before.

It was only trees and undergrowth around her at first glance. But when you looked a little closer, you could see there was a shack. It was set back from the fire by merely something like a dozen yards, except your eyes brushed across it easily at first, scarcely taking it in, because it was the same color and texture as the rest of the surrounding forest.

It was only small and had no windows. Presumably, no water or sanitation either. And she wondered how anyone could live like that. But then, George didn't strike her as any kind of normal person. He was far more like a natural force, relaxed but solid, calm and wise, the surprises that life threw at you not even bothering him a touch because he knew such things were fleeting.

He had wandered off by this time. And that bothered her, since it was genuinely getting dark. She couldn't hear him moving about in the surrounding woods, except occasionally there was a dragging noise. And it sounded as though he were picking something up.

That was confirmed when he came wandering back. He had a heavy pile of deadwood clasped between his arms. He dumped it several feet away from the small, dwindling fire, then selected three dry branches, broke them up and dropped them carefully into the center of the flames. He blew on them and they licked up, a flickering orange glow dancing across the little clearing.

"Build the fire good and strong," he smiled at her. "Keep the shadows and the creatures that dwell in them at bay. Humans have been doing this thing since Prometheus."

"You know about Prometheus?" Lindy asked him, quite surprised. "But that's Greek legend."

George just pulled a face and told her, "We call him Blazing Arrow instead. But it's all the same thing."

She took that in, then stared off between the tree trunks. They looked like solid rods of black drawn on a sheet of gray by this stage. Where they ended and thin air began was getting harder to discern with every passing minute. Dusk was closing like a trap, obscuring the boundaries between what was real and what wasn't.

Through a gap in the treetops, the pale disc of the moon had already appeared. It was only very faint, but she could see the mottled markings on it.

On his shoulder, back when she was maybe four, a couple of years before the incident with the baseball bat. Out on that same weed-strewn back lot on a summer's evening, so far back in her past that it appeared to her like another dream. Him smelling faintly of Scotch, but in an agreeable mood, so that the soft odor was comforting and sweet.

Both of them staring right up at the purple, darkened sky and sharing the experience.

"Isn't that beautiful, Lindy?"

"Yes, Daddy, it is." She pointed at the moon. "But what's it made of?"

And he grinned so hugely she could feel it down her side. "Why, don't you know? I thought that every little girl knew that. It's made of cheese."

"Really?"

"Yeah, of course!"

He'd laughed and kissed her on the cheek.

Lindy blinked, her eyelids slapping together with what sounded like a heavy thump.

They'd been so close. Why had he begun to hate her, not long after that? What had she done to cause it?

That was the wrong question and she knew it. She'd been far too young to be guilty of anything herself. But she'd never once been able to stop herself from asking that. She really was messed up, and had been so almost all her life.

Easy pickings for the stuff out in the shadows.

***

A shrill shriek, far off in the distance, brought her shuddering upright, her eyes straining as they tried to pierce the gloom.

"Only a night bird," George Greentree murmured.

He had resumed his place on the far side of the dancing flames. But his words didn't reassure her, and she kept on peering off into the forest.

"Will they come for me?"

"They said they would, and so I see no real reason to doubt it."

"Even here?"

She shivered.

"Especially here."

"What am I going to do?"

"What I say, if you're smart."

"Few people have ever called me that."

"Well, now's the time to start."

Trees and air had merged by now. The darkness had become a solid entity, obliterating all the boundaries that were imposed by normal vision. Overhead, a few stars had come out. And off to their edge, Lindy could make out a tiny cloud.

The night bird called again. She quivered. Jesus Christ, it sounded like someone in pain. It sounded like a little child being hurt. She found herself wondering why she'd even come out here.

Because you've nowhere else to go, the answer came back at her.

The night bird started shrieking again, then abruptly stopped. And when she looked across at George, his face had gone stiff in the firelight.

He was not staring in the direction the call had come from, but off to his right hand side. She couldn't hear anything there, but apparently he could. His expression became thoughtful and he chewed a moment at his top lip with his yellowed teeth. And then he started getting to his feet with what looked like arthritic slowness.

He motioned her up as well.

"Start backing toward the shack," he said. "And stay behind me at all times. You got it?"

37 – Revisitation

By the time they'd reached the front door of the shack, the moon had risen a touch higher and become a little more defined, casting its light down at a slightly different angle so that shards and slivers of it now appeared between the massed, surrounding timber. Not that that made anything much clearer. Very little in the way of a definable shape sprang out. All that swam to Lindy's gaze were sections of overlapping dimness, nothing out there moving unless moved by her imagination.

But then, she thought that she caught sight of something. A sliding motion in the darkness of the forest. Her face jerked toward it, but it was already lost among the blackened tree trunks.

Then it came again, a little closer in. She gulped down a tight breath.

It had only been in plain view for a fraction of a second before sinking into darkness once again. But it appeared to be a patch of mist, standing out clearly against the universal blackness of the woods, its upper edge catching a thin ray of the moonlight and breaking it up into silvery scintillas before moving out of range.

George was looking in the same direction. They both twitched as it vanished.

When it appeared a third time, it was maybe a dozen yards closer. It was almost perfectly round, the same height a tall man would stand, its bottom edge clear of the forest floor. And it was moving over to them with an almost casual smoothness, in spite of the fact that there was no breeze. As Lindy watched, it passed through one of the narrower tree trunks without changing its shape in the slightest.

It almost reached the edge of the small clearing they were in. And then it stopped.

Began to disperse, bleeding outward from its edges until it had merged completely with the dark.

A pair of sharply glowing, bright green eyes appeared where it had been.

Nothing else. Not the dimmest hint of a surrounding outline.

Merely those.

***

Part of her was – once again – already wishing this was all over. Wishing she were dead, so that she didn't have to be so frightened anymore. But George seemed to sense that. Reached back with one of his gnarled hands until it closed round one of hers, and gave it a reassuring squeeze. His other hand, his right one, was already occupied. He'd pulled the larger amulet back out from underneath his plaid shirt and was holding it to the full limit of its leather thong. His face was fixed on that green gaze, unshifting. And he'd lifted himself higher than he normally stood, no weary, aged curve around his shoulders any longer.

"Who *are* you?" he called out. And his voice, although still croaky, was much firmer, stronger than was usual. "Give me a name to call you by!"

"You mean my *real* one," came John Hunter's chuckling voice, "so that you can exert influence on me, old man? I think not."

George reacted to those words by turning his head slightly. Mumbling to Lindy low, out of the corner of his mouth.

"This one's very, very ancient," he said. "I can smell it on his breath."

"I can hear you, George!" John Hunter laughed. "I know your name. I've passed through these woods many times before, in different guises."

Lindy was still trying to force her mind to work. She found it difficult to tear her eyes away, but managed it at last, her gaze sweeping through the interlocking shadows, trying to spot any more motion out there.

"There were *three* of them," she whispered to George. "The other two were women."

"I can't sense any others. There is only him, and him alone."

"Damn right!" the voice out ahead of them crowed. "Do you think I'd bring either of my daughters along on my final date with Lindy?"

Daughters?

John sounded so lighthearted, happy, as though he was savoring every moment of this. And she realized that was the truth. The way he'd treated her … he'd savored every second of it. They were food and drink to this kind of monster.

208

She'd taken her own amulet out by this stage, and her fist had closed around it in a bloodless knot. But …

"Who do you think that you're protecting, George?" he was calling out. "Anyone decent? Anyone good? You've got *that* wrong! She's nothing but a twisted nymphomaniac!"

"That so?" George grunted, shrugging. "Well in that case, I wish I'd met her thirty years ago."

And that small show of defiance was almost like a signal to the creature. John Hunter had gone entirely silent now, and it was practically oppressive in the darkness of the woods. No footfalls could be heard, no slightest rustling. But that green gaze started moving closer, smoothly and assuredly.

"Into the hut," George hissed.

Lindy didn't want to turn her back, but had to crane her head around to find her way in through the door. It turned out there was a crude latch. She pulled at it, and they went tumbling through.

But as she was shutting the door behind them, something startling happened. They had been plunged into utter lightlessness. Except George mumbled a few native words, and a yellow glow began to filter out around them.

It was coming from a battered, glass-and-metal storm lamp that was set atop a small crude wooden table in one corner of the room. And when Lindy looked more clearly, she could see there was no licking flame, only a bright amber glow.

Shock washed through her, driving off the fear for a few seconds.

"How'd *that* happen, George?"

Then her attention went around the inside of the shack. Aside from the table, the only other pieces of furniture in this place were a low, rickety-looking chair and a crude pallet with a bolster at one end, a pile of shabby blankets piled up at its center. There were a couple of cook pots hanging from one wall. A fishing rod in another corner, along with a hunting rifle that she thought might be a Winchester but looked pre-War.

Then her focus went up higher. There were dozens of strangely-shaped objects suspended on cords from the wooden roof. Some of them she recognized – dreamcatchers and larger, flatter versions of the amulets that she and George were wearing. But there were also masks of barely human faces. Peculiar constructs made of polished balls of mottled stone and clumps of feathers. There was even a stuffed eagle.

Her mind tried to absorb all that. And then her gaze went back to the storm lamp, which was still pushing out an even glow.

"Are you some kind of shaman, George?"

Despite the trouble they were in, a little of that impish light came back into his pupils, the edges of his withered lips rising a touch.

"Don't go telling Ellen Hamp," he told her. "She finds out, she'll drive me nuts."

But then he looked back at the door and moved away from it, taking Lindy with him.

"The wendigo is directly outside," he said.

"Can he get in?"

"Unless we do something stupid, no."

The next thing that came to her ears was the sound of footsteps. Hunter was making them, whereas he'd not before. He had moved away from the front door and was making his way around the outside of the shack. And the fact that she could hear him now could only mean one thing. He *wanted* her to hear him. He was plucking at her nerves. It was the way he worked.

Every step was like a cannon shot, leaves crunching and grass buckling underneath his tread. His stride was confident but idle. He could wait all night. He reached the rear wall of the hut and started ambling along it.

As he started coming up the other side, she found herself looking at the crude table again. Apart from the storm lamp, there were several other objects on it. A pipe. A clean and empty dinner plate, the plastic type you took on picnics.

And a small, crudely-formed dagger, that looked like it was made from the same iron as the amulets.

She went hurriedly across and snatched it up. It felt slippery to the touch at first, but then she realized how damp her palms had become.

Hunter was progressing to the front left corner once again. And Lindy had been staring at the shack's walls long enough to understand the barrier they formed was not completely solid. There were knotholes in the wood, and there were places where the boards had warped and gaps were showing. She ought to have been able to catch some glimpses of the prowling creature outside, but the glow of the storm lamp was working against that. And so she asked George if he could turn it down, and he muttered a few more words.

The light dropped to a whisper of its former self, ochre-textured dimness closing in around them. Lindy was now facing the front wall again, and could make out small patches of dancing orange from the campfire out beyond it. The branches George had added were still burning fiercely.

Then she saw a partial silhouette moving across it. And the shape didn't appear to be John Hunter's. The frame was narrower. The arms were longer, practically simian. She took all of that in within a bare split second, but it anchored itself in her mind, even when the shape moved on.

His footsteps hadn't changed their tempo one tiniest bit. She caught several more glimpses of him as he made another circuit. The face seemed longer and the chin more pointed. The legs were spindlier, the knees prominent and lumpy. Hanging down almost to them – he was apparently naked – was a very thin and flaccid cock. Revulsion pushed its way into her throat and stayed there, and her face pulled out of shape.

She'd been to *bed* with this thing? It was an effort just to hold herself together.

George was staring at her worriedly.

Lindy looked down at her hands and saw that she had clasped them together, so that the dagger was now tightly gripped between them. It occurred to her to burst out there and plunge this blade into the creature before it could even …

George put both hands gently on her shoulders.

"It'll know you're coming before you even take your first step outside. And in its natural state, it moves real quick. Almost faster than the eye can follow. So the sensible thing to do is wait."

Hunter's steps had almost reached the door again when they came to an unexpected halt. Lindy and George both froze up. There was utter silence outside for a few breathless seconds. Then his voice came drifting in.

"You like things simple, Lindy? There's a children's story that I'm thinking of right now, about a wooden house like this one."

He paused to let that sink in.

"I can't make yours fall down by blowing on it, no. But I can burn it down."

His footsteps started up again. They were moving away from the shack this time, in the direction of the fire.

38 – Fireflies

Once that she was fairly certain he was moving off, Lindy took a chance and moved up closer to the wall, shutting one eye and peering through the largest gap.

She could make out his whole diminishing outline now. It was picked out stark and hard against the bright glow of the campfire. And was mostly human, albeit ungainly, tapering in places where it ought not do, so that his frame looked like it was diseased or malnourished. But then she started to pick out certain features that were wrong.

The fingers were way too long. The feet, when they came flapping up, looked the size of frogmen's flippers. She thought that she could make out strands of wispy hair around the skull, except the dazzle of the firelight made that a hard thing to be quite certain of. And along the creature's shoulders, there was some kind of weird fringe, made up of spines perhaps.

Her anguish and revulsion were forgotten by this stage. She didn't care what it had tricked her into doing … all that concerned her was what it was going to do right now. Lindy gripped the iron dagger so hard it dug into her palm. She heard herself gasp as the creature reached the campfire and bent down.

It put its hand directly into the bright flames without so much as flinching. Dabbled about in there a while, then selected a large branch and lifted it out. The fire immediately enveloped its misshapen hand, but that didn't bother it either. It straightened and turned.

A dancing ochre glow ran up across its belly, revealing a chest with no navel or nipples. It would have been childishly smooth, except that ribs were showing through. The monster's face was still mostly obscured in shadow, though, its green eyes shining like a pair of lanterns. But there *was* hair around the skull, a fair amount of it. It was straggling, stringy and uneven. Silver-gray, so that it glowed with the same eerie luminescence as a nighttime cloud pierced by the moon.

George had told her it was very old. It looked it.

It paused a moment, staring straight in her direction. Lindy got the feeling that it knew that she was watching, and she fought the urge to pull away,

The scrawny muscles in its arms tensed, and the branch snapped in half with a startling crack. A swarm of embers flew up when that happened, and she got a brief impression of its face, there and gone in less than the time it took her eyes to blink with shock.

It was flatter than it should have been. The cheekbones were not there, although the brow was ridged. There only seemed to be a shadowy hollow where the nose ought to be sitting. But below that, she picked out some small glitters of white. And they were most probably fangs inside its partly open mouth.

It held up one half of the broken branch and twirled it, so that another shower of sparks flew up against the darkened sky. The other half, in its left hand, went down by its side, resting against its bare thigh. Its stance was casual, now.

George had crowded in beside her, pressing up against her shoulder, and was seeing the same things that she was. When she looked around at him, his face was very grave and he looked deeply lost in thought.

"Will the charms still keep him off?" she asked.

George shook his head uneasily.

"They'll stop him touching the shack with his hands. But then, he doesn't have to do that, does he?"

Out beyond the gap, the figure took a casual step toward them, then another, both of its hands still ablaze. And George seemed to come to a decision.

"I'm going to have to go out there."

When Lindy tightened further up, he grabbed her by the shoulder.

"Whatever happens to me, stay inside. Please ... promise me you'll do that."

***

Next moment he was on the move, with a fluidity and swiftness that she had not seen from him before. His back straightened up and he reached for the ceiling, snatching one of the weird feather-draped constructs down. It was flat and circular, and turned out to be a small shield. Then he went to the corner where the fishing rod and the rifle were propped. He swept them both aside. A long and narrow painted rattle was revealed.

It hummed like a beehive when he picked it up. Then he was heading for the shack's front door.

Lindy stared out through the gap again. The wendigo was halfway to them.

George went plunging through the doorway, and for a brief moment she lost sight of him altogether. But she couldn't abandon him completely. She needed to stay inside, for sure. But she moved over to the door herself.

George and Hunter were facing each other, barely eight yards in between them. The shaman was holding the shield out in front of him. The rattle was above his head and setting up a constant rhythm

Lindy felt off balance – listening to that sound – as if she'd been transported someplace else. It was like listening to waves breaking on a beach of shingle. Or perhaps hearing the breathing of a deep, echoing cave.

It seemed to hold the creature spellbound for a moment. And then George began to chant.

She didn't understand the words, but she could sense the power in them. His pitch rose and fell.

As she watched, the air halfway between the two male figures … it began to glitter. There were only tiny motes of light at first, as though some fireflies had arrived. But then the glittering grew more intense, and everything beyond it seemed to ripple. So some type of wall was forming there. Some barrier of magic force. Her mind didn't even try to stop accepting that.

The creature knew what it was seeing too. It suddenly came lurching forward, dropping the two shafts of burning wood and reaching out with both its hands. Those long fingers of its were tipped with curving claws. And they swiped at the barrier, trying to slash it.

At first, they did not succeed. But then the middle talons on the right hand broke right through. The barrier rippled wildly, flickering. George tipped back his head and chanted louder and far faster than he'd done before. But Hunter would not let go.

He kept his right hand where it was and brought his left one up to join it, every movement purposeful and steady. The barrier was still wavering, and he began to work on the small gap he'd made until he'd torn it wider.

It was like watching someone make their way out of a tent by simply cutting through the canvas. He'd gotten a whole arm through before too much longer, then his head. And the dancing light was beginning to fade, the entire barrier breaking down.

It brightened for a second, closing round the creature's flanks. But then it gave an abrupt flash and vanished altogether.

There was *nothing* languorous about John Hunter now. A few swift strides and he would be on George. Even if the shaman turned and ran, he'd never make it back.

And before she even knew what she was doing, Lindy was pushing herself out into the open, yelling senselessly at the top of her voice.

She clenched her teeth. Could feel her right hand going back across her shoulder. There was no world beyond this clearing now, and no time but this single moment.

She was sucking in cool forest air, then hurling the knife.

39 – Phone Call

And she was dead on target.

She could actually see – as though in fine slow motion – as the iron spike went plunging through the air directly at John Hunter's chest. All that she was watching was his silhouette by this time, her vision contracting so she couldn't even make out George. She heard a single bumping sound, one of her own heartbeats. She'd gripped her lower lip between her teeth, could taste a spot of blood there.

All that she could think was, *DIE!* She wanted to see Hunter fall. The blade closed in. He didn't have the time to move. She'd caught him out, and this was over.

And then suddenly, the outline she'd been looking at was no longer there, although it left behind a blur. The knife went sailing through that blur and went out past the fire, finally dropping into the undergrowth beyond.

Lindy jerked back into full awareness, her head craning round. She'd *missed*. Or rather, he had dodged the blade, vanishing altogether. George had warned her they were very fast.

The shaman had come unfrozen too. Urgency gleamed in his eyes. And when she moved forward, he put out an arm insistently to stop her.

"I need to find that knife again!"

"No time," he snapped. "Get back inside. I'll join you shortly."

And then he turned to the twin pieces of lit branch, stamping on them quickly till they were reduced to glowing dust. That done, he advanced on the campfire.

Lindy forced herself to retreat inside the shack, but didn't make it much beyond the threshold. She could only stand there watching while George used his heavy boots to kick the fire apart. He trampled back and forth till there were only a few shining embers. Then he came hurrying back, as fast as his legs could carry him.

He was shaking when he got indoors, and fighting for breath. And so he propped himself against the doorpost, wheezing a while until the tremors in his frame had slowed.

"Thank you. I'd have been done for if you hadn't acted."

He pursed his lips and jerked his head in the direction where the fire had been.

"He can *use* flames, but he can't create them. Nothing supernatural can. Fire was a gift to Blazing Arrow, from the gods to humans, them alone. And so he cannot get to us by those means now."

Which left the question, *What else might he use?*

Both of them went still and quiet, their skin almost pricking as they stared back out at the surrounding forest. No green gaze came back at theirs. The timber was so still it might as well have been a painting of a woodland, black layered on deeper black. There was not the faintest rustle from the undergrowth. The battle that had taken place had hushed the creatures in the woods, so much that the pair of them might as well have been the last two living creatures on the planet.

"Where's he gotten to?" Lindy finally whispered.

"We don't even know he's gone. He might be watching us right now."

They were tricksters – right, she knew that. And they had no sense of time at all. And maybe she was losing hers as well, because she could scarcely remember what this place looked like in daylight. Could almost feel the darkness leeching inward through her pores. And Lindy shuddered.

The campfire might be gone now, but the old storm lamp continued glowing, letting out a gentle fizzing noise. It was as though they were both huddled on some tiny amber raft that was just sitting on a huge, dark ocean.

They seemed to be utterly alone out here.

***

Another hour passed, as slowly as a glacier moving. Lindy felt her body starting to rebel. She suddenly felt flushed and began trembling. Her eyes got sore and stung and kept on playing tricks on her.

She had been on numerous stakeouts during her career, and had always believed that patience was a part of being a cop. But this was an entirely different thing. *She* was now the one who was most likely being watched. She was the target. And it wasn't anything that she'd been used to since she had left home.

She leant exhaustedly against the wooden wall beside the door, her eyelids slipping shut. That old apartment in Brooklyn came rushing back to her, some of its furniture overturned and her father's crazed voice roaring in the background. If none of that had ever happened, if she'd had a normal childhood … would she even have wound up out here? She just didn't know.

A hand settled on her shoulder.

"Try to stay awake," said George.

She blinked, a little angrily. "What difference does it make?"

But then she listened carefully as the shaman explained how dreaming brought you closer to the supernatural world. Except this *all* felt like an eerie dream, one that she might never wake from.

"Can't you do anything more?" she asked George. "I mean … if you're a shaman, can't you drive him away?"

He smiled at her sadly.

"You saw what happened when I tried to stop him. I could barely hold him back a minute. And it's not that I'm weak, no. It's that he's very, very strong."

"So what's he waiting for, exactly?"

"Maybe he's just waiting for the sake of doing that. Tonight will be followed by another one, and then the next. So he's got time."

And it was just too much. She could feel that she was sinking. Her knees were bending of their own volition. She was hunkering up into a tightened ball.

Her head went down, and she began to sob.

***

A pair of soothing hands alighted on her in another while. George massaged her neck and shoulders softly, saying not a thing because there were no words. She very rarely cried, but didn't feel ashamed of it. He seemed to understand that.

How long had it been since any man had laid his hands on her this gently? She couldn't remember, and that was partly her own fault, she knew. But she wiped her eyes, looked up at him and tried to smile.

"Thank you."

He looked puzzled.

"For what?"

She reached up and took hold of his wrist.

"Just thanks."

But then her gaze went past the doorway once again.

The woods out there were still black and entirely quiet. Only this time, she forced herself to remember that the world simply did not end where the treeline melted off to seamless shadow. There were people out *beyond* this place. Towns and cities and lights and traffic, the rituals of normality still being played out beyond this clearing.

For the first time in hours, she started to think about the place she lived, the office she worked in, and the people who she knew.

Maxi!

It was almost like an instinct, it struck her so quickly. Lindy fumbled in her pocket, pulled her cell phone out. She oughtn't be able to get a signal out here, but when she thumbed the red switch the display screen lit up.

Maxi had tried calling her a second time, but hadn't left a message. Under George's pensive gaze, she dialled his number.

Nothing. His was switched off, and she'd never known him do that.

"That thing shouldn't even be working," George was pointing out.

And she understood that. But she couldn't seem to absorb it properly. A peculiar urgency had gripped her. She tried dialling Maxi's cell again, but still got no response.

"Who're you trying to call?" George asked. "And more importantly, why?"

His crumpled expression had become very concerned, and when she shrugged, the corners of his mouth turned down. He took in a slow breath, like he could feel that there was something coming.

"The idea just popped fully formed into your mind? Right?"

And she nodded.

"And you didn't stop to wonder who exactly might have put it there?"

And she was still taking that in, when the cell phone started ringing in her palm, so abruptly that she almost dropped it.

And the display was telling her that it was Maxi. So – rather warily – she answered.

40 – Negotiation

"Lindy?" came his harried voice out of the speaker.

Her heart pounded and she stood right up.

"*Maxi?*"

"Don't listen ta him, gal! Do not do a thing he says! I –"

But his words were overtaken by a sharpened scream of pain. There was a clatter as the cell phone at the other end was dropped.

Scuffling after that. It sounded like an enclosed space, some kind of echoing room.

Maxi started shouting, "*No!*"

But he was away from the cell by this time.

Was he still in New York, or had he tried to follow her out here? Except in that case, he'd be somewhere in the open, wouldn't he? Lindy kept on calling out his name.

She could hear a hand sliding around the other cell phone. A faint rattle as it was picked up. Then someone's breath against the small device. And she was not sure why, but she could almost sense the smile behind it.

"Hello again, Lindy," John Hunter said.

***

Goddamn it, *this* was why the woodlands had been silent for so long! He'd gone back to New York!

She could still hear scuffling noises back behind John Hunter's voice. Maxi stopped protesting and let out another scream. Lindy was trembling by this stage, her teeth clamped with anguish. John – in counterpart – sounded cheerful and sublimely calm.

"Do you really think that I would be so mean as to leave you cooped up in that squalid shack for … how long? The rest of your life, perhaps? There's a whole wide world waiting for you out here, Lindy. And there's someone that you genuinely care about."

Maxi was the *only* one. And Hunter had to know that. The s.o.b. had gotten inside her head again. She felt further violated, and her panic began transforming into rage.

"What are you *doing*?" she demanded.

"To him? Personally? Nothing at all. But my daughters are introducing him to … shall we say, the *darker* side of sexuality?"

There was another scream, far higher-pitched than the ones before.

"That's something that you're used to, Lindy – yes, I know. But Maxi here appears to be a novice."

It knocked her sideways to hear both those things, Maxi's pain and Hunter's words. But the professional side of her kicked in. So she went very still and asked, "What do you want?"

"You. Here. Away from that damned shack and that old man."

"You'll let Maxi go?"

"Of course I will. I have no interest in him."

She could tell that he was smirking. *Liar*, she thought. But that was the thing with negotiations. You had to at least *pretend* that you were trying to forge an honest deal. The only thing she had to offer was herself, and they both knew it.

"Where are you?" she snapped.

His words came oozing down the line like treacle laced with poison. "You're the detective, aren't you? And so, figure it out."

"What are you *playing* at? Just tell me!"

"Well, I'm near the park, of course. And I'm high up. In a place that is unoccupied, and has been since this started."

And she got it.

"You had better hurry, Lindy. If you don't get here by dawn, we'll have to leave. And we'll be taking Maxi with us."

Immediately he'd said that, he hung up.

Sheer exhaustion was written into every single one of George's wrinkles when she looked at him again. He'd tried so hard to save her, but it seemed that he had lost.

She pocketed her cell phone. Took her badge out of her purse and clipped it to her jacket. Transferred her gun to a pocket too, for all the good that that would do her. Checked that the amulet was still hanging against her breastbone, and then fumbled for the keys of her renter.

"Gotta go?" George asked her, very quietly.

And she nodded.

PART FOUR

FIGHTING BACK

41 – Up

Dawn was almost breaking by the time the city came back into sight. And it was a dawn the like of which she'd rarely seen, the opening of a truly, brutally hot day. Like the world had somehow swiveled on its axis, and the northeast coast of the United States had moved far closer the Equator.

The day's first light was usually mild and gentle, all pale lemons, bleached blues and dove grays. Whereas the glow emerging at the east horizon now was deep. Was harsh. It was a rich, thick yellow with a burnished quality. The towers of Manhattan stood in blackened silhouette against it. And the river passing underneath her – it was like a sheet of bronze.

She had the pedal to the metal and the renter was doing well over a hundred. And she knew that cameras would be picking her up, but didn't care. *All* that she could pray was that she stayed away from her own kind and didn't wind up with a cruiser on her tail.

Her side window was slightly down and she could hear the roaring of the air outside the car. And some of it was coming in and she could feel it round her face and neck. In spite of the fact that it was moving fast, it already felt tepid. Sweat was beading on her upper lip and brow. She didn't even try to wipe it.

Neither did she bother with the FDR once she'd hit the island. She simply hammered along 125th, then took a left, jumping every stoplight in her way.

That goddamned ugly yellow glow was starting to ooze out along the streets that she was passing. But so far as she could tell, the sun had not risen fully above the horizon yet. So there was still a load of shadow left and – this being the place it was – that would remain the case for quite a while. Shadows were like caves that John Hunter could wait inside. And he would wait for her for as long as he was able … she believed she knew that much about him.

The Sirius Apartments were now coming into view. She stamped the renter to a squealing halt in front of them. Then she was outside in a flash, her right hand going to her gun. She made sure that the little amulet was in full view against her chest. And then she started running over.

But her legs slowed down within a bare couple of seconds. Somebody was waiting for her just inside the entrance.

And it wasn't John.

***

It was the same doorman she'd spoken with a few nights back, only he was framed behind the glass doors now. Fuller. Or Fullman, something like that. The night the Callum guy had died.

The doorman looked mostly unchanged since she had first met him. Just as gaunt and angular, his broad nose like a hatchet and his long hands with their swollen knuckles poking out from beneath the cuffs of his uniform jacket. Except his nervous manner was entirely gone. His gaze was blank and very still. He was perfectly upright, rigid. And he didn't even seem to notice she was there at first.

Then he blinked, and his face inched around until it was angled at her. The corners of his mouth came up in a tight parody of a welcoming smile. He pulled back one of the doors for her, and then bowed to her in a mock-courteous fashion.

She had no slightest doubt John Hunter was controlling him.

But she ignored that and went on past. How much time did she have left?

Elevator doors were hanging open right in front of her, dim illumination on inside. But with *three* of those damned creatures in this building, she'd no sooner step into a confined box than push her arm into a flame. And so she took the stairs instead.

Her footsteps clattered, echoing around her as she headed up. She kept on going, her breath hot and heavy in her lungs. Again, she couldn't hear a single noise from the apartments she was going past. So the creatures had influenced *these* people too.

What was happening felt barely real. Like all of this was taking place upon some multi-storied stage. But Lindy screwed her face up and she pushed those kinds of thoughts away.

No! This was not a game! Somehow, she was going to get through all of this. Get Maxi through it too. She didn't care what George had said. She was going to *destroy* John Hunter.

She'd reached the final flight before she'd even realized it. Slowed down, grasped the handle of the safety door and pulled it back.

The doorway to the penthouse was wide open in the corridor beyond. And there was nothing but darkness to be seen beyond it.

42 – Almost Fully Day

There was not a sound coming from inside the place. And that tensed her up worse than she already was … all she could hear was the hiss of her own breathing and her pulse pounding inside her skull. This was New York City, wasn't it? And there was *always* noise, whatever time of day. This wasn't merely the city that never slept, it was the city that never shut up. As her eyes adjusted, she could make out that the sliding glass doors to the roof terrace were partway open. So there should have been the murmur of a passing car, at least. But there was absolutely nothing.

She felt like she had stepped out of the world and straight into a new one. One where the old rules didn't apply. Where sound and hearing could be altered as though with the simple flicking of a switch. Which begged the question … what else exactly could be manipulated that way?

She could. She already knew that. It was her fault she was here today. But Maxi was an innocent party in all of this. So she took as deep a breath as she was able, then stepped in.

Her eyesight wavered, and then solid images formed around her.

This apartment didn't look as if it had been redecorated since the mid-Eighties. The huge glass dining table with its tubular black legs. The bulky sound system over in the corner. But apart from the furniture, this massive living room was wholly empty. Not a soul in here but her.

She caught a sudden movement. Swung toward it, instinct taking over once again. Drew her gun, clasping it two-handed, although her arms were shaking so badly that she could barely aim.

All that it turned out to be was the edge of a drape near the open window that was being pushed at by some current of warm air. The gentle fluttering motion caused the light to pulse. The daylight. It was growing stronger.

Am I too late?

The notion struck at her like an electric shock.

Is this Hunter's final torture? To make me come so far, so fast, so urgently, only to find that Maxi has already gone?

"How could you believe that I would be so cruel?" came a familiar voice, off from her right-hand side.

Her training kicked in and she swung toward it, straight-armed, crouching slightly lower.

There was nothing there but a blank, hessian-covered wall.

Lindy blinked and her eyes swiveled, trying to catch what they were missing.

"How could you believe I'd go away without you? And what use to me is Maxi? No, I'm here for you."

The wall seemed to ripple and then bulge. And John Hunter stepped right on through.

***

He was dressed exactly the same way he had last been when she'd seen him in this city. But his face had changed again. The features were all there, except that they had been compacted and compressed. The nose was larger and more prominent than it ought to be, protruding almost like a snout, and the rest of his features were pressed in around it, as though she were looking at him through a fisheye lens.

His eyes were glowing a brilliant green again.

Lindy's finger started tightening on her trigger. But then she saw how useless that would be. And the gun went slipping from her nerveless grasp. She barely even noticed as it hit the floor. She was transfixed.

When Hunter smiled, his teeth were very narrow and more numerous than they ought to be, and needle sharp.

"Aren't you even going to say hello?" he asked.

Lindy tried to push some breath up through her throat, except it felt like it had closed up tight. She wasn't even sure what she was trying to say. Her mind was no more than a vapid blur.

"You could always ask where Maxi is," Hunter suggested, taking a slow step toward her.

She pulled back when she saw that. Felt her shoulder-blades hunch up against her spine, sweat flooding between them. But she snatched the little amulet up, holding it to the length of its leather cord.

Hunter's eyes narrowed a little.

"That won't save your friend," he smiled.

The tightness in her throat finally eased a touch, and a sound came drifting up that was a *ng-ghh* sound. She steadied herself and tried to clear her head. Managed to get three words out.

"Where *is* he?"

"In company. And being taken care of."

Hunter nodded at a spot directly behind her.

And she didn't want to turn her back on him. It took every ounce of strength she had. But – almost painful though it was – she managed to swivel. Managed to shift her head around. She'd only meant to look away for the briefest of seconds. But the sight that came froze her completely.

A door that had been closed before had now swung fully open. There was barely any light inside the room that was revealed. But somehow, she could see in pretty clearly.

And it had to be the master bedroom. The furnishings were even more dated than out here, red velvet everywhere you looked, erotic prints up on the walls. The kind of bedroom she immediately thought of as a cheesy-looking place.

The huge bed at the center was perfectly round. The quilt and pillows were in rumpled disarray and mostly on the floor. But lying at the middle of it was Maxi – her heart leapt when she saw him. He was splayed out like a starfish on the mattress. Only it wasn't by his own choice that he was that way.

His shirt was off and there were bloody scratches all over his chest and shoulders. And his feet were bare. His skin was so slick, top to toe, that it was glistening like he'd just been in a swimming pool. And his head was tipped right back. His eyes were very wide. They fastened on her urgently.

The two women were with him, the blonde and the brunette, their skin so pallid that it could have been composed of vapor. They were both wearing diaphanous robes of no discernible color, somewhere between blue and green and gray. The outlines of each of their figures were clearly visible through the filmy cloth, their hips and nipples and the shadowed triangles between their legs.

They were both crouched over Maxi, their long hair hanging down like tiny waterfalls. And their slender hands were everywhere, pinning him in place.

The blonde one had a palm clamped firmly over Maxi's mouth. They each had hold of one of his wrists. The brunette's free hand disappeared beneath his jeans. As Lindy watched, the fabric moved, and Maxi's face creased up with agony and something else.

And she was yelling out before she even knew it.

"*Stop that!*"

Then her gaze swung back to Hunter, who was grinning.

"Make them *stop*!"

"Only you can make that happen." And he gazed across her shoulder rather wistfully. "My daughters are wonderfully well-skilled in bed. I know that from personal experience. The only problem is, their fingernails are awful sharp."

From behind her came a stifled moan. She didn't turn around again, but her whole body shuddered.

And then Hunter did something strange. He slowly lifted his right arm in the direction of the window.

And the outside world came flooding in.

She could suddenly hear traffic noise. She could hear birds singing in the trees. And she jerked her head in that direction.

Sunlight had begun pushing in across the roof terrace of this apartment.

"Almost fully day now," Hunter said. "Which means it's almost time to go. But we're not going from here empty handed, Lindy. The only genuine question is, which one of you are we taking with us?"

And she struggled to think straight, but that turned out to be impossible. Mostly because what was being asked of her *was* utterly impossible. What kind of choice was *this*? Let her friend die, or offer up her own life in his place. Or perhaps it wasn't even death that was involved here.

All those times her Mom had taken her to church came rushing back. All those sermons that the priest had given. Would she be dropped into eternal flame? Or lost in some dank, bottomless gray gloom forever?

And she couldn't help it. Tears were dripping down her face again, her entire body crumpling.

"Take the amulet off, Lindy."

"Please, haven't you done enough?" She didn't even recognize her own voice, it was so choked up. "You've had your fun. Can't you just leave me be?"

She'd never begged for anything, but she was begging now. She could make out through the shimmering blur of her own tears that he'd stepped in a little closer.

"It doesn't work that way," he said. "There has to be a resolution. Ours has been an interesting story, Lindy. But what use is a story if it doesn't have a proper ending?"

And her mind was going round like a small rodent in a cage. Trying to find a way out, but she could see none. This wasn't fair! It wasn't right! She knew that she was far from perfect, but she just didn't *deserve* this!

John was glancing at his watch.

"Ah well. It looks like we're going to have to make do with a man."

"*No!*"

One of his eyebrows came up.

She tried to ignore that, glancing back at Maxi, who was still firmly in the women's grip. And a sudden calmness took hold of her out of plain nowhere. She could still feel teardrops running down her face, but was aware that she'd stopped shaking.

None of this was Maxi's doing. He wouldn't even *be* here if he hadn't been her only friend. And when she turned her face back to John Hunter once again, her head was slightly bowed.

The first moment she'd walked into that hotel room, she had stepped willingly into a trap. It had closed around her very slowly, that much was for sure. But now its metal jaws were tightening behind her, and she had no choice but to accept that for a fact.

She gave a brief tight nod, her breathing very shallow. And then reached up for the amulet's cord with both her hands.

Stopped.

Once she had the necklace off, what was to stop these damned creatures from taking them both?

"Let him go first," she said, as firmly as she could manage.

"This is no time to be making demands."

But there was a faint tone of surprised amusement to his deep, dark voice, and so she set her teeth.

"Let him *go*. It's *me* you want, and we both know it."

Hunter raised two fingers to his chin and fixed her with a smile again.

"You have a point."

And then he gestured to the women on the bed. They both frowned petulantly but they edged back a little, setting Maxi free.

He immediately came stumbling to his feet, except his limbs were nerveless. He was staggering around and almost tripping the same moment he was up. He was staring at the carpet stupidly, his head going around. Trying to find something, like his shirt and shoes maybe. Perhaps even his gun. He wasn't acting sanely, and she had to snap him out of this.

So she yelled out: "Forget all that! Get *out* of here!"

His eyes went to her and his brow creased up. He reached out with a hand and tried to speak. His lips moved but no sound came out.

"Forget about me, Maxi! Go!"

His head shook, a spastic motion. He came teetering out of the room. Only his eyes weren't vacant any longer. There was agony, but strong determination too. He simply wasn't going to abandon her.

And she could see it in his gaze, for the very first time. He actually believed he loved her.

She let that sink in a second. Then she snatched up her gun where it was lying at her feet and pointed it at him.

"Go, or I'll kill you myself!"

The haunted look on his face burned itself into her memory as he registered that. And then he turned away, did as she'd said, the front door swinging almost shut behind him as he stumbled past it.

She could hear him going down the stairs a moment later. Listened to those noises fade.

And after that she went silent herself, since there was nothing left.

43 – Epiphany

Maybe she had always known this, that it would end very badly for her.

Maybe it had always lain there, like a dark kernel of knowledge at the bottom of her soul. Had her father sensed it too and *that* was why he'd hated her … understanding he had passed his genes on to a vessel that was headed for a dark dead end?

She certainly hated herself, didn't she? There was little other explanation for the way she lived. The drugs and drink. The constant work. The solitude. The meaningless encounters and the escalating roughness of them, and the way she had encouraged and connived in that. Who *did* that to herself? She'd been a piece of flotsam carried down a fast, unruly river for a long while now, and she'd done nothing in the least to stop it. Not a single thing.

In a strange way, she'd always imagined it would be like this. Not the precise circumstances … there was no way *anybody* could imagine that. But she'd always believed that – in her final, faltering moments, staring her extinction squarely in the face – there would be …

What was the word that she was looking for?

Epiphany. A revelation. A final few seconds of utter clarity, quite crystalline. When at long last she could see herself for what she truly was. Understand the world around her and know her place in it. Then glance back across her shoulder, and plainly see the whole path that had brought her to this terminus.

Crystal clarity. Here it was.

She drew in a breath that was as clean and cold as though it had been filtered through newly-fallen snow, and then let her gun slide from her hands again.

That apart, she was incapable of movement. And the creatures in this room were closing in on her. Both women had come out of the bedroom and were standing either side of her, back past her shoulders, so that she could sense them more than see them. And Hunter had stepped up to her as close as he dared. He was barely a yard away. And she wondered dully what they were all waiting for. But then it came back to her through her swirling thoughts.

The amulet.

"A deal's a deal," John Hunter smiled. "I've kept up my end."

"Just a few more seconds," she heard herself mumbling.

"And what difference will a few more make?"

"I want to be sure Maxi has got out okay."

"He has. He's standing on the sidewalk, shirtless and shoeless in the sunlight of a New York morning."

"And I'm supposed to take your word for that? Can I go take a look?"

One of his hands came up, the palm out flat. He had stopped smiling.

"And let you out into the daylight too? Do you believe I'm stupid, Lindy?"

And he had a point. There was no way that she was going to fool him. She was surrounded and cut off. The game was up. There was no sense trying to fight this any longer.

So – as slowly and as smoothly as she had done anything in her entire life – she reached up for the cord that held the amulet again.

It felt tight against her neck. Felt like it was digging into her skin. Almost as though it was trying to hold on. As though some power inside the sacred metal didn't want their bond to break. But she ignored that, kept on prying at it till she worked it loose. Then it was slipping up, only it tangled with her hair.

She set her teeth against the pain and yanked it free, a couple of red fibers going with it.

Held it out toward John with her forefinger and thumb.

And she was readying herself to let her fingers part and drop it.

When the apartment's door came slamming open so hard it was almost like a violent explosion.

Peter Renzo – wild eyes gawking from his stubbled face – was standing framed there in the gap that it had left.

***

His suit was rumpled and his hair askew. He looked like he had been up the whole night, the same way she had. And Lindy couldn't understand why that should be the case. But she knew one thing for certain.

He'd be dead in seconds if he kept this up. These creatures would turn on him and take him apart like a carcass on a butcher's slab. He had nothing to offer them, and no protection either.

Then she saw what he had brought with him. Not the gun in his right hand ... that he'd be holding one was obvious enough. It was a big revolver, with the hammer cocked.

But he also had a silver crucifix between the fingers of his left hand. A length of chain was dangling from it, so she guessed that he had snatched it from around his neck on his way up here. A pendant he had always worn, perhaps? Except she'd never seen it before, never known a thing about it. It was pretty large for something that you wore against your chest, around four inches tall and with a clear, spread-eagled figure standing out atop it. What would make a person carry such a thing around with him, pressed up close against his heart?

Lindy heard the two women behind her jerk toward the little man and hiss. But Hunter was more measured in the way that he reacted.

His head came smoothly over. One thick eyebrow lifted, and the grin returned.

"Ah, really? A Christian? But you're not dealing with vampires here. You do understand that, don't you?"

"*Don't* tell me what I'm dealing with."

Renzo's face had turned to stone, his eyes like flint.

"I *know* what I'm frigging dealing with."

And he edged a few paces into the room.

"I'm dealing with scum. I'm dealing with shit. Detritus from the bottom of the barrel of existence. And it doesn't matter what you're called. It's all the same. You're from the dark side, and you're dirt. Whereas this, if you believe –"

And he held up the cross a little higher.

"This is cleanliness and light, and will defeat you."

Even in the state of mind that she was in, Lindy couldn't quite believe what she was hearing, seeing.

"Peter," she tried to call out, but it only emerged as a shallow whisper. "*Please. Leave.*"

His gaze met hers. And he looked completely in control, like he knew precisely what he was doing. But how could that be?

"Maxi's safe," he told her in a quieter tone. "He's down in my car. I got a quarter of the story out of him, then figured out the rest."

"You have to go yourself."

"And leave you here? No way."

"They'll *kill* you if you don't."

"No, I don't think so, since what are they really? Figments, from humanity's worst nightmares. Scary, but they're little more than shadows when you look at them straight on. And the light from this can sear them."

He brandished the crucifix again.

"There's a prayer going through your head right at the moment, isn't there?" Hunter asked him with another smirk.

And Renzo nodded almost proudly. "You're damned right there is."

"Yea, though I walk through the shadow of the Valley of Death? That old one? How very unimaginative."

But Lindy noticed that he wasn't moving any closer to the smaller cop. The truth was he was frozen to the spot, as though the soles of his shoes had been stapled to the floor.

"The Lord walks beside you?"

"That's right," Renzo hissed.

"You will fear no evil?"

"That's fucking *right*!"

And Renzo held the cross above him at full arm's length.

A chink of sunlight – a tiny beam that had found its way in from between the drapes – struck it abruptly. And the silver pendant broke it up into a thousand shards, so that the crucifix flashed brilliantly and the room's four walls were covered with bright sparks.

Lindy was aware of both the women drawing slightly back. But Hunter held his ground.

"It's only a piece of metal, Christian," he pointed out, although he did it with his eyes half closed, his face becoming darker. "Why would you believe that it has any power?"

"It doesn't matter what the object is," Peter came back at him instantly. "What matters is the person with it."

"Is that so?"

"Yeah, that's *exactly* so." And Renzo jerked his head at Lindy. "She's trying to believe right now because she's desperate and has no choice. But I believe because I know the truth. Light will *always* defeat darkness in the end. That's not just religion, ghoul, it's science too."

And he started moving again, carefully but quickly. He wasn't coming any closer, but was circling around their little group. Moving crabwise, his gaze not dropping away for a second, his gun aimed squarely at the creatures and the crucifix still held defiantly aloft.

At which point, Lindy noticed something so bizarre she could only imagine that her eyes were playing tricks on her. Peter was in semi-dimness, now. And had moved right away from the little shaft of sunlight.

But the silver crucifix … it still seemed to be glowing, had a lambent, almost living sheen. Pulses of pale luminance seemed to be spilling across it.

"Stay right where you are, sarge," Renzo was saying to her. "Keep hold of that amulet for all you're worth."

But he couldn't have things his own way forever.

Hunter murmured a word in a guttural tongue. And on that signal, both his daughters stiffened up and bared their pointed teeth. And then the pair of them went lunging at the little cop. And he stopped dead, thrusting the cross out at them.

It flashed again, even in the darkness. But it didn't sear them after all, as it turned out. It was suddenly like they were moving underwater, their movements becoming very slow. The passage of their arms and legs left after-images behind. They ought to have been on him in an instant, but they couldn't even seem to reach him. And they appeared to realize what was happening, because their bright green eyes went wide with shock, the edges of their wide mouths stretching back.

They looked as though they'd been drowned, the next second after that. Both their frames became translucent. All their savage beauty sloughed away, revealing them for what they really were. Faces that were merely fanged skulls, mummified skin stretched across them. Narrow, withered arms that ended with disfigured claws. Hair that wasn't blonde or dark or really hair at all, more like some kind of wispy fungus.

These were monsters from the darkest side of nature, being shown in their true form.

"See how the light strips away the lies?" Renzo was announcing to the room in general.

He was blinking quickly and perspiration was running down his face, but his tone was just as solid and convinced as it had been when he had first arrived. He started edging sideways again, though he kept his focus on the women.

Hunter blurted out a couple more of those strange words. Both the sisters looked across, then ground their jaws and tried to get at Peter in one massive final effort. But their movements became even slower, when they attempted that. And they suddenly recoiled. They bounced away as though they'd hit a rubber wall. Instantly went back to their human shapes, but they were flailing away from the little cop.

Hunter hadn't left the spot in all this while. His green eyes were burning, frustration oozing off him like a viscous liquid. He'd thought he had won. He'd *known* he was the victor. And was there anything more painful than that kind of certainty dissolving?

Renzo reached the drapes. Shoved his gun into his pocket and then grabbed the cloth. Yanked it backward from the glass, the runners letting out a piercing shriek. A wash of dazzling yellow sunlight poured into the living room.

The three figures near Lindy faded to the briefest outlines and then vanished altogether. But Hunter's lips were moving again, just before he left. And his last words seemed to linger … seemed to echo on the air around her.

"Ah, well. Not this morning perhaps, but we've all the time in the entire world."

And he grinned a final time, the outlines of his eyes fixing on Lindy.

"I'll be seeing you again. Real soon."

44 – The Church

And after that, it wasn't so much a matter of moving, running, as of falling. Tumbling headlong into a vast gravity well of motion. Hammering past the front door. Slamming through the fire door as well. Almost risking broken limbs on the wild descent down the concrete steps. Lindy's joints had become spastic, her limbs trying to fly off in every which direction, and if Peter hadn't been supporting her she would have collapsed long before she'd reached street level.

The ragged sound of their own breathing followed them the whole way down. As if a pack of wolves were following them closely. The insistent rhythm of it drove them even harder.

And then they hit the lobby. The doorman who had ushered Lindy in seemed to be back in control of his own mind. He was sitting slackly behind his desk, rubbing at his face and obviously trying to remember what had happened. As they burst through, he looked up. Tried to straighten. Tried to call out. But they just ignored him.

Daylight was ahead of them, beyond the glass doors. And they kept pushing toward it.

The sidewalk banged beneath their feet. The hardest paving slabs of any city in the world, more like steel than stone. And it jolted them. Seemed to wake them from the nightmare they'd been living through. The combined sounds of a Manhattan summer's morning washed across them.

Why were they still running? Hunter and the others were gone. But common sense was just a distantly recalled thing, sheer adrenaline controlling them. Their only impulse was to get away, put as much distance as was possible between themselves and this damned place. And so they kept on going.

Peter was directing her toward an aged Mitsubishi station wagon by the curb. It had pink primer on its wheel arches, and scuffed paintwork. But she could make out Maxi's slumped shape on the rear seat, so this had to be Renzo's car. He yanked open the passenger door and helped her in.

And then he was behind the wheel. Hitting the ignition. Stamping on the gas. When he swung out, there was a squeal of brakes and hooting from behind, but he took no notice of that.

He hit the intersection with 59th and took a violent left. And then he had his cell phone out, was talking on it.

As they sped across the East Side avenues, Lindy felt her breathing slow. The shaking of her limbs slowed down. Her mind started to return to something approximating normal. She'd almost died – or worse – back there. And she had accepted that and even bowed her head. And that can change you.

It was almost like she'd been reborn into this world, a place she'd thought she'd never see again. But here it was, still around and staring back at her. She blinked, trying to take it in. Had it always moved as fast as it was moving now?

And then she stared across at Peter, who was still discussing something on his cell. He looked the way he almost always did, compact, formal, with a thin shadow of stubble on his chin and jaw. But his eyes were no longer gleaming now that the threat was behind them. His face had turned a little slack and shapeless, all the savage determination gone.

The kind of guy she wouldn't even take a second glance at, usually. Mr. Ordinary. But he'd saved her.

He mumbled "Yeah, sure," several times, then pocketed the phone, put both hands on the steering wheel, and pushed the station wagon even faster so its chassis rattled. They were headed out across the Queensboro Bridge, the silhouettes of skyscrapers behind them.

Lindy tried to think of something to say, and finally realized what it had to be.

"How'd you know we were in trouble? How'd you even find us?"

He glanced at her briefly before staring straight ahead again.

"First, there was the sheer damned weirdness of the cases we were working on. And the other violent stuff as well, all very far from natural. Then, there was the way you acted to me in the coffee room … I've known you years, and that ain't you."

He paused to let that sink in. He had somehow sensed she'd been possessed?

"And then you disappear completely off the map. And I keep on trying to get hold of Maxi, and it turns out I can't raise him either. And so I get your cell phones pinged. Guess what? You're – for no reason I can think of – both at the same place where this thing started."

"That can't be the whole of it. Why'd you come in brandishing that cross?"

His head dropped for a few seconds, but when it came back up his face had regained some of its fiercer tautness.

"I'm not sure you'd understand."

"Well try me."

"Have you ever been religious?"

"When I was a little girl, perhaps. Not these days, obviously."

"So then you think of evil as a mental thing. The act of choosing one course or another. Whereas to me, it's physical, a real and living force. An entity that takes on many forms. And I've been sensing the presence of something like that ever since this all began."

When he glanced across at her again, he even managed to force a tiny, quirky smile.

"It's not something I suspect a lot," he pointed out. "In fact, this is my very first time. And believe me when I say I never thought – not for an instant – I'd actually wind up having to confront something like this. But I have Faith. And Faith, like all things, has a dark flipside."

He'd simply accepted the idea that there were supernatural creatures out there in the night? Who *thought* like that these days? But then she saw the truth. An awful lot of people did, right the way across the world. It was modernism that was quite uncommon.

She remembered Maxi and stared back at him. Still bare-chested, he was folded like a limp rag across the rear seats. His eyes were only open a crack, and he seemed quite oblivious to everything around him.

"But I've gotta know the whole of it," Peter was saying to her. "Tell me what's been going on, from start to finish and in exact detail."

Which was going to be embarrassing, to say the least. But when she tried, it was the oddest thing. Her rational mind kept trying to recoil. Kept refusing to recall stuff straight. Insisting it was all a dream. She had to struggle and dig hard to retrieve *any* memories, so that she ended up recounting only small, disjointed fragments. It was as though she had been heavily drugged. Only a few stark images stood out clearly.

"You remember nothing more than that?" Peter asked her, with a note of sharpness in his voice. "You being straight with me?"

"Completely. But I can describe what John Hunter looks like when he's not in human form."

"Wendigos, huh?" he nodded. "Just one of the thousands of names in this world for a bunch of goddamned demons."

"But what do we do about them? Run? Hide? Fight?"

"None of the above," was the small man's response, taking a sharp right onto an unfamiliar street in Queens. "First, we rest. They won't be back till night and that's a way off, so we've time."

***

The building that they finally pulled up in front of proved to be a church, although you wouldn't have known it from the outside. It was just a single story place, whitewash on its outer walls and with a low roof that was patched and tarred in places. A medium-sized, gray-haired man with a bald crown was waiting for them by the entrance. He was wearing a bottle green short-sleeved shirt and old beige slacks, and had on an anxious expression. So this was obviously the person Peter had been talking to during the journey here.

"Lindy," Peter told her, "this is Father Stuart Donnelly, a friend of mine."

The priest favored her with a soft, guarded smile, then ushered her inside. And when she looked back, she saw that Peter had returned to the station wagon to fetch Maxi.

It was very plain and quiet inside. Like this was another small enclosed world all of its own, a million miles from the racket of Manhattan. The walls were painted matt off-white. The floors were a hardwood whose sheen had been dulled down the passing years. There were individual wooden chairs instead of pews, a simple podium at the far end instead of a pulpit, and a crude table that had to double as an altar. A distinctly humble place.

Donnelly showed her to a chair, then pulled another one across so she could set her feet up on it. A woman of about his age came hurrying across with a blanket, which she arranged over Lindy.

"Genuine creatures from out of the dark?" the priest was asking Peter.

"Three of them, as real as me."

Then Peter crouched down next to Lindy.

"Stuart's done some exorcisms," he explained, "so he believes this stuff as much as I do."

But she was barely taking all this in. Her mind seemed to be closing down. Her eyesight had blurred, and the voices she was hearing sounded very far away.

And so it sounded pretty stupid, even to herself, when she told them, "I don't think I can rest."

"You must," said Father Donnelly. "You've the hardest night of your whole life ahead of you."

Hadn't she already been through several of those? Something cold and hard was being pressed against one of her hands – a glass of water. And something much smaller was being dropped into her other palm.

"Diazepam," the priest explained. "Mostly I rely on prayer but there are times when chemistry is much more useful."

45 – A Handful of Hours

Curiously, she did not dream. Or at least she didn't remember doing so, like her mind had cut out activities of that sort while it was trying to repair itself.

But she awoke with a start, everything rushing back the moment she hit consciousness. Being stalked the entire length of midtown. Being besieged inside her flat. And then the battle in the woods. And trying to save Maxi.

She sat up sharply, her heart thundering, and stared across at him. He was set between two chairs the same way she was, had a blanket over him as well. Was fast asleep. Looked peaceful. Someone had put iodine and Band Aids on his wounds, and she was pleased to see that. But did he *genuinely* believe he was in love with her? She'd never known that.

They were alone in here, no sign of the aged priest or Peter.

She got up very slowly. Her whole body ached. She thought to look at her watch and it was now gone two in the afternoon. She couldn't understand how she had slept so soundly for so long until she remembered the pills.

But night was only a handful of hours away. And it couldn't be the case that Peter had run off. So where exactly was he?

She found him sitting on the front porch stoop, in the shade of an awning. His coat was off, his back to her and – curiously – he was smoking a cigarette. She'd never seen him do that thing before. When he heard her footsteps coming up behind him, his head turned slightly but he didn't look at her. He simply sat there, bent over slightly, waiting for her to join him.

It was a *brutally* hot day. The street was bathed in light so yellow that she had to squint, the towers of Manhattan wavering like ghostly mirages in the distance. But she ignored all that, lowering herself painfully till she was sitting next to Renzo.

"Didn't know you smoked," she said.

"Used to. Gave up many years ago, except I miss it every day. So – circumstances being what they are – I thought I'd treat myself. Dumb, really."

He offered her one and she took it, and then peered around as best she could at her surroundings. This was a deeply average area of Queens, all single story houses not too different from the building they were sat in front of, not much traffic passing by.

"This where you live?" she asked.

Peter creased his face up wryly and then shook his head.

"Bring those assholes anywhere near my wife and kids? Not likely. I live in a different district of this borough. Happen to know Father Stuart from some church outings I've been on." And he paused thoughtfully, pursing his lips before speaking again. "And you're Brooklyn, right? You were brought up there?"

"Yup."

"And when that male demon appeared to you, one of the shapes it took on was the shape of your dead father?"

She recalled telling him about that in the car. It had been one of the few things she'd remembered clearly. But Peter seemed to be driving at something, and she wondered what. His head had gotten noticeably bowed.

"I don't think I've ever mentioned this," he said, "but my Pop was a beat cop too. He knew your old man. Patrick Grady, right?"

"They were friends?" she came back at him a little edgily.

"No, not exactly." And Peter wasn't even looking at her anymore. "My Pop didn't think too much of yours. It must have been rough, growing up around a man like that."

And so her Dad had had a reputation that had spread out far beyond the walls of their family home. She hadn't even guessed at that. God, what had she ever done to deserve any of this? She felt a sense of helplessness begin to overtake her, but it was a familiar one, coming from her past. And she'd always done her best to bury that, and so she fought against it once again, holding back what felt like the onset of tears.

And tried to answer like a calm, sensible adult.

"It was … pretty bad."

"I'm sorry. Am I prying here?"

"I … sort of. I mean, no. I mean, I don't quite see what you are trying to lead up to."

Peter took one last draw on his cigarette, scowled at it pensively and threw it away, following it with the rest of the pack. And then his head bobbed up a little.

"It's just, I was talking to Father Stuart while you were out. Talking about these creatures and the way they operate. And they often prey on people with bad pasts. People with bad childhoods. Use that stuff against them, since it's primal and goes very deep. All this didn't happen by accident, Lindy. You were chosen."

That last word cut through her like a knife and she became extremely still, just listening to him speak.

"We're going up against them in a few hours' time. And they'll use this stuff to try and hurt us. So it's best you tell me what exactly is the worst that they can throw against us."

And he still wasn't looking at her.

"Worst?"

"I'm not sure you even know this. I feel pretty awkward mentioning it now. But your father didn't only have a reputation with his fists. He ..."

Oh my God ... be brave.

"Go on."

"Used to force hookers to do stuff, so he wouldn't bust them."

Christ! An image of her Mom's face, bruised and bloodied, sprang up in her mind's eye. He'd been doing that to her, and he'd been cheating on her too?

"And when the club scene started up, he used to do the same to chicks with coke or exes in their purse." Peter paused to rub his face with both his hands. "That isn't the behavior of a man who likes sex, Lindy. That's the behavior of a man who hates women. So I have to ask."

And he finally looked straight at her.

"You? Ever?"

A few times in her adult life, usually very late at night and when she couldn't sleep, she'd suddenly imagined that that kind of thing had happened and she'd simply blocked it out. And that idea had frozen her like nothing else could. Turned her to a living block of ice, barely able to so much as blink.

But no. It wasn't real. The more that she delved back, the more that she was sure of it. He'd only ever struck her.

And so she shook her head.

"He wasn't interested in me that way."

"Sure of it?"

"I'm certain."

"Well, that's good to know," Peter nodded gently.
"Do you believe in previous lives?"
"That's Hinduism that you're thinking of."
"It's just, I keep on wondering what awful thing I might have done in a previous life to get born as the daughter to a man like that."

Peter reached across and gripped her very lightly by the shoulder.

"You don't get to choose who your family is. The only thing you get to choose is who you are, and what you do with that."

"But doesn't one thing shape the other?"

"Only if you let it."

And then a noise brought them both turning round. Maxi was standing in the church's doorway, still bare-chested, his face glistening with sweat. He blinked at them, then peered around.

"Queens? What the hell is I doin' in Queens, mon?"

Then his strength seemed to desert him and he slumped against the doorpost.

"Tell me that were all a dream las' night?"

Lindy looked away, and Peter looked apologetic.

46 – Crusade

After they had washed and straightened themselves up, they traveled a few more blocks in Peter's station wagon. Maxi now had on a pale yellow shirt and a pair of poorly fitting Hush Puppies from the church's thrift collection, and he didn't look too pleased about it. But Peter had given him his back-up piece

None of them was exactly happy. Lindy caught a few pale, dim reflections of herself in the station wagon's windows, and the expression on her face was largely the same as Maxi's. She looked stunned and apprehensive.

How'd it come to this? She couldn't understand how normal life, however twisted and confusing, had been transformed into this damned thing. This nightmare become real. This new reality where all the rules had broken down. She might have been dragged along to church a few times, but she'd been schooled mostly in logic, science. And had grown up believing all the legends of the past, all those strange beliefs and superstitions, were merely stories told around campfires, nothing more.

And now the flickering shadows cast by those old flames had steadied and solidified. Had taken on a tangible form and stepped in her direction. She'd been through *so much* awfulness, the past couple of nights. More than enough to convince her what was happening was genuine. But there was still a small part of her mind that refused to accept it.

Only Peter – hunched over the steering wheel – looked certain. Grim. Full of resolve. And by this stage, she thought she understood why that was.

He was on a mission. Maybe even a crusade. He truly believed in Evil in its physical form, and now that he had been confronted by it he was going to beat it. Prove that his religion was far stronger than the things out in the night. Yeah, Jesus Saves.

When they pulled up to the curb again, it was outside the frontage of a rifle store. *Sam's Happy Hunting*, read the sign above the plate glass window, and there was a heavy metal grid pulled down across it.

"But we've already got guns," she pointed out.

But Peter cut her off with a brisk shake of his head. He'd obviously been thinking this whole matter out in detail.

The sound of their doors clacking open as they got out made a bunch of small Hispanic kids – at play on the opposite sidewalk – stop what they were doing and then stare across. The mid-afternoon heat battered at Lindy like a hammer, turgid with humidity, so heavy that her lungs seemed to struggle as they drew it in. The air was wavering and, when she cast her gaze off further down the street, she could see a silvery shimmer spreading out across the pavement.

The inside of the store smelled of wood shavings, oil, and metal. A middle-aged man was standing behind the counter in a camouflage shirt and gray jeans. He had a slightly sunburned, rather rumpled face, a broad moustache, and hair down past his shoulders. But he acknowledged Peter with a friendly nod and then peered curiously at she and Maxi.

"Another church-group friend of yours?" Lindy asked, *sotto voce*.

"Yeah."

And Peter shook hands firmly with the man, introduced his companions, and then explained what he wanted.

***

Sam took them through to a room at the back, which had a wide desk with tools laid out on it. Pliers of several different sizes. Molds. A Bunsen burner, and a vise.

Peter said to her, "And now I'm going to need that amulet of yours," and held his palm out.

Lindy stared him in the eyes, unsure what was going through his mind. But he'd come through for them so far, so she reached up for the leather cord and took the thing off from around her neck. Handed it carefully to him. He turned it around between the tips of his fingers, his gaze becoming quizzical.

"Matchi Manitou, huh?"

"It's supposed to translate into 'Great God.'"

"There are nine billion names for God," Sam put in. "Science fiction feller wrote a whole story about it."

Peter passed the metal shape to him.

"How many do you reckon you can get squeezed out of this?"

Sam studied it himself, then produced a pocket knife and cut the cord away in one swift motion, which made Lindy jolt.

"Just hold on a minute!"

Except that Peter grasped her gently, pushing her arms back. She was forced to watch in numb silence as Sam produced a little set of scales and weighed the thing.

"Real heavy for something that size. Heavier than normal iron."

"From sacred ground, apparently," Peter told him.

"Yeah? Maybe it has moral weight, then."

Sam lit the Bunsen burner, put the amulet into some kind of long-handled deep metal spoon and then held it over the flame. And after a short while of that, the face of the Matchi Manitou began to glow an increasingly bright red.

Lindy started to feel panic overtake her.

"Hey, that's the only thing that –"

When she tried to stop this, though, Peter took hold of her upper arms again.

"It's the only thing that's kept you safe so far. And yeah, I get that."

His face was very close to hers, his features rigid and his dark eyes burning with a cold assurance.

"But as an amulet, it only works defensively, and that isn't good enough. We need to go on the attack. We have to take the fight to them. Which means we need some kind of *weapon*, not merely a shield. If the metal's sacred, then it shouldn't matter what shape it is in."

"You *sure* of that?"

As she watched, the features of the Matchi Manitou began to flatten out and blend into each other. And within another minute, it had been reduced to just a glistening blob of molten iron.

"Caliber?" Sam was asking.

"We're all .38s, I think."

Lindy steadied her thoughts and nodded jerkily. Sam selected some molds from a stack of them at the rear of his desk and began tipping the heated metal in.

"Just about enough for three slugs," he informed them, "and that's stretching it."

Which made Peter's eyebrows come bobbing up almost comically.

"There's some math for you," he breathed. "Three rounds. Three of us, and three of them. So each of us gets just one shot apiece."

"We can't afford to miss, in other words."

He nodded.

"I'm afraid that means we'll have to let those things get right up close. And do you think that you can live with that?"

Lindy looked away a while. She'd been letting John Hunter get right up close this entire week. And now that she knew what he really was, the memory of that repelled her. Sickened her. But angered her as well.

It wasn't only Peter who was on a crusade by this stage, since she was ready for revenge.

"You'd be surprised what I can live with."

47 – The Park

In the end, it had to be the park. It was where all this had started, after all. And besides, where else would it be?

These things that they were hoping to face down ... they weren't from anywhere around here. Hadn't sprung up from the heated, clunking sidewalks. Hadn't taken shape between the shadows of the tall skyscrapers. They had come here from the countryside. They were a form of darkness that had started off as green. Nature's aberration, not a man-made thing. More at home among the foliage and trees.

The three detectives waited on the Rustic Bridge awhile, propping themselves against the stonework, fidgeting uncomfortably. Casting glances out across the huge, grassy expanses. Squinting again, since it remained bright initially. The surface of the pond beneath them captured the sun's yellow light and threw it back like molten gold. Tiny winged insects were pulled this way and that by the rising thermals. Tourists, dog-walkers and families went by. Even the little kids were sluggish, whiny in the stifling heat.

But then the sun was going down, the number of passers-by was thinning. A woman went past them in full jogging kit, perspiration streaming down her face, kept on going for another hundred yards, then floundered to a halt and doubled over. Yanked her baseball cap from off her head and mopped her brow with it. Gave up and went hobbling away.

Off to the west, the sky had turned a vivid carmine color, so unbroken that the buildings standing up against it looked completely black.

"Not the time to let your guard down yet," Peter murmured to the other two. "It's coming."

And he meant the night, and they all knew it.

He'd brought a bottle of water along and they passed it in between them, taking heavy gulps. And when it was empty, Peter found a bin to toss it into.

"Hate littering," he tried to grin.

"You could be facin' death here," Maxi asked him, "and you bothered about bein' tidy?"

"Don't even think about that. Don't even *think* about the possibility of losing."

Maxi gawked at him

"All that I can think about is turnin' round an' runnin' till I reach Jamaica."

"Nothing's keeping you here. You can give me back my gun if you like."

Maxi thought about that for a second, and then his face tightened up. His head gave a quick shake that set his sweaty cornrows flying.

"Strength in numbers, yamman?"

"Yamman. Yes indeed."

Peter shrugged, then looked away. They were completely alone on the bridge by now, no one even coming near them. And the carmine sheen away to the west was bleeding off along its edges, navy blue replacing it. Streetlamps had started coming on.

Everything out here that could cast a shadow was casting a longer one. And they stretched out until they merged, fusing into one gray blur. There was a final red flash as the sun went down. Then they had moved into the night, and there was no way back.

The traffic noises of the city drifted to them faintly. It was like they were standing on a dark and square-edged island that was sitting in a sea of badly fractured light, thousands of lit windows – great ascending columns of them – off in the distance and streams of headlamps passing by. Normal life was still close at hand, but they'd been separated from it somehow, like a huge glass barrier had just come sliding down.

"Why's there no one?" Maxi asked, almost in a whisper.

And the others knew exactly what he meant. Things weren't the way they had been back in the Seventies any longer. People didn't flee the park as soon as darkness fell. There ought to be, at very least, a couple of kids with skateboards still, a pro dog-walker or some people simply wandering. But there was nothing like that.

Peter reached under his shirt and pulled his crucifix out into view, letting it drop down against the fabric.

"Either people sense there's something going down, or they've been *made* to sense it. Those things want us out here on our own, since we're the only people in this city who know what they really are."

"But where are *they*?"

Lindy seemed to come to life and looked around.

"It's too bright here," she announced. "I was told it by an expert. They cling to the darkness."

Both of her companions stared into the deeper shadows.

"You wan' us to go further in?" Maxi asked. "Ya sure that's wise?"

"I don't see that we've got any choice."

"They're *giving* us no choice," said Peter grimly. "Damn, this hasn't even really started yet, and they're already calling the shots."

He gnawed his lip with his front teeth for a few seconds. Then he straightened up.

"Stick together at all times. Our lives depend on it."

They nodded.

***

She'd never been afraid of the dark. She'd always seen it clearly for precisely what it was, a primitive thing, your ancient instincts screaming at you. *Wild animals here!* And there'd been none before.

But it was screaming at her violently now, because she knew that there were real predators out there in that murk.

The deeper Lindy got into the darkness then the more that she could feel herself shrinking. Getting ever smaller till she felt like she'd been reduced to the size of a child again, the weight of the night compressing her inward. She was shaking and could barely breathe. There was something clogging up her throat -- it wouldn't budge however much she swallowed. And her eyesight kept on flickering, blurring. Not that there was much to see.

When she glanced back across her shoulder, the pool of light around the Rustic Bridge had been reduced to a mere blot. The lines of streetlamps on the roads that transected this park looked like fairy lights hung in the windows of a house a mile away. A little of the traffic noise still reached her, the occasional horn. But mostly it was a muffled sound, similar to waves breaking on some distant shore.

She could hear her footfalls on the turf. And could hear Maxi's hissing breath, the words he kept on mumbling.

"Strength in numbers," he was saying. "Strength in numbers, strength in numbers."

Like a mantra, endlessly and mindlessly. He had been petrified last night, even more terrified than she had been. And now, that fear was devouring him all over again. And that being the case, why was he pushing on beside her? Had what she thought she'd seen deep in his eyes last night been real? She felt the urge to glance across at him, but decided against it.

They didn't have their guns drawn yet. Didn't want to show their hand too early. Lindy started wondering how clearly these things could read minds. They could manage it to some extent ... she was certain about that. But when she'd been out in the woods with old George Greentree by her side, both of them had done things that had managed to surprise John Hunter.

Maxi began to lose his bearings, started wandering off course. Peter saw that, reached out startledly and grabbed him by the shoulder.

"Strength in numbers, pal," he murmured.

They went round a large gray boulder.

There was a small bunch of trees directly ahead of them, no more than an uneven black shape against the darkness. Lindy got an instinct, felt herself draw to a halt and sensed the others do the same.

Three separate patches of pale fog moved out and floated just above the grass in front of those dark trees.

They stopped moving. They did not change shape. Simply hung there with their edges swirling. Waiting.

All six of them waiting, now. The humans and the other things. The three detectives were standing practically shoulder-to-shoulder, their arms hanging by their sides. Lindy's instincts told her to keep quiet. Except the impasse just went on and on, and they couldn't stay like this forever.

So she forced herself to croak out, "Peter?"

"Let's see what they do," he said.

"They're not going to do anything. The bastards are just taunting us. It's what they're best at."

Peter sucked air in between his teeth. Maxi started moving for his piece, but Peter reached across again and stopped him.

Then he seemed to come to a decision.

"Hey!" he yelled out at the balls of fog. "You're awful quiet?"

He balled his fists and thrust his chin out.

"Remember me? I'm the guy who robbed you of your prize, last night! You know all three of us, in fact! We certainly know *you*! So why don't you just show yourselves and get this whole thing over with? We'll be done with you before you know it!"

Which was smart, trying to taunt them back. She knew how full of pride John was. Except the balls of fog remained in place, as milky as three blinded eyes. This was an ancient wisdom they were dealing with.

A drop of sweat fell off her nose. And when she looked across at Maxi, his face was drenched too. Peter's expression was the only one that was holding steady, but it was very pale.

"Aren't you even going to *say* anything?" he shouted. "What, you don't like being stood up to, and so you're sulking?"

The faintest noise came lilting out. A laugh, not even in a human voice. That even made the small Italian jerk. But the balls of fog … they stayed precisely where they were.

"Patient sons of bitches, ain't they?" Peter hissed under his breath. "We've got no options left. We *have* to get in close."

"Together," Maxi said.

"Yeah, man, side by side. Let's go."

But taking that first step was the hardest thing to do. Not just for Lindy, but for all of them. Like each of them was waiting for the other to go first. Even Peter kept on trying to lift a foot and then replaced it.

And dammit, this was down to *her*! They wouldn't even *be* here if she hadn't let herself be gulled. She wasn't letting this pass for another second.

Anger drove her forward, and the others followed.

The turf was crashing underneath her feet now. She could practically hear the blades of grass snapping. Her breath was seething in her nostrils and her pulse was thudding in her skull. The others had caught up with her by this time, and the three of them were moving like a single entity. No doubts now and no hesitation. They were going to *end* this.

"Strength in numbers," came John Hunter's mocking voice.

The words were very loud this time, and Lindy jolted to a halt. The ground seemed to vibrate, then lurch sideways under her feet. As though the world had tilted on its axis. It was so unexpected that she felt her jaw drop.

What had happened?

The question flowered in her mind, then moved down to her lips. And so she turned around to ask the others.

Except that she was all alone now in the dimness of the park. Maxi and Peter had both vanished.

48 – In Darkness

Peter felt the ground beneath him tilt and shudder too. The whole park seemed to lurch, and when it stopped and steadied, things had changed.

Lindy and Maxi were no longer either side of him. He swung around, trying to find them. Went around in a full circle, but they were no longer there.

The next breath that he took was icy cold, and seeped through his lungs and banged against his heart, making it flutter wildly. And he almost lost his nerve and ran.

He'd been so full of certainty up until this moment. Sure that his Faith would protect him. Positive that he could beat these things if he kept goodness foremost in his mind. But what exactly had he been expecting ... that they'd simply, casually walk up to him and let him shoot them? They were more than likely very old – he forced himself to remember that. And wise in the ways of men. Full of dark experience when it came to tricking human beings.

And that was what this had to be. A trick and nothing more than that. Nothing that Lindy had told him, nothing that he'd ever heard, indicated that they could make objects move or vanish, much less people. They couldn't have spirited his companions away. But they could fool with your perceptions, he was sure of that. It was more than likely that the other two were still close by. Except he couldn't see or hear them any longer.

His heart kept pounding unevenly, though. His lungs were having trouble drawing enough air in. And he could feel how wild his gaze was as he gawked around.

He looked back the way that he'd originally been staring. And the three large patches of immobile fog ... they were no longer there. The outline of that clump of trees was like a hole torn in the dimness, and the city lights beyond it looked like stars right at this moment, shining bright and beautiful but impossibly distant.

Peter thought of taking out his gun, but forced himself to hold back on that.

This can only be the first part of the trick, he told himself. *The opening of the act. Wait for more before you move.*

Something shifted in the shadows of the trees. A paler shape within the blackness. And the instant his head jerked toward it, sweat ran down into his eyes. He rubbed at them, but they kept stinging.

Something, yes. *A human shape.* And it kept moving closer through his blurred-up vision.

Lindy had described two women. This had to be one of those. The one with dark hippy hair, tall and pallid as a snowbound winter's morn. Her hips undulated as she moved. She was approaching him as casually as though they were both out for a stroll. But in the darkness, with his smarting eyeballs, he could not make out her face properly. Not until she was much closer.

And then …

The name dropped involuntarily from his frozen lips.

"Marcy?"

And he felt another violent jolt. But it came from *inside* him, this time.

His wife of fourteen happy and contented years was moving up to him. But not the way she looked these days. Not the way she'd looked when he had last walked out through their front door. No gray hairs appearing and no crow's feet round the eyes. No slightest tiredness to her smile. Her pale brown irises were crisp and bright. And her figure was back to the way it had been before she'd borne him their children.

This was Marcy as his high school sweetheart, a couple of years before they'd gotten married.

And Peter told himself immediately: *Trick!*

What was *this* supposed to prove? Did these creatures really think him quite that stupid? She got within five yards of him and stopped.

And the wattage of her smile increased.

"Hello, Peter," she said, her voice lilting.

"Go to hell."

Her face went slack.

"I know exactly what you are," he snapped at her.

"And how do you know that for sure? Do you have the first idea what beings of our kind can really do?"

He tried to think of some way to answer that, but couldn't. So he simply blinked at her, quite numbly. And her smile came wafting back.

"You think about me this way often, don't you? And you get quite focused on that memory. When it's hard to pay the bills on time. When one of the kids has gotten sick. You lie awake in your largely sterile bed, your exhausted wife snoring by your side, and you think about the way it used to be, back when things were so much simpler and romantic. You regularly have waking dreams about that simple, easy, carefree life you used to live."

He ducked his head so that he didn't have to look at her directly. This was bullshit. Worse than that. Of *course* he thought about the old days sometimes. Every father with a family did. But time moved on. You couldn't stop it. People got older and they changed. It was the natural way.

"Ah, I think I understand," Marcy was saying now. "You're *proud* of how your life is now."

He set his jaw and answered, "Yes."

"You shoulder your responsibilities without complaint. You're an excellent father and a good and faithful husband. You've never cheated once, though you've had many chances. Even with the members of your own church group."

And wasn't that what really sucked? Three times – maybe four that he could think of – women from the parish he attended had come on to him, attracted by the fact he was a cop. They knew that he was married, but they didn't seem to care. Did they even understand the teachings of their own religion?

"It's human nature, Peter," Marcy was saying. "Your bible tells you this. You are innately sinful, all of you. And 'all' includes a certain Peter Renzo."

Which was true. It was why he went to church as often as he did, and said his prayers, and attended confession. He did all those things to stop the badness in him from eating him up.

"You try to fight against it. I admire that in you."

"Another lie."

"But what happens when you get older, Peter?"

He ought to try and shoot her now.

"Gray and gaunt and broken like a stick, the weight of life bending your back into a question mark?"

She wasn't too far away, and he'd made a clean shot from much greater distances. His hand started moving for the pistol he had tucked into his waistband. But it started shaking too. This creature looked *so much* like Marcy.

"Do you remember how your father ended up?" she asked him.

And that hit him where it really hurt.

Mom had perished of a slow brain tumor. His father was forced to watch. Pop had finished off his life a lonely alcoholic, sitting in the same armchair practically every hour of every day, just staring into empty space. All his decency had been for nothing. All his honesty had gotten him plain squat. And you could see the question in his eyes, the final couple of years. *Why did I even bother?*

Peter had always been afraid that he'd wind up like that. But Marcy had already changed the subject.

"I'm thinking about our Prom," she told him.

Final night of high school. The Academy awaiting him. They'd danced and hugged. And after that, when it had broken up, about a dozen of them had climbed into a couple of cars and driven out into the countryside beyond the city. They had found a clearing, lit a fire. And a joint had gone around.

He and Marcy had waited till nobody was looking, and then stolen off into the woods. And afterwards – lying side by side and staring up – they had talked about the future, what it held for them. The stars had never been so bright as they had looked that night. And when they'd stepped back out, the horizons seemed boundless.

The world had shrunk a whole lot smaller since then ... there was no denying it.

"Back then," Marcy pointed out, "we didn't even understand what 'disappointment' meant."

He ground his teeth. He'd never understood until he'd been a couple of years on the job just how bad people could be. Human beings *were* animals on a basic level. And the question that had always nagged at him was ... why did he believe that he was any different? He was flesh and blood, wasn't he? Came from the same origins as everybody else. And so if they were capable of shameful things, then so was he.

Marcy had stepped in a little closer.

"You think you can destroy me? All you'd be destroying are your own most precious dreams. You'd end up in an even worse state than your father was towards the end. But I can take you right back to that Prom night."

And she was even closer. He could smell the perfume she was wearing now. The exact same fragrance Marcy had worn all those years ago. He'd drowned in it when they'd been making love. He'd wallowed in it, and it drew him now.

If he looked up, would the stars be dazzling again? He wanted to raise his head, but couldn't. He was staring at the ground instead. Her hands were going round his neck, her touch extremely warm and soft.

He felt her breath against his cheek. It was sweet-smelling and carried with it the heat of her body. And would it be so bad to let himself slip back to those simpler times for just a little while? Set himself free again, the weight of the world off of him?

But you can't do that! a tiny part of his mind screamed. *You cannot turn back time!*

He cursed and pulled his gun out. Pushed its muzzle up against her chest.

"You'll kill the best part of yourself if you do that," she said. "Because the best part is called 'hope,' and you'll have nothing left."

And then she touched his thoughts, and an image sprung up. Himself in his father's place. Sitting in that same armchair and clutching at an empty glass. Hair white. Head bowed. Eyes that had the constant gloss of helpless tears in them.

"Know what one of my favorite songs has always been?" Peter asked her, staring hard into her face and seeing it for what it really was. "*'Que sera sera.'*"

And he pulled the trigger.

***

She went stumbling back, clutching at her breastbone, her eyes wide, her mouth as slack as a rubber band that had lost its elasticity. And for a brief moment, horrible guilt and pain tore at him.

But then her face started to transform.

It turned into another dark-haired face, but one he did not recognize, flatter and more Latinate, its lips painted darkly.

Then it gave up on its human appearance altogether.

Two incisors sprouted up like tusks. It was hard to tell in this poor light, but had that frizzy hair turned a dark green? The eyebrows expanded till they turned into a fuzzy V. There was a wispy beard dangling from the creature's chin now. And its clothes had disappeared, revealing a pair of breasts that were little more than bestial dugs.

The eyes were not merely a sickly green. They didn't simply glow. They glittered, coruscated, seemed to spin. Captured your attention, held it, trying to take your mind to places that it didn't want to go.

Help me, they were telling Peter right now. S*ave me.*

And for the briefest moment the young Marcy started coming back and he edged forward.

Except he checked himself. He took a breath. He blinked, and the monster returned.

The creature's eyes slipped shut. It let out a strange noise, somewhere in between a gasp, a sigh, a sob. And then its outline transformed altogether.

There were no real features anymore. Just a mass of natural debris that had formed into a vaguely human shape. And the leaves in it were very pale at first. But then they changed color.

To mottled red and yellow, first. And then to brown. They crinkled up.

And then the entire structure came apart, fragmenting into dust.

Peter tottered backward, swiping at the stuff in an attempt to prevent it from choking him. His head was dizzy, and the park around him seemed to sway. But he fought to get himself back on the straight and narrow.

Where the hell were the others?

His eyes tried to penetrate the darkness, without much success. But then a scream of pain came springing from his right-hand side. A man's voice. *Maxi!*

So he started running off in that direction.

49 – In Dreams

A horse-drawn buggy was headed out across the park. Maxi could make out its outline on the transverse up ahead of him, and was surprised to see it. It was so far away he couldn't make out many details. But the driver – in a top hat – had his head bowed low. A small lamp beside him swayed and bobbled with the carriage's motion. The large horse out front seemed to have a plume of feathers attached to its brow. The buggy itself was a rectangle of shadow and he couldn't make out who the passengers were, if any.

He tried to forget about it, his gaze flicking back to the small copse of trees and then going to either side. His breath froze hard in his throat and he could feel the tiny muscles in his face all trying to twitch. Where precisely had the others gone? He wanted to run, but did the same thing that he always did whenever he felt that impulse. Maxi drew his gun.

And then a low bumping noise brought his head around. The buggy had now left the transverse, crossed the sidewalk – which was what he'd heard – and was heading down across the grass toward him. He had never in his life seen one of them do that, and felt astonished. He could hear the rattle of its springs as it drew closer. The rumble of its metal tires on the dried-out turf. The rhythmic pounding of the horse's hooves. It *was* wearing a feathered plume and, after another while, he could hear it snorting as it pulled the carriage.

He couldn't see the driver's face, however close the buggy got. All that could be made out was that shiny black hat, blocking out the fellow's features like some carefully placed inkblot. But the inside of the carriage started coming into view. And he could only see one person there. A woman, short, and blonde-looking at first. But then the color of her hair started to change.

To red. A very familiar shade of that particular color.

Less than twenty yards away, the buggy swung around at right-angles and then drew up to a creaky halt.

A long, slim, tapering leg came reaching down.

And Lindy stepped out.

***

She was dressed in a long, dark robe, fastened at the throat with a large, rather ornate silver clasp. She'd not been dressed like that before. In fact, he'd never seen her wearing anything like it. So this had to be another trick. He'd been warned these creatures were adept at that. He shivered and then raised his pistol, aiming it as steadily as he could manage.

Lindy had been smiling when she'd stepped down from the carriage. But now, her expression transformed. Her pale face slackened and her full lips parted slightly. And her eyes filled up with a dismay that kept trying to take on liquid form.

"You aren't going to hurt me are you, Maxi?"

And she said it very quietly, but the words seemed to reverberate around him.

"Damn right I am. You not be her."

She took a step toward him.

"Are you sure?"

Another.

"Can you be completely certain?"

"Yar." And he gripped his gun double-handed. "It not *possible* ya're her."

She shook her head. And took another step.

"Maybe you're both right and wrong. It's possible that I'm the 'her' you've always wanted her to be."

As she kept on stepping softly through the grass toward him, she reached up with both her hands and unfastened the silver clasp. The cloak dropped away behind her like the shed skin of a snake. She was completely naked underneath.

Maxi tried to keep on staring at her face, except the pale body beneath it kept on drawing his gaze down. Because it was precisely as he had imagined it would be. And he'd imagined that an awful lot. He could still remember the very first day that he had met with Lindy Grady.

'Beautiful,' he'd thought. One of the most beautiful women he had ever seen.

His heart tripped over when she shook his hand. His skin had tingled, and his head had swum. And he'd lain awake late – that same night – trying to understand why that had happened. And had finally arrived at something like the truth. He'd fallen in love with her, not spiritually but physically, the first moment he had laid eyes on her.

None of that had ever faded. It had never stopped ... but what to do about it? If he ever dared to tell her what his feelings were, then what would happen? She'd be shocked – offended even? She would laugh into his face and put him down? Or she'd sleep with him, but that would not last long. Not the way she was, the way she lived.

And so – like countless men who find themselves in love with a woman who they cannot have – he'd made himself her friend instead. It was the only way to stay up close to her. The only way to have her round him as much as he needed. Only it wasn't quite enough. He dreamed and fantasized a lot. He imagined, and did other things as well.

He was single, just like her. And he frequented bars as well. His tall Jamaican looks attracted good numbers of women, but he always turned most of them down, just waiting till a redhead came along. In bed with her, he'd partway close his eyes and then try to pretend that she was Lindy.

And now here it was. What he'd always wanted. When the present day came swimming back, a pair of soft, warm hands was pressed gently around his own. The muzzle of his gun was pointed in between her naked breasts. Her face was very close, and her eyes seemed enormous.

"Is this all that you can think to do with me?" she asked him quietly, sadly. "Put a bullet through me?"

He'd started shaking again, teardrops running down his face. Because he *really knew* this was a trick. He *knew* that he was being had. But he'd imagined something like this every single day for years. And pulling on that trigger now would kill something inside him that he wasn't quite sure he could live without.

She'd started stroking his hands with her fingertips. And it felt so wonderful, merely that small intimacy. He found himself losing control. His fingers started parting. And before he even knew it, his gun was tumbling to the ground, forgotten.

And then she was pressing up against him, the impact so swift that he tottered back a couple of steps. Except she moved with him. One arm was going up around his neck. Her breasts were flattening against his chest. Her hot breath slid down his neck. The perfume of her hair and body filled his skull.

And Maxi was crying like a baby now. This was what he'd always needed, but he knew what it was leading to.

If this be my final moment in this world, then please just make the end come quick.

He closed his eyes and pressed his head against her shoulder.

But then the pain started kicking in, and he realized how cruel she was. In the earlier murders, the heart had been shredded. Whereas she was concentrating lower down. Agony erupted round his navel. Something like a set of knives was being pushed slowly through and past it. And when he looked down, he could see it was her fingers, going through his yellow shirt and burrowing smoothly through his skin.

He howled desperately and tried to pull away. Except the arm around his neck had taken on a vise like grip. He tried to break it, but it was like steel. And Maxi writhed furiously, but couldn't get free.

Something hot and wet was slopping down his pants leg now. And was that simply his own blood, or could it be a portion of his guts? He wailed, a very high pitched sound. His head came slamming up.

Her eyes were green and sparkling and whirling. And she had no hair or eyebrows any longer. No nose either, simply a triangular space where it should be. Her skin was ashen, gray and dead. And there were canine fangs protruding down across her lip.

Maxi felt his spine arc as her fingers pressed a little further in. She had to be shredding his insides by this stage. His mouth was still hanging open, but no further sound was coming out except a curious bubbling noise.

The park shrank to a dot the size of a pin's head. And everything outside that dot was purest black. There was a fire burning in his belly now. And he had no option but to feel its progress as it spread out through him.

When there was a sudden, deafening thud. A gunshot, right up close. The grip around his neck evaporated, and the creature that had hold of him began to slide down, falling away.

Revealing Peter Renzo standing there behind her, with the gun that Maxi had dropped firmly in his grip.

He was holding it at head height, with its muzzle smoking.

***

Maxi went stumbling back himself a moment later. His knees buckled and he hit the dirt. The pain closed down on him real hard and he curled into a fetal ball, clutching both hands to his stomach in a vain attempt to staunch the flow of blood.

Peter was stripping off his jacket and then wadding it up, pressing it to the wound.

"Hold onto this," he muttered. "As tight as you can."

And then he was standing up and bellowing into his cell phone.

"Officer down! We need paramedics in the park, just south of the Sheep Meadow!"

After which, he was on his knees, feeling for Maxi's pulse.

"Can't do nothing more till they arrive, pal."

"Go *help* her!" Maxi managed to get out through his gritted teeth.

"Right. Just stay alive, okay? Just lie still and hold on tight and breathe."

And then, he was back on his feet and jogging off into the darkness, yelling at the top of his voice.

"*Lindy!*"

50 – In Truth

As soon as she found herself alone in the darkness, the truth hit her. Ever since she'd been rescued – and grateful though she was – she'd had the strongest inkling it would still come down to this.

The link that had been formed between herself and Hunter was too strong. Peter and Maxi had genuinely tried to help her. Had been determined to stick by her. But when push came to shove, there was nothing they could ultimately do to save her. This was *her* business. She had to face it on her own.

A cold shudder went through her, but she held herself up straight. Took out her gun and grasped it with its barrel angled at the ground. And she began to advance slowly, casting her gaze about her, the same way she might do when entering a suspicious building. The same way she might do when hunting for a fugitive. Because she got the certain feeling, now, that that was going to be the only thing that got her through this. Behaving like no one's lover anymore. No one's daughter either. Simply acting like a cop.

Somewhere very far off in the distance, she could make out someone shouting. And it *might* be Peter, but the voice was much too far away to tell. It was possible her name was being called out, but she didn't even turn her head.

No ... focus!

She was sensitive to every sound, her skin practically picking up tiny vibrations on the air. Every time she thought she saw a movement, her eyes flicked to it and fastened there. Except she saw the reality after she'd done that several times. The darkness and the distant lights were playing tricks on her. And the state of her nerves wasn't helping much. When genuine motion came, she'd know it. She was sure of that. She stopped and waited.

It was going to be John Hunter coming at her from the gloom. She understood that too. But in what form? The patches of fog had disappeared. The ragged outline of the clump of trees stared back at her like the opening to some cave. And there was no telling what was going to emerge.

"What *is* your real name, John?" she suddenly called out. "I don't have the first clue how to use it against you, so there's no real harm in telling me."

But she heard no voice coming back at her.

"What do you get called back in the dark place that you come from, John? 'Hunter' is a joke, right? And the joke's on me – I get it. But everything in this world has a name, and so what's yours?"

The only answer that she got was the flat echo of her own voice in the open meadow. The traffic noise was still there, except quieter than it had been, almost subcutaneous. The only place that really counted was right here, right now. Lindy was suspended in a frozen moment. All keyed-up and quivering like she had taken PCP. *You gonna make me wait?* she thought. *I'll wait all night if need be.*

As though in response to that thought, something pale started shifting deep within the shadows of the trees. It was pretty small, and less distinct than the patches of gray fog had been. But it was moving steadily toward her.

A human outline began to resolve.

If it's my father again, I'm gonna blow his head off first chance that I get.

But she remembered what Peter had said about needing to get right up close, and kept her gun down low.

No bald pate came into view. No bullish shoulders or muscular frame. This figure was shorter, had a mop of tangled hair. And …

What the hell?

It was a woman's shape teetering in her direction, taking little, birdlike steps. She was dressed in a shapeless cardigan, a floral smock beneath it. And was wearing carpet slippers. Lindy still could not make out her face.

But instinct took her once again, by the scruff of her neck this time. It shook her violently, so that her resolve started melting. Because she couldn't quite believe …

Had never expected …

Never for a moment thought …

The shadows started bleeding away from the face approaching her.

The figure stopped.

It was her mother peering at her through the dimness of the park.

***

She ought to have been ready for anything – she knew that. But how much of 'anything' can one mind take?

Lindy stared across at the figure and went numb, the speed of her pulse dropping away, the shaking in her limbs becoming slower, almost flaccid. It felt like a cold and viscous liquid was filling up her veins and replacing her blood. Mom looked terribly small from this distance, but she could make out every detail clearly.

Another illusion, she tried to tell herself. And yet the sight tore at her heart.

There were patches of darkness all over the woman's face that were not simply shadows. They were bruises, mottled purple marks. Her upper lip was split, a little dried blood smearing down from it. Her hair was frizzy and unkempt, standing up in bunches. And her eyes were very wide, a dull, haunted expression in them.

Her mouth moved. A whisper came rushing at Lindy like a gust of wind across the wide expanse of grass.

"We're the same thing, you and me."

But no, that wasn't so! She'd spent a good part of her adult lifetime trying to prove that wasn't so. She had *no* husband to put her down or beat her up. She was free and independent and a damned good cop.

"You protest too much, Lindy," came that same whispering voice. "And you always have, with every word and every action."

Which was when it struck her. There was one thing she had always been extremely afraid of, and it wasn't getting hurt. She was terrified of being weak, the way she'd been when she had been a little girl.

That Texan in the nightclub, just a few evenings ago. Had she actually been *daring* herself, playing chicken with her body and her soul? If so, then she'd been doing that thing ever since she'd first left home. Every last encounter with a man. Every time she took drugs and risked getting caught. She'd always told herself she did those things because she liked them, except ...

Was that really so?

She tried to fight against it, but she couldn't stop the raw emotions welling up. Her childhood did more than simply haunt her. It still *dominated* her.

Her eyes went damper and her vision blurred. Her head started to throb so powerfully she couldn't think straight.

Her mother had come a few yards closer.

"I know what you'd really like to do."

Lindy tried to grit her teeth. Tried to raise her pistol. But her arms and her shoulders had gone numb. Her whole body was rigid.

A soft set of fingers alighted on her shoulder, only it was painful when she tried to jerk away.

"Take your *hand* off me," she managed to grate out.

Her voice sounded very choked and hoarse. Her eyesight hadn't cleared up any. Her mother was only a dim image at first, pale as mist against the surrounding darkness. But then her face came into focus once again. It was clear of any damage and was smiling.

"I know what you really want."

This was all a trap, and she had to drag herself away from it and come back to reality. Except the words that she was hearing ... they were sinking deep into her like a row of tiny fishhooks. Capturing her attention and then pinning it in one small place. What *did* she really want? She wasn't even sure herself.

"You want to start again."

A person can't do that!

"You want to go back to before the time when the trouble with your father started. Back to when he cared about you, and he wasn't violent. You remember what that was like, don't you? You still think about it sometimes."

What the hell do you know about my thoughts?

"You can start again and make yourself a different life. A happier, more stable one, with none of the loneliness you now have to endure."

"That can't be done!"

"Says who?"

"To turn back time? To be reborn? Millions of people want that, but it simply isn't possible."

And her mother smiled extremely gently.

"Well, girl, it would be a miracle, for sure."

Miracle. That word resonated in her skull. And set up soft vibrations there, so that Lindy felt her eyelids trying to slide shut. The church she'd been to as a little girl came rushing back. The stained glass and the candles and the way the whole place echoed to each tiny noise. The Bible there in front of her. The illustrations of the twelve disciples and the saints. And that had been an entire *age* of miracles, now hadn't it? They'd happened all the time, as regular as clockwork.

But none happened these days, not a single one. No angels appeared to save the slaughtered of Damascus. No seas parted to set the starving and the enslaved free. And why was that? It wasn't even fair.

All she'd ever hoped for was one stupid little miracle. One tiny magic moment that would change her life. That bare apartment where she lived. The bars she spent her evenings in. The men whose names she never even asked. She wanted that all ... was 'gone' even the right word?

No. Cleansed. Erased. A new start. A clean slate. But that could only happen if her childhood changed.

And however much she wanted that, it wasn't *possible*!

Her eyelids came back open.

51 – And in the End

Those light fingers were still resting on her shoulder, but her mother's face was gone. Another one was staring back at her.

It was her own.

And yet not quite.

The eyes not nearly as tired and strained as she usually saw them in the mirror, clear and fresh and sparkling instead. Pleased. Not a hint of tension to the muscles of her features, with a relaxed air, a relaxed smile. A gentle, almost carefree grin. Pink around the cheekbones, and her skin glowing with health. This was not a person who worked too hard or turned to drugs.

Lindy glanced briefly down and sideways, to see that one of the fingers that had settled on her shoulder had a wedding band on it.

And words started resounding through her head, in her own voice.

Seven years now. Married five. Engaged for two.

She flinched. But found that – otherwise – she couldn't move.

I have three children, two girls and a boy.

Which was something she could not even imagine the reality of. She had barely gotten through her own childhood, let alone preside over another one.

I quit the force a few years back. Stopped trying to prove how strong I was. Stopped trying to show myself that I was better than my father said. Things like that are just the kind of games that fools play. I'm far happier now.

And this was just the biggest trick, the biggest lie of all, wasn't it? Because a Lindy Grady of this kind had never once existed.

He's called Josh. I love him dearly and he loves me back. We're all going to Europe in the Fall.

And a very vivid image sprang up in her mind. Herself, this way. A handsome man beside her. Two small children in tow, and a baby in her arms. And they were walking down a boulevard toward the Eiffel Tower. They were all in Paris.

She'd sometimes thought of traveling, but had never gotten around to it. And it wasn't merely that she'd never left the States. She'd hardly ever left New York.

How'd her life become so small? How'd her world contracted to a few streets, a handful of bars, her cramped apartment and the station house? She couldn't understand how she had let it get that way. It was almost as though she was continually hiding.

Something started moving down her face. She twitched again, then realized it was a single tear.

The smile in front of her grew slightly broader. Then the lips parted, and her own voice came issuing out.

"Am I the version of yourself you really want to kill?"

And she knew – the moment that she heard it – that it was the truth. What she was staring at was not just happiness, but real fulfillment. The past locked away in a cellar that would never be reopened, and the need to prove herself forgotten. She would rather put her pistol to her own head than destroy it.

So why not do that? Happy Lindy asked her, in her head.

She felt her right hand moving, carefully and smoothly now, any hint of numbness gone. The weapon felt very cool and solid in her grasp. The heat of the night was pushing in round her oppressively. She hadn't noticed it in quite a while, but was horribly aware of it right now. As though the very air was trying to choke her.

She wanted it gone. Wanted an end to all of this. This stifling heat. This stifling life. Maybe if she blew an extra hole in her head she would be able to breathe a little better.

She felt the muzzle of the pistol settling against her brow.

And then – off in the distance – she thought she heard someone calling her name again. And was that Peter?

She could barely remember who he was, apart from his name. Barely remember anything of the previous days and hours. Brief, staccato flashes started coming back at her. A naked body lying in this park. A long drive into woodlands somewhere. A fox staring in at her through her windscreen. And being on a bus, and pretty scared, at night.

George Greentree's rumpled face.

Then Peter's rather ordinary face rushed into view.

They partially merged into one.

And they were smiling at her gently, their eyes sad. Their lips were moving soundlessly. She got the sense that they were trying to give her some kind of advice. And that was then it struck her.

She wasn't wholly alone in this world. *No* – there were people in it who still cared about her and wanted to help her, despite all her faults. They understood how damaged she was, but they didn't shy away. She was fallen, but they kept on trying to pick her up.

Which made her part of something. A part of the human race. A broken part, for sure, although ... wasn't that true of almost everyone?

But she was larger than the boundaries of her own existence. She was not an isolated being, but a member of a mighty tribe. All of them with fragilities. None of them even *approaching* perfect. But there was a unity between them, and they looked out for each other.

Whereas this perfect, happy, smiling being stood in front of her ... was merely an illusion. Was no more than dust.

Its hand was still resting on her shoulder. But it was an 'it' now, not a 'she.' Lindy started swinging the gun around. And the illusion's face distorted.

Didn't simply crumple up with fright. It changed. The female aspects vanished from it, the hair melting back. For a brief moment, it was John Hunter's face staring at her once again. But after that ...

All of the hair vanished, leaving just a naked scalp with bumps and ridges on it. And the nose went the same way. The ears reduced themselves to tiny stumps. The lips melted back and the mouth went almost round, pointed teeth revealed inside it.

And the eyes ... they went round too. Had no lids or lashes. They were very large, and seemed to glow. And she could see her own reflection in them clearly.

Then the thing began to grow, swelling up massively above her until it was practically three stories tall. Its arms had become simian in length, with one hand remaining on her shoulder. And its grip began to tighten, claws now digging in. It started dragging her to one side, pulling her off balance. And she yelled with fear and pain.

But – even while she was being swung helplessly around – she kept a firm grip on her gun. The creature's face was coming down at her. It looked the same size as her whole apartment. The inside of the thing's round mouth was darker than the night. Perhaps there was a vacuum there and she'd be sucked into it, wholly gone.

It was closing down over her. Swelling vastly. Filling up her vision. Here was the oblivion a part of her had always craved. But something else inside her fought against that.

Look away!

She could feel its breath skirling around her, as dank as the deepest part of a primeval forest. There was just pure blackness over her, a circle of it, ringed with teeth. And she understood she barely had a second left. She let that knowledge move her.

Forced her eyes off past the circle to the hunched body behind it. Angled her gun higher up, for where the thing's heart ought to be. Let her training and her long years of experience guide her. There was nothing else she could rely on.

Lindy made her body settle into perfect stillness. And she fired.

Just one shot.

And if I've missed ...?

The pressure on her shoulder vanished. And abruptly, there was nothing left above her but a cloud of swirling, thick black powder.

***

Lindy found herself folding her arms above her head alarmedly. Expecting that powder to come rushing down across her, smothering her, coating her in black. And then finding its way into her lungs. Maybe that would change her, making her less than human.

But it didn't seem to do that thing. The night sky appeared to be rippling slightly now, except it wasn't that. Each individual speck of dust was melting into the darkness above, winking out of existence.

The next thing she knew, her legs had lost the last of their strength. Her knees were buckling, she was going down. She managed to tumble onto her backside rather than going the whole way. And she sat there numbly, swaying as though she were on a ship. She drew her knees up to her chest and clutched them tight.

The park had gone away by now, and so had the surrounding lights. Her mind felt blank. Her eyes were almost blind.

And the only thing that she could hear was Peter running up behind her.

EPILOGUE

BEYOND THE NIGHT

By mid-morning, Maxi had been operated on and was lying in a bed, tubes hanging from him like he had been halfway changed into some kind of organic machine, although his face was at peace, his eyes shut. The staff all knew he was a cop and were checking up on him constantly.

"How long till he wakes up?" Lindy asked an intern.

"I wouldn't hold your breath. He'll pull through, but he's still weak. He lost an awful lot of blood."

She stayed for a while longer, nonetheless. And – a few minutes before she finally decided to leave – Maxi's eyeballs started moving underneath their lids. So he was dreaming. She could only imagine about what.

Peter had already gone back home to his family, which meant she was alone again. She squinted fiercely when the sunlight hit her on the sidewalk. New York City was reduced to a constant noise around her, the rumble of traffic, the parping of horns, a siren somewhere in the distance and the thunder of a passing truck. All this movement. All these people. They lived as tightly-packed as microbes, but lived wholly separate lives, rarely knowing what the others did or what was passing through their minds.

How weird was that? It barely seemed to make the slightest sense.

But the real question nagging at her was, *Where now?*

She could go home to her apartment, but it barely even counted as a home. Just a place she slept in sometimes. And she wasn't nearly ready to put in an appearance at the station house. So she just stood there for a while, people walking past her like she'd turned into some kind of ghost.

And then she finally made her mind up. She walked to the nearest subway station and waited for an express train that would take her off the island.

Brooklyn had changed a lot since she had been a child here. But she thought that she could still detect familiar odors. Cooking smells. The aromas wafting from cafes and delicatessens. She wasn't even sure if any of that was real, or only her imagination.

She was staring at the sidewalk now, not even looking where she was going, simply letting her feet travel where they wanted.

And when they finally decided to stop – when her head finally lifted – she was outside the apartment block where she'd grown up.

It had been shut down, condemned, windows boarded up. She stared up at the grimy, blinded building for a while, then made her way round to the back.

There were even more weeds out on the back lot than she remembered from her earliest days. They yanked at her ankles as she walked through them, as though the past were tugging at her. This was where there'd been the incident with the baseball bat. This was where her father had punched out Kevin Mitchell, shortly after Kevin had given her her very first kiss. This was where the damage to her life had first begun, and there was nothing she could do to change it.

Helplessly, she sat down on the weeds and crabgrass. But she didn't cry, and not the slightest moan or sigh escaped her lips. Stuff like that was pointless. It would alter nothing, and she knew that for a fact. She simply sat the way a little child would sit, oblivious to the bustling, revolving world around her. The thoughts going through her head were all about the past.

Until a voice dragged her back into the present day.

"You okay down there?"

She looked slowly up, the sunlight catching her at an odd angle first so she could only see a human outline.

But he stepped in a little closer, and the man who was finally revealed was definitely not her type. Tall and about her own age, sure, but with shoulder length hair and a beard and dressed in rumpled jeans and a collarless shirt with the sleeves pushed up, a small stack of folders tucked under one arm. Some kind of serious-minded type, by the look of it. He had a gentle smile though, and was showing it to her right now, even though his dark eyes were concerned.

"What makes you think I'm not okay?" she asked.

"Grownups who want to sit down usually do their best to find a bench, or at least a low wall."

She'd been through so much that her head still hurt. What had happened down the past few days still had its grip around her. Except … it was over now. She'd come through to the other side.

She had the whole rest of her life to live, and perhaps this conversation was where it began. So ...

"What makes you think I'm a grownup?" she came back at him.

The concern left his eyes, and his smile transformed to a grin.

"None of us really are deep down, now are we?"

And wasn't *that* the truth? She relaxed and let out a small laugh, and the normal world came rushing back to her with her next breath.

They wound up going to a nearby coffee shop. And since she didn't want to talk about herself too much, she listened as he told her about his own life so far. His name was Dean, and he'd grown up in Brooklyn too. He'd been on Wall Street till some two years back. Had worked sixteen hours a day and spent most of the other eight living the high life. Till he'd finally burned out and given all that up. These days, he taught business studies at a community college not too far from here.

"Mostly kids from poorer backgrounds. On my better days, I like to think I'm giving them the chance of a decent bite at the Big Apple."

"And on your worse days?"

The answer that bounced back at her was gently self-mocking. And he certainly wasn't the kind of guy she usually went for, but she found herself beginning to like him. He was smart and well-meaning and funny, only he didn't make a big deal out of any of those qualities. And he was quite good looking too, beneath the beard. And old familiar urges started stirring in her.

His hands were on the table in between them, and she started reaching for them with one of hers.

But then she stopped herself. Her head swum heavily and then she stood straight up. Dean peered at her in a rather worried fashion, obviously concerned that he'd said something to offend her.

Lindy steadied herself and stared at her watch.

"It's seven minutes before one, right?"

Dean confirmed that, looking slightly nonplussed.

"On a Thursday."

"So far as I'm aware."

The expression on his face was asking what kind of peculiar game exactly she was playing.

"Are you going to be in town next week, same time?"

He blinked, turning that over. "I don't travel much. So, sure."

"And will you wait for me?"

"Did you say 'wait'?"

"Here, in one week's time. Right at this very table."

"I'm not sure I understand."

"What's not to? I'm leaving now. But I'll be here same time next Thursday. Will I see you here when I turn up?"

His eyes went slightly glazed, but then he saw what she was driving at. His face went very pensive and he briefly pursed his lips.

"I can't imagine why not."

"My work keeps me busy, so I might be late. Will you hold on a while if that happens?"

He smiled gently and nodded. "For hours, if need be. What work do you do?"

"I'll tell you next Thursday."

And then she turned away and was about to walk off, when she heard:

"Here's the obvious question. Why?"

Lindy glanced back across her shoulder.

"Almost no one my entire life has ever bothered being patient with me."

"Including yourself?" Dean asked.

That question followed her the whole way back along the sidewalk to the subway station. But her step was a good deal lighter than it had been before. And she was smiling to herself – a tiny, very private smile. She was already looking forward to that other Thursday seven days ahead.

***

By the time that dusk had begun to paint Chinatown ochre, Lindy was drawing a bath. This was really shower weather, but what the hell. As the small, round tub filled up, she lit a few candles and set them around its edges. And she hadn't done anything like this in quite a while.

She hadn't slept since she had gotten home. Still felt too wired, too full of thought. But she hadn't taken any coke, and perhaps would take the momentous step of not using it tomorrow morning either.

Perhaps she'd be able to sleep after she'd soaked in the hot water for a while. She undressed in her bedroom, put her bathrobe on. And when she went on through, the tub was almost full. She turned the faucet, closed the door and slipped the robe back off.

And she was lowering herself into the steamy water ... when she felt something. A sensation in her abdomen.

What the hell had *that* been? It felt almost like a kick. And that couldn't be.

She lowered herself the rest of the way. Folded both her palms across her belly. And it came again, very distinctly.

She had still not climbed out by the time the water had gone cold. But she'd reached an understanding of two things, by then.

However hard you work at it, you cannot really beat nature.

And ... beyond the latest night that you have traveled through and managed to survive, there is always another one, sitting and waiting at the world's outer edge. And then another, and another.

And you could not ever escape them, however desperately you tried.

Lindy's head dropped, and did not come up.

***

Sometime around the middle of that night, a patch of fog – around eight feet high by eight feet wide and gray as a dead dream – drifted into New York City, though there was no wind. It came skimming in from the high northeast, pushing its way across the fringes of the Bronx and then crossing the Harlem River. Kept on going till it reached the edge of Central Park. It went across a couple of the broad traverses and the reservoir.

And finally, it began to slow, coming to a halt beneath a little clump of trees. Where it was joined by another, and then a few more, each of them arriving from the same direction.

Until there were more than a dozen of them.

All of them drawn into the city by the smell of easy meat.

More novels from this author:

UNDER THE ICE

"Out at the edge of the ice, something dark appeared, rising from the water and then closing downward on the frozen surface. I squinted. And was sure it was a human arm."

David and Bobby are a pair of twin brothers both in love with the same woman. But on a trip to Finland, the matter gets resolved in the worst way imaginable – Bobby drowns in the icy waters just outside Helsinki. Two years later, David is still in that city and living with Krista, when a supposed magic artefact comes into their possession. And when David makes a wish upon it, dark things from the past begin resurfacing. Things like old-time sins and misdeeds. Like guilt and awful memories.

And things like Bobby himself, two years drowned and trapped under the ice ... but still here with us.

Under The Ice was voted one of Horror Novel Reviews' TOP TEN BOOKS of 2013.

"Under the Ice is a stellar tale ... brilliant, well thought out and perfectly delivered by Tony Richards, who understands the balance that must be upheld between fantasy and reality. The story boasts numerous layers and a final curveball that's going to leave readers pleased. Whether you opt to label this one a revenge tale, a ghost story or a zombie tale, matters not. It's original, creative, and successfully blends all of the aforementioned classifications, wrapping a plethora of ideas into one novel. This is an excellent read, and you want to get your hands on it as soon as possible!" – Horror Novel Reviews.

"Richards conjures a wonderful atmosphere of cold and cold beauty, coupled with some wonderfully drawn characters.

From beginning to end I couldn't put this book down. The story powers along and is told with great style by an author at the height of his powers. He's every bit as good as the best you'd care to mention. Download Under the Ice now. It absolutely cannot be missed!" – Matt Williams.

THE NIGHT MANAGER: A GHOST NOVEL

There it stood beside the pebbled shore, a massive old Victorian hotel out on the edge of Birchiam-on-Sea. And it was late October when author Alex Morland took a room ... the place was way off-season and extremely quiet. But that was fine by him, since he was hoping to complete his latest novel.

As the weeks slipped by, though, he began to realize he was not quite so alone as it had first appeared. There were brief but strange encounters in the gardens and the hotel bar. There were sounds of running in the corridors at night, and then loud screams.
And then there were the dreams he kept on having about The Grange's night manager, Mr Jakes, all leading him finally toward the aged hotel's dark and deadly secret.

THE ELECTRIC SHAMAN

In the not too distant future, the Dark Continent has changed. It's become Federal Africa, with all of the old countries now united into one great nation. The separate tribes are gone, technology has boomed ... it is a very modern place.

But if you think that it's completely changed, meet Lieutenant Abel Enetame of the Zimbabwe State Police Force, a single father with a great deal on his plate. He doesn't only have the usual crimes to deal with, murders, assassinations, kidnappings. There are violent Black

Supremacists. There are fanatics like the Tribalists, who want to take the whole place back to the old days. And there are egotistic billionaires and power-crazy politicians.

And when those kinds of people start getting their hands on brand-new devices that can do startling things, like change the past, for instance ... well, that's when the sparks really start to fly. Because the future of the whole of modern Africa might well rely on one police detective.

Tony Richards' latest short stories can be found in this brand-new collection:

NIGHTCRAWLER & OTHER TALES OF DARKNESS

Enter a strange world where swimmers keep on disappearing from a perfectly calm stretch of sun-drenched coastline. Where the fog around you seems to come alive. Where a mother will do anything her small child wants. Where a group of people on a beach are not quite who they seem to be.

A Halloween mask turns out to have awful powers. An empty room is not completely that. A ghost appears just once, but haunts you for your entire life. A tiny, petite woman commits awful crimes of violence she scarcely seems capable of.

And what exactly is that crawling around on your roof at night?

13 new tales of supernatural suspense and terror from the author of *Three Dozen Terrifying Tales*.

More short fiction from Tony Richards:

THREE DOZEN TERRIFYING TALES

An old man makes a deal with the Devil. A woman proves to be a lot more dangerous than she first appears. A dark lake holds a deadly secret, as does a dismal housing project and a beautiful secluded beach. Learn the origins of Abraham van Helsing. Visit the circus and face your worst fears. What in heaven is a 'lighting dog'? And surely crows can't hurt you ... can they?

There's some gore, murder, and mayhem, but an awful lot more atmosphere and psychological horror in these tales, all of which have seen publication in professional magazines, anthologies, and e-zines.

"A hell of a writer, one of today's masters of dark fiction" – Horror World.

13 GHOST STORIES

Do you just see ghosts in graveyards and old houses? Not in this collection of breathlessly dark tales from an author described as 'a master of the art.' Here you will find ghosts in Greenwich Village, in the suburbs of London, the American Midwest, Paris, Tokyo, and even on the Far-East island of Penang.

Ghosts seeking justice. Ghosts out for revenge. Sad phantoms still looking for companionship. Spirits who refuse to believe they're dead. And even a ghost with a cunning plan.

Your journey into the night-world of eerie hauntings and dim, chilling apparitions has just begun.

The complete Raine's Landing supernatural series from Tony Richards, available to read in eBook, paperback, or on Kindle Unlimited:

DARK RAIN

Raine's Landing has a brand-new visitor. He's an ancient demon who has adopted human form. He loves to control people's lives, and feeds on their fear. And when he starts his deadly games, not even the town's adepts – magicians descended from the genuine witches of Salem – can stop him. So the job is left to ex-cop Ross Devries and his Harley-riding sidekick Cassie Mallory. They don't have any magical skills, just their guns and fists and their sharp wits. But will those be enough?

"It will keep you on the edge of your seat. A definite must read for those into fantasy, paranormal fiction, or just a good book" – SF Revu.

NIGHT OF DEMONS

A crazed serial killer called 'The Shadow Man' arrives from Boston, fleeing from the law. But once in Raine's Landing, he acquires some magic powers of his own and begins using them to terrible effect. He has a local adept on his side, a malcontent who hates the town. And together, they begin to – literally – rain down Hell upon the Landing.

"Multi-dimensional characters ... action-packed and constantly keeping the readers on the edge of their seats" – Amazon reviews.

The action is fast and furious, with plenty of witchcraft, magic, and supernatural beings. Once you start you will find it hard to put down" – The Monster Librarian.

MIDNIGHT'S ANGELS

Raine's Landing is facing its worst peril yet, monstrous flying creatures in the service of an evil older than the Universe itself. They have an unpleasant way of getting people on their side. Their powers keep on growing until little can withstand them. Most of the major adepts succumb ... there are only two left to defend the place.

And the town's chief troubleshooter, ex-cop Ross Devries, has an enormous challenge on his hands. He needs to get his former sidekick, Cassie, back into the fight. And if they are to have any slightest chance of winning through, they're going to have to make some very strange new friends.

"I absolutely love this series. It has plenty of supernatural creatures in it, along with some great heroes and heroines" – Amazon reviews.

"Excellent series. Very enjoyable with an interesting twist on the urban fantasy template" – Amazon reviews.

DEADLY VIOLET

It's late December now. People are getting ready for the holidays, scarcely guessing what is coming their way next. Because a psychic beggar girl in the town's Victorian past has gotten hold of a magical jewel that massively expands her powers – she has reached out with her mind through time itself, making contact with Raine's Landing in the present day.

The only problem is, she's warped the fabric of reality by doing that. Rows of houses begin vanishing, with their occupants still inside. Bizarre creatures, some of them extremely dangerous, start to roam the streets. And if Ross,

Cassie, and Doc Willets are going to stop their hometown from disappearing altogether, then they're going to need an awful lot of help.

"Richards is a master at suspending disbelief and combining horror, fantasy, and humor in a way that will mesmerize readers from cover to cover" – RT Book Reviews.

SPEAK OF THE DEVIL

It's only early February, and the town should still be in the grip of winter. But the air has turned unseasonably warm and an unexpected thaw has come. And as the snows begin to melt back, bodies start to be discovered, murdered human corpses, each with strange ritual markings carved into their flesh.

At first another serial killer is suspected, but it is not that. The markings are satanic ones. Somebody inside the town is practicing black magic of the foulest kind. Demons have been summoned, dark spells cast, doorways opened into deeper realms. And then the Landing's adepts start to be attacked.

And with his sidekick, Cassie Mallory, unable to help him, ex-cop Ross Devries is facing the toughest and most brutal fight of his entire life. Because this time, he is battling the Hordes of Hell.

"This is what modern dark fantasy SHOULD be. I'm officially hooked" – Goodreads.

"Tremendously entertaining. I thoroughly recommend this to all fans of the paranormal genre" – author Gaston Sanders.

WITCH HUNTER

"But I am innocent, I tell you! I am not a witch!"

"Well, we shall soon find out the truth of that. Prepare yourself for your ordeal."

Back in 1687, Verena Oakemont was put to death by the notorious witchfinder Thaddeus Firman. And – despite her protestations – she really was a witch, and a powerful one too, the daughter of a demon.

Three centuries later, she's escaped from Hell and returned to Raine's Landing. Death has made her magic powers far stronger than ever, and it's not merely the town that she wants to subdue. Her gaze is fixed upon the world beyond it.

But that's not the biggest problem Ross and Cassie have to face. Something even worse is coming in Verena's wake, the servant of an ancient force that would destroy the Universe itself. And the only person who has any chance of standing in its way … is Cassie's brand-new daughter, May.

A vengeful witch. A brutal hunter. And a magically-empowered child. These are the ingredients for the most climactic Raine's Landing adventure yet.

"If you love the fantasy genre, you will love this series as well! I hope (it) never ends!" – Amazon reviews.

CIRCUS OF LOST SOULS

"Freak Show, read the placard at the top. And in the shadows off beyond those bars I could make out the dim shape of a full-grown man. What kind of circus in this day and age even had a freak show anyway? I knew for a fact

that it just didn't happen. No one took a crazy guy and put him in a cage. My hand was still around my gun and I knew right away what I was going to do. I'd draw it as I started going forward. Shoot away the padlock that was holding the cage shut and haul that poor guy out of there, and the hell with any consequences after that."

Is this the end for Raine's Landing?

Not one but two extremely mighty entities have arrived in the town, each of them with their own way of getting what they want. Both are strong enough to control the entire population, and their magic is so vast Raine's Landing's usual protectors – adepts descended from the real witches of Salem – do not stand even the slightest chance of stopping them.

And with Cassie Mallory trapped under the power of one of these ferocious beings, ex-cop Ross Devries finds himself completely on his own, battling against forces that no normal man could ever hope to beat.

"By weaving this fantasy into a modern setting, Richards creates something unique" – Alternative Reads.

"The rest of us stand on the sidelines with eyes wide open at his audacity and wonder what he'll do next" – Black Static magazine.

Printed in Great Britain
by Amazon